# A QUEEN
# IN HIDING

# A QUEEN IN HIDING

## Sarah Kozloff

**TOR**

A Tom Doherty Associates Book

*New York*

This is a work of fiction. All of the characters, organizations, and events portrayed in this novel are either products of the author's imagination or are used fictitiously.

A QUEEN IN HIDING

Copyright © 2019 by Sarah Kozloff

Excerpt from *The Queen of Raiders* copyright © 2020 by Sarah Kozloff

All rights reserved.

Edited by Jen Gunnels

A Tor Book
Published by Tom Doherty Associates
120 Broadway
New York, NY 10271

www.tor-forge.com

Tor® is a registered trademark of Macmillan Publishing Group, LLC.

Library of Congress Cataloging-in-Publication Data

Names: Kozloff, Sarah, author.
Title: A queen in hiding / Sarah Kozloff.
Description: First edition. | New York : Tor, a Tom Doherty Associates Book, 2020. |
   Series: The nine realms; 1 |
Identifiers: LCCN 2019041244 (print) | LCCN 2019041245 (ebook) |
   ISBN 9781250168542 (trade paperback) | ISBN 9781250168535 (ebook)
Subjects: GSAFD: Fantasy fiction.
Classification: LCC PS3611.O85 Q44 2020 (print) | LCC PS3611.O85 (ebook) |
   DDC 813/.6—dc23
LC record available at https://lccn.loc.gov/2019041244
LC ebook record available at https://lccn.loc.gov/2019041245

Our books may be purchased in bulk for promotional, educational, or business use. Please contact your local bookseller or the Macmillan Corporate and Premium Sales Department at 1-800-221-7945, extension 5442, or by email at MacmillanSpecialMarkets@macmillan.com.

First Edition: January 2020

Printed in the United States of America

0  9  8  7  6  5  4  3  2  1

*To Dawn,*
*who believed in this the most*

to the ice towers

# Ennea Món

Mapped by Thalen of Sutterdam

Northvale

Crenovale

Vittorine

Pattevaur

Brallick

Weirandale

Woodsdale

Lakevale

Naple's Mill

Andrale

Guttown

Barston

Cascada

Bay of Ciada

Riverine

Maritima

Queen's Harbor

Prairyvale

Pigtل

Wigلt

Githyan

Yosta

Jigat

Sutterdam

Vigat

The Ribbon

Sutterdam

Melgellia

Metos

Drintoolia

Melladrin

Width of the Mountains

Threecaster

Needle Pass

The Iron River

Fenturan

Oromondo

Fourcaster

Sevencaster

Tar's Basin

Istulpa

Alpetar

Fivecaster

Pexlia

Posted

to the hot zones

## Hidden Talents

What talent hides unseen within each breast?

Begrimed, bejeweled, and all the rest,

Till soothing sun calls forth a sleeping bud

Or rain reveals the gold beneath the mud.

# PRELUDE

## Cascada, the Capital of Weirandale

Four catamounts stalk the Throne Room, their black-tipped tails scribbling unease in the stuffy air. They linger near the Dedication Fountain, lapping the water that spills down to the pool.

Catamounts have guarded the throne for centuries.

These beasts pay little attention to the guards who check the room or the women who periodically sweep the floor. If the maid is sobbing over a slap or a kick, they do not care. They do not attend to the night shrieks of prisoners in the cells, and though they can't hear the children's hungry fretfulness in the city below the palace, in any event the catamounts would ignore their plight. People in general hold no interest to these mountain lions: they live solely for their devotion to the queens of Weirandale.

But no queen has occupied the Nargis Throne for more than a dozen years, not since Queen Cressa the Enchanter's terror-driven flight. Now the only thing the cats can do is sniff anyone who dares to enter the Throne Room, seeking a familiar scent. Their menace holds off any usurper foolish enough to attempt a coronation at the Dedication Fountain.

Sometimes the catamounts rub against the throne's arm or leg.

Sometimes they dash through the room, their tawny coats sliding over heavy muscles, chasing a beam of light or a speck of dust. On occasion they roar to relieve their boredom and frustration. But no queen appears to take her rightful place, and the years slip by.

The chair sits empty. Locked tight, the Throne Room shouts only stillness and quiet. The catamounts wait, their yellow eyes gleaming, lashing their tails.

# PART
# ONE

*Reign of Queen Cressa,*
*Year 8*

EARLY
WINTER

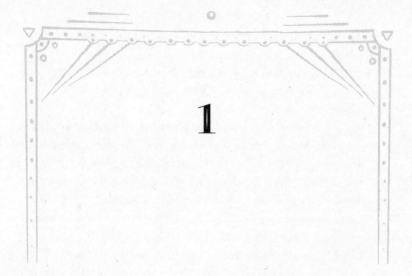

# 1

## Cascada

"Have you noticed anything different or unusual about the princella since our last conference?" asked Chronicler Sewel.

"Not really," Queen Cressa had to admit with a sidelong glance at her daughter, who was perched—with a sullen mouth—on the chair beside her in the chronicler's private office. His desk, bookshelves, and stiff-backed chairs made the modest room cramped, or perhaps the queen's physical discomfort arose from the subject at hand. This was the fourth time she had brought Princella Cerúlia for her Definition, and again the visit boded to be a failure.

"She hasn't shown extraordinary perception or navigational ability or skill at archery?"

"No," Cerúlia spoke for herself. "I haven't."

Sewel nodded. His quill scratched against a piece of paper, his hand shielding his words.

"Princella, do you know what I've written?"

"Now, how could I know that?" she answered, the front of her shoe just reaching the floor, which allowed her to scuff her toes.

"How would we recognize, Sewel, if she manifested as a *puppeteer*?" asked the queen.

"That's easy enough. Princella, use your mind to make me clap my hands."

Sewel's hands didn't move. Cerúlia made a sound of disgust.

"What about a *far-viewer*?" Queen Cressa suggested. "Cerúlia, can you see your father?"

"Mamma, I would have told you if I could." Although she didn't move her feet, her mother heard the tiny snort through her nose and saw the way her upper lashes slammed against her lower.

"Indeed," said Sewel, rubbing his sparse goatee. "I imagine that you've become acutely aware of past queens' Talents."

"Grand-mamma was Defined at four summers, and Mamma at six, and here I am at eight, and I can't do *anything*."

"I highly doubt, my princella, that after having endowed all the queens of Weirandale with a special Talent, Nargis would abruptly discontinue the practice with *you*." Sewel gestured toward the indicia of Nargis in the room: a waist-high, white marble column that broadened at the top into a bowl shape. Water continually overflowed the bowl, falling into a ribbonlike trough that circled back down around the base. "We must just not have recognized your ability."

Cressa found Sewel's surety comforting. "We keep expecting that you will be an Enchanter like me," she said. "We may be overlooking something obvious or something rare."

"Mamma, can't you use your Enchanter's Talent to figure it out?" Cerúlia asked. Her face looked drawn in the pale light of a winter morning.

"I wish I could. My own Talent is so limited."

"If you'd read more in *The Queens' Chronicles,* Your Majesty, you would realize that all Talents grow over time. They typically start quite narrow, and then as the queen matures and faces challenges, she discovers that her Talent spreads into adjacent areas. Nargis does not want to overwhelm her queens with Powers they are not yet ready to wield." Sewel's gaze grew distant and he rubbed his chin again. "Though no Talent is limit*less*. Each queen inevitably discovers blockages and exclusions. I've often wondered if Nargis places these there with some kind of design. . . ."

"Yes, yes. I know I must make the time to look at the books on other Enchanters," the queen acknowledged with a touch of frustration. "At any rate, I take it we can make no further progress today toward Defining the princella?"

"Princella," Sewel addressed her directly and leaned forward, "is there *anything* you can do that other people can't?"

"Last time I told you I like to make up stories—but lots of people can do that. And nothing happens when I tell tales; I mean, the giants don't become real or anything like that."

Sewel nodded.

"She's got a good ear for music," said Cressa. "But, we discussed this last year and I've paid close attention ever since; music may be a comfort in her life, but not a magical Talent."

"I can talk to my horse?" Cerúlia offered hesitantly.

Sewel leaned back, his head—because he was so slight of stature—not even reaching the top of the chair back. A smile reached his gray eyes. "Ah, *that* childish fancy."

"It's *not* a 'childish fancy,'" said Cerúlia, with an extra swing of her foot.

"Oh, I didn't mean on the part of Your Highness; I was referring to my own fancy, when I was young, that I could talk to my pony." Sewel's neat-featured face lost its habitual shrewd expression. "I used to whisper in his ears by the hour and imagine he understood me. I think such a belief is quite common among children."

"And he talks back to me," Cerúlia said.

"Out loud?" asked the chronicler, sitting up straighter.

"No. In my head."

"Does he speak the Common Tongue?"

"No, not really," her daughter faltered a little. "He just . . . well, thinks at me."

"Hm-mm," Sewel shook his head. "My pony conveyed that he wanted a treat, or he wanted his neck scratched. Animals are remarkably good at communicating their desires nonverbally, aren't they?" The royal chronicler brightened. "But this may show that you are on the way toward developing a branch of Intuition—which is a subset of Enchantment. Your Majesties, I'd suggest you stay alert for any more definitive manifestation. In the meantime, I will do a little research." He waved his hand at the arched doorway behind his desk that led from his office into the Royal Library.

"Very well, Sewel." Cressa rose, Cerúlia followed suit, and Sewel jumped to his feet. "Cerúlia, run along to your lesson chamber—Tutor Ryton will be waiting."

Once her daughter had left them alone, the queen, standing with her hands on her chair back, addressed her chronicler. "Sewel, tell me, should I be worried? Has this ever happened before?"

"We must have faith. The Waters flow on the path they choose," he replied. However, under her continued intense gaze, he withered. "Ah, no. Not to my knowledge. Usually a princella's Talent is marked by five, or six at the latest."

"And after the chronicler Defines her," said Cressa, "he hoists the Queen's Flag, so that everyone knows that Nargis has again blessed the line with some extraordinary power as a mark of the Spirit's favor. That the whole palace marks us visiting you and yet the flag is never raised—this is becoming hard for Cerúlia." She meant to excuse her daughter's pouts; she didn't add that the uncertainty also undercut her own rule; Sewel would understand this.

Sewel made a helpless, baffled shrug. "As you said, Your Majesty, we must be overlooking something obvious or something rare. Nargis grants the Talents, but it is up to us to recognize them, and then it is up to you royals to learn how to wield them."

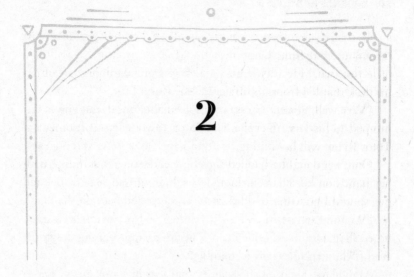

**2**

Two days after her humiliating visit to the chronicler's office, Cerúlia looked up from her work to gaze at the reflections from Pearl Pond that skittered about on the ceiling. The small lake on the side of the palace had no pearls in it; it just reflected the building's white stone.

Tutor Ryton coughed deliberately. She shot him a grin and he responded by raising his eyebrows at her. Instead of picking up her quill, Cerúlia crossed to the window and surveyed the scudding clouds.

"Princella!" reprimanded Tutor Ryton.

"I want to see if it's still fine out, 'cause we talked about going out later." Really, she wanted to see if the blue bird was perched anywhere in view, but she caught no sight of it.

"Princella, please return to your task."

Cerúlia sighed dramatically and turned away from the window. She stopped to pet her little greyhound, Zizi, who was toasting herself in a tight circle in front of the fire.

*Zizi, do you hear me?*

Getting no response, she crossed to the large desk, where Ryton traced another map for her to work on.

"How far do you think I can tip this inkwell before it spills?" she asked, reaching across his work to the filigreed brass pot.

Ryton merely cocked an eyebrow.

Cerúlia tipped it once slightly, then again more vigorously. The third time she cried, "Oops!"

Ryton sprang to his feet to get away from the liquid—but the inkwell still stood upright in her little fingers.

Cerúlia giggled at Ryton's jump, but her tutor just shook his head with a sorrowful expression. She decided he looked somewhat like a hound, what with his sad round eyes, long nose, and big ears.

"You're no fun," she said. Teasing him never made him laugh; it just made him sad. Reluctantly, Cerúlia returned to her stool and began writing in names of the capitals of the duchies on the blank map of Weirandale on her own table. She'd filled in three more when she heard her mother's quick footsteps approaching down the tiled hall toward her lesson chamber.

Most days, her mother or nursemaid would look in on her—especially since Tutor Ryton had mentioned the princella occasionally behaved impudently with him.

"Your Majesty," said her tutor, bowing, as her mother walked in.

"How does our pupil today?" asked Mamma, coming to stand behind Cerúlia, with a hand resting on her shoulder.

"She's been applying herself well enough, Your Majesty," he answered, though he lifted his brows a bit at Cerúlia again.

"See, I've filled in all the Western Duchies—I've only got the Eastern ones left."

Her mother stroked her hair. "After you write in all their names, Tutor Ryton will tell you about the major crops in each. Don't you think that would be wise, Tutor?"

"Very wise," he replied.

"But Mamma, I was almost done with this! Why'd you have to make it harder?"

"Hush, Cerúlia, you will study as Ryton and I see fit: you'll need to know so many, many things someday."

There was a knock on the door, and then a guard allowed Tiklok, mother's favorite messenger, to burst in.

"Beg pardon, Your Majesty," he said as he bowed.

Her mamma took the fat envelope Tiklok offered on a silver

tray. She always treated him gently, even if he did have that awful hole in his cheek and whenever he spoke he made an odd noise that sounded half huffing and half whistling.

Cerúlia ran to Tiklok to play their "Giant-Go-A-Walking" game: he held out his hands while she stood on his large boots. She balanced on his feet as he took long steps. It took him only five strides to cover the whole length of the room.

"Faster," ordered Cerúlia while her mother pulled out several pages of thick vellum. But she found that the game was not as much fun as when she was little, before she was the only Undefined princella in the whole history of the realm. And her mamma looked stricken.

"Mamma. What's wrong?"

"Hm-mm?" said Mamma, scanning several pages ahead. She turned to Tiklok. "You must find Councilor Belcazar and tell him to meet me in my closet.

"I must attend to this matter," she continued. "Ryton, I've changed my mind. Instead of working on the duchies, have our girl look at larger maps. Teach her to identify the Great Powers and their major cities."

Her mother swished out, leaving only an overlooked token of her presence, like when the blue bird dropped a feather. Cerúlia picked up the discarded envelope. The sealing wax shone red, and when she folded the flap back in place, she made out an imprint showing many jagged shapes.

"What's this, Tutor?"

"That's the signet of Oromondo. Those symbolize the eight flames of their Magi."

"Flames?" asked Cerúlia.

"Yes, in Oromondo they worship Fire."

"Not the Waters of Life?"

Ryton shook his head; he was preoccupied with pulling out a giant scroll and laying it out on the big easel table with weights to hold down the corners.

"Come here, Princella; we will study Queen Catreena's map of the Great Powers," he said, moving a stool so she could stand on it. "I will show you where your father's ships are now."

"Will you show me this country, with the red flames?"

"Of course," he said, patting the stool.

She didn't like the way this letter had troubled her mother. "I'm coming," she said, still staring at the red wax.

"Prin-*cel*-la."

On her way she detoured to throw the envelope into the fire. "There," she said, with satisfaction. "That's the end of *them*."

The fire flamed up so intensely around the envelope that it almost caught the hem of her skirt as she turned away.

# 3

"You sent for me, Your Majesty?"

"I did, Belcazar. Close the door behind you." Cressa didn't want any of her overly curious retinue listening in on their conversation.

Belcazar complied and took a chair at the table across from the queen. He was a husky man, pockmarked, with hair crimped into tight curls, light brown but streaked with amber when hit by the light. Now in his fifties, he moved carefully, thought deliberately, and talked precisely, so that consulting him often drove Cressa to distraction. But she had learned to value his analysis. His family held a midsize estate in Vittorine, and years ago he had traveled to Cascada to entreat Queen Catreena to adopt a more equitable tax formula on landowners large and small. This formula impressed her mother because it quelled many irritating complaints. Later she asked him to come up with a solution for clogged drainage ditches; the lattice screens he designed were still in use all around Weirandale.

Queen Catreena had appointed him to *her* Circle Council twelve years ago. Cressa had asked him to continue serving; indeed, out of all her councilors, she trusted him the most.

"I received this—this missive. I would like your opinion on it."

Belcazar nodded and without fuss began to read the long document she placed before him.

His gray eyes paused over every word so Cressa sat alone with her thoughts. She wished she could ask her mother's opinion. "Catreena the Strategist," the people now called her. Her Talent had become blazingly obvious early on when as a toddler she bested all adults in Oblongs and Squares.

Cressa judged her own Talent a paltry weapon for the present circumstances. At the comparatively late age of six summers her mother had taken her to Rowatag, the former royal chronicler, for her own Definition. Her mother had told him, "The princella is able to change people's memories."

The ancient functionary had tested this assertion: he had called in a young assistant, asking him to fetch a certain herb they all saw from the window. When he returned, Cressa had been asked to erase the assistant's memory of his errand. She had climbed down off her chair and touched his dry, ink-stained hand. When questioned, the man vehemently denied that he had left his work desk all morning; showing him the stalks of chives and the mud on his boots did not bring back his recall.

How well Cressa remembered that later that afternoon, her mother had taken her outside to see that the Queen's Flag—silver droplets falling into a silver river, on a backing of blue silk—had been hoisted onto the top of the palace and had rippled in the wind! Some Talents were publicly announced; others (especially related to Enchantment) were kept private to increase a queen's opportunities to learn to wield them. But at least everyone knew that Nargis had graced Cressa with its favor.

Rowatag explained that Cressa's Talent was a variety of Enchantment. He had spoken at length about other queens in Weirandale's past who were also Enchanters, though their specific abilities varied. One had been a *memory enhancer;* she could make people remember in minute detail events they had forgotten. Another was a *compeller;* she could force people to act against their will. Still another queen could read people's thoughts. Often, over time, Enchanters developed several ways of affecting people's minds and memories.

Cressa grasped how *compelling* would be useful: she would

just compel the Oromondians to do as she bid. Though she always needed to be touching her subject—would she have to touch all the citizens of Oromondo?

But "making people forget" had not as yet proven particularly useful. As a child she had sometimes made Nana forget that she had already had her candied fruit and she would get another one. Thus far, she had had few real occasions to practice her Talent for something of consequence.

Belcazar had only turned over half the pages. Cressa stood and paced around her comfortably appointed private audience chamber, her closet, with its deep blue rug and white velvet wall hangings.

*Plink.*

The water feature in this room, named the Weeping Swan, was a glass and gold bowl, above which rose an enameled swan's neck and head. The beak dropped one drop of Nargis Water at a time; usually Cressa no longer registered the sound of the droplets.

Her mother had been the Strategist; always looking five steps ahead, calculating what would happen before her every move. Catreena had married the widowed King Nithanil of Lortherrod because she deduced that someday an alliance with Lortherrod would be of utmost importance to Weirandale.

*Plink.*

Ironically, the only thing Catreena had not seen in advance was that she herself would die in her prime. Caprice struck with random cruelty, heedless of the harm it wreaked. Catreena's horse had stepped in a gopher hole and thrown her. She had broken her neck and died instantaneously, a look of surprise frozen on her face. Cressa had been only twenty-three summers; she had been five moons into her pregnancy with Cerúlia. She had not felt ready to assume the throne: she had wanted some years of private life. She did not feel ready now for this challenge.

*Plink.*

Finally, Belcazar deliberately straightened all the pages, then straightened them again and moved them to the side. He drummed his fingers on the table, one at a time. The queen stifled her urge to scream at him and sat down on the opposite side of the glossy mahogany table.

"Troubling," he said.

"I realize."

"This was . . . hand-delivered this . . . morning?"

"Yes."

"Did the servant see *who* brought it? Did Envoy Thum come himself?"

"I don't know. Why does that matter?"

"Well," said Belcazar thoughtfully, "perchance it doesn't. But we have received other communiqués from Thum and this . . . doesn't convey the same tone."

*Plink.*

"What do you mean?"

"Thum shows belligerence and . . ."

"—aggression. Like all Oros." Cressa often found it impossible not to fill in Belcazar's pauses, though doing so never sped up his delivery.

He nodded. "Oromondo has been a militaristic realm forever and a day. It respects discipline above all."

"This is not surprising," said Cressa. "Their country is volcanic, and the populace must be taught to heed warnings of eruptions. And they rely on mining, a venture that requires strength and fearlessness."

Belcazar nodded slowly, looking at his fingernails as if the answers to all the world's troubles were written in their ridges.

*Plink.*

He continued, "But in past years we have always been able to treat with Thum. Oh, he'll evoke the great divinity of their Eight Magi and . . . chastise us for being nonbelievers, but that rhetoric merely covered his true goal. Since the War of the Priests we have traded amicably."

Belcazar took out his handkerchief, blew his nose, and deliberately put the kerchief back in his sleeve.

*Plink.*

Cressa massaged her forehead with her fingertips in impatience.

"We suspect Oromondo has been paying the Pellish pirate fleet to raid for foodstuffs, but we have found no proof. But here"—Belcazar pointed to a passage—"and here, and here, the religious zeal rings so fervent." He read aloud:

> Ye have offended the Magi and pure Oromondians with thy putrid heathen practices. Weakling scum of the earth, reeking with corruption, soiled with thy guilt, worshippers of water, idolaters of a line of Witch bastards, rats puffed up with trifling vanities and unclean luxuries—the Magi will tolerate thy meddling NO LONGER.

"I skipped over those flourishes," she said. "I think the crux of the matter lies in the rice shipments—the rice they claim was poisoned, the rice they say caused stillbirths and drove cows mad."

*Plink.*

"The rice wasn't poisoned," said Belcazar.

"Could someone, somehow have tampered with it?"

Belcazar rubbed between his brows with a forefinger, and Cressa again became conscious of the drip of the water.

*Plink.*

"Consider, Your Majesty, how *much* poison it would take to taint four full holds of grain. And mix it through? Hardly probable. And to what end?" More finger drumming. "Nevertheless, before the full Circle meets, let's inquire if any of the shipmasters rest in port. And question the grain merchant."

"The Circle meets after noonday so I will send the messages now." Cressa went to the door and spoke to her servants.

"I hardly think," she said as she turned back to Belcazar, "that Thum, or anyone, would simply invent the notion of women losing their babes."

"But one does not feed rice to milk cows," he countered.

"They might if they had no other grain. Look you, what do we know about Oromondo? For some years it has groaned under mysterious blights and suffered a food shortage. That is why they trade for foodstuffs. Didn't Tenny tell us that the Oros have numerous procurement contracts with the Free States?"

"True," replied Belcazar. A long pause while each finger struck the wood. "These blights. These illnesses, no one knows their cause."

"But why blame us?"

*Plink.*

Belcazar repeated drumming each finger on the table. "Why do villagers turn on their neighbors . . . when misfortune strikes? People need answers, and they will blame whomever they suspect wishes them ill. Someone . . . paranoid . . . wrote this letter; someone bursting, exploding with religious zeal."

"I don't think it matters who dictated it. What matters is that Oromondo demands that I relinquish the throne, we return the gold and the jewels they sent, and we send eight more ships full of grain on tomorrow's tide, or it will declare war on us."

"Yes," said he. "You've got the meat of it." Then he went on to recite a passage from the letter:

> Thy streets will run with blood, thy Witch will meet justice, we will take what we are owed by the force of the Magi's glorious Power.

"What shall we do?" Cressa's face stiffened with anger.

"Hmm? Do? About what?"

"Any of it. All of it."

Belcazar, whom she knew to be a peaceable, imperturbable man, for once answered quickly. "We prepare for war."

*Plink.*


Queen Cressa steadied herself for a moment before entering the Circle Chamber where her council awaited her. Over the last year, more and more she dreaded meetings with this group.

Oh, she trusted Belcazar and sweet, elderly General Yurgn. But lately she guessed that her councilors didn't always tell her the full truth, or that they met separately to strategize how to "handle" her. And all shrank away from any physical contact with her, as if they had heard a whisper about her Talent and feared her touch.

Steward Matwyck, the councilor she had once leaned upon the most, had to be the head of the opposition. Or at the least, she could not imagine the others working against her without his tacit approval. She could be mistaken in her suspicions. She had the authority to dismiss her Circle, but such a drastic step would require that she present incontrovertible evidence of *crimes* to the court and the populace. And she had precious few allies.

The underlying problem, she knew, lay in how little time she had spent in Cascada and how little time in court: she had not won her subjects' personal loyalty. They held little true regard for her, either as a woman or as their queen. When Catreena died, Cressa had abruptly succeeded a ruler who was known and respected for her sagacity. Cressa herself had never earned their acceptance, much less their esteem or love, other than by virtue of her birth and station.

*Well, it will not do to dally in the hallway any longer in front of my watching ladies-in-waiting.*

Cressa raised her chin and told Duchette Aubrie to announce her.

"Your Majesty," the six councilors murmured as they bowed and curtsied. They stood around the council table in the high-ceilinged, round turret room, the winter morning chill chased away by fireplaces at both sides.

Queen Cressa crossed to her high-backed chair, cushioned in blue velvet, at the honey-colored oak table shaped like a hollowed-out circle. By some earlier monarch's design, she had her back to the light coming in the mullioned transoms, so that it shone full on her councilors' faces. Water flowed constantly in a circular pool in the middle of the table, creating a light background murmur. She seated herself, and General Yurgn pushed her chair closer.

"You may be seated," she said. "I take it you have investigated this situation?"

Lord Steward Matwyck, placed on her right, ran these meetings because he held the highest rank on the council. In Weirandale the country's landowners elected a steward every ten years. Matwyck was a handsome man of medium height and graceful build, with soulful dark gray eyes and short mid-brown hair boasting only a few threads of amber. He habitually wore well-tailored but modest attire, usually of muted color.

"Your Majesty," Matwyck said, as he took the floor with an incline of his head. "I hope you are not distressed. How wise of you to turn this matter over to us."

For many years Matwyck's compliments and concern for her well-being had soothed away any disquiet Cressa harbored. Today, however, she found herself more immune to his charm.

"What have you discovered?" she asked, just a tad abruptly.

"We have interrogated the grain merchant and the seamaster of one of the trade ships. The merchant and her family have been eating rice from the same shipment for moons with no sign of illness. No other customer has complained about the rice being tainted. She has supplied many shops, even the palace, with this fall's harvest. In point of fact, we have *all* eaten from her granaries.

"Moreover. We found one of the shipmasters of the transport in port. He swears that no one went down in the hold from the time the rice was loaded until the ship reached harbor. And the ships made no unscheduled stops.

"So we have looked into this matter thoroughly and found nothing amiss. I conclude the charges are specious."

"I cannot fault your logic," Cressa said. "But then why has Oromondo sent such a challenge?"

"Your Majesty, forgive me," Matwyck continued, "but we know the Oros better than you do. This bluff is in decidedly poor taste, but not a cause for anguish."

Belcazar broke in. "I have already said my piece, Matwyck. You know I . . . disagree. I believe that the army must be mustered now and . . . all defensive measures put in place. We can't take the Oros lightly. And this letter contains . . . outright . . . threats."

"But Belcazar, Your Majesty," said Duchess Latlie, vigorously shaking her double chins, her uncovered hair coiffed in an elaborate ringlet style too young for her advancing years. Her hair shone the gold/orange/tan color commonly described as amber. (On many noble heads the amber strands interwove with brown, but if Latlie grew any brown hairs she had her maid pluck them out.) "I do believe that they have sent threats of this ilk in past years, under dear Catreena's rule. She could not be taunted into overreaction, and I do trust that you will follow her wisdom."

"What do you mean by 'overreaction,' Duchess?" asked Cressa, miffed by Latlie's air of superiority. Latlie always grated on Cressa because she had served as her mother's lady-in-waiting for a year and habitually presumed on this slight connection.

"Just that we would hate for you to muster the army or cause all sorts of uproar over this scrap of—of rubbish. And any military move would mean that you would have to raise tithes, dear Majesty. And that would be so unfortunate, even unwise. We would hate for you to have to do that again so soon after the ambitious road project you advocated last year."

"As I recall, Duchess, this council unanimously and enthusiastically approved the repair of the royal roadways. Are you saying now that you begrudge the monies?" Cressa recognized that behind the polite words lay a threat: if you raise levies on the gentry, you will alienate them. "By the way," she continued, hoping to sound like Queen Catreena, but fearing she mimicked Cerúlia on a petulant day, "didn't I ask to see the account books on that project some time ago?"

"You may have," admitted Councilor Prigent, who served as the royal treasurer, a narrow-shouldered, somewhat dull young man whose prematurely thinning hair (the dead brown of a frozen dirt path) was too lank to hold the curled style popular among courtiers and fell lifeless into his pudding face. "If so, please accept my most abject apologies, Your Majesty. An accident with a wineglass spoiled some pages. I will get the ledgers to you as soon as—"

"Prigent! Tsk! Tsk!" Matwyck interrupted in a mock-scolding tone. "Send for the ledgers this instant! That is, if in the present serious circumstances, Your Highness would still like to satisfy your curiosity. . . ."

*How much have they padded those expenses? Dare I push this issue today?*

Cressa assumed what she intended as an icy stare. "Let us return to the issue at hand, which is not roads, nor taxes, nor monies, nor account books, but the Oromondo grievances and threats. Is there aught we can or should do to reason with or placate them? What response do we offer?"

General Yurgn coughed into his age-spotted hand. "We might consider sending them a shipment of rice. Gratis. That would be a gesture toward peaceful relations. If you calculate the price, any mobilization or hostilities would end up costing all of us much more than a shipload of rice."

Matwyck steepled his hands, a characteristic gesture that connoted his thoughtfulness. He had long and shapely fingers. He kept his hands spotlessly clean and reportedly asked his valet to sand his nails nightly. The other councilors, who coveted his approval, looked to him for his reaction.

But Belcazar broke in. "No amount of rice will make up for lost babes . . . or what they see as deliberate . . . insults toward their sacred Magi."

Cressa agreed with Belcazar, but she had no chance to say so, for Matwyck was already speaking. "Oh, Belcazar, do you want us to return the two emeralds and the sapphire too?" Matwyck gave a wry chuckle. "My friends, we need not placate. We just ignore this screed. The Oros will see our silence as a sign of strength. They may bully other countries, but *we* cannot be baited or intimidated. In my considered opinion they will go back to mining their metals and bowing down to their Magi and leave us alone until their need for grain forces them to recommence trading—in which case we may be able to make more favorable terms. Oromondo lies hundreds of leagues away. It doesn't have a navy. Unless, my esteemed friend, you fear the Magi's 'magic powers'?"

Cressa suspected that the Magi's powers should not be sneered at, but she felt boxed in by Matwyck's dismissal because to say so now might make her sound weak or frightened.

"The army's force is always at your disposal, Your Majesty," General Yurgn quietly interjected into the awkward silence.

The queen looked at the two councilors who had not yet spoken, Lady Tenny, her councilor for diplomacy, a sharp-nosed, well-traveled woman whose hair was pulled back in a severe style showing the rusty amber at the temples and the chocolate brown of her widow's peak, and Lord Retzel, bushy-browed and hard of hearing, but the largest landowner in the realm.

Lord Retzel spoke first. "I agree with Matwyck, eh? He's investigated. He's added everything together; he's so clever. I agree completely. Your Majesty." Lord Retzel spoke, as always, too loudly and too forcefully, as if bluster would compensate for lack of brains.

*Of course you do. You serve as his lapdog, or if occasion warrants it, his bulldog. I hate the way you thunder at me.*

Lady Tenny made a snort, conveying that the whole meeting had been a waste of time. "Your Majesty, we have gone round and round on these issues. May I make a suggestion? Before you decide what action to take"—she held up her hands to ward off interruption—"if any, we might demand an audience with Envoy Thum and see what he has to say? Questioning him might offer us more information. We might at least"—here she inclined her head in Belcazar's direction—"be able to determine if he himself wrote the ultimatum or if he just acts as a messenger from the Magi."

Lady Tenny's diplomatic proposal made sense, but most of all, it provided a way for Cressa to escape this room. She did not know which was worse: the way her councilors cajoled, talked over, or threatened her.

"Very well, Lady Tenny," she replied, working to keep her voice steady and her tone calm. "Pray arrange an audience with Thum tomorrow. After Tenny, Belcazar, Yurgn, and I question him, I will discuss this matter with the Circle once more."

"How wise you've grown, my queen," Matwyck smiled as he spoke, but Cressa was not at all sure whether the compliment was genuine or patronizing.

"Rest assured that I will never 'overreact'"—she spoke with an edge in her voice—"but neither will I overlook threats to our sovereignty nor insults to the throne."

Cressa rose to the top of her paltry height and swept out of the room. She was trembling, but hoped they would not notice.

# 4

"Oh my!" said Stahlia, staggered by the sight before her. "How magnificent!"

The Nargis Fountain, situated in the center of the Courtyard of the Star in Cascada, was fashioned of blue and white quartz, with a five-pointed base. Each of the star's points referred to a different manifestation of fresh Water: lakes, rivers, springs, rain, and mist. The icy Waters of the Nargis River arced high up into the sky, balancing aloft a gemstone of Nargis Ice, which refracted the slanting light. The water drifted down, tracing elaborate patterns of water droplets in soft rainbows, falling into an intricate series of stepped pools. Dew trembled in the air around the Fountain.

The Courtyard of the Star hummed with visitors of all stations, but when people neared the edge of the pools, they would fall quiet, listening to the Waters' patter and splash. They would dip one hand into the turbulent lower basin, letting droplets fall off each of their fingers in turn as they muttered the five prayers for Health, Home, Safety, Comradeship, and the Future of the Realm.

Travelers journeyed many leagues just to gaze upon the Fountain, but desperate pilgrims, afflicted with illnesses, also ringed these lower pools. Some wore finery and trailed clouds of sandalwood in their wake; some sported stained woolens, and fleabites flecked their skin. It was said that drinking the Waters might lift the spirits of the depressed, ease grief, or mend a broken body. Yet the Waters behaved capriciously; they did not often work their magic. For every person healed, many more walked away deprived of their last hope.

Stahlia of Wyndton hung back a little from the basin's edge, with her husband and daughter beside her. They had changed into clean outfits and dropped their light cases at the Traveler's Ease as soon as their ship had docked. Stahlia and Wilim had brought their daughter, Percia, to the Fountain, for the chance that it might heal her leg. She was their only child—now nine summers old—and her incapacity grieved them like a throbbing toothache. Stahlia grabbed Percia's hand.

*She'll still be my Percia, even if the Waters refuse to magick her leg. But I can hardly credit that a hobbled future lies in store for her.*

Stahlia watched, barely breathing, as a careworn mother in front of her dipped a battered metal cup in the Nargis Basin and gave it to her toddler to drink. She then spoke distinctly, "Can you hear me, Jeren?"

At the same time, an elderly man with twisted fingers kept plunging his hands into the swirls. "I needs me hands to work," he pleaded. "I needs me hands to work." When his infirmity remained unchanged, a Sister of Sorrow in her gray habit glided to his side, speaking softly to him.

Gathering her courage, Stahlia said, "Come, lamb," to Percia and brought her up to the side of the basin. Wilim pulled out of his waist the embroidered white linen kerchief that had been one of his late mother's prize possessions. Barely daring to breathe, Stahlia dipped it into the Waters, wetting it thoroughly to absorb the enchantment. She took the sopping cloth and rubbed it up and down Percia's damaged leg under her ankle-length woolen dress.

"Ooo, 'tis so cold!" giggled Percia, cringing. "Look! I see a bird way high up, taking a bath!"

"I see it too, my girl," said Wilim, but Stahlia didn't look up.

*Has the crooked bone straightened?*

For good measure Stahlia dipped the kerchief again and repeated the application. Then she rose from her knees. Wilim had taken off his hat to show respect: the upper skin of his forehead showed less weathering than the rest of his face, and his medium brown curls had caught some of the mist. Stahlia's eyes met his, as they were of the same height. She could read what he was thinking, because it was what she was thinking: *Through the Grace of the Waters, let our girl be cured.*

Percia gazed around the teeming courtyard with wonder. At that moment a nearby vendor opened his stall; his display of multi-colored silk ribbons fluttered out gaily into the wind. "Oh! Look!" cried Percia. Irresistibly drawn, she pulled away from her mother's side and ran to the vendor's stall.

*She runs gracefully, as if she'd never been crippled!*

"Steady on, steady on," called Wilim, running after her. Stahlia fell to her knees. She rested her forehead on the basin rim, her face wet with a mix of tears and spray.

*Nargis. I can never repay You for what You have done. I worshipped you unthinkingly before: for the rest of my days, I am Yours.*

Wilim scooped Percia up joyfully, and when she realized that she had run without limping, she shouted, "Look at me! Oh, Papa!"

Of course Wilim bought her the silk ribbon of her choice, which Stahlia carefully wove into her plaits. They looked around at the wares of other vendors and the food stalls and the tourist amulets filled with drops from the Fountain.

When their joy and giddiness wore off they wanted to leave the courtyard, which had grown much more crowded as the day lengthened. The little family struck out on one of the streets, believing that it would lead them in the direction of the textile marketplace Stahlia longed to visit. The broad, cobblestoned avenues and august buildings spoke of centuries of peace and prosperity. Down one street they spied a distinguished structure of gray marble.

"Could that be the palace?" asked Percia.

A man walking by in a brocaded cloak overheard and chuckled, though not unkindly.

"No, little one. That's only an office of the Cascada Bank," he told her. "The palace is at the top of the slope. Look," he said with a pointing gesture, "you can see its white towers in the sky."

Although Wilim had a good sense of direction, they were too shy to ask about routes, and the family soon lost its bearings. Eventually, the travelers found themselves in a quiet neighborhood of stately homes, each surrounded by unfriendly walls.

"Well, Master Wilim, which way now?" Stahlia teased. On another day, she might have been peeved, but today even this mischance seemed marvelous.

"I apologize to me missus," he replied with his typical easy mockery, sweeping off his hat and bending his knee. "I have led us astray. So I must give up the leadership of our little troupe. What do you advise, Percia?"

"Let's go that way." Percia pointed to the left, and Stahlia and Wilim shrugged their shoulders over her head and followed her lead.

After a short way a blue tanager swooped down and alighted upon the cobblestones in front of them. Stahlia had seen the scarlet variety before, but even the red bird rarely nested in the Eastern Duchies.

"That's a tanager, lamb!" she told Percia. "I have never seen one so close. And never a blue one. What's it doing so far north in the winter? Stand still; don't scare it."

The three of them froze, but the bird acted oddly calm in front of the humans. It cocked its head several times, as if looking closely at Percia. Then it turned around and hopped away a few feet, stopping to twist its head to see if they followed.

"Mama!" whispered Percia. "The bird likes me."

And so it appeared. They took a few tentative steps forward, and the bird continued hopping in front of them; after a few moments it flew to the top of a nearby metal gate cut into a high stone wall.

Percia ran ahead and pushed the gate, which swung open at her touch, grating harshly. She dashed through, the bird leading her forward.

"Percia! Hold on now," called Wilim. But she was many steps

ahead and either did not hear or heed him. Wilim rushed through
the gate with Stahlia a few paces behind. On the other side they followed a path that twisted around a thick row of hedges, and then all
at once the three tumbled out into a clearing.

In front of them stood a little girl, a head shorter than Percia,
dressed in an old-fashioned play smock that covered her up from
chin to toe. She also wore a queer white bonnet with a narrow brim
but a deep crown tied under her chin with a broad white ribbon. She
was *talking* to the blue tanager.

"But I didn't ask you to find me a playmate! You can't highjack
people off the path," she scolded. When the tanager sang a few trills,
she acted as if she were listening. "That gate is never left unlocked!
You unlocked it yourself!"

Percia approached the odd little girl wide-eyed. The girl looked
at the tanager and pretended to translate its song.

"He says you're just what he's been looking for and much too
perfect to resist!"

Percia laughed in delight, and the odd little girl joined in.

"I'm Percia."

"I'm very pleased to make your acquaintance," said the girl, with
a little dip of a curtsey.

Stahlia took in that they stood in a beautifully manicured park.
Under a massive oak tree, a little creek burbled along, crossed by
a footbridge and bordered by flowerbeds, neatly readied for winter. Stone benches lounged in the oak tree's shade, and rope swings
hung from its branches. A child-size house with a painted door and
shutters drew an enthralled, "Look, Mama!" from Percia.

Almost invisible in the light shade, an older woman in a black
dress and white cap and white shawl sat watching from one of the
benches.

"Oh! Pray excuse us!" cried Stahlia. "Mayhap we aren't supposed
to be here. Are we intruding?"

"No, no. Ye be welcome."

"We are visiting from the Eastern Duchies and such strangers in
your great city that we quite lost our way," Wilim explained.

"Call me Nana," the woman said. "People have called me Nana for so long ye'd think I never had any other name. Chickadee is so lonely for a child to play with. Could yer daughter keep her company for a while?"

"Is she your grand-babe?" asked Wilim.

"Oh no! I'm her nursemaid."

Stahlia and Wilim sat near the older woman. Stahlia saw Percia lift up her dress and show her new friend her healed leg and turn around to display her silk ribbon. The girls giggled as they ran back and forth across the footbridge chasing one another: Percia was long-legged and graceful, but her new companion was both quick and quick-witted, darting behind obstacles to escape her reach.

"I'm Wilim, and this here is my wife, Stahlia. We live in Wyndton, in Androvale. I work as a peacekeeper for Duke Naven, while Stahlia is a weaver. Her tapestries hang in all the great halls of the Eastern Duchies." Stahlia's cheeks grew warm; she wished that Wilim wouldn't boast about her work so often or so fulsomely.

Then Wilim, always personable and talkative, described their visit to the Fountain and Percia's miraculous cure.

"She had an accident, you see," Stahlia added. "She was dancing last Planting Fest and a wrong-footed boy tripped her. The healer warned us it might not knit well. But now! We can put that sorrow behind us!"

"Will ye be staying in Cascada long?" Nana asked.

"We can't." Wilim shook his head. "It took all our savings just for the passage, and Duke Naven wants me back. Stahlia yearns to search for yarn and thread but we will head back on the ship on the evening tide tomorrow."

Chickadee had escorted Percia all over the little park, pointing out all its features. Now they stood in front of the grown-ups. "We're hungry, please Nana," said Chickadee. Stahlia noticed the girl had velvety brows and long lashes framing warm brown eyes. Gray was the most common eye color, but Stahlia found Chickadee's unusual looks appealing.

"Yes, we're hungry," said Percia, taking on the role of echo.

"Ah, good thing I filled my basket," Nana replied with a cheerful wink, pulling out from the shade beneath the bench a wicker basket filled with a variety of small turnovers. The girls grabbed one in each hand and ran away to have a private feast in the cunning little house.

"Can I offer ye a bite as well? The ones with glaze are sweet, and the ones without are savory."

Stahlia bit into a savory turnover, discovering a mixture of spicy sausage and melted cheese. She hadn't realized she was so hungry; she couldn't resist scarfing it down in quick mouthfuls. Nana urged her to take another: this was filled with black currant preserves, but a hint of lemon rind brought out the currants' tang. Just as Stahlia realized she was thirsty, Nana produced a cool jug of apple beer, which the three adults passed between themselves with sighs of satisfaction.

"How many summers has Chickadee?" asked Stahlia.

"Eight," answered Nana. Stahlia expected Nana might take the opportunity to boast a little about her charge, for the child was clearly imaginative, but all Nana said was that she was a touch willful, but that was understandable, for her mother drove her hard on her lessons.

"How old is Percia?" Nana asked.

"Nine," replied Wilim. "She'll be tall like her mother. And almost as pretty," he said, winking at Stahlia.

Stahlia waved away his flirting and leaned back on the bench, relaxing her tense shoulder muscles in her contentment and the winter sunshine. She only half listened to Wilim's description of Wyndton to Nana as she watched the girls, her own heart leaping each time Percia bounded about like a frisky goat. The playmates climbed on a ladder into a platform in an oak and pretended they were sailors on lookout. Then they scampered down a thick rope. They took turns pushing one another on a swing. When they weren't screaming with laughter, they whispered in each other's ears. Their faces glowed.

"Weaving takes so much skill; do you come from a family in the trade?" asked Nana.

"Not really. My father accepted a loom as payment for a debt," Stahlia replied. Wilim carried on with the tale of how the loom had sat unused and dusty in the barn until a spate of bad harvests; how Stahlia's father had, in desperation, pulled it out and learned to weave simple blankets. Wilim's pride colored his voice as he related how Stahlia had taught herself to form pictures and figures.

All of a sudden Chickadee called out, "Stop me! Stop!" Percia grabbed the swing's ropes, and the high-class child jumped off and ran up to Nana. "Mamma is coming," she announced.

Percia ran over behind her. "How do you know?" she asked, since they heard and saw no one.

"Um, I hear the horses."

Stahlia heard nothing. Nana, however, took her charge's report seriously. She got up, doused a cloth in the stream, came back, and started carefully wiping Chickadee's hands and face clean of dirt and black currant juice. Percia glanced sideways at her friend and turned to Stahlia, requesting, "Neaten me too." A little worried about whether this noble matron would approve of their having trespassed into this play park and wanting to make a good impression, Stahlia obliged. She also combed out Percia's honey-brown bangs; she told Wilim to brush the pastry crumbs off his beard; she patted her own hair under her coif and straw hat, wiped the dust from her boots, and shook out her creased frock.

Meanwhile, Nana had helped Chickadee out of her smock. The white blouse underneath had a wide collar and cuffs of the finest lace. Over the blouse she wore a short weskit of dark green silk embossed with an intricate design, and below, a split skirt of the same. Stahlia was admiring the costly fabric when she heard hoofbeats in the distance, coming on fast.

Then Nana untied the girl's bonnet, and the child's long hair, all of which had been stuffed inside the deep crown, tumbled down.

In all the known realms of this earth, only the queens of Weirandale had hair of that color: the cerulean blue of the icy Nargis River—the blue of a blue tanager. In the shade it could look almost turquoise, but it was bluer than the gem; in the sun it could look sky blue, but always with a light green shimmer.

*"By her hair ye shall know her."* A snatch of an old lay played in Stahlia's mind. This was not just "some child" from one of the neighboring mansions. Percia had been romping all afternoon with the princella herself, Cerúlia, heir to the throne.

Wilim caught her eye and sprang to his feet. Stahlia called her daughter and held Percia against her own body, her arms protectively crossed about the young girl's chest. Nana cast them an amused glance and started to say something, but they could not hear what, for at that moment a squad of six of the Queen's Shield, equipped in breastplates embossed with silver droplets and blue cloaks, came thundering up on tall black horses. Stahlia glimpsed additional horses behind the phalanx. The soldiers—five men and one woman—had hard faces, and they did not look happy at finding interlopers with the princella.

The silence stretched long, broken only by the horses' fidgety shifting of their hooves, their blows, and the sound of leather creaking.

Then the front soldiers pulled their mounts aside to let a particularly fine beast walk forward. Nana and the little girl fell into deep curtsies; Stahlia and Wilim more awkwardly followed suit, while Percia just stood awestruck. In the middle of the riders, a petite woman, garbed in a white riding habit, her blue hair (slightly darker than her daughter's) peaked out from under a tiny hat with a trailing, embroidered bag-coif, kicked her feet out of the stirrups. Her Royal Stone, a hexagon of Nargis Ice, shimmered from her brow, where it was held in place by an extremely thin, transparent circlet. She declined the proffered assistance of a guard and slid gracefully to the ground. The man jumped forward to grab the reins of her mount.

"What have we here?" asked Queen Cressa, not unpleasantly, but with a slight wariness in her tone.

"Mamma, I should like to introduce you to my friend, Percia of Wyndton," responded Cerúlia. "We have had such a grand time!"

"Pleased to make your acquaintance, Percia of Wyndton," said the queen, using a soft tone to the child, who finally responded to Stahlia's tug and made a deep and graceful curtsey. The monarch then turned to the nursemaid. "Nana?" Stahlia's anxiety over their trespass escalated so that her legs quivered.

"Let me present her parents, Your Majesty," said Nana in a bit of a rush. "Good folk," she added, "Wilim and Stahlia, visitors from Androvale."

"Your servants, Your Majesty," mumbled Stahlia and Wilim, trying to bow even lower.

The queen considered them a long moment. "Please rise. If Nana cannot judge who are safe companions for the princella, the realm is indeed in peril."

"If you will permit me, the real question, Majesty, is how did they get into the palace grounds?" asked a man who wore a tall feather in the middle of his helm.

"The West Gate was unlocked," answered Chickadee.

"The West Gate is never unlocked."

"I regret to contradict you, Captain, but today it was," Wilim dared to answer.

"Seena!" the captain barked. "Check this out." The female shield slid off her horse and disappeared into the hedges.

"Don't be mad, Captain Stern Face," said Chickadee. "Mayhap the squirrels unlocked it."

Everyone laughed, breaking the tension, as Stahlia suspected the clever child intended. The queen then spoke to them graciously, inquiring about conditions in the Eastern Duchies. She questioned Wilim closely about any crime or troublemakers in his ward, the toll of last winter's grippe, and how the autumn yields had shaped up. She moved on to the purpose of their visit to the capital, congratulated them on Percia's recovery, and elicited the story of their losing their way.

Stahlia stood beside Wilim as he conversed with the queen, stealing little glances, wanting to remember forever the pattern of the embroidery on her cuffs, the drape of her collar, and the shimmer of the clear jewel on her forehead.

"Is this your first time visiting the capital, mistress?" The queen tried to include her in the conversation.

"Oh—um—yes. That is, no, I've never been here before. Ma'am. Your Majesty." Stahlia nearly died of embarrassment at her fumbling answer.

The queen smiled graciously and turned back to Wilim. Stahlia looked around to see what the girls were doing; bored with the adults, they now were feeding the princella's horse stalks of dried grass.

"This is Smoke," she overheard the princella tell Percia. "Smoke, this is Percia of Wyndton."

Stahlia watched apprehensively as this beast, so much more dangerous-looking than farming drays, gently lipped bits from her daughter's hands. The artist in Stahlia registered the horse's black coat and the girls' brown and blue hair, gleaming in the slanted light.

When the horse finished the last offering, the princella grabbed Percia's hand and rushed over to the circle of adults.

"Mamma, come see the fishing hole we found."

They all trooped over to the little stream that meandered through the play park. Stahlia, still under the spell of the morning's magic, felt drawn to kneel on the bank and dip her hand in the babbling quicksilver. She let the water drip off each of her fingers as she silently chanted prayers to Nargis.

She could feel the queen's gaze upon her.

Stahlia cupped the water in her hand and took a sip. It tasted like any stream water but was somehow more refreshing. Stahlia held the next swallow in her mouth longer, savoring its cool, woodsy wetness, the flavor of pebbles and pine needles.

The princella, so much bolder than Percia, impatiently tugged her mother's hand in both of hers and pulled her the last few paces. "Mamma! You're supposed to look at the fishing hole!"

"I see it, Cerúlia. It's rather deep. Someday we'll rustle up a fishing rod for you and give it a try."

"Sergeant Bristle's probably your man for fishing, my princella," said the captain. "He's always telling tall tales about the fish he caught back in his wastrel youth in Lakevale. But it's too dark now to see if anything lurks down there."

The queen glanced up at the lengthening shadows. "The days run short, and we've dallied much longer than I intended." She instructed the captain to make arrangements for two shields to escort the family out of the grounds and to their inn. She waved away their thanks, saying it was the least the throne could do for their services entertaining the princella.

"Bid your friend farewell," she said to Chickadee.

Somehow, it hadn't occurred to either child that they would have to part.

"No!" they shrieked simultaneously, wrapping their arms around one another.

Shocked silence greeted the unthinkable impertinence of contradicting the queen. The two little girls, standing in the waning light, clung to one another like the sole survivors of a shipwreck.

Several of the shields looked away or down at their feet while the nursemaid and the queen both appeared nonplussed at such disobedience. Stahlia moved first, kneeling, talking to the girls quietly, rubbing their backs, making promises she knew were lies—that *they* knew were lies—about how they would see each other again soon. After a few moments, Percia transferred her teary embrace to her mother's neck.

Stahlia worried more about the princella, who ran to bury her head in Smoke's flank, keeping her face hidden. The horse turned around to nibble at the little girl's collar, stamping his back hooves.

Queen Cressa thoughtfully stepped back to the country travelers and drew them a few paces aside from everyone else.

"Would you grant me a boon?" she quietly inquired.


"Nana," Cerúlia asked, as the two of them rode toward the palace and a cold wind started to blow in their faces, "did Mamma enchant Percia and her folks? Did she make her forget me?"

"Aye, I suspect she did. Their faces changed after she touched them and they left without seeing us."

"How could she do that? *Why would she do that?*" Her voice rose higher.

"I don't know, Chickadee. You'll have to ask *her.*"

In her anger, Cerúlia kicked Smoke into a gallop.

# 5

When she returned to the palace, Cressa had no chance to attend to Cerúlia's distress because numerous clerks and two ladies-in-waiting besieged her, the former wanting her approval of various documents, the latter the opportunity to show themselves essential. She allowed herself to be led to the Administration Salon and seated herself at a generously sized table. A servant poured her a glass of wine while Cressa worked her way through the matters presented to her, distracted by her ladies' commentary and their half-successful, half-irritating efforts to prove their worth.

Cressa had never learned how to use the ladies-in-waiting efficiently because she refused to appreciate the necessity of keeping on top of court rumors. She hated having these attendants bobbing around her and suffered them with ill grace, which made their days difficult and made her feel guilty and churlish.

"Let me blot that before you get ink on your cuff, Your Majesty," offered Duchette Lumetta. (Cressa found Lumetta particularly suffocating, but she was Councilor Latlie's kinswoman.)

Lady Fanyah had picked up a report on the grain yield from Prairyvale, her home duchy. "These figures look low to me," she commented.

Wondering whether Fanyah was being helpful or deliberately

sowing discord, Cressa said, "Good to know. I will have the bushel count rechecked." Turning to the clerks she asked, "Are we done now? That's everything that can't wait another day?" Receiving their assent, she addressed Lumetta and Fanyah, "Ladies, you are also dismissed for today."

"But Your Majesty, wouldn't you like us to dine with you?" asked Lumetta. "I heard the juiciest story today!"

"Might I suggest—" Fanyah began.

"Ladies!" Cressa interrupted, "sometimes I need solitude just to think! You may attend me tomorrow."

Accompanied only by Shield Branwise, she walked through the building to the Royal Library and bid Branwise fetch Sewel. Her chronicler rushed to greet her, the key of his office swinging round his neck on its golden chain.

"You were right," she said. "I need to consult the volumes of other Enchanters—the sooner the better."

Once inside, he swiftly lit lanterns. The library was situated on the ground floor of a corner turret; bookshelves stretched up for two stories, separated by window slits. One large window—it faced west—consisted of two panes of glass with water continually, silently, running between them: a waterfall trapped inside a window. The water inside the glass did not add moisture to the room full of the most precious records of the realm. In the afternoon light the Sunset Waterfall refracted pink and orange hues; now, however, because the sun had fallen behind the foothills, the swirling water caught just a hint of the lantern gleams.

*The Queens' Chronicles* stood bound in red velvet, bolstered by filigreed bracing. As Sewel laid them out for her Cressa looked back and forth between them, cross-checking one story against another. Sewel watched her closely, but instead of pestering her he merely noticed when she needed more light and patiently held the lantern closer to the pages covered with beautiful—but fading—script.

When she let the cover of the last volume slap closed, Sewel winced at her less-than-gentle handling of his treasures.

"It has been some weeks, Your Majesty, since you favored me

with your thoughts. Might you have a moment now?" Chroniclers held a specific function in Weirandale. The Brothers and Sisters of Sorrow chose a person from their order based upon his or her meticulous attention to detail. Sewel's life work lay in compiling *The Reign of Queen Cressa;* like previous chroniclers he would intermix pages devoted to public records or witnesses' testimony to her deeds with sheets dictated by the liege herself.

Cressa felt pressed for time, but also duty-bound to leave for the future some intimation of her present predicament. Sewel could write as fast as she could speak, so for several moments she chose her words with care as his quill flowed across a page.

Cressa waited until the quill stopped scratching. "Sewel," she mused, "if I were to dismiss one of my councilors, could I appoint you instead?"

"Your Majesty, I would serve you in any manner you requested, although chroniclers know precious little about daily political issues. Our expertise lies in the past. But if you mean to ask if chroniclers have, in Weir history, ever sat on a Circle Council, this occurred only once to my knowledge: in the reign of Queen Cymena the Proud, when Cymena beheaded all of her Circle and then needed to form a temporary replacement."

"Beheaded? Not a happy precedent."

"They had been plotting against her, and at this time the Rorthers were mounting raiding parties against coastal villages. She had to present herself as indisputably in charge."

"Should I behead anyone who is rude to me?"

"I'm not certain, Your Majesty"—Sewel weighed his words—"that beheadings work to win the love of the people."

"Did my mother ever have enemies killed?" Cressa asked.

"Domestic adversaries?"

"Yes."

"Not to my knowledge," he answered. "None are recorded in *The Life of Queen Catreena* by Rowatag, and Rowatag was most scrupulous."

"But then my mother wouldn't have needed to. Everyone was afraid of her."

Sewel only nodded. He didn't need to add, "and no one is afraid of you," because they both knew this to be true. Cressa sighed and nodded a farewell.

As Cressa left the library, Shield Branwise shadowed her, one step behind, when she headed toward the front of the palace and the formal double staircase that led to the Royal Chambers. Ahead of her Cressa spied a blue cloak and called out, "Captain Clemçon!" The leader of her personal guard, a square-face man with light gray eyes, froze halfway up the staircase and turned around.

"Your Majesty?"

"I wish you to put one of the catamounts on patrol in the Royal Wing tonight and continue until I tell you otherwise."

"Do you know of some threat?" Clemçon's body tensed, and his hand instinctively sought his scabbard.

"No, this is just a precaution. A diplomatic argument has raised tensions."

"Oh. Then possibly just doubling your shields would suffice. To be frank, Your Majesty, being around the mountain lions makes the men nervous. They weigh as much as a man, and they can take down a buck solo."

"I understand that disquiet, Captain. But what is special about catamounts is that they can't be bribed or threatened; they live for their loyalty to the line of Nargis queens."

"I can assure you that all twenty-four of your shields have been handpicked and tested. They are steadfast. I have personally investigated each—"

"Captain. I intend no slur. I am sure the Queen's Shield is all that I wish and more. I've just been reading some bloody bits of history. Please, indulge me in this."

"To follow your commands is not an indulgence, Your Highness. 'Tis my duty and my pleasure." Captain Clemçon made a stiff bow and strode off to get one of the four great cats from the Throne Room. If the catamounts knew a court officer, and if he addressed them with the ritualistic phrase, "The Nargis Queen desires," they might (or might not) obey a request of this ilk. If they didn't comply with Clemçon, Cressa would have to gather her courage to entreat them herself.

Cressa continued to the princella's suite. These had been her rooms until her mother died and the rooms had been converted back into a nursery.

Her portraits of her father and half-brothers and the landscape painting of a typical Lorther windswept beach at sunset no longer hung in these rooms. Sometimes she missed her other homeland, another of the Great Powers, yet a chilly clime, where Tidewater Keep, situated on a seaside cliff, always smelled of brine. Once, Cressa's collection of seashells had been propped beside the Princella's Lullaby, the open rivulet of water—about knee-high—that coursed along one wall, tiled to look like a rushing stream.

At the present time, following Cerúlia's wishes, the rooms boasted a colorful stencil of all the beasts of the realm. The stencil, however, was superfluous, since the chambers burst with a throng of live dogs and cats. Indeed, Cressa had to nudge them with her knees to make the waves part. While Nana tidied up the day room, Cerúlia, dressed in her nightshift with her blue hair in a sleeping snood, sat in the window embrasure. From the looks of the matter, she was teaching one of her cats to ride on the back of one of the dogs, like a rider on a horse.

"Mamma!" she cried. "You're so-oo late! The moons have already climbed high. And I've been waiting to talk to you."

"Now, dearest," Cressa kissed her brow. "My day has been busy, yet I did come to fetch you from West Garden. Into bed now and I'll chat with you awhile. Nana, feel free to get yourself some supper while I sit with her."

Her daughter obediently bounded into her four-poster bed and pulled the feather-stuffed quilt up to her chin as Cressa pushed the curtains aside and sat on the edge. But as soon as Nana left the room, her daughter turned on her fiercely.

"Mamma, why did you enchant Percia and her parents? I didn't want you to do that!"

"Several reasons. The most important was to protect them. You know the throne has enemies. I thought they would be safer if they couldn't talk about their afternoon with us."

This took the force out of her daughter's complaint; Cerúlia's tone instantly turned from accusation to grief. "But the tanager chose her to be my friend, my best friend."

"Did he now?"

"You must believe me about this."

"Hmmmm," Cressa said noncommittally, thinking about her daughter's lively imagination as she stroked her hair.

"So how will I see her again, if she doesn't remember me and she's sailed away?"

"Perchance when this trouble with Oromondo is over we'll invite her and her family to visit."

"Mamma, could Percia be *my* lady-in-waiting like Lady Fanyah is yours and live at the castle?"

"We'll see."

"How long will *this* 'we'll see' last, Mamma? I don't want to visit Duchess Latlie's grand-niece again."

"Why not?"

"She's nothing like Percia. She's stupid and mean. She pinched me. Look." Cerúlia kicked the quilt down and pulled up her nightshift and pointed out each little bruise mark darkening her brown thigh.

"How did this happen?"

"Yesterday at midmeal she pinched me under the table because everyone was admiring my hair."

"Why didn't you tell me yesterday?"

"The marks didn't show until today."

"Sounds like an envious little beast." Having duly admired each bruise, Cressa tucked the quilt back up around the girl. "What did you do after she pinched you?"

"I moved my chair so that the leg came down on her boot. Then I said, 'Did I hurt you? I'm *so* sorry!'"

Cressa exhaled to keep from laughing. "No, you need not visit her again."

"Good," said Cerúlia, yawning. "She taught me such a funny rhyme though. I wonder why Lady Fanyah never shared it with me. Do you know it?"

Cerúlia sat up and sang tunefully, though she broke into giggles two-thirds of the way through:

*Rorther red upon each head.*
*Lorther gray they do display.*
*In days of old, Iga was gold.*
*In years back, Wyes wore lilac.*
*Alpie yellow shows your fellow.*
*Isles' bright green could be foreseen.*
*Mellie plum to hail your chum.*
*Oro white they hold upright.*
*Pellish pink because they stink.*
*Weir amber is the grander.*
*Precious blue for only two.*
*Muddy brown in every town.*
*Common brown is all around.*

Cressa regretted that Cerúlia had been exposed to this ditty, though she could hardly keep the girl in ignorance forever. Although all peoples the known world over shared a skin color of wheat brown and eyebrows of a darker walnut hue, whether from bloodlines or diet (or if legends were accurate, as a mark of their Spirits' favor), in olden times citizens of many countries displayed a characteristic hair color. But the more their people traveled and intermarried and the more foodstuffs traded freely, the less these colors appeared. Brown hair—of varying shades and textures—had long become the norm. Some people had haphazard streaks of their country's original Old Color.

Nowadays, polite people considered it old-fashioned and narrow-minded to focus on Old Color and deeply offensive to imply that one hue was preferable to another. However, conservative families—like

Duchess Latlie's—still fixated on tracing their "pure" lineage. And they held on to Old Color requirements in arranging marriages.

"I don't approve of that song," said Cressa. "I don't want you to repeat it. Brown hair is just as nice as any other color. Think a bit: Percia's hair is brown, and Duchess Latlie's is full-on amber. So color of hair means nothing. Latlie's a fool and a snob; she disapproves of your father because of his hair."

"My father is one hundred times better than her!" Cerúlia protested.

"Indeed."

Cressa pulled her daughter closer, enjoying the smell of the elderberry soap that Nana used to scrub her, and listening to the soothing murmur of the Princella's Lullaby.

Meanwhile, Nana herself returned from the kitchens carrying a supper tray for herself. Nana had a snug room of her own off of the princella's bedchamber where she would eat in front of her fire. Cressa nodded to her as she passed through: Nana had always held a special place in her heart.

One of the smaller dogs jumped up on the bed and pawed vigorously at the quilt, succeeding in pushing its slender muzzle underneath. It crept beneath and snuggled next to Cerúlia. Cressa didn't particularly like dogs and would never have wanted one in her own bed. But her daughter clutched the creature against her chest and yawned again.

"Goodnight, Cerúlia. May Mother Moon and Daughter Moon watch over your dreams." Cressa kissed her daughter, lingering, wanting to draw the moment out, and then drew closed the bed curtains, blew out the candles, and left her to sleep.

Passing down the stone hallway filled with flaming torches, she saw a doubled contingent of the Queen's Shield. And a catamount, lying in the middle of the floor, impassively staring at her with its yellow eyes, which caught the flames and sent them back again.

# 6

Cerúlia's biggest dog, Aki, prodded her with his cold nose, which he had wiggled under the bed curtains. She rolled over, but then Aki pawed her back with his nails.

She sat up in bed, still sleep-drugged. Cerúlia felt a pressure on her mind, something akin to wings beating against a closed window. She "opened" the window, and Aki spoke to her for the first time. *Danger,* he sent.

*Aki! You can hear me?* Cerúlia delighted in her new connection with a dog. *Can I talk to the other dogs too? What about the cats?*

*Little princess! Danger!* Aki sent.

*Is there a fire?* she asked, yawning.

*No. Strange men. Stink of fear. On the roof. Coming closer.*

Cerúlia twitched the bed hangings open. Zizi, Faki, and Naki growled softly. Pakki, who was so old that he didn't even react to his name, was the only dog not on alert. Her house cats had arched their bodies and their tails twitched. Cerúlia snapped alert.

A short interior corridor connected the queen's chamber and the princella's. Her mother had told her it was built so that mothers and fathers could check on their daughters in the middle of the night without walking in the public hall undressed. The passage wasn't a secret, but because after nursery years it stood dark, cold, and airless, everyone generally avoided it. Platsy, the maid, had once referred to it with a shudder as the "Passageway of Lost Babes," and Nana had scolded her sharply. Reluctantly, she explained to Cerúlia that the name stemmed from the fact that parents used it most when newborns were ailing.

Tonight Cerúlia raced through the black passageway barefoot, the dogs panting on her ankles. She shook her mother.

"Mamma—wake up! Wake up! There are strangers on the roof."

"Um, what?" Her mamma reached for her sleepily and asked, "Are you ill?"

"No Mamma, listen! The dogs say that there are attackers on the roof."

"The dogs say—*the dogs say*—Cerúlia, what kind of nonsense did you wake me up for?"

"Mamma! I swear men are coming to kill us! Look!" Cerúlia grabbed a narrow brand from the fire and held it up so her mother could see her dogs: their heads hung on low, rigid necks, their ruffs stuck straight up and their lips were pulled back from their teeth.

Her mother darted up, taking the burning wood from Cerúlia. She crossed through her sizeable Reception Room, where a maid dozed before the banked fire, and opened the double door to the main hallway. The two shields outside turned to her mother's urgent call. Faki and Naki took advantage of the cracked door to slip out, racing away at full speed, ears flattened, low growls deep in their throats.

While her mother spoke with the men and they called their fellows patrolling the hallway with sharp halberds, Cerúlia saw the catamount push at the window shutter, first with a paw and then with her nose. Cerúlia sprang out into the hall and opened the shutters, which led onto a balcony; the catamount jumped through in one graceful bound.

Two of the shields ran off in the direction the dogs had taken.

"Platsy." Her mother shook her maid and lit two candles with the brand before throwing it into the fire. "Take this. Go back to your quarters and lock your door. You won't get in trouble for leaving your post. Go now!"

Sergeant Bristle and Shield Seena came into her mamma's rooms, their stern expressions and the quivering light making them look like strangers instead of old friends. Bristle bolted the doors to the big hall and wedged a chair cockeyed on two legs against it. Then he led them into Mamma's bedroom and again secured the door. He and Seena crossed through the passageway and locked the door from Cerúlia's rooms to the corridor. They looked around for a sturdy chair to brace against the door but didn't find one to their liking.

"Wake up, Nana!" said Seena, who had gone into Nana's room and shaken her. "Trouble afoot."

Bristle had been examining the door fastenings of the Passageway of Lost Babes. "You ladies go in here," ordered Bristle. "I'll stand watch on the queen's side; Seena, you take this side. Bolt the doors from within and stay quiet there until I give you the all clear."

"Can we take a candle?" asked Nana, rubbing her eyelids.

"Best not," said Bristle.

"Wait!" Cerúlia pulled elderly Pakki and her delicate little greyhound into the protected space. Aki, nostrils twitching, moved beside Seena.

Minutes passed so slowly. Locked in their black, shut-in space, with only glimmers of firelight slipping around the doorjambs, they couldn't tell what was going on. Cerúlia grew bored, and her feet were so freezing she picked them up off the icy stone and rubbed them. She noticed that her mother and Nana wore night clogs; she wished she'd left hers neatly by her bedside as Nana always told her to.

Still they waited. Cerúlia wanted to complain about her feet, and she wanted to call out to the shields to check that they were still close by, but she held her tongue. She wondered, with a shudder, if the lost babies' souls surrounded her in this dark corridor, but she pushed down her rising panic.

The thoughts of Zizi, the knee-high greyhound, battered inside Cerúlia's mind for the first time. Startled by the strange sensation, Cerúlia jerked.

*Zizi?*

*Danger! Men with death in their hearts.* The dog trembled against Cerúlia's calf so intensely that her whole body shook.

*You're all right, Zizi. I swear I'll protect you.*

In the distance they heard shouts and the noise of swords clanging, higher-pitched yells, and then the sound of a woman screaming into the night. She screamed and screamed and screamed.

The noise ceased, and for long moments they heard nothing more. Cerúlia strained her ears, but all she could hear was Mamma and Nana breathing quickly. She took her mother's hand and patted it.

Abruptly, Aki growled. The noise of a blade splintering wood cut through the dark.

"See-na!! I'm coming!" Bristle shouted from behind them.

People had burst through the outer door into her rooms! As terror coursed through her, Mamma crouched down and enfolded her in her arms.

*Intruders! This is one's territory!* Aki's warning splashed into Cerúlia's mind.

Seena shouted, "For the Nargis Throne!" and the clash of sword hitting sword rang out.

But Cerúlia couldn't make out anything further because all at once the air was sundered by ear-splitting yowls, rising in pitch.

The noise became so loud and fearsome that Nana covered her ears in her hands and cried out, "Nargis, protect us!" Mamma pulled Nana down and wrapped her arms around her too. But Cerúlia yanked herself free of the embrace, jumping up and down. She put her mouth to her mother's ear, "It's the cats! I have five cats in my room!"

Her delight in the cats joining the battle only lasted a second. Without warning, something extremely heavy struck the door to their passageway hideout. The door shook, and a chink opened between two planks!

Without meaning to, Cerúlia screamed.

They heard catfight screeches, Aki's growls, and human shouts of pain. Heavy footsteps came thumping down the hallway. More sword clashes and yells and curses. Pakki, finally realizing something was wrong, started woofing, his deep voice echoing in the enclosure and deafening the shut-ins.

"DROP YOUR SWORDS IF YOU WANT TO LIVE," roared Captain Clemçon's voice with such authority it rose above the chaos.

A clattering noise. The cats cut off as if someone had thrown a basin on them. *Shut up, Pakki!* Cerúlia sent to him without even realizing she had done so, and the old hound was so surprised to hear her thoughts in his head that he too ceased his barking. Cerúlia caught the noise of moans and men talking over one another. Someone pounded on the door on the queen's entrance to the passageway.

"Your Majesty, are you unharmed?" came Sergeant Bristle's voice.

Mamma unbolted the door that opened into her own bedchamber. "Yes. Tell me."

Bristle looked wild; he'd lost both helmet and cloak, and dark sweat stains spread under his arms. Nana went to the wardrobe to pull out a night cloak to cover her queen's nightshift. Cerúlia grabbed a fringy coverlet off a chair and wrapped it around herself.

"A band of intruders penetrated the palace grounds," reported Bristle. "They went from the terrace to the roof and were making their way to the Royal Wing. Eight have been killed. Hard to survive when a catamount has broken your neck or a dog ripped out your throat. Two broke into the princella's rooms. They were fought off by Seena and all the animals."

"Who are these intruders?" asked her mother.

"We don't recognize 'em."

"But are they Weir citizens?" she pressed.

"As far as we can tell. Course, we'll be asking these questions of the captives."

"I would see them. Nana, keep her here." Wrapping her cloak around her, Mamma left the suite through the public hall. Nana reached out for Cerúlia's shoulders, but Cerúlia was too quick—she slid out right behind her mother.

Cerúlia's eyes opened round when she saw her own rooms. Five shields and Captain Clemçon were crammed inside, and all her furniture had been tossed about. In the light of flickering torches she saw red splattered everywhere and pooling on the floor. The cats perched here and there, briskly and innocently licking paws and coats. Aki's eyes were locked on two men on the floor, his lips pulled back in a snarl, his fur puffed out like a porcupine. The men on the floor wore dark colors; their clothes were torn; their faces twisted.

*Aki, what—*

Cerúlia broke off contact with the dog to attend to the human conversation. Captain Clemçon had gone down on one knee to the queen, not noticing that he knelt in a puddle of blood.

"How did these men infiltrate the castle grounds? How did these ruffians enter *my daughter's rooms? The princella's bedchamber!*" Her voice got higher, and some spit sprayed out of her mouth.

"I swear to you, Your Majesty, we will find out." Captain Clemçon pulled out his sword and laid it hilt-first across his thigh, keeping his head bowed low. "This happened on my watch. My liege, would you like my sword?"

"Don't be a noble ass, Clemçon, just get to the bottom of this." Mamma studied the wounded men. All Cerúlia could tell was that one was big, the other tall and lean. Cerúlia saw their faces bore wicked scratches and their hands had little punctures in them everywhere from the cats' bites. Their trouser legs showed Aki-size tears. A gaping wound—*a sword slash?*—cut across the bigger man's belly, pulsing blood.

"I don't know them," said her mother.

"Nor do we," replied Clemçon. "We will bind them up so they don't bleed out here and take them for questioning."

"Did you get them all?" Mamma asked.

"We're searching the grounds now. I've gotten the rest of the catamounts to help."

Clemçon turned to a shield. "Yanath! Get healers in here! We have to keep these two alive by all means."

The thinner man on the floor noticed Cerúlia staring at him. His eyes locked on hers. She experienced his hatred like a blow. His lips moved. Cerúlia couldn't hear what he was saying because Aki started growling low, but she guessed he cursed. His ill will alarmed her; she ducked behind her mother, holding on to her skirt.

Captain Clemçon caught sight of Cerúlia. Again he went down on one knee, "Princella, my deepest regrets."

When her mother realized that Cerúlia had snuck into the room she asked Shield Seena to take her back to the queen's bedchamber. But Mamma bent down and whispered to her, "I wish you to keep all the dogs with you at all times."

Cerúlia was glad to escape the wounded man's hatred. Nana disapproved of her running off, but she held her lips together and didn't scold this time. As Cerúlia crossed to warm her feet at the fire, she saw that the dragging length of the coverlet dripped with blood. She threw it off with a shudder and a little yelp. Aki, who had followed them into Mamma's room, thrust his nose into her neck.

"Nana," Cerúlia said, "my stomach feels really bad. Like I ate an old shoe."

"Saw more than she should've," Seena told her nursemaid.

Nana got down on her knees and hugged her tight. "There, there, my Chickadee," she said. "I'll set you to rights."

Nana sat her down on a footstool and rubbed her freezing feet in her warm hands. She sent Tiklok for a sleeping draught with lots of honey, which tasted comforting.

When Faki and Naki scratched at the door, Shield Seena cautiously opened it and let them in.

"Naki's bleeding!" Cerúlia pointed, with a little shriek of distress.

"We'll take a look," said Seena.

"Sit still, Naki," said Cerúlia. Nana held a lantern close to his middle and wiped off the blood, while Seena probed the injury along his ribs with her fingers.

"Good boy," said the shield, and Cerúlia noticed that despite the sprays of blood across her forehead and breastplate—despite everything that had happened that night—her voice and hands were steady.

"It's only superficial, Princella."

"What does that mean?"

"It's only on his skin, not deep into his body. He's going to be fine."

Then Cerúlia felt embarrassed for screaming over a little hurt. "How does *your* stomach feel, Shield Seena? Would you like some of my tisane?"

"My stomach? Thank you, Princella, I'm fine."

"Seena's trained for this, Chickadee," said Nana. "Now drink the last bit and hop into bed."

Cerúlia let all of them—Aki, little Zizi, Faki, injured Naki, and even no-good old Pakki (Seena had to pick up his stiff hind legs)—get up on Mamma's big bed with her. Nana said that this once, her mother would not be angered. In the morning she would talk to Aki more and see if she could converse with all the dogs. But now the bed was warm, and Zizi felt soft and her little heart thumped against Cerúlia's chest rhythmically.

# 7

The queen dozed restlessly for a few hours and then woke with a start. The sun was threatening to rise. Five dogs breathed peacefully on her satin bed coverings around Cerúlia; one of them snored loudly. Nana slumbered in a chair, her feet up on a footstool, with Cressa's oldest winter cloak spread over her face and body.

Cressa got up off the couch, tiptoed to her adjoining washroom, and as noiselessly as possible dressed in a skirt and tunic simple enough for her to pull on without assistance. As she moved back through the room, two of the dogs opened their eyes and regarded her. The large one merely closed its lids; the small one stood and circled round on the quilts before settling back down with an elaborate exhalation.

Cressa perched in a window seat, cracking open the wooden shutter for the sight of the light's first fingers touching the snow-capped Nargis Mountain. The Nargis River tumbled down from this single peak, and then flowed underground through Cascada, showing itself only in the Nargis Fountain in the middle of the city and the Dedication Fountain in the middle of the Throne Room. But the palace's wells drew on Nargis Water, thus so did the water feature in her bedchamber, the Queen's Waterwall, a spot where water flowed down a rock surface to an enameled pool in which floated a cluster of jeweled water lilies. The water lilies swayed in the slightly undulating water, today providing no comfort.

*Intruders made it into my daughter's room. What connection lies between this attack and Oromondo? Are any members of court involved?*

Little waves of panic intermittently coursed through her body, sometimes making her give little jerks. She desperately wished for Ambrice at her side, but he was hundreds of leagues away, pursuing Pellish pirates as her Lord of the Ships.

Cressa's parents, whose marriage had never been convivial, had separated after the death of her infant brother on his sixth night. King Nithanil had returned to Lortherrod and his two sons by his previous marriage, while Catreena had remained in Cascada. Her mother had sent Cressa every summer to visit Lortherrod for an extended stay. Doubtless, Catreena considered herself bound to maintain her daughter's ties to her father. Unfortunately, the long sea voyages and absences made Cressa a stranger both to the nobility and the lower ranks of her homeland.

Cressa's own marriage had not brought her more allies. Ambrice was not a king, nor duke, nor even a member of a rich merchant family. He had been the seamaster of *Sea Sprite,* which had taken her to Lortherrod when she was nineteen. Broad chested and tall, calm with a dry sense of humor . . . By the time the ship had finished the long voyage back to Weirandale, she had fallen in love. In Ambrice's arms she had found her home.

She had thought her mother would bar the match, seeing no advantage in it for the realm. But rather than be the pawn of one of her mother's stratagems, Cressa had been determined that—if only in this one matter—she would follow her heart. She had entered her mother's closet with clenched jaw and balled fists, ready to defy her mother and sovereign. Oddly enough, Catreena had merely looked pensive at Cressa's announcement and then wished her joy.

The lightest tap on her bedroom door roused Cressa from her memories and worries. The dogs did not react, so she loosed her hand from the dagger she had instinctively thrust in her belt after robing.

She opened the door quietly, glancing behind, and noting with

relief that Nana and Cerúlia slept on. Captain Clemçon and Sergeant Bristle, both unshaven and unchanged, though with freshly
scrubbed hands and faces, stood in her Reception Room, along with
several servants and all four of her ladies. The ladies fluttered about,
and one of them handed her a sealed note. Ordering fastbreak, she
motioned for the men to follow her and led the way to her closet
down the hallway so that voices would not disturb Cerúlia. The
same catamount—or it might have been one of the other three—
sprawled in the hallway on its side. It supervised the humans' movements without expression.

A fire blazed in the room, providing a semblance of comfort. As
soon as the door was closed, Clemçon broke out, "I bring ill tidings,
Your Majesty. The prisoners are dead. They died before we could
question them. We believe they were poisoned."

"Tell me."

*Plink.*

"We summoned healers to them where they lay yonder." Sergeant
Bristle spoke rapidly, pulling on his mangled left ear, deformed by
some long-ago altercation. "Two of them did some stitching up and
bandaging; the other gave them what she said was 'a fortifying tonic' to
build them back up after their blood loss. We carried 'em down to the
cells. They moaned as we shifted 'em, then by the time we got 'em
down there, both got quiet-like. But when we tried to question 'em,
their faces went queer, and they spoke only gibberish. A half hour later
they were like in a deep sleep. We couldn't wake 'em, not with water or
shaking. Nothing roused 'em." *Plink.* "We sent for healers, and they
said the wretches lay a-dying. In a wee bit, they was dead as dirt."

"I'm at fault. I called for healers." Clemçon was loyal to the bone
and willing to take responsibility for everything that went wrong.

"If it had not been the healer's draught, they would have found
some other way to deal with any captives," said Cressa. "They would
have poisoned their water, or your food, or started a fire. Think
about the planning that must have gone into this attack: they were
prepared for any eventuality. You hardly had a chance of interrogat-
ing any assailants left alive."

*Plink.*

"You're probably right," Clemçon replied, scratching his lip stubble. "Whoever 'they' are."

"Have you identified the healer?"

"A dark-haired woman," said Bristle. "We've asked. Neither of the others knows who she was. Each thought the other knew her, and it was all rather confused last night. No one thought to question the pig-fuckin' *healers*—begging your pardon, ma'am."

A knock on the door announced Lady Dinista carrying a tray with bread, cheese, and fruit for their repast. The full pot of holly tisane emitted a welcome fragrance. Dinista poured out cups.

"Will there be anything else, Your Majesty?"

*Plink.*

"No, Dinista."

"Wouldn't you like me to stay and take notes for you?"

"That will not be necessary. You may leave now."

They ate and drank in silence, all too tense to sit down. The water droplet from the Weeping Swan hit the surface below it in the quiet room.

*Plink.*

"Did you find out anything from examining the bodies?"

"Aye," replied Bristle. "All ten fit and not so young. Men who might have had some experience fightin'. Scars on their bodies. Highwaymen, could be, or could be mercenaries."

"And we found these," said Clemçon, "sewn into the bottom seams of their trousers." He reached into a purse hanging around his waist, pulled out a leather pouch, and turned it upside down on the mahogany table. Gemstones spilled out: emeralds, diamonds, rubies, and sapphires. A queen's ransom.

*Plink.*

More than the news of the poison, the sight of the fortune gave Cressa chills. *Someone wants me dead enough to pay this much! Who has this much wealth?*

While Cressa toyed with the gems, the guards poured themselves more strong tisane.

"Why would they have kept their payment on their persons?"

*Plink.*

"No one's going to leave that treasure in a stash house. There's more," said Clemçon. "Last night a footman saw a set of men being let into the compound through the front gate by palace guards—"

Bristle broke in. "*Palace* guards, ma'am, not the *Queen's Shield.*"

"Which means the palace guard is bought off?" Cressa breathed.

"Or the assassins had a pass note from someone unquestionable," Clemçon said. "We'll be asking."

*A pass note from someone from her council?*

"But if the palace soldiers have been bought, or some portion of them, why wouldn't *they* attack? Why hire assassins in the first place?" asked Cressa.

"Soldiers' sense of honor," said Clemçon. *Plink.* "'Tis one thing to open a gate and look the other way, or accept a pass note and let in strange armed men. 'Tis quite another thing to take a sword to your queen yourself. Look how much they had to pay."

"So the intruders were well-funded. They had been chosen carefully. They had a plan. Why didn't they succeed?"

"Your forewarning, my shields, and all the animals."

Bristle emitted a low whistle. "Of the eight kilt on the roof, terrace, and the stairs, the beasts took five." *Plink.* "You should see what was done to 'em—chewed 'em up right proper. Two died from both blades and teeth and only one in a proper fight—that is, a human fight. That was Dallek's kill, rest his soul on the Waters."

"Dallek?"

"Fought off one of the intruders," Clemçon answered. "Put him down too, but the bastard snagged an artery before he died."

"I regret I neglected to ask if all my shields were safe," said the queen.

"Did his duty, Dallek. Honorable death." Clemçon shook off the sympathy.

"Yes. Well, they underestimated us once. They won't do that again. Now what? Will they poison the dogs and the catamounts?

They can't kill the catamounts—catamounts have served as guardians of the throne going back for hundreds of years."

*Plink.*

"If the plotters are treacherous enough to threaten your life, Your Majesty, I doubt they will scruple over mountain lions, no matter how entwined with legend."

"Yet the catamounts are so deadly. . . ." The queen clung to the thought of their protection.

"I wager some steady bowmen could put them down. In daylight, that is," Clemçon shrugged. "Same with the dogs." He drank more tisane.

*Plink.*

Cressa envisioned the mountain lions, each pierced by a score of arrows. "I see," she replied, feeling somewhat faint.

A long silence blanketed the room. Cressa felt her eyelid twitch. To cover this up she started pacing. "Who amongst my shields fought most bravely last night?"

"Seena stood her ground. She did real good," Bristle said.

"And Pontole—on the terrace—fought like a demon," added Clemçon. He addressed his sergeant, "You would have been proud of his attack. And his parries!"

*Plink.*

"Fine. I would like those two assigned to protect the princella. I want to send them with her out of the palace today," ordered Cressa. "With her dogs. Have them ready in an hour.

"Captain," she continued, "once my daughter is out of the palace I wish the ten men's bodies displayed in the middle of the courtyard. Strip them naked. Let all see what happens to those who attack the throne. And could be someone will recognize them.

"Finally"—the queen swept up one of the gems and handed it to Bristle—"Dallek must have had some kin. Make sure that this is sent to his family, with my compliments and condolences. I would like that done right away." She picked up a green stone cut with unusual facets that caught her eye. "And I have use for this too. Keep the other gems on your person, Captain."

"Now, if you will excuse me, gentlemen, I have an important audience to hold."

After they left, Cressa lingered over the food a minute. She had only nibbled while she conversed, and she needed to fortify herself for this day.

She poured herself some more tisane. *Plink*. As she supped, she recalled the note handed her by Lady Fanyah. It read:

Your Majesty,
I could be of such comfort to you at this trying time. Send for me so I can assist you.
Your most obedient servant,
Matwyck

Cressa crumpled the note and threw it in the fireplace. As she watched it flame up, she held her hands to the extra heat, thinking about how fire both destroyed and warmed.

She returned to her bedchamber and woke up Nana and Cerúlia. She hustled her daughter into a riding habit. Cressa told her ladies to stay behind and escorted the princella down to the stables, personally giving the two shields their instructions. They were to leave the palace grounds and ride leisurely in the western hills on unpredictable paths; they were to buy food and drink at wayside carts or inns; they were to keep the three big dogs with them at all times. Their little party must return, as quietly as possible, just before dark.

By the Grace of the Waters, Cerúlia showed no ill effects from last night. Her daughter thought this was a big adventure—to ride off on Smoke all day long!—and Cressa felt relieved to get her away.

The queen hurried back to her chamber and sent Nana to supervise the scouring and setting to rights of the princella's suite. Then she called her maids and ladies and told them to lay out one of her most magnificent gowns and fix her long blue locks with extra care.

"Your Majesty, are you all right?" asked Lady Fanyah, devoid of witticisms this morning.

"What happened? We've heard all sorts of wild things," Dinista chimed in on top of her.

"What did your shields have to say?" asked Lumetta.

Cressa had no strength to be tactful. "Ladies, I had very little sleep. I need quiet while I dress."

Rebuffed, they attended her in tight-lipped silence and left the room sullenly once she was robed.

Later, when Geesilla, her youngest and sweetest maid, was alone in the dressing room fixing her hair, Cressa reached for her hand while inwardly, she reached for her Talent. She experienced a queer sensation—something akin to unexpectedly tapping into a large, still pool in an underground cavern that had been there all the time, just waiting for her.

"Geesilla, are you loyal to me?" she asked.

"You have treated me with kindness, Your Majesty," Geesilla spoke as if bewitched, "but Lord Retzel pays me double and has promised my beau a job as overseer if I report everything I know to him."

Cressa's pulse galloped. "I see," said Cressa. "You will forget I asked." She dropped the girl's hand.

"Oh this style is so fetching!" said Geesilla, putting in the last ornament. "Is there anything else I can do for you, anything at all?"

"No," said the queen. "That will be all."

Alone in her dressing room, Cressa stood up. Anger made her sway for a moment.

*They've played me for a fool and a weakling. Indeed, I've acted the fool and the weakling.*

A short time later, clad in a gown of pale yellow, a cap with a yellow veil, and a coordinating long lace train held up by Lady Dinista and Lady Aubrie, Cressa entered the Throne Room via a side entrance. Three of her councilors—Belcazar, Lady Tenny, and General Yurgn—expected her, concern etched on their faces, which was unsurprising because news traveled quickly around court. Envoy Thum awaited their pleasure outside the formal doors of the East Entrance. Cressa seated herself on the Nargis Throne on the dais.

The Throne of Weirandale (and thus the surrounding palace)

had been built precisely here because of a natural spring of Nargis Water. Centuries ago Chista the Builder had had a tall, jagged quartz pinnacle strategically placed so that the Water sprayed up one side, and then cascaded like a waterfall down the other, carving a smooth channel, tumbling to fill the golden Coronation Basin, set at waist height. The Water spilled over the basin's rim into the floor-level Dedication Pool and was carried away by pipes laid under the floor. The slight mist, which gave Cressa its characteristic tingle, cooled the twitch of her left eye.

The four catamounts lounged by the Dedication Pool and the Coronation Basin. Nargis Water exerted some mystical pull over them: sometimes they bathed in the spray of the Fountain and they drank from the Pool. At night, in turns, they might leave the Throne Room through their tunnel exit—discreetly set in the Throne Room floor—to hunt in the wild hills that abutted the palace. But in general they preferred to stay close to the Pool, Basin, Fountain, and Throne. Mostly they ignored people in the Throne Room, but even while sleeping, they radiated an aura of protectiveness over the queen.

Colorful historic tapestries hung along the walls on the lower level. Interior balconies where the gentry stood to watch notable occasions ringed the mid story. Above the third story Queen Cayleethia the Artist had designed a vaulted roof of stained glass in a pattern of tiny clear, white, and blue panes. Daylight and moonlight streamed into the Throne Room through these panes, refracting into multicolored arcs. To stand inside the Throne Room was to feel as if one sat inside the rainbows made by the Nargis Fountain in the Courtyard of the Star.

General Yurgn approached Cressa and bent a knee. "Your Majesty, I have seen too much bloodshed in my life. Peace is always preferable to war as life is always better than death. Yet the Oros must pay for this outrage against you and your daughter."

Cressa nodded, touched by his protestation, but not trusting herself to speak.

Her councilors seated themselves in chairs on a step below the queen. Cressa arranged to have trouble with her long lace train tangling between her foot and the throne, a simple low-backed chair, well-proportioned for a woman, made of white gold and upholstered in white velvet.

"Lady Tenny, would you assist me?" Tenny obliged, and when Cressa, in shifting her weight off the train, reached for Tenny's hand to steady herself, Tenny offered it without hesitation. *Good, but not conclusive.*

"Tenny, you will start the audience and question the envoy. Lady Dinista, pray tell the caller we are ready for him now."

The palace caller announced in her most ringing tones, "Envoy Thum of Oromondo!"

Thum, a thick man rigid with muscle, with snow-white hair brushed straight upward, walked ponderously down the long approach. Of his armor, he wore only a ceremonial breastplate, adorned with the eight red flames of Oromondo, but it looked extremely heavy. When he reached the dais he bowed his head slightly but did not bend his knee. The four catamounts sprang erect from their negligent poses. Their tails lashed and four sets of eyes pinned him like prey. Cressa couldn't help admiring the way Thum stood his ground without shrinking backward.

Though Yurgn kept his face a mask, Belcazar's eyes hardened with anger. The councilors looked at Queen Cressa; she lazily circled her hand to proceed.

"En-voy Thum," said Tenny, biting each syllable. "What is the meaning of the document you delivered to Her Majesty yesterday?"

"Can you not read?" he replied.

"I can't read rubbish!" she snapped. "How dare Oromondo propagate such calumnies against Weirandale and against the throne? Civilized countries do not resort to insults, threats, and far-fetched accusations. In all my days I have never read the like of this letter. Did you write this yourself?"

"Civilized? What do you know of being civilized?" Thum retorted with a sneer.

Tenny stared at him, dumbfounded.

"Civilized countries do not worship witches and poison food," Thum continued.

"Weirandale has never—and would never—poison foodstuffs!" said Lady Tenny. "You've been stationed here—what? Five years? Don't you know us Weirs by now?"

"I don't know *her*"—he pointed his chin at Cressa—"at all."

Cressa had attended numerous tedious gatherings with international envoys. But at the moment she couldn't recall whether she had made a point of building trust with Envoy Thum.

"What makes you think the rice was poisoned? Why would we do such a thing?" General Yurgn asked.

"As to the why, I do not pretend to fathom. Those who scorn Pozhar have no spark. Those who refuse the Divinity of the Magi have no morals or souls. Need I remind you of the Initial Crime?"

"The Initial Crime occurred four hundred years ago—how long are you going to use that as an excuse for your enmity toward Weirs!" asked Yurgn.

"It is still revelatory of your barbarism and hostility," Thum answered.

"But the rice. Ah . . . blights have affected Oromondo for many decades," said Belcazar, joining the conversation for the first time.

"True. And we recognize these as the curses of the witch queens. I know the rice was tainted because when I was last in my country, I ate some myself. Look at my arm!" He rolled up his red silk sleeve: oozing sores covered his forearm. "They do not heal," he said. "They stink and fester and cause constant pain. And yet my infirmity does not compare to the anguish of our children in their little bellies. Weirandale's underhanded aggression has caused great suffering throughout the Land."

Cressa thought the arm looked nasty indeed.

"When Weirandale wants to be aggressive," said General Yurgn in a steely tone, "believe me, Oromondo will know it. Poisoning foodstuffs that children eat is not our style. Underhanded is not our style. Our armies fight with honor."

"But." Belcazar held up one finger. "We investigated the shipments and . . . found them clean. Why do you believe it was the rice that did this or sickened the . . . children, rather than . . . some plague or . . . something else you ate?"

"Because the rice is the only new food brought to the Land. And the only item we imported recently. Do you think we be fools?"

"Yes, I do think you are foolish," Cressa broke in. She couldn't claim the intelligence or wisdom of her mother, but she possessed a certain instinct for self-preservation, now fully engaged. "Because you pay your assassins with gems so easily traced back to Oromondo." She had been clenching the jewel in her fist; now she threw the emerald down on the ground at Thum's feet. He picked it up and glanced at it with shock.

"Don't deny that this is the cut of an Oro jewel-smith," she warned him. "We can prove as much."

Thum didn't deny it. He opened his mouth, but no words came out.

"We found that on the person of a man who attempted harm to the Nargis Throne," she said. "What do you know about a gang of assassins sent under cover of darkness?"

Thum held himself up absolutely straight. "I know nothing about assassins," he replied. "When Oromondo wants to kill we do not send assassins in the night. That is without honor. 'Underhanded is not our style.'"

"And yet you call the queen a witch, threaten her, and then assassins strike in the night. Quite a coincidence," snapped Lady Tenny.

Thum shrugged.

"With your permission, Your Majesty, I can't listen to these insults another moment. Guards! Hold this man," called General Yurgn.

"You would arrest an envoy? That's a violation of diplomatic protocol!" Thum sputtered.

Cressa laughed genuinely. "So is trying to kill the ruler of the host country. Or even just threatening her. Take him away. Give him naught to eat or drink, and keep four guards on him at all times."

While General Yurgn stooped to pick up the dropped emerald, Captain Clemçon and Sergeant Bristle entered by a rear side door.

Clemçon stepped forward to supervise the confinement of the diplomat. Bristle remained behind and looked at the queen meaningfully.

Cressa descended and walked over to him, out of earshot of everyone else.

"Your Majesty, one of the scullery gals recognized two of the dead men. They have been delivering wine the last few moons. They was not the regular carters—she knows this because she's sweet on one of 'em. The regular one, I mean. She says he vanished from this job after Summer Solstice Fest."

"So they have been scouting the palace for some five moons?"

"Mm-hmm."

"Bristle, Captain Clemçon refuses to believe ill of any of the Queen's Shield. But you quarter with them. Tell me: has anyone acted differently recently? Anyone you worry about?"

"There's one chap." Bristle's brow wrinkles deepened, but his eyes did not waver.

"What concerns you?"

"Gathleigh loves to gamble, but he always loses. Always borrowing coin from everyone who will put up with him. Then about three moons ago, he stopped borrowing money. Even paid back his debts. Said his luck had changed. But when we play cards, he still loses like a duck, even to Seena, and she's the worst card player I've ever met. Truly, the worst."

"Where was Gathleigh last night?"

"Ma'am, he left the grounds last night. Something about a family matter."

"Gathleigh . . ." she mused. "I should know him."

"Awfully good with a bow. On the young side. Straight, dark brown hair. Wears a little mustache."

"I remember him now."

"So I take him down for questioning with the envoy?"

"No," Cressa replied, thinking. "No. I want you to send him alone to check that the West Gate is safely locked. Right now. And then get your horse and Nightmist saddled. The queen needs a ride to get some fresh air after these events."

"You have a plan, ma'am?"

"Indeed. But if mine should fail—who is better at close quarters fighting?"

"Me."

She surveyed her sergeant appraisingly. He looked beefy but not young. Seeing doubt in her eyes, he added, "I'm more experienced."

Cressa nodded and ended the conversation. Her councilors had lingered at a respectful distance, awaiting her instructions.

"Yurgn, I will meet with you later. Thank you, Lady Tenny, that was most . . . enlightening," she said, dismissing them. "Belcazar, after such excitement I feel a tad unsteady. Pray, give me your arm, and escort me to my chambers."

Belcazar rushed to her side and offered his thick forearm for her to lean against. With a brushing-away motion of her other hand, Cressa indicated that her retinue should follow at a distance.

As they walked down the vaulted passageways and up the Royal Stair, she spoke to Belcazar softly so no one would overhear.

"Can you think of a plausible reason to journey quayside?"

He took several steps before responding. "Umm . . . I love fresh bass, and I often go to the docks . . . to pick through the catch myself?"

"A trifle odd to go fish-mongering on such an eventful day, but that will have to do. Buy some fish. But then locate the current master of *Sea Sprite*. Tell him to call in his crew, provision the ship, and be ready to sail tonight. He should do this quietly, but not so furtively as to cause suspicion. If anyone asks, he is to say that we are sending a private ambassador to Oromondo. I may not want *Sprite;* I may not need it; but I'd like to have it prepared."

Belcazar took three steps in meditative silence. "*Sea Sprite,* not *Queen Carra*?"

"*Sprite.* I would suspect the royal galley is being watched."

They had reached the outer door to her chambers. Belcazar bent and kissed her hand. As he did so, he muttered, "I detect your mother's craftiness in you, my queen. And even more daring."

When the door of her personal room closed behind her, Cressa ripped off the yellow gown, reckless as to laces and seams. She got into her riding clothes without calling for any of her maids.

Sergeant Bristle waited outside the stables with her Nightmist and his own black mare. The queen spoke loudly about how a ride in the fresh air would cure her headache, just in case anyone listened.

The afternoon had started to wane. They rode hard on the path toward the West Gate, which lay a league from the palace proper, through grounds of carefully curated oaks, elms, and birches and banks of wide shrubs. Bristle chose a stand of thick-trunked willows where the path came around a curve to bide their time.

Cressa found the waiting difficult, so she tried to distract herself with small talk.

"Just yesterday Cerúlia played outside without a cloak," she said, pulling her fur-lined cape closer about her.

"Yesterday may have been the last fine day," Bristle grunted. "See that bank of clouds coming in from the north? Dark with weather."

As soon as they heard Gathleigh's horse's hooves returning, they rode out to meet him at a leisurely trot.

When they came abreast, everyone reined up. Gathleigh swept off his hat and bowed.

"Well, man, what did you find?" asked Bristle.

"All locked and secure. Clemçon has a heavy plank bolted across the gate now."

"That rules West Gate out as an entryway," said Cressa. "Shield, I would like to dismount a moment. You will assist me."

"My honor." Gathleigh jumped off his own horse and came over to hold Nightmist's head. But instead of sliding off by herself—as was her practice—Cressa reached toward the guard. Automatically, he held up his arms to grab her waist and assist her down. Once she was on the ground, Cressa kept her hand touching his shoulder.

"Gathleigh, who paid you to give information?"

"Treasurer Prigent's man," he answered in a flat voice.

"Do you know why they wanted this information?"

"They said 'twas to double-check on your safety."

"You aren't stupid, Gathleigh. Who else is working with Matwyck?"

"I spoke only with Prigent's manservant."

"What was the plan?" The queen's fingers dug into his uniform.

"Your Majesty was the killers' target—they wanted to capture the girl."

"Why would they move against me and why now?"

"I do not know for a surety, but I think because Matwyck's term is almost up. Another election for a new steward at midsummer."

"Did anyone tell you that, or did you figure it out yourself?"

"Stands to reason." Gathleigh shrugged.

"And what is in it for the others?"

"Riches. Buckets of jewels. He paid me with a diamond. A real diamond. Had a pig-fuckin' time finding a merchant to change it into coin."

"Who else is working for them?" Cressa pressed. "My ladies?"

"I think. Though I'm not sure about the one from Maritima— what's her name? The one with the lyre. The others delay until she leaves the room to whisper together."

"Any more from the Queen's Shield?" Bristle interrupted, his voice rough-edged.

"No," said Gathleigh.

"The palace guard?" Bristle asked.

"The palace guard follows orders," Gathleigh answered ambiguously.

"What do you know about Oromondo?" the queen asked.

"Oromondo? Nothing firsthand. Heard a whisper about a letter yesterday."

"Are any further actions planned for today?" Cressa inquired.

"No one has said naught to me. I'm thinking they might need to regroup."

Cressa looked up at Bristle on his horse, asking with her glance if he had any more questions. He shook his head and started to reach for his sword. She brushed him off: if Gathleigh went missing now, someone might notice.

"Shield, give me a lift back into the saddle. Then you will ride back to the palace. You will remember only that you carried out Bristle's command and that West Gate was locked. You never saw me on this path, and we never spoke. Do you understand?"

"Yes."

He bent and hoisted her left calf to give her more momentum into the saddle. Then he remounted and rode off as if he didn't see them.

Bristle let out a whoosh of air. Cressa wiped her cheeks and forehead with the hem of her cloak.

"I ken you're queen and all, but I didn't know you could do *that*," Bristle said.

"I was not sure myself. But as the chroniclers say, you find the Talent when you need it."

"We should have *you* question the envoy," said Bristle.

"Aye. If we can do so without anyone knowing. I need to keep this Talent secret."

As they rode back to the palace, Bristle began muttering under his breath.

"What?" Cressa asked.

"This will just madden the captain," he said. "Fuckin' asshole traitor! I would've gladly run him through on the spot. Oathbreaker! Pig fucker!"

Cressa nodded, but she was less shocked by Gathleigh's perfidy. "Words will only hold those who want to be held." Her mind lingered on the import of what they had learned.

*The election. Matwyck will be expected to step down graciously because the typical term of service is one ten-year cycle. But if the queen were dead and the princella only an unprotected child, would he dare postpone the vote?*

*A man who would kill his queen would dare anything.*

*He intends to rule through Cerúlia.*

*Whatever happens, he must never get his hands on her.*

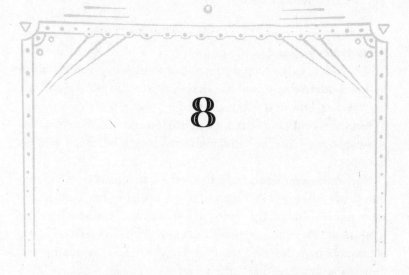

# 8

Belcazar gestured to the fishmonger that he should move the bass on the top of his cart to allow him to see the ones beneath. The fish below had pinker gills and clearer eyes. More hurriedly than his wont, the councilor chose one and gave the delivery boy his West Park address. He waited to pay for his selection until he saw the boy wrap it up and set out on his way. Having spent the first four decades of his life in a landlocked estate, fresh fish still exerted a strong appeal.

He'd left the carriage a block from quayside partly so he could stroll the dock area without being observed by palace coachmen. Belcazar stared, unseeing, at the lively wharf, swarming with ships, bustling with men, and crammed with goods. The Weir capital was located here to take advantage of trade: Cascada boasted the most extensive seaport in the realm, though Queen's Harbor, in the south, came in a close second.

Because the Nargis River emptied into this basin, the water in the cove sparkled with crystal clarity, and the Weirs strove to keep it that way. Foreign sailors soon learned that tossing refuse or filth in any water source was an unpardonable offense in a country whose motto was "The Waters of Life." Belcazar could see down to the sandy bottom of the bay teeming with minnows and spot a few seashells. Today, however, his thoughts strayed far from water quality.

*Catreena, what would you have made of the Oro letter, the assassination attempt, and Thum's behavior?*

Unbidden, rather than the myriad of formal occasions on which he had conferred with the late queen, he recalled the sight of her face on the pillow next to him, framed by a cloud of disheveled blue. When she was thinking hard, a dimpled indent formed between her straight brows. Once, he had dared to reach over to touch it with his forefinger.

He could never figure out why Queen Catreena had invited him into her bed that summer night. He knew that he had cut a handsome figure some fifteen years ago but lust could not have been the motivation. The queen appeared to enjoy their conversation afterward more than the sex. Cressa was away that summer, visiting her father; the marriage had died some years earlier. Belcazar often wondered if Catreena had been lonely.

Belcazar woke from his reverie to walk down the quay to the harbormaster's hut. The figureheads, paintings, and flags of the assorted ships at dock today stared back at him with pride or challenge. With the winds of Ennea Món so unpredictable and challenging, all had both oars and sails in varied configurations depending upon their function. Oceangoing traders had deeper keels for cargo and long, multiperson oars to get them out of harbor or row them to more favorable breezes, while passenger ships had shallower hulls and more comfortable below-deck designs. Naval galleys, either escorts or war vessels, warned away attackers with their hull-shattering rams and bristles of oars, which made them capable of high speeds and adept maneuvers. Dodging dockers pushing carts laden with dry goods and livestock, Belcazar noticed *Queen Carra,* the royal war galley—named after Weirandale's first queen—at anchor in the bay, her three masts of lateen sails furled, her gilding flashing in the sun.

"I have a query for Seamaster Bashkim," he told the officer on duty in the harbormaster's hut. "'Tis merely a trifle, but do you know where he is to be found?"

"He's in port. He leases a little house on the north side of the harbor, sir. Would you like me to send a runner to fetch him?"

"Is that so?" Belcazar meditatively rubbed the bridge of his nose. "It really is . . . not that important. But if you could send a lad to say that . . . I'm going to have a drop of ale at First Call, and—if it doesn't inconvenience him—I'd be pleased to meet him there . . . I would take this as a kindness."

"Just so, sir. What name should the runner give the seamaster?"

"Name?"

"Aye, sir. So Bashkim knows who wants him, see?"

"Oh, of course. Tell him . . . ah . . . Lord Bass."

He could have kicked himself for this foolish name. He should have had a better answer at the ready.

He strolled out of the hut, walked a ways, and then leaned against a crude wooden wagon to pull the wrinkles out of his hose. When he glanced up he spied one of his own coachmen clumsily ducking behind a dockworker carrying a bale on his head. The man had followed him, spying. Belcazar deliberately straightened the other hose while he thought through how to handle the situation.

Belcazar decided to broach the coachman directly. He walked straight up to the abashed servant. "Left the coach unattended, have you?"

"Ah! Oh no, sir. My mate still holds the horses."

"Good. Why aren't you with him?"

The poor man squinched up his cheeks and stuttered for long seconds.

"Beg pardon—ah—you see—sir—ah—"

The man's tongue-tied stutter gave Belcazar time to pretend he didn't know the servant was working for Matwyck. "Oh. I see. Well, there's no shame in needing to find the jakes.

"Now, return to the coach. I am stopping at First Call but I won't be long . . . and I'll not want to wait on you."

Belcazar quickened his pace, pleased that he had handled this situation adroitly.

He thought that Cressa's plan of placing herself out of reach until the palace danger settled showed prudence. Not what Catreena would have done, but the daughter had not the mother's strength.

The mother had had a strong nose and a firm jaw; Cressa's features were more delicate. But the daughter was showing surprising craftiness in this present emergency.

*Poor thing: her elevation came so unexpectedly. I told Engeliqua her sobriquet should be "Cressa the Reluctant" or "Cressa the Unready."*

Belcazar felt certain that Tenny and Yurgn would side with him against Matwyck and Treasurer Prigent. And he was certain he could count on Lord Retzel and Duchess Latlie too, now that the game had turned so serious; despite their constant caviling surely they knew their duty. Together they would uncover Matwyck's plot and force him to resign, and then send a message to *Sea Sprite* that the queen could safely return.

"One bowl of chowder, one pitcher of ale, and two tankards," he called to the proprietor as he entered the tavern, so gloomy after the glare of the sun on the water. He slid onto a beaten-up wooden bench facing the door. As far as Belcazar could tell, none of the people inside paid any attention to him; he didn't recognize any as Matwyck's men.

*Queen Cressa will be pleased with my service to the Waters. She might be grateful enough to see that my sons receive some slight preferment. I would so like to see my children well set up.*

The rushed barmaid plunked the pitcher down so hard it sloshed. Belcazar poured a tankard but stared at the bubbles, worrying over the strange concatenation of alarming events.

Then his mind circled back, as it did too often for a married father in his fifth decade, to that one summer night.

*Why could I not stir you to pleasure? Engeliqua always seems satisfied.*

A server set the chowder in front of him, breaking his reverie. A group of sailors at the bar jostled one another with rowdy high spirits.

"I have the most powerful thirst," crowed one of the sailors. "We've been out forever. Keep 'em coming, as fast as you kin pour 'em. For moons, I've dreamed of nothing but ale."

*Men want what they cannot have,* Belcazar realized, and this old truism struck him with renewed force. *I cannot have Catreena. Even when she lay within my arms, she withheld herself.*

*What is it that Matwyck wants that he cannot have?*

*What do the Oros want that they cannot have?*

A voice intruded on his study of the oily film on top of the chowder, which made the soup unappetizing.

"Lord Bass?" said Seamaster Bashkim at his elbow.

# 9

Nana had called in the palace's best scrubwomen to deal with the blood that stained the tile grout and splattered up the walls. The idea of would-be killers fouling the princella's bedchamber deeply offended her. She had the room emptied of furniture and then got down on her hands and knees beside the scrubwomen and brushed with vigor. One of the reasons the palace servants respected her so was that though she was the closest to the royal family, she never put on airs and she was never above getting her own hands dirty. More than that, she genuinely understood and appreciated their labor and skill.

Nana had lived in the palace nearly thirty years. She had grown up on a humble dairy farm in the western duchy of Crenovale, but she had soon discovered all that lay ahead for her at home was the endless boredom of pitching hay, pulling teats, and lugging milk pails either for her parents or for some future husband. By sixteen summers she was heartily tired of living ankle-deep in cow shit.

A traveling carnival stopped in a nearby town, and its bright-colored costumes and cheery cymbals made it the most exciting thing she'd ever seen. The second night she visited, a young carny worker started flirting with her. The third night Nana ran away with him without a moment's hesitation. Yet by the time she'd traveled two weeks with the carnival she had seen through its cheap and gaudy tricks, just as she discovered her lover's dull wits and habit of gambling away all his pay. By the time the show reached Cascada, she was fed up with the traveling life. She took a job as a kitchen worker in the palace.

One day long ago the young princella, Cressa, was fretful, and her nursemaid could not get her to lie down for her nap. The nursemaid walked about the palace, seeking to distract the fussing child. In the kitchen, Nana charmed her by blowing soap bubbles. The next day and the day after the princella demanded to visit her friend in the scullery. Nana began looking forward to these visits, making the lonely child little toys out of carved soap bars. Soon the nursemaid found it easier to bring the princella down to splash in the wash bucket with Nana while she enjoyed a glass of mead and a long gossip with her friends at a kitchen table.

It did not take long for the palace chamberlaine, Teonora, to discover the truth of the matter. She sent the official nursemaid packing and installed Nana in her stead.

As the eldest of six siblings, Nana had experience with children. She raised Cressa. Wherever Cressa went, Nana went too—even if it was on a damnable voyage to Tidewater Keep in chilly Lortherrod. From a start as a dairymaid, she'd spent an awful lot of her life in castles and among nobility. And she'd discovered that the gentry generally smelled better than commoners and spoke highfalutin words, but that was about all you could count on. Some were dumb, some were tricky, and many weren't worth cow slobber.

She never had a child of her own, but in every way, she bonded with her charge. That Queen Catreena was a cold one who had paid scant attention to her daughter. But Cressa had been an easy child, turning to her nursemaid's affection as a sunflower twirls to sunlight. The only issue in her whole life that Cressa ever put her foot down about was her choice of Ambrice as husband, but Nana judged him a fine match for her girl—any fool could see how he doted on her.

Now, Cressa ruled and Nana had reached her late middle years, slightly stout and getting stouter, with a frizz of brown hair and a perfectly oval face set off by the white lace collars she habitually wore. She took care of Cressa's daughter, who already showed more spirit than her mother and needed a firmer hand. Cerúlia also depended upon Nana less than Cressa had. For one thing, her Cressa was a more attentive, more loving mother than Catreena had been: Catreena the Strategist spent her time amongst her gentry, watching them with narrowed eyes, while Cressa snuck away from all those fawning courtiers to play in the nursery. For another, Cerúlia had all those beasts!

"I don't mind the cats, I tell ye," Nana said to the footmen who carried the four-poster back into the freshly scrubbed room. "They keep themselves so clean. Kind of fancy a cat purring in front of the fire. Cozy-like, you know? But them hounds with their dirty paws!—Aye, you, Zizi! Pakki, shift yer old bones. Git out of the way of the table!" She used her foot to nudge the elderly dog, but her touch was gentle. "There now, all back in order. So much better! Just put that chest over there, Tiklok."

"The floor's a mite damp, Nana," he said. "I'll build up the fire to help it dry. I've some applewood logs that should chase away the lye smell."

"Thank you, Tiklok. I'll leave the window open too. I do thank ye all, lads. Tell Cook Besi I ask her to give ye each one of her meat pies."

The helpers left, leaving the door open to air out the room, and Nana got busy resettling all Cerúlia's little treasures where they belonged. The cats, who had been hiding from the bustle, draped themselves around the suite, watching Nana with eyes of green and gold as she moved about.

"Ah, Nana! I was worried about you," came Lady Fanyah's voice from the doorway. "How fare you, my dear?"

By the time Nana whirled around and dropped a curtsey, she had pulled her face out of the scowl that had set in when she recognized the vixen's voice. "So kind of you, milady."

With her amber-and-brown locks artfully arranged and dressed in silk with mink fur around cuffs and neck, Lady Fanyah leaned against the open doorjamb, the picture of ease and privilege. "Ah, but you didn't answer, Nana. Weren't you frightened by the uproar last night? Was it terrifying?"

Nana was not about to discuss her feelings with a chit of a lady-in-waiting whom she didn't trust as far as she could throw her. "Not too bad," she replied. "How may I serve you, milady?"

Fanyah was not as thickheaded as some; she heard the curtness in Nana's reply. She got to the point. "Where is our *darling* princella today?"

"Out riding, milady."

"Oh, so thoughtful to remove her from the scene of the crime! When will she return?"

"I'm not certain, milady."

"Excuse me," interrupted Tiklok, who had returned with a basket of applewood. Lady Fanyah stood in the doorway in his way. Proper etiquette would be to wait silent and still until a lady moved on her own accord. Nana was surprised and gladdened by Tiklok's boldness.

"Oh! I'm so sorry to inconvenience *you*," said Lady Fanyah, moving aside, her condescension rewetting the floor. "When she does return, Nana, I'd like to be notified. I'm dying to see her. In fact, I've got the prettiest little bracelet to take her mind off last night's unpleasantness."

"So kind of you, milady."

"You will send for me, Nana, the moment she returns?" Lady Fanyah pressed, with authority in her tone.

"Of course, milady," said Nana, curtseying again. Lady Fanyah regarded her sternly, and Nana dropped her eyes.

Tiklok finished sweeping all the fireplace ash into a bucket and stood up to carry the bucket out of the room, but Lady Fanyah still blocked the doorway. This time Tiklok waited politely and quietly, but his tall body loomed.

"See that you do," Fanyah replied, twirled on her heel, and left.

Tiklok set the bucket outside the door and built up a roaring fire.

"Is there anything else I can do, Nana?"

"Help me lay the clean bed linens, lad? I don't mind telling *you,* I'm rather tuckered today."

They remade the bed, and then Tiklok sped off to other duties. Nana was pleased that the room was set to rights, but she felt deeply unsettled. Her Cressa was in trouble—trouble that she could not fix with lye soap.

Nana tossed a blanket around her shoulders and dashed outside to the grand stables set in the rear of the Administrative Wing of the palace. The stableman Hiccuth and she had settled into an "understanding." It was not quite a love affair and certainly not a marriage, but it suited them both.

She found Hiccuth, a short man with a broad smile whose considerable belly strained the ties on his shirts, oiling some harnesses in one of the rear tack rooms. The place smelled like straw and horse piss, but Nana found the odor familiar, even comforting.

"How are you?" he asked her.

"Weary. I slept but little last night."

He wiped the neat's-foot oil off his hands carefully and gently kneaded her shoulders with his strong, callused hands.

"Those vermin!" he said. "The staff talks of naught else. I heard you weren't touched, but I've been hankering to see you. A bad business."

"Aye. I was awful scared."

"Have you seen their bodies?" Hiccuth asked.

"No, and I don't wanna."

"You should give them dogs a bone, Old Beauty. Some of them bites are dog bites. I'm real glad you have them by."

"Do the servants know what 'tis about?" Nana asked.

"If they do, they're keeping mum," he said. "Lots of gossip but little sense. I've asked around a bit, casual-like, but as you know, since Teonora took ill Retzel hired most of the help. If you ask too many questions these days, you find yourself out on your rump."

"'Rat's Skull,' I calls him," she muttered. "Don't stop that rubbing."

"Under your breath, I wager," Hiccuth said, grinning. "I'd like to see you call him that to his face."

"I'm not afeard of any of that lot," she said, tossing her head. "Leastways, not for meself. For the queen and the little one, I am deathly afeard. Rub a little lower, would you?"

"When will the Lord Consort return? 'Twould be helpful to have him about."

"No one knows," said Nana, scrunching her brow. "That's the worst of it. Not bloody likely they would have tried something like last night if Lord Ambrice was in the house. He would have bashed their skulls with his bare hands."

"He's a brave man, I'm not denying, but swords will beat out hands any day."

"Hmm. Hanging around waiting for something to do makes me fidgety, and then my heart starts beating all quick-like again. I'd fain visit Besi and Borta in the kitchens, but they'll be into the supper rush."

"Aye. You'd best stay out of their way." Hiccuth gave her shoulders a concluding pat. "Why don't you visit the Church of the Waters? You always find comfort there."

"Aye. That I do. I'll pop round thataway and say my prayers. I'll pray for the queen and my Chickadee. And I'll pray for Lady Fanyah to fall down the stairs and break her skinny neck."

Nana turned to leave the tack room and then came back and threw her arms around Hiccuth. He held her close, murmuring in her ear, "There, there. Overtired you are, my old gal. We just do our best, and the rest is not our business. By the Grace of the Waters, all will end well."

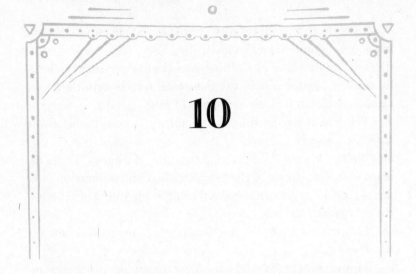

# 10

When they reached the palace after their encounter with Gathleigh, Cressa recognized Branwise, one of the Queen's Shield, loitering near the stables. Sergeant Bristle rode over to talk to him while Cressa, with deliberate nonchalance, turned Nightmist over to the stableman with a compliment about the fancy ribbons in her mane. Bristle and Branwise fell in behind her as she entered the palace proper.

"Cap'n needs to speak to you, urgent-like, ma'am," Bristle muttered under his breath.

"Not my chambers," she said, trying not to move her mouth.

"Duty room?" suggested Bristle, behind a hand that was casually rubbing his face.

"No." She walked a few more steps, considering. "Bring him to the princella's lesson chamber."

Bristle peeled off to get his captain, while Branwise stayed by her side. The queen tried to move without apparent nervousness, acknowledging bows and curtsies as she usually would.

Duchette Lumetta and Lady Dinista lay in wait for her where two main corridors crossed. Although the palace proper boasted more than three hundred rooms, the queen's circulation through the building could be predicted.

"Ah, Lumetta. How kind of you to watch for me," said Cressa with a forced smile. "Here, take my riding gloves and hat. Do me the service, Duchette, of alerting my maids that I long for a hot bath? And Dinista, would you begin to lay out some gowns? I have an important meeting with my Circle Council, and you choose so well. I will be up presently."

The ladies looked pleased at being given commissions, no matter how trivial. Cressa crossed the palace and climbed a back stair to the now-deserted lesson chamber. Chafing her cold hands in the room without a fire, with Branwise watching the door, she paced until Bristle and Captain Clemçon shuffled in. Lines of stress seamed her officers' faces.

"So, here we are again," she said, making a feeble attempt to lighten the mood.

"Your Majesty, this note appeared on my desk in the guardroom," replied her captain, all business. "Several servants came in and out during the day, delivering drink and sandwiches; one of them may have left it."

Cressa unfolded the scrap.

Wash there Hare.

"I don't understand," said Cressa.

"Took me a few minutes too," Clemçon admitted. "The writer is unlettered, or wants us to think so. She wants us to wash the *hair* of the dead assassins."

Fatigue made Cressa's mind slow and numb. "But why?"

"Because not all of them have brown hair. When we brought out buckets and soap we saw that one man's hair had been darkened with mud. His brown is mixed with white."

"An Oro."

"Aye."

"And what about the rest of them?"

"We checked carefully. All the rest have brown hair."

Cressa had been leaning against the cold fireplace, and now she whirled around. "I am surrounded! The palace guard, the Queen's

Shield, Oromondo, my own ladies, the councilors . . ." She paced a few steps, feeling her eyelid twitch. "Have you made any headway with Envoy Thum? This is further evidence of Oro perfidy."

"Not yet. I regret we're not very experienced at extracting information."

"I wouldn't have it any other way: your job is to protect me, not torture people. Perchance I should try my Talent. Can you get me down to the cells without the whole palace noticing?"

"That would be tricky," Bristle warned.

"Aye. I thought so." Her eyelid jumped. "I have a meeting with my Circle Council in a little while. Afterward, we'll see if 'tis necessary."

"Should we question all the servants to find out who left the note?" asked Clemçon.

The queen considered. "Someone is trying to help us. I'd like to know whom, but it might put that person in danger. Let's leave that for now."

Back in her chambers Cressa gathered assistants to change her out of her riding habit and ordered a pot of tisane.

"Lady Aubrie, your lyre would sound soothing while I bathe. The rest of you, work on finding me the perfect outfit with a high cap."

Aubrie plucked a soft melody and thoughtfully refrained from peppering the queen with questions or comments as she marinated in the copper tub. Cressa relieved her gritty eyes and twitchy lid with a warm, wet cloth, which her lady-in-waiting refreshed with hotter water whenever it cooled.

After her bath, Lady Dinista offered her a bloodred gown that she recalled as too tight or the black velvet studded with sea pearls, but the latter she judged too somber. She ignored Lumetta's lobbying for a white dress with feathers. In the end she and Dinista settled on a light gray gown with darker gray sleeves, an outline of the Nargis Fountain embroidered in blue threads that matched her hair color on the front panel. She held her arms out as her ladies started to robe her.

"Are you hungry, Your Majesty?" her maid Geesilla asked with what a day before Cressa would have chalked up to sweet concern. "Have you supped today?"

Cressa realized she had not eaten since early morning, but the suggestion also gave her an idea.

"Aubrie, pray fetch the chamberlaine. Lady Dinista, put away these other gowns. Lady Fanyah, you may choose my slippers. Once you've finished with those laces, Lumetta, you are all dismissed for today."

"I'm sure you'll have a restful night tonight," said Lumetta, with a smile that showed all her rodent teeth, "and tomorrow all our troubles will be over." She closed the door as the ladies swished out.

Geesilla had settled a gray velvet, stiff-brimmed circlet with a trailing scarf on the top of Cressa's carefully coifed hair when the chamberlaine arrived, leaning on a cane.

For more than thirty years Chamberlaine Teonora had super-vised all the servants' hiring, firing, and training as well as the mini-city's provisioning and repairs. Her efficiency and organization made the palace run smoothly, and her formidable presence made grown men quake. But last year healers had found tumors in her belly. The woman used to carry a bosom like a bed bolster, but now all the starch and plumpness had fled her chest, while her middle poked out, grossly distended. Teonora's normal walnut coloring had taken on a greenish tinge, but she held herself as straight as ever.

Cressa hadn't seen her for moons, and she felt a rush of pity and regret that she had let her sicken so without offering comfort. But also wariness. Could she trust her?

Teonora curtsied as if the movement took all her balance. "Your Majesty, I have hoped all day that I could be of service to you. If you must be in danger, at least let me help. What can I do?"

Cressa's gaze met Teonora's in the reflection in her looking glass as her maid threaded her aquamarine-and-diamond earbobs. The chamberlaine's gaze held steady, and she nodded her chin ever so slightly. Cressa found herself wondering whether Retzel could have bribed Geesilla and her ladies if Teonora had been as strong as in previous decades. If she'd reached out to Teonora earlier, would she be in such trouble today?

"That will do, Geesilla; leave us now," said the queen. Then once the maid was out of earshot she decided to take the gamble.

"I need your assistance during this upcoming meeting, Teonora."

The dying woman said, "Tell me, Your Majesty."


An hour past the appointed time (it never hurt to make her councilors wait for her), Queen Cressa entered the Circle Chamber with her head high, her back as straight as Teonora's, and her gray headpiece adding a thumb's length to her height. Although numerous candlesticks glowed about the room, she felt the winter night's darkness flowing in through the transoms as an oppressive weight. The Circle Pool in the middle of the room looked black; tonight the candle flames could not make the swirling water sparkle. As Yurgn seated her, she motioned for everyone to take their places.

Matwyck struck with a tone of injured pride warring with deep concern. "Your Majesty. I regret I must lodge an official protest. The gravest events of my term have transpired and you have not seen fit to confer with me. I was elected by the realm's leaders! I must be kept informed of such matters as intruders and attacks upon the palace! Please, allow me to do my job. Please, allow me to assist you."

"Steward, calm yourself. Here I am; I am conferring with you now." Cressa smiled what she hoped was a disarming smile. "You must understand that the day has been rather busy and fatiguing."

"Matwyck, in your zeal you press too hard," chimed in Duchess Latlie. "The queen has had a terrible ordeal. In the absence of your dear mother, I do hope you won't scruple to lean on me. Two can bear loads too heavy for one. Armed intruders in the princella's chambers! How is the moppet? We hope she isn't fearful or distressed. We haven't seen her about today."

"The princella has a strong constitution; no need for alarm," replied the queen, keeping her smile fixed on her lips.

"We have seen ten bodies. Have they been identified? What was their aim?" said Matwyck, tapping his fingertips together to show his concern. "Where did they come from? How did they get into the palace? How did they die?"

"Captain Clemçon, the head of the Queen's Shield, is in charge of the investigation, as is the proper chain of command. He has all the details."

"Then let the captain appear before us now and answer our questions."

"Oh no, Matwyck, I fear he is too occupied for that. You wouldn't want to interfere. In due time. Wait until the morrow or the next day."

At this moment the door opened and several servers appeared bearing trays of delicacies, including cured meats, fish roe, special cheeses, pickled vegetables, and carafes of wine.

"How is this? Now is not time for a fest," protested Matwyck. The servers, befuddled, started to back out.

"Stay," said Cressa. "After such a trying day, you must all agree that a light repast is in order? As for myself, I haven't dined today. I wish to share these tidbits with you."

"Oh, how very thoughtful of you, Your Majesty, to think of us even in the midst of such trials," Matwyck yielded, and despite herself—out of years of yearning for his praise—Cressa almost basked in his compliment. Almost.

The servers provided plates for the councilors and began filling them. And Cressa ordered, "Wine all around." The servers' orders (per her arrangement with Teonora) were to continuously refill the councilors' gold flagons whilst filling her own with berry juice.

"Hmm. This is delicious: do try the duck sausage," said Cressa, "and the creamy cheese." Teonora had raided the palace stores for the best fare; Cressa had been hungry and she felt the food renew her energy.

"Oh, I just adore these olives!" said Latlie, tossing one after another into her mouth.

The queen patted her lips on her napkin. "Now that we have all been served, Lady Tenny, pray recount our interesting audience of this morn."

Tenny glanced around. Four servers had remained in the room, standing at attention with their backs against the wall. Yet Circle meetings, by strict custom, were always held completely private, without even a secretary to record them. Tenny glanced at Matwyck for guidance as to whether she should protest, and Matwyck shook his head ever so slightly.

As Lady Tenny relayed the story of Thum's rudeness and arrest, Retzel drank his glass down in a gulp. Yurgn, Prigent, and Latlie started on the cold meats and pickled quail eggs—which had been purposely chosen for their saltiness and spiciness—and then reached for the fine vintage, with the servants assiduously refilling their flagons at the least diminishment. Matwyck sipped his wine more carefully, while Belcazar merely toyed with his goblet.

When Tenny had finished ten minutes later, no one asked any questions.

"I would appreciate your counsel concerning Envoy Thum," said the queen.

"Has he given up any information to Clemçon?" asked Yurgn.

"I've heard he isn't speaking," said Cressa.

"As I said a dozen times, Oros are very hardy," said Retzel, licking his fingers. "They will hold up under any physical inducement, eh?"

*A dozen times you've reassured the others?*

Her councilor for diplomacy turned to Cressa. "I've been curious: How did Your Majesty know that the emerald was of Oro fashioning?"

"More wine, Lady Tenny?" Cressa stalled.

"No." The councilor put her hand over her flagon's top.

"Oh, but it helps one relax after such a trying day." Cressa laughed just a little, as if the wine was already affecting her.

"Thank you, but I slept poorly last night," Tenny replied. "More wine and I would nod off here at the council table—I'm already light-headed. Your Majesty, the emerald?" she prompted, staring at her intently.

"Oh, yes. One of my shields told me. Guardsmen seem to have experience with many forms of payment." Cressa kept her tone light and turned her attention to her fried clam. Only her heightened alertness allowed her to notice under her eyelashes that Prigent clumsily bumped his knife against his plate.

Tenny began coughing.

"Are you all right? Something caught in your throat?" said Matwyck, directing everyone's attention toward her and away from Prigent's anxiety. Tenny coughed dramatically a few more times; Matwyck jumped up and offered her his wine flagon. Tenny drank, cleared her throat ostentatiously, and smiled to indicate that she could now breathe unimpaired.

*Tenny too.*

"Footman, pour Lady Tenny some wine. It is never a good idea to eat without liquid," said Cressa.

"Your Majesty, I have heard your Shield now has a vacancy," said Matwyck. "So sad. Although I trust the danger has passed with the arrest of Thum, I have several excellent candidates to recommend."

"You are very kind. Though surely you realize the selection of the Queen's Shield lies in the hands of her captain." Cressa turned to the servers, ordering, "More wine."

She continued, "We didn't discover who wrote the threatening letter. But the attack last night denotes a direct escalation of the Oro threat. Of course, we should consider the possibility that Thum has lost his senses and could be plotting on his own. Before we 'overreact,' might it be politic to send an envoy to Oromondo, to treat with them directly? What do you think?" She strove to sound eager for advice and counsel.

"A noble plan, Your Majesty," said General Yurgn. "Noble. Peach—at all costs—we must have peach." He seemed unconscious of the fact that he had just referenced a fruit. "But who could we send?"

Matwyck steepled his hands, as if considering deeply. Cressa kept her face somber and took advantage of the pause to eat a fig.

"The only person I know who is brave enough, overwhelmingly loyal to the throne, and obviously has Your Majesty's confidence would be our esteemed colleague Belcazar," Matwyck pronounced.

"Excellent plan, eh?" said Lord Retzel, wiping his mouth with the back of his hand. "Matwyck, what a clever fellow you are! You always arrange everything so neatly." He waved his bejeweled hands expansively, not noticing that he sloshed drops of wine on the table.

"A most sensitive diplomatic mission and an honor to be chosen," added Lady Tenny, with downcast eyes, as if she could no longer meet Queen Cressa's gaze.

Belcazar did not speak, but his brow crinkled as his fingers traced the circle his flagon had left on the table. Cressa looked around the table. It occurred to her that Prigent had been silent thus far. Her eyes met his; he blinked and averted his eyes.

*Drought-damn you all.*

"What do you think, Belcazar? Of course you would not need to leave tonight," Cressa said to him. "You would want to spend time with your family. Get some of your affairs in order. Would two weeks be ample?"

Belcazar met her gaze, looked down, and then looked at her again. His forefinger rubbed the space between his brows. "I was Queen Catreena's servant and . . . I am yours . . . to command."

"Excellent wine!" Yurgn smacked his lips. "Which cask did you tap?" he asked the servant who had just refilled his flagon too.

"Teonora chose one of the reds from Prairyvale distributed by Red Rooster, General."

"Perfect choice! Red Rooster is my company, you know. One of my canniest investments. A great vintage last year."

*Yurgn supplies the palace's wine through one of his business interests. Yurgn hires the carters who deliver the wine. Yurgn has thrown in with Matwyck. The head of my army is a traitor.*

"Oh indeed, General Yurgn? How fortunate. Let us drink to your health," remarked the queen with her sweetest smile.

The general threw back a full glass and smacked his lips again.

Matwyck took a contemplative sip. "I wonder, just as an extra precaution, would it be wise for Your Majesty and the girl to move to a new location for a few days?"

The insolent way Matwyck referred to the princella infuriated Cressa, but she could not allow herself to show her feelings.

Latlie dabbed at her mouth with a napkin, missing the pastry crumbs flecking her chin. "I would be honored to host you at my manor house in Vittorine and I do believe I'd make you most comfortable! The princella would have playmates! We could sneak you away in the middle of the night and make this our secret!" She giggled with the wine. "Wouldn't that be a lark!" She wiggled her hands in a shiver of excitement.

Retzel, drunk enough to treat his liege as a servant girl, wagged his finger at Cressa. "You'd be a fool not to consider—"

Cressa interrupted Retzel, saying, "How exceedingly kind of you, Duchess. But I'm sure that isn't necessary. And I feel safest in Nargis's palace."

"As you should, Your Majesty. Let me insure you—*reassure* you the palace guard are on alert! My guard will die at my command." Yurgn pounded his fist on the table. "I am morda—mortified by last night's events. Simply mor-ti-fied. If I live to be a hundred, a hundred and one, I'll never recover from this, from this, from this . . ."

"Treachery?" Cressa smiled at the general she had trusted so gullibly, then gave in to an enormous yawn. "Oh pray, excuse me. What a difficult night and an exhausting day. Lady Tenny, I probably should have followed your wisdom about the wine.

"Councilors all, I prefer to pick up this conversation in the morning. I fear I simply must retire now."

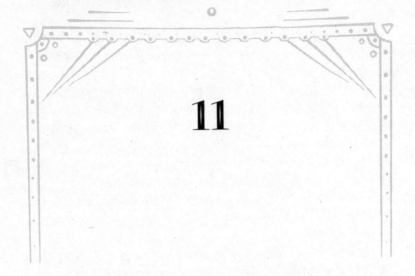

# 11

Many things confused Tiklok. He didn't understand the order of courses at High Table. For a long time he'd gotten lost in the palace's corridors and couldn't figure out which staircase or which entrances to use. He never understood why gentry and servants alike made such a fuss about precedence whenever they lined up, and he could never puzzle out where he should stand.

But one thing he was certain of: Nargis had anointed him as her Agent some years ago.

He still thought of the Spirit as "her" even though Nargis had told him Spirits weren't women and they weren't men. They had no hands or feet or bodies, so they couldn't be male or female. And because they had no hands, they needed people like him to work for them. Nargis asked him to do little commissions for Her—It.

"But why'd you choose *me*?" Tiklok had asked, as drops of Fountain water dribbled into the ticklish places in front of and behind his ears.

*Thou art faithful and humble,* said the voice in his head, a voice that was low-pitched for a woman, or high-pitched for a man, and which, at any rate, did not sound human.

Tiklok hoped he was faithful and humble, but he knew he was also clumsy, cautious, and not as clever as other people. Being Nargis's Agent didn't make him graceful or smart or grant him any magic powers. Nonetheless, he did whatever the Spirit asked with a willing heart.

Only two others had any claim upon that heart. The first was Queen Cressa. Tiklok couldn't recall how old he'd been when the queen altered the stream of his life—he had started to stretch out but he had yet to sprout any beard. His father, a butcher by trade, had been beating him again; this time Tiklok's misdeed had been allowing a bloody hindquarter of calf to slip from his grasp to the dirty street as he fetched it from the cart to their stall. This beating might not have been worse than countless previous ones, but since it took place in the Central Market a considerable crowd had gathered to watch.

One of the Queen's Shield had grabbed his father's meat hook as it swung high in the air for the next blow.

In the stillness that descended, the queen, mounted on her magnificent black horse, had said in a cold voice, "Who is responsible for this lad?"

"Your Majesty," said his father, doffing his cap and falling on his knees, "he's my dolt of a 'prentice. Always fumble-fingered. Look what he's gone and done."

"Not any longer," said Queen Cressa. "I find I need another page. Bristle, pay the man two catamount coins for the boy's indenture. Then take him to the Fountain to wash his wounds and see if Nargis will ease his hurts."

Sergeant Bristle had put his arm around Tiklok and half carried him the few blocks to the Courtyard of the Star. He liberally splashed water on his face and borrowed a cup for him to drink Nargis Water. The Fountain had instantly eased his agony, but it did not erase the scars and misshapen bones that already studded his body, nor close up the triangular rent just torn by the meat hook through his cheek.

Though the wound healed with neat edges, ever after Tiklok's speech and eating were damaged. But the queen had ordered that he be treated kindly, so Tiklok's life started over with clean uniforms, light jobs, warm rooms, and without constant terror. A few of his fellow servants taunted and bullied him, but since Tiklok grew tall and broad, and since he never reacted to their teasing—which really scarcely bothered him compared to his own father's brutality—they gave up their sport.

Whenever Tiklok had free time he would return to the Fountain to thank Nargis for his rescue. And one day the Spirit chose him by anointing him with a spray of water. Chose *him*—just as he was.

When he grew too old to be a page, Chamberlaine Teonora promoted him to lackey. As a lackey his uniform was of coarse canvas, though still warmer and more comfortable than anything he'd owned as a butcher's boy. He never served at table or helped guests, but he did many behind-the-scenes chores.

The other person who owned his heart was Kiltti, a scullery maid with a merry laugh. Kiltti, who had pox scars all over her chest, said that Tiklok's disfigurement didn't bother her, and she let him kiss her. And then she let him do more. Tiklok felt that lying with Kiltti was a more glorious prize than he'd ever expected out of life.

Kiltti had ambition—she wanted to be promoted as a cook someday—and to rise she needed to read recipes. So in their free hours (whenever they weren't sneaking away to an unused attic with a straw mattress), Kiltti and Tiklok would practice their letters on the big scrubbed table in the servants' common room. If Cook Besi or the head baker, Borta, chanced by, they would correct Tiklok's and Kiltti's mistakes, and give them a new cookery word to learn.

Tiklok dutifully copied down "custard" or "boil," but he preferred the eight-page chapbook of nursery rhymes that Tutor Ryton lent them. He had "The Water's Choice" by heart.

All the while Nargis spoke to him intermittently. He performed tasks as the Spirit instructed, without question and as well as he could.

One of his first orders had been to take over preparation and delivery of Chamberlaine Teonora's afternoon tisane. The undercook who handled this task previously had been puzzled, angry, and resistant, but Tiklok insisted, "This is my job, now." Lord Retzel's man even spoke to him about this, but Tiklok would not budge, and in the end they all gave up and let him do it.

When he took the sick lady her tray, sometimes he tried to learn more about how the world worked. Teonora, after all, had many years of wisdom.

One time he asked her, "Is Nargis the only Spirit?"

"No, boy. But Nargis is the Spirit that cares about Weirandale."

"How many other Spirits are there?" he asked, pouring out a steaming cup.

"Seven. Though some say eight."

"And they care about other countries far away?"

"That's right." Teonora took a long sip.

"Do Spirits have people who work for them?"

"Do you mean like the Sorrowers, who lead church services and help the afflicted? Priests and the like?"

"No, I mean regular people the Spirits talk to."

"Lots of people talk to Spirits, Tiklok. Just go to the Fountain in the Courtyard and you'll see scores of folk begging Nargis for aid. But I don't know of anybody that the Spirit ever replied to. The Waters know I've asked about my tumors many a time and received silence as an answer. Spirits don't have to explain their doings to *people*. Nargis provides us the Waters of Life. That's enough."

Tiklok pondered this information. But in the meantime Nargis told him to keep his eyes open. At first Tiklok found this perplexing, because he hadn't actually been walking around his days with his eyes shut. But now he noticed so much more. He saw Teonora slump over with pain when she thought no one was about; he saw Councilor Prigent stroke Geesilla's cheek; he saw Lady Dinista pull a ruby bracelet hidden under her sleeve out and turn it admiringly; he saw the Lord Steward's man, Heathclaw, and the treasurer's clerks working on account books in the late hours of the night. And more than once, he saw Lady Tenny walking alone in the garden worrying a kerchief so hard he thought it would tear in two.

He told Nargis all these things, though he didn't understand what they meant.

Some moons ago Nargis had ordered him to patrol the corridor outside of the Royal Library all night with a broom. If anyone came, he should say maids reported a mouse nest and Teonora assigned him to watch for the varmints. Twice that week Tiklok saw men whom he suspected worked for Lord Matwyck casually strolling down the hallway in the wee hours. He didn't know what devilment they could be up to, but when they saw him they hurried away. He was awful glad they had not questioned him; he didn't know how well he could lie.

A few weeks ago, Nargis had told him to gather acorns from the grounds and boil the nuts to make a dark brown liquid in a kitchen pot.

Today he had looked at the naked bodies in the courtyard in fury and disgust. Nargis bid him leave a note under a pitcher of ale he took to the shield's duty room.

This afternoon, the Spirit had instructed him to locate a jug of coal tar in the kennel master's cupboard. Then he'd obtained some bergamot oil by telling Kiltti that Teonora had a craving for the spice to flavor her tisane. Pilfering a good bottle with a strong stopper from the healers' shelves presented no difficulty for a lackey whose duties took him all about without anybody paying him the slightest mind.

The scariest part of his orders involved getting the bottled mixture into the queen's bedchamber, because her special guards were quite jumpy after the attack. Tiklok didn't think of himself as possessing any guile or smarts, but the solution lay easily within his grasp.

Shield Yanath, his face strained with fatigue, stood on duty.

"Hey, Yanath," said Tiklok, though the "th" sound came out with a horrible hiss. "Brought more wood to build up the fire. Gonna be a cold one tonight."

"Fine, Tiklok. Platsy's in there, straightening up, but Herself is not."

Tiklok nodded. He built up the fire in the Reception Room first, taking his time, stacking extra wood painstakingly while listening to Platsy move around in the bedroom. When she came out and smiled at the warmth he'd created, he pulled his cap at her and ducked into the interior chamber. More quickly he added logs to the fireplace there.

His glance fell upon the queen's dressing table.

*Nargis? You'll tell me if this is wrong?*

He carefully took the bottle out of his wood basket and set it on top of the note behind a hairbrush. Then he left the bedroom. He was leaving the outer room when Platsy stopped him.

"Tiklok!"

He shied. Luckily, everyone was accustomed to his strange mannerisms.

"If you see Geesilla would you tell her to get her arse up here? She's on duty next, and I'm tired of covering up for her lateness."

Tiklok nodded and pulled his cap to Platsy and Yanath.

As he strode down the hall he pondered why his heart raced so. He whispered, "I've got nothing to be scared about. I belong to Nargis, Queen Cressa, and Kiltti."

And he would gladly sacrifice this mangled body for any one of them.

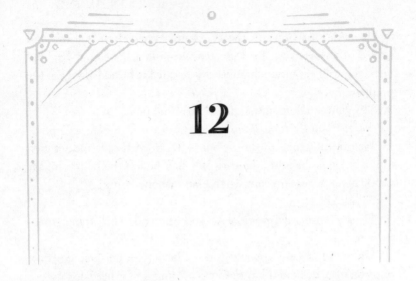

# 12

As she walked back toward her wing of the palace, Cressa added up her knowledge and guesses.

She had instinctively made her decision hours earlier; now she had to hope that her performance for the Circle Council had thrown them off enough so that she would have sufficient time to act.

She recognized the soldier escorting her as a member of her Shield. And two more stood outside her suite. She heard laughter from Cerúlia's chambers.

"Mamma!" Cerúlia rushed to her when she opened the door. "Seena and Pontole are so much fun! I am teaching them to play Oblongs and Squares. Will you order them to play with me more?"

Cressa knelt to hug her daughter.

"I am so pleased you passed a pleasant day. I want you to tell me all about it. Just one moment."

Cressa drew the soldiers to her. In a low voice she said, "Seena, find Captain Clemçon and tell him I need all the Queen's Shield to ride with me *now*. Then give Bristle this precise message: ''Tis time to finish the matter we discussed on our ride today.'"

"Very good, Your Highness," said Seena. Turning around, she said, "Princella, we have some duties, but we will play with you again soon."

Brushing off Cerúlia's protests, Cressa crossed through the Passageway of Lost Babes into her own bedchamber. A lantern glowed, and a bed warmer peeked out from under the foot of her bed. Her nightclothes warmed on a screen in front of the fire. She felt exhausted; the room looked so toasty and inviting.

Nonetheless, she grabbed a traveling case from the top of her wardrobe. She stuffed in some under smocks and hose, a nightshift, a cloak, her boots, and her dagger.

She moved to her dressing table to grab those jewels that were at hand, rather than in the royal vault. Next she grabbed a hairbrush. On the table stood a bottle filled with a dark liquid. When she picked it up, she saw a note below it that read:

Hare dy. Akorns coal tar berGamot oyl.

Cressa heard a quiet rap on the door and then the sound of someone opening it without waiting for response. She just had time to drop the traveling case behind her full skirt and stand in front of the dressing table as Geesilla entered and curtsied.

"Your Majesty, I thought I heard you in here. Why didn't you ring for me?"

Normal procedure would be for a maid to undo her hair and help the queen undress.

"Ah, Geesilla!" Cressa replied, forcing her voice to sound casual. "I'm not quite ready yet. I'd like—I need to dictate a letter. Go fetch Chronicler Sewel for me."

Geesilla took another step deeper into the room. "Why don't I send Tiklok, Your Majesty? I just saw him down the hallway. That way I can start on your hair while we wait for him. Or Lady Fanyah writes a fair hand, and her quarters lie much closer. That way, I could help you unlace and—"

"Geesilla," said Cressa, forcing herself to sound calm. "I'd like you to go. It is very late to be summoning my chronicler; sending my personal maid shows respect, as does keeping myself dressed. I would rather not receive him in nightclothes.

"Just do as you're bid, now," the queen added, in a tone that accurately conveyed her weary impatience. Geesilla departed with a flounce.

Cressa placed the stoppered bottle in the traveling bag. For an instant she thought of changing out of her gray gown, but it would take too long to unpin, unlace, and unhook, especially without help.

Crossing through the passageway to the princella's room, she instructed Nana to add similar things of Cerúlia's to the case, while her daughter looked on, confused. Cressa felt the seconds ticking away.

Cressa drew Nana to her in a deep hug. First, she wiped Nana's memory of the afternoon at West Garden. Then she whispered, "I have always loved you, my Nana. You have been dearer to me than my own mother. You have been my rock and my refuge."

Nana rubbed her back. "Oh my own, would that I . . ."

Reluctantly, the queen broke away. She addressed her daughter, "Cerúlia, give Nana a hug. We are off adventuring for a while."

"But, but—what about my cats and dogs? Can we take them with us?"

"Surely Nana will take the best care of them until you return."

"Can't we go tomorrow?" The child looked toward her four-poster.

"No, Cerúlia. We must leave right now."

Nana knelt. Her daughter hugged her distractedly, her lip just starting to tremble. "Watch Naki's cut. And make sure Zizi doesn't get fat."

"Give me a kiss, my heart's own," said Nana.

Cerúlia kissed her and then stroked her wrinkled cheek, staring at her solemnly. "I'll miss you, Nana," she said.

Over Cerúlia's head, Nana said to Cressa, "May the Waters keep ye safe. I will be waiting right here."

Cressa touched three fingers of her right hand to her lips, then to her Royal Stone that glimmered on her forehead, and then spread the palm toward Nana: the Queen's Blessing, a fare-you-well gesture only used at special partings. Then she grabbed Cerúlia's hand and rushed her out of the room.

Captain Clemçon and three other shields awaited them in the hallway. All the guards had turned their cloaks inside out so that instead of showing the bright blue royal insignia, they looked black. Some had rucksacks on their backs. Clemçon took the case from the queen and handed it off to Shield Kinley. Then he took her elbow in one hand and Cerúlia's hand in the other, and set off down the corridor.

Cressa looked over her shoulder. Tiklok emerged from the shadows of a doorway. When he saw her glance, he bowed low. Cressa mouthed, "Thank you" to him.

# 13

Clemçon's thorough knowledge of the palace served him well. He led the royals down one of the narrow back servants' staircases. To bypass the bustling kitchens, however, he took the broad corridor past the public meeting rooms, which typically stood quiet in the evenings, disturbed only by ticking clocks or the inaudible songs of the water nymphs painted on their ceilings.

Matwyck's secretary was just backing out of an administrative chamber, his arms filled with ledger books. Clemçon opened the nearest door, pushed the royals inside, and followed them himself, hand on his sword hilt, peering through the door crack. His shields kept on walking steadily; quick-witted Kinley managed to chuckle as if her companion, Dariush, had just told her a joke. Heathclaw concentrated on juggling his burden and getting the door to lock with a balky key. He had not seen the royals, and he paid no attention to Queen's Shields nonchalantly striding down the hallway.

When the man disappeared, Clemçon led his party into the Great Ballroom, so empty tonight that their own reflections in the mirrored walls kept catching his eye and their footsteps echoed hollowly. In the corner, painted over so as to be almost unnoticeable, stood the wooden door used by footmen to fetch firewood. Clemçon had a master key.

The stables lay to the west of the residence. The small group walked quickly, turned a corner of the building, and collided with a palace soldier pacing his rounds. Dariush pulled his dagger and poked the man in the side while Yanath grabbed his opposite arm in a vise grip. "Shhh!" whispered Dariush with a wicked smile. They dragged the shocked man between them.

Clemçon experienced a stab of fear when he spotted no horses in the yard, but soon discovered that the stableman and his helpers held them out of sight, saddled and ready, in the capacious central aisle of the stable.

About half of his troop had already gathered, and the others arrived swiftly in clusters of two or three. Some of the men and women had brought belongings; all had their weapons. Yanath tied his captive up tightly, gagged him so he couldn't call out, and locked him in a horse stall.

Clemçon helped the queen and the princella mount. His liege whispered to him about the extreme need for haste. He counted heads; one was missing.

"Don't wait for Gathleigh—he won't be joining us," Bristle said in an undertone. Clemçon experienced a shock; he shook it off.

"Bristle and Dariush," the captain called, "shed your armor and ride leisurely to the Arrival Gate. Get the palace guards to open it for you. We will walk the horses until we are away from the buildings and then follow you. Your job is to get the gate open."

Bristle pursed his lips. He took a flask of liquor out of a saddlebag, took a swig, and offered some to Dariush. Next, he deliberately spilled some on his clothing. They rode off talking in rowdy voices about taverns and tavern wenches.

Handing Nightmist's reins to one shield and Smoke's to another, the captain led the way, pulling his horse out of the yard. The temperature was just cold enough for their breath to condense in white clouds. Clemçon turned around and saluted the stableman.

The horses kept remarkably quiet; none nickered or whinnied. He waited until they reached the winter-brown grass a ways from the palace, where movement would be more muffled than in the flagstone courtyard. Then he passed the whisper to mount up. He pulled his horse alongside Her Majesty. "Where are we headed?" he asked.

"The quay."

Clemçon checked behind him. Shields Seena and Pontole flanked the princella. He kept the pace slow, heading to the left of Arrival Avenue.

When they were close enough, he halted them in the deeper shadows of the ancient elms that lined it. From what he could overhear, Bristle had encountered difficulty. His sergeant's voice grew strident.

"Come *on,* you goat-fuckin' jackasses! Me and me mate have *leave.* There's *ladies* waiting for us." They couldn't hear the guards' reply.

Clemçon counted fourteen on duty tonight, more than the normal contingent. And he noticed they all had horses picketed at the gatehouse. He looked back at the palace: several torches flitted back and forth through the Royal Wing, so there was no time to circle around to the Kitchen Gate.

"Since when, you pig-fuckers?" complained Bristle. Another answer they couldn't make out.

"Well then, fetch your squad leader off his lard ass and get *him* to authorize it." A guard passed through the arched door of the gate tower and came back with an officer. At this distance, even though numerous torches lit the gate area, Clemçon could not be sure, but he thought the officer might be Lurgn, one of General Yurgn's sons.

Bristle started a heated argument with Lurgn, but clearly Lurgn wasn't going to yield, no matter how much Bristle cursed. Clemçon made a snap decision. He whispered to his best bowmen to pick their targets. The palace guard wore helms and breastplates, so his archers knew to aim for faces, groins, and thighs.

"Ready? Now!" hissed Clemçon.

Eight arrows flew, slicing the cold air. Seven connected with solid thuds, but not all put their targets completely down. Men started yelping in pain and fury. Bristle's and Dariush's swords flashed, and the rest of the Queen's Shield galloped to their aid. If the palace guard had all had their long halberds at the ready, the horsemen might have fared worse, but some of their wicked hooked pikes leaned against the wall. Metal clashed in wavering torchlight. Dariush cut a young guard's throat, and blood spurted in a wide arch. Bristle head-butted Lurgn. With a solid swing of his own sword Clemçon beheaded a young soldier who stood stock-still, frozen in shock at an attack from his own comrades.

The skirmish lasted only moments, but noise rang out as the palace guards shouted and cursed their attackers. And the princella started screaming, "Mamma! Why? Mamma! Make it stop!"

When all of their adversaries lay dead or dying his men winched up the heavy metal portcullis that barred entry during the night-time hours.

"Ride! Ride!" Clemçon shouted, raising his own bloodied sword into the night.

All the Queen's Shield spurred their horses. Nightmist and Smoke shot off as if released from years of unjust captivity.

They galloped recklessly, right through the middle of Cascada. Clemçon thought he heard a yell of "Stop them! Stop them!" but nothing could halt their momentum down the sloping avenues. A few arrows flew in their direction; one lucky shot connected with the side of Pontole's thigh.

As they rushed headlong through every turn, anything or anybody in their way scattered like affronted chickens. On a winter's night the city was comparatively quiet, but a number of folks were still out and about. The two dozen horses leaped over obstructions, and citizens dashed out of harm's way. People screamed. One of the shield's horses slipped, fell heavily, and made no effort to rise; Dariush circled back, and Yanath, evidently not seriously hurt, leapt up behind him. They clattered at full speed through the Courtyard of the Star, the Fountain pulsing water above them into the black sky.

Clemçon kept watch on the royals. He knew the princella could ride well, but he marveled at how Smoke and she moved as one. He would rather have had the royals surrounded by his soldiers, but no one could catch up with their superior mounts. The queen and princella led the way, their cloaks billowing out behind them, as their horses sped down the hill from the palace, down through the city streets, and down toward the harbor. A dark hat and veil flew off Queen Cressa's head and floated into the air behind her.

Hooves clattered on wooden boards as they reached the quay. They pulled up the horses, who balked and skittered at the sudden change of speed, men and beasts panting and looking around. After the stress of the flight it felt anticlimactic that all was silent and gloomy under the two cloudy moons—as it would be, this time of night. The only things to see were some stray cats prowling for fish scraps, a limited glow from the hut of the harbor watch, and the dark hulls of sleeping ships, some boasting watchmen dozing over braziers. From up the hill, back toward the palace, came the sounds of pursuit.

"There!" shouted the queen, pointing to a ship berthed a distance to the north. Now Clemçon too saw a man standing on the dock, waving a lantern. They galloped off in that direction.

A smallish though deep-hulled ship stood with its gangway down and its sailors already in motion to loosen her moorings. Clemçon recognized the figure with the lantern: the queen's councilor, Belcazar.

"Get the princella and your men aboard!" Queen Cressa ordered him.

A man he assumed was the seamaster appeared on the deck, shouting. "Ten horses! We have room for only ten."

Clemçon dismounted, as did his soldiers. Smoke, with the princella still astride, trotted right up the gangplank as if the gelding climbed shaky planks every day. Seena and Pontole led the other horses up. Clemçon protectively held on to the queen's elbow, his hand on his sword hilt.

"Belcazar, well done," said Queen Cressa. "Captain, give me a gem."

Though his fingers had become thick and clumsy, Clemçon fished the leather pouch out. The queen gave Belcazar a giant gem—the color indiscernible in this light—that he tried to refuse.

"I insist. You may need to leave Cascada and hide for a while."

He started to kneel and kiss her hand.

The noise of an immense troop grew; it was getting closer to the quay.

"Your Majesty!" insisted Clemçon, tugging her elbow. She gave Belcazar the Queen's Blessing as Clemçon hustled her up the gangplank.

The sailors pulled up the plank and unfurled the sails, using their oars to push off from the dock.

The twelve two-person oars on each side of *Sea Sprite* moved them out into the harbor with practiced strokes while the sails just lay flaccid. Clemçon sought to detect wind on his cheeks, but he was too flushed to feel anything.

A hunting party of at least forty soldiers with more reinforcements streaming down the hill burst out onto the quay and headed toward the ship like wolves sighting their prey. The horses that had been left behind spooked, milling nervously around in a tight cluster, providing a buffer of chaos that the councilor used to slip away into the shadows of some crates.

The sailors pulled on their oars, moving the ship farther out of the harbor's shelter. Then the sails filled, and the ship gained speed, headed deeper into the Bay of Cinda.

The first mate attended the royals while shields saw to the horses they had loaded. Captain Clemçon looked to his wounded; Pontole's arrow came out of his thigh easily, and he stanched the bleeding with pressure. Others had taken slight injury in the mêleé at the gate, crashed into low-hanging signs, or twisted joints; most just needed a bandage and a word of comfort or reassurance. As the shoreline receded from view and no chase ship put to sea, Clemçon puffed out his breath with relief and rolled his knotted neck muscles.

"Captain," Kinley interrupted, "you're needed." She led Clemçon to where Sergeant Bristle cautiously perched on a keg. Bristle held his hands clamped over his belly, black liquid rapidly seeping around his fingers.

"What's *this?*" Clemçon asked. "Damn you, Kinley, fetch a lantern I can actually see with."

Bristle grunted. "Cow-fuckin' Lurgn! I sunk my sword into him, but he still managed to stick me right and proper." Clemçon pried away his sergeant's hands to examine the wound as gently as he could, discovering that a blade had gone in its full depth. It hadn't cut a major artery, or Bristle would not have been able to ride, but whatever it had nicked bled steadily.

Clemçon sucked his breath in through his teeth.

"I know; you can do naught for a deep belly wound," said Bristle. "Lost a lad this way in that bread riot . . ."

"Drought and damnation! We should have been quicker to the gate!" Clemçon straightened up and put his hand on Bristle's shoulder. "How about a drink for the pain?"

"Never say no to a good drink. But Cap, you make a wretched tavern wench."

Clemçon sent for the ship's rum. Although Bristle needed the liquor for his pain, no sooner had he drunk it than he vomited it back up. The shields made their companion as comfortable as they could, and took turns watching over him. Clemçon retired to one of the bunks, but despite his fatigue, whenever he closed his eyes he saw Gathleigh, the young Weir soldier at the gate, or Bristle. He was just as glad to give up trying to sleep when Yanath came to fetch him, telling him that Bristle's condition had worsened; now he fevered and gasped for breath.

Clemçon sat by him during his last hour, clasping his longtime comrade's hands tightly. Bristle's agony was fearful to behold.

"Together we saved the royal family," Clemçon said softly, though Bristle was past talking. "I couldn't have done it without you, Sergeant. You did your part so stoutly. You will forever live in my heart with honor. Sleep gently on the Eternal Waters."

Shortly after the sun rose on the Bay of Cinda, Bristle gasped his death rattle. Within a moment, his old friend was gone, replaced by inert flesh.

# PART
# TWO

*Reign of Regent Matwyck*

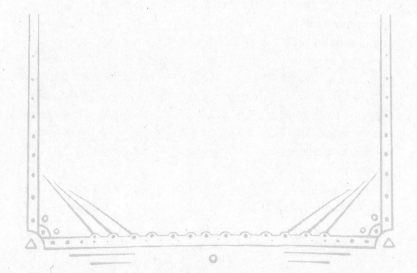

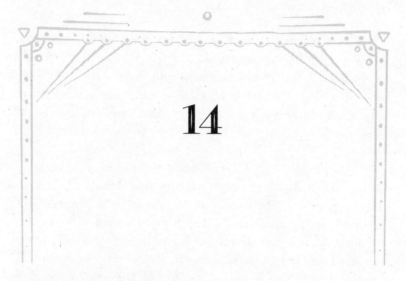

# 14

## Sutterdam, The Free States

Thalen didn't want to race, but Harthen shouted, "Go!" and took off, his short legs pumping. Strictly speaking, this was not really fair, because Harthen gave himself a head start.

Thalen and Hake sped off after Harthen, traversing the narrow, winding streets. Hake pumped his arms, trying to catch their little brother. Thalen, however, loped along easily, distracted by sights and sounds at intersections, such as a man with a basket of greens on his head or a street performer playing a lute.

*When you pick lettuce does it die instantly? I love that tune.*

Sutterdam was the biggest city in the Free State Vígat, part of the Alliance of Free States; it sat astride the Sutter River, which looped about and embraced so many tributaries that one could hardly move ten minutes in any one direction without crossing an arched bridge. Barges bobbed across the rivers and canals moving materials and finished goods, while their pole workers yelled a cacophony of warnings and disputed right-of-way with an impressive variety of oaths. Such a widely mixed population peopled Sutterdam that Old Colors had long ago blended to make brown hair of every hue and texture—coily, curly, or straight—the established norm.

Thalen bumped into a vegetable cart, banging his knee; then hopping, rubbing his new bruise, he tripped over the base of a waterspout. By the time he caught up with his brothers on the other side of Cobblers Bridge he looked disheveled, and his unruly hair, which had started neatly tied back like Hake's, had pulled loose.

"What happened?" said Harthen. "We've been waiting for you *for-ev-er.*"

"Never mind," said Hake. "But from here on we'll walk together." Then, knowing that Harthen always overflowed with energy, he amended, "We'll *march* to the Square of the Martyrs. Like soldiers." And he led his brothers on at a swift cadence.

The Square of the Martyrs sat in the middle of Sutterdam: the tree-lined, cobblestoned plaza boasted an assortment of weathered, life-size statues. Four centuries ago "The Martyrs" had approached King Iga VII with petitions about corruption amongst the nobles and for alleviation of their dire poverty. Using his Power of Transformation, the king had turned them into stone figures that couldn't pester him.

The brothers were on their way to meet the Long Roads Cart bringing their teta Norling to Sutterdam. She was their father's older sister. The boys were not supposed to know that some moons ago her husband had "run off with" the barmaid of their inn. Their father, Hartling, had written, begging his sister to join their Sutterdam household, saying they were having a hard time managing, what with the family pottery business having so many orders to fill. This pretext had the advantage of being truthful, but Thalen suspected that his father also did not want Norling to live lonesome. During the winter, even though the Inn at Spruce Valley sat bestride the Post Road, some days no custom stopped; he overheard his father tell his mother that Norling "just rattled around that empty ramble alone, with no one to fix a leak in the roof."

The brothers shared affection for their teta. During hot summers when they were young, their parents would take them for extended visits out to the inn, where the spruces scented the breezes. The city boys learned to ride on the inn's horses and to swim in a nearby pond. And Norling's blueberry tarts were legendary. In recent years, though, their parents had been so busy at the pottery that the brothers had only seen their relatives at holidays.

Long Roads Carts between locales in Vígat rarely arrived at the appointed hour. This one, however, had come *early* and had already dropped Teta Norling off in front of the Golden Bridge Tavern. A long-faced woman with a thin nose, she sat on her cases looking around under a bare tree near the Statue of the Martyrs. Though she wore her innkeep's merry black-and-white-striped gown with a red apron, his aunt looked older and forlorn, as if all the cheeriness had been sucked out of her cheeks.

Young Harthen, spying her, dashed ahead to give her a tight hug. Hake greeted her, "Welcome to Sutterdam, Teta Norling. We trust you have not been waiting long." Ashamed that she had been left waiting alone, Thalen just kissed her soft, deer-colored brow. He noticed that now he had to bend his neck down.

"My, my, how you have all sprouted up!" said Norling. "Three fine young men! And so fine looking, with your mother's blue eyes."

"I've been practicing with a sword and dagger!" Harthen pulled up his sleeve to show his muscles, which Norling admired.

Hake apportioned out the cases amongst the brothers. They set off to the factory first, so their parents could welcome their aunt. Because the distance was so short—really just over Coopers and Farriers Bridges—Harthen barely had time to act out a vicious street fight he'd witnessed yesterday and boast about how much fun he'd had with his pals dropping eggs on bargemen from Scriveners Bridge before they arrived.

Sutterdam Pottery hummed with the activity of a thriving concern. Housed in an extensive brick building, it made everything from plain jugs for transporting oil or cider to fine pieces commissioned by wealthy patrons. The fancy pieces enthralled their father, Hartling: he designed all manner of shapes, glazes, and patterns.

In the outer yard workers packed up crates while others shoveled coal for the kilns. The boys dropped Norling's belongings in an out-of-the-way corner. Inside, they threaded their way around to find

Pater at his wheel, his precise hands forming a pitcher while his kicks kept the wheel turning. He grinned broadly at Norling but could not stop at that moment, so Hake and Thalen took her up a flight of narrow stairs at the back to their mother's business annex and the rooms that accommodated employees who stayed to tend the kiln late into the night. Harthen remained on the floor to help Pater.

"Norling!" said Mater, getting up from a table piled untidily with lists of commissions, bills of lading, and invoices, in front of a wall filled with cubbyholes of similar papers.

"Jerinda, my dearest!" The women embraced and exchanged greetings, and Mater told Norling about how many orders the business had, how many workers they now employed, and how many hours the kiln kept burning. Thalen didn't listen to their words, but compared their demeanors: Mater so bright and pretty, Norling so careworn.

Presently, Mater turned to Hake saying, "Eldest, I must calculate tomorrow's payday. Stay to help me."

"Of course, Mater. Thalen and Harthen can escort our teta home."

"Truly, I'm so relieved you've come," said Mater. "With me so busy, Harthen gets into new mischief every day. And I can't keep the boys in hose or shoes."

Thalen and Norling retraced their steps back to the factory floor. Harthen, who as his pater said "had the hands," now sat at a nearby wheel fashioning a wet lump of clay into a flagon that mimicked the shape of the pitcher. He grinned up at them, happy with his skill and the activity.

Pater, wiping his hands on his work apron, now had a moment to greet his sister, which he did, Sutter-style, with kisses on both hands. Hartling, with his medium height, muscular physique, and sober business wig (a headpiece of brown hair tied simply at the back, worn by Free States men who began to go bald), always conveyed a certain economy of motion and a grace that Thalen envied. His father and brothers seemed to know exactly where their limbs had strayed; *they* never crashed into things. Thalen concentrated on staying out of the way of the busy bustle that surrounded them, warily eying a shelf of pots as if any minute he might crash into it. He'd had unhappy experiences with shelves before and was determined not to get caught again.

"Harthen, I could really use you," said Pater. "We must get all of the order for Olet in to fire today. I'm sorry to steal Youngest, Norling, but Olet's Olive Oil and Spicery is one of our best customers."

"Sure," said Harthen, "Thalen can take Teta Norling home."

Losing both brothers posed a problem for Thalen; he couldn't carry all four of Norling's cases by himself. However, he spied a wheelbarrow in the yard that would serve nicely.

As they trundled back toward home, Thalen found that balancing the wheelbarrow, avoiding bumping into pedestrians, and not letting the cases slip on the downward slope of the bridges took most of his concentration. As he started to get the hang of the job Thalen politely asked Norling about closing up her inn and whether she felt tired from her long trip.

"Those carts, they sure give a body a thorough jolting," Norling said, avoiding the first topic.

"I wish we could turn them into swan boats," said Thalen, "that would glide passengers along smoothly."

"Aye, it would be nice to have the Power of Transformation," said Norling.

"I've read that with the eradication of Iga's line, no Earth Magic lingers in the Free States."

"Though your own father," said Norling, "turns one thing into another."

"Well, all craftsmen do. That's not the same as turning a bag of pebbles into a bag of gold."

"Isn't it?"

Thalen grinned sidelong at his teta's cleverness, and she winked at him.

"Excuse me," said Thalen to a woman with a tray of fried dough who stood in the way of his wheelbarrow. She moved enough for him to get by. The crooked streets overflowed with people going about their business on this winter day, and Thalen had to pay close attention.

"Tell me, Thalen, what about you?"

"Harthen would make a really good potter, but he has his heart set on becoming a soldier. I don't think I would make an adequate craftsman, nor do I want to fight. Someday, Hake will take over the pottery. My mind wanders when I should be doing figures, so I doubt any merchant would hire me as a bookkeeper. Pater asks me to load carts, but I don't envision life as a carter." He set the wheelbarrow down a moment to wipe his hands on his trousers.

"En-vi-sion," Norling repeated, tasting the word. "I didn't ask what work you will do," she said, offering him a kerchief, "I want to know what interests you."

"I like to read books," said Thalen.

"What kind of books?"

"Histories and nature the most. But I'll read anything I can find. Have you read *Tales of the Rorther-Lorther Wars*? Or, last week I got *Of Trees, Shrubs, and Plants*. The difference between trees and shrubs is not just a question of size, you know, which many people believe."

"I didn't know. Where do you find such books?"

"My schoolmasters loan them to me. Or I spend my carter's wages. Did you bring any books with you?" He nodded his chin at the cases as they started on the downside of Silversmiths Bridge.

"Only two: a cookery book and a book of Weir ballads. You're welcome to both. Now I wish I'd brought some of the books from the inn. Sometimes instead of paying their fare in coin, travelers traded in possessions."

"Did you have any histories?"

"I don't recall. I had a whole pile of things to barter. I got rid of it all."

Thalen had to put his back into pushing the wheelbarrow up the slant of Tailors Bridge and so hid his frustration over the lost books.

"Do you do well in your studies, Thalen?" asked his aunt.

"Aye."

"How well?"

"I come in first in most of the subjects," he answered as he crested the top. "But I'm not trying to best the other kids; I just always end up remembering what we've studied."

Norling nodded. "You don't strike me as competitive. What else do you like besides reading?"

"I love music! I would like to learn to play."

"Have you asked your parents?"

"No—you know them. They're practical people. They would think it frivolous. . . ."

"Tsk," said Norling. "We hired many a troubadour for the inn for busy seasons. Music lifts the spirits. I brought my flute in the black case. I can teach you a few of the standard lays and how to play."

"Oh Teta, that would be splendid!" He paused. "And I like to eat."

Norling eyed him with a measuring glance. "What are you, thirteen summers? I'll bet you grow taller every day. You might be the tallest of the lot. Take after our grandpater, I think, not your parents. But you look a little thin. Are you hungry all the time?"

"Just talking about eating makes me hungry," said Thalen. "Especially being with you and thinking about your pastries."

"Well now, that's something else I can do for you, boy. No one has ever left my table with his belly flat. In fact," she said, starting to roll up her sleeves because she recognized Lantern Lane, the curved row of narrow, middle-class homes they had turned onto, "just let me at your pantry."

"Not today, Teta Norling. You should rest from your long trip and get settled. We added on a room just for you by pushing the wall out into the space behind the house. We all worked on the construction, and Mater bought a rug. It's small but kind of cozy. Will you be comfortable here after all the inn's spaciousness and privacy?"

"Spaciousness can be a blessing or a curse," said Norling with a grim look.

Thalen considered this apparent contradiction for a moment and smiled sideways at his aunt when he understood it.

"Are you sure I can't get into your kitchen?" his aunt asked as they halted at his stoop.

"We've got food in the larder. Not as good as yours, of course, but it will suffice." Thalen lifted the first case to lug it into the house.

Norling tugged his loose hair affectionately and then grabbed a second case. "*Suffice,* will it?" she said, teasing him about his word choice. "What a sweet lad you are, Thalen. Harthen, I fear, is destined for scrapes, but whatever your future holds, I'm certain you'll stay out of trouble."

# 15

## Cascada

"Really, no one has seen *Sea Sprite*? None of the lighthouses spotted her?" Matwyck and his confederates conferred in the private sitting room of his palace quarters in the midafternoon of the day following the queen's escape while wispy spits of snow whirled in the wind.

The room mirrored his preferences: unostentatious, but actually very costly, with a rug of surpassing softness because it was made of baby rabbit pelts.

Matwyck regarded his confederates, weighing their strength and resolve. Treasurer Prigent, a compliant sycophant, nervously brushing his hair off his forehead, was always the easiest for him to handle. Underneath his upright demeanor, General Yurgn had a straightforward motive—money for his populous family, which Matwyck was happy to provide. On the other hand, Duchess Latlie and Lord Retzel needed their exculpatory fictions stroked. Lady Tenny had presented the only formidable obstacle, and Matwyck had struggled to find the right pressure point; he smiled inwardly at the recollection of the day he had broken her with threats of public calumny over a long-buried transgression.

"All the reports from our people confirm. The ship faced out to sea, probably heading to Lortherrod or the Green Isles," reported Prigent, who, befitting his stature as the only councilor without a title or riches, stood while the others occupied the limited seating options. "No word from Maritima yet, though I've sent couriers."

"I made a grave mistake, underestimating Cressa's terror," said Matwyck, steepling his fingers together in front of him as he sat at the card table. "We should have struck posthaste after the first attempt failed instead of considering a second plan to affix the blame on the Oros. Who'd have thought she would flee like a squeaking mouse? This headlong flight just proves, Tenny, she does *not* have the temperament to rule."

"No balls, eh?" said Lord Retzel, who sat near the fire, slumped down with his feet stretched close to the flames.

Tenny, perched lightly in the window seat, nodded but made no response. She held her body rigid, poised for flight, and looked steadily out the window, as if gazing away from her confederates distanced her farther from them.

"Cressa had assistance," said General Yurgn, who sat next to Matwyck at the table, "in the form of her pig-fuckin' shields. Her shields and that traitorous shit Belcazar."

"I know." Matwyck placed his hand on his ally's forearm. "General, we all feel the loss of your brave son and can only take comfort that his sacrifice was for the realm. Unfortunately, the shields are out of our reach for the present. Now, Belcazar . . ."

"Matwyck!" Lady Tenny whirled around, speaking firmly, "You pledged no bloodshed or reprisals. You gave me your solemn word."

In a soothing tone Matwyck said, "Calm yourself, my dear. My pledge is as sturdy as Nargis Mountain. Besides, I find unnecessary violence so distasteful. I have an alternative idea. What I would like"—Matwyck turned to Retzel—"is for your people to start a little whispering about the illicit liaison between Queen Cressa and Belcazar. Weren't they seen arm in arm and him kissing her hand?"

Retzel nodded. "Seen by a palace guard and a maid, eh?"

"Good, good. Then whenever Belcazar creeps out of his hidey-hole his character and his stories will be tarnished. And if we fail to intercept her and she raises an army to march on Cascada, she too will have to answer for this adulterous affair, an episode that besmirches the honor of the Nargis Throne."

"By the Waters, man. You are a clever soul, eh?"

"Which is why, my friends, the queen named me regent whenever she left the realm for more than a day. Councilor, have you the proclamation?"

"Yes, right here," said Prigent, flourishing the parchment. "I found it easy to get her seal in the midst of a stack of appropriations!" Responding to Matwyck's arched eyebrow, he confessed, "Well, Duchette Lumetta distracted her, and Lady Fanyah told her this parchment was just an extra copy of the previous one."

"Still, Prigent, we would not be here without your invaluable assistance," Matwyck obliged his underling's need for more praise. He kept the irony in his voice so very light none of the lackwits caught it, though Tenny shot him a sharp glance.

"But how will we explain the sudden absence of the queen and the girl?" asked Duchess Latlie from the half-reclined position she had assumed on a couch, twirling her amber curls around her finger, as if all this trouble was almost too much for a lady of quality to bear. "Everyone saw them riding like fury toward the quay."

"The princella has gone to visit her grandfather. She will return in good time."

"Her grandfather!" said Latlie, bolting upright on the divan. "*He's* really responsible for all of this. Cressa was corrupted by her visits to Lortherrod—the Lorthers infected her with their foreign ways."

Once Latlie got started, no one could turn her from her favorite theme. "She married a vulgar, brown-haired seaman! She ignores all protocol and precedence! No wonder we are getting these outrageous petitions from this so-called Parity Party!"

General Yurgn turned so only Matwyck could see his face and rolled his eyes with impatience.

"Of course you're right," said Matwyck, humoring the duchess and laying a calming hand on the general's sleeve. "This shows a shocking lack of breeding and discernment."

"Cressa traveled so often she never learned how things are done here," the duchess continued. "She doesn't understand that social order depends upon respect for rank. If you dissolve that, you invite unrest. And she has snubbed *all* of my Planting Balls. My balls are the highlight of Cascada society, and she has not once graced my house with her presence! I've told you what she wrote me as an apology?"

"I don't recall the exact wording."

"I wish *I* could forget: 'Although I have heard that your Planting Ball is a delightful recreation, I'm sure that—being a mother yourself—you will understand that whenever affairs of state do not consume my evenings, I prefer to spend the time in the company of my child.' My balls attract the very best people; I offer the very best meats, the very best wines and conversation and entertainment in the realm! Never mind that I have swallowed my pride and reinvited her every year that husband of hers was at sea—because, naturally, I simply can't have *him* in my house. Lord Consort or no, I do believe that standards must be maintained or we'll have anarchy!"

"Naturally. I appreciate how spectacular your hospitality is, my duchess, because for the last two years you have done me the great distinction of inviting me," Matwyck commented.

"I would have guided this young queen for the love I hold her mother; I could have taught her; but she spurned all my offers of friendship."

"You have done all you could and more," Matwyck agreed. "I have been astonished by your generous forbearance."

"What about the queen?" asked General Yurgn, unable to sit through more of Latlie's tirade.

"Do you mean, where has she gone?" asked Matwyck. "Why, our brave, impetuous liege has herself pursued the would-be assassins' escape ship."

"Will the people swallow this?" asked Lady Tenny. "It doesn't explain the dead gate guards, nor the chase down to the quay."

"The regent has declared that the massacre at the gate arose from a drunken brawl," said Yurgn, with a glare that took in all the room. "As for the chase: palace guards attempted to recapture those who fled after such a horrid breach of discipline. His story besmirches the honor of my dead son and his unit"—Yurgn turned his scowl on Matwyck a moment—"but we'll have to stick with it now."

Matwyck poured a glass of claret for Yurgn. "I *am* sorry, my dear friend. But *we* know the truth and honor their bravery.

"Tenny, you need not worry that the court or the people will question or fret," he continued. "None will weep for Cressa; she is not loved."

"And a few gold catamounts will work wonders on any doubters," Retzel offered with a chuckle.

"What about her personal attendants?" Latlie asked. "Her maids and so on? Do they know anything? Will they contradict us?"

Retzel threw his head back to laugh. "I have had the maids inside my purse for years, eh? Her shields held loyal, but they left with her."

"All except the one, that is. How did they discover Gathleigh worked for us?" Prigent asked.

The councilors chose to overlook this reference to the man found stuffed in a clothes press with his throat cut, as if Prigent's question strayed into indecorous territory.

"And the ladies-in-waiting?" asked Yurgn.

"Mine," said Retzel, grinning.

"Excellent. And the tutor?" asked Yurgn.

"What tutor?" asked Retzel, instantly defensive. "No one ever said anything to me about a tutor, eh?"

"*Tutor Ryton* instructed the princella. I think the man's too weak-kneed to cause any trouble," said the general. "But just in case, in a few weeks he may enjoy the hospitality of one of our cells." Lady Tenny started to speak, but Yurgn glared at her, and her protest died on her lips.

"Teonora, poor soul," said Duchess Latlie. "I've heard she couldn't get out of bed today. This blow will be the end of her, I do believe. Really, I don't know how she's kept going this long. Some people just *refuse* to die."

Prigent giggled at this.

"Only an idiot laughs at pain and death," Tenny snapped, not looking at her fellow councilor.

"Tough old bird," chimed in Retzel, speaking on top of Tenny.

"But what about the nursemaid called Nana?" Latlie asked. "I do believe she is quite popular around the palace. Quite a fixture, I do believe. It would look ill if anything happened to her. She may be untouchable."

"Then I will have a chat with Nana myself," said Matwyck, "to take her measure personally. In the meantime, when should Thum escape? Tenny, I will need your assistance renegotiating with him. He feels rather ill-used and will not like our terms. A light woman's touch will be so salutary."

"Then the sooner he gets out of a jail cell the better," she said. She resumed gazing out the window, her face a mask, her hands gripping the sill.

"As you wish, as you wish," replied Matwyck. "So we all know our next steps?" He gazed at each of his confederates in turn.

Latlie responded, "I am going to scour every noble house, looking for the princella or signs that some royalist has aided her."

"Indeed," said Matwyck. "The search for her is our highest priority. We *must* find her. Start with Maritima, her father's native duchy, then move on to the Eastern Duchies. Use whatever means you must."

"I will communicate with the Pellish to search for *Sea Sprite*," Prigent said.

"We've always had people stationed in the Green Isles, haven't we? What about Lortherrod?" Matwyck asked.

"The Isles serve as such a transit hub," Yurgn answered, "that every country sends a strong contingent of spies there. Tidewater Keep now, it protects itself with suspicion—those Lorthers distrust their own shadows!—but I'll see if I can place someone there or in the nearest town, Liddlecup."

"I will spread the delicious news about Belcazar, eh?" said Retzel.

"And I," said Matwyck, "after I visit this 'Nana' creature, will have the proclamation read and posted. Tonight you will toast Weirandale's new Lord Regent!"

With the meeting breaking up, Tenny headed quickly out the door, her expression hooded. His other four confederates offered polite applause and then, quickly or ponderously, departed to put their plans in action.

Matwyck left his quarters humming under his breath. He walked through the Administrative Wing to his office chambers, discovering Heathclaw engaged in whispers with a knot of other agitated clerks.

"Heathclaw," Matwyck said, drawing him into the privacy of his chamber. "You must arrange for all of the palace servants to gather for an announcement in the Great Ballroom this evening at moonrise. The palace caller will read this proclamation; then I will say a few words."

"That's good, milord. Rumors are flying."

"Also," Matwyck continued as if his clerk had not spoken, "you will have copies of this proclamation posted all throughout Cascada and send one to each duchy, posthaste."

"Very good, Lord Steward," said Heathclaw, taking the rolled-up parchment.

"Lord *Regent*," Matwyck corrected him.

"Lord Regent, sir!" said Heathclaw, with an extra low bow.

"And you will send a message to my wife in the country, telling her that I request her presence in the capital, as soon as convenient."

"Very good, Lord *Regent*," said Heathclaw.

"We will be very busy in the days ahead, Heathclaw. We have double responsibilities now. See that you keep up."

With renewed alacrity Heathclaw bowed himself out of Matwyck's office and returned to his table in the outside salon.

By habit, Matwyck approached the paperwork stacked on his table of glossy burled walnut and dispatched some routine matters, returning his desk to its usual pristine state. He had finished the last chore when he overheard Lord Retzel thunder at his clerk in the anteroom.

"Milord"—Matwyck rushed to open his door to his fellow councilor and the richest man in the realm—"do come in." He ordered Heathclaw, "Go to the kitchens for tisane for Lord Retzel. You will remain to see to everything yourself."

"Matwyck—" Retzel looked as if he was going to say more, but as he strode into the office his mouth chewed on remarks he couldn't spit out.

"It is normal," Matwyck supplied as he closed the door, "to have second thoughts. Your scruples do you honor, milord." He gestured that Retzel should be seated in one of the two matching chairs in front of the fire.

Retzel's belligerent jaw lost some of its sharp definition.

"It's just—damn the Waters, Matwyck—she is *queen*."

Matwyck played a card he rarely used—honesty. "I will admit to you that I myself have had to steel my nerves." And he allowed himself a nervous gesture: he tapped the three long fingers of his right hand into the folds between the knuckles of his left fist so that they made a soft, plopping noise.

"But," Matwyck continued, "think of the chaos and harm she would have done if she acceded to the Parity Party and compelled higher wages for laborers. How would the crops be planted, tended, or gathered? She would bankrupt the noble estates and reduce them to a shadow of their luminance. Then Nargis's people would go hungry."

"She wouldn't really have done this, Matwyck. We talked her out of it once, and she hasn't raised the subject recently; we could do so again, eh?" Lord Retzel toyed with the rings that decorated his stubby fingers.

"Dare we take that chance, milord? And she's young; she could reign for twenty, thirty years. She is soft and soft-hearted. I, who come from the folk, know that the lesser classes must be treated with a firm hand—that's all they'll respect. If I had left the council, could you handle her whims alone?"

Retzel smacked his hand against the chair's arm at a long chafed-over memory. "Catreena's Lorther consort, so tongue-tied he could barely get out a sentence, he said to me, 'My sailors eat better than your laborers. Hungry people make bad workers.' That's what he said to me!"

"It's not her fault, poor Cressa," Matwyck admitted, "that she was subjected to foreign notions and foreign propaganda. The Waters know, I've tried to straighten out her thinking, but I only made slight progress. But we can't let the country suffer from Lorther customs. Drought-damn it, milord, this is Weirandale, not Lortherrod!"

"Right! Right you are." Retzel stood up, satisfied.

Matwyck pressed his point. "Even yesterday, we saw her less malleable, more authoritative. She snubbed us over the meeting with Thum. She's poking around in the account books. We had to act, especially *now,* when we've lost valuable cargoes to the Pellish and the shops have raised prices. Our little folk look to *us* for decisive action."

His voice grew persuasive, because Matwyck almost believed that their strike—which some might call treachery—actually showed a higher bravery and loyalty. "The Lorthers worship seawater, not fresh water. We are saving our country from a taint that would make our Waters undrinkable."

"Right. You phrase things so well, Matwyck. But I was the one who recognized your abilities and put you forward for steward. You won't forget that, eh?"

"I will be forever grateful to you, milord." And indeed, Matwyck inwardly acknowledged a debt. Of course, if it hadn't been Retzel, he could have found someone else to sponsor him, but Retzel had done his part.

"Excellent. I'm going now. The others don't need to know I dropped by, eh?"

"Of course not, milord. Though I think your scruples do you credit. More than anything else they prove your intent is disinterested."

"Just so."

The lord took his grand self out of Matwyck's office before the tisane arrived. Matwyck heard Heathclaw's voice drift in from the hallway.

"I'd appreciate that," he said to someone. "Here, I'll get the doors."

That wretched lackey—the one with the ghastly hole in his face—carried in the tray.

"Put it on the table," Matwyck ordered.

Matwyck settled himself back in the chair made of unusual leather; it came from the soft skin of fawn bellies, cured, dyed black, and stitched into an elaborate diamond pattern by artisans in Vígat. Retzel had not noticed the chair's qualities, but Matwyck savored the texture each time he sat in it. The leather had the qualities that pleased him most: unostentatious but covertly costly and unique. He sipped the perfect tisane—steaming, sweet, and tangy—staring sightlessly out his window at the early-winter afternoon.

Afterward he strolled through the palace, taking the temperature of the workers' anxiety and letting them see him relaxed and in control. Although he took pleasure in Heathclaw's adulation, he would have liked someone from his past to witness his elevation.

His past. His pa must have had some noble blood—probably passed down outside of a marriage bed—as evidenced by his isolated strands of amber hair. His ma had no letters, but she was quick enough, and it was his ma who had kept their little provisionary shop afloat and cadged together unsellable goods to fill seven children's bellies. His folks had both been harried, but they'd been proud of their middle child's keen mind and found the fees to send him to Tannery Row Upper School; they'd even asked a neighbor to mind the shop so they could attend the closing ceremony at which he'd beaten out all the snobby tradesmen and middling professionals' children to come in first (the other students so dense he'd hardly had to cheat). The upper school awarded him a prize of a silver tear and a volume of Weir history.

Luxuries never appeared in his home, and necessities were hard to come by. During his school years Matwyck had taken to stealing things from street vendors as he distracted them with some ruse, or—when he could catch them alone—intimidating smaller or younger children to hand over whatever they possessed of value. His mother had eyed a new cap of his but said nothing. The next day, however, she had provided a demonstration he never forgot.

A relatively prosperous neighbor had entered the shop, buying two overflowing baskets. As soon as the man had left, his ma turned to Matwyck. "Run after that gent and in your sweetest way, give him this copper drop. Tell him I overcharged him by accident and I sent you with my deepest apologies."

Matwyck did as he was bid. The neighbor was surprised and decidedly pleased.

When the door had slammed behind him, his ma had looked at him sharply. "Well, lad, do you still think you're so smart?"

"No, Ma. Your way is better. From now on, you can overcharge like a bandit and that man will swear to the city watch that you're the soul of honesty."

His ma had looked proud. "Mind me now, boy. The best way (the only way that works long-term) is to build a reputation for honest dealing. And behind that reputation—and fix it so no one knows they've been rooked—you make sure that you get what you want in this life."

Matwyck's eldest sibling, a boy whom his parents had doted on, had died in a scuffle with the city watch. Of course his older sisters had decamped from the crowded, vinegar-smelling loft above the store to husbands or lovers as soon as they could. When Eyevie ran off, Matwyck lost the only person who could keep up with his wit and his sole partner in the puppet plays they staged to entertain the young ones. His two little brothers (whose faces he could barely recall, though he remembered their puppy-like bodies clinging to him during thunderstorms), both died of the bloody flux. Their deaths must have broken his ma's heart, because a trivial illness carried her off soon after. And then, two years later, his pa, who'd been in his cups even more since she passed, just moved too slowly when a tavern brawl broke out: an accidental stab wound putrefied, and the old sod died too.

Matwyck could have run off when he was fourteen or fifteen summers, but he'd bided his time. Then all of a sudden at seventeen he had owned a shop; certainly not a giant concern, but he had no debt, no partners, and no bosses.

All he had to worry about was a baby sister. Fortunately, she was comely, and Matwyck had found a family down the street willing to take her off his hands.

Matwyck passed some scribes clustered in the hallway of the palace. They bowed low to him with cowed faces. He smiled benignly at them, lost in remembrance of the first killing he had made in the grocery, which had involved parlaying a cask of rare lemons into ten silver tears. He had sipped the heady cup of success as he steadily bartered and forged deals, all the while assiduously studying upper-class dress, customs, and speech.

Sometimes on the streets or in the line of job applicants at the castle he thought he spied Eyevie, his favorite sister; he might enjoy having someone from his past marvel at his triumph. But when the woman who vaguely resembled his sister turned out to be a stranger he felt both disappointed and a little relieved, because Eyevie would likely prove an embarrassment or encumbrance.

Matwyck walked on toward the salons and into the Royal Wing. He had no designs on the sumptuous rooms of the royalty; he would keep them intact as an outward sign of his devotion to the Nargis Throne.

He entered the princella's suite without knocking. The day-room and the adjoining sleeping nook were tidy, but the air hung stagnant. In a small adjoining chamber, he spotted a plump, older woman wearing a lace collar. She sat in a chair by the fire with a cat in her lap. An old mutt and a little greyhound asleep on the hearth filled the space with animals.

The servant did not stand up when he entered. Matwyck smiled to himself; he found such petty games an amusing challenge. He pulled up a chair across from her and sat in it backward, calmly crossing his arms on the chair back. Matwyck did not favor casual deportment; for him to sit this way conveyed contempt. He stared into her eyes for long moments; she met his gaze levelly, insolently. If she was intimidated, she was remarkably good at covering it up.

"Do you know where the queen and her girl were headed?"

"No." The lack of the honorific "milord" hung in the air between them.

"Did they say anything to you about their plans?"

"No."

"Do you have any idea of where they would hide?"

"No."

Matwyck drew two golden catamounts out of his purse and toyed with them between his long and shapely fingers.

"You know, Nana," he spoke confidingly, "I don't mean to criticize Queen Cressa specifically, but I've noticed that royalty habitually take advantage of their position. Oh, it may not be their fault—some habits are bred into them by years of tradition. They know how much we yearn to look up to them. We ache to show our loyalty, to be recognized for our faithfulness. And those raised to rule inevitably exploit these yearnings, even when they don't intend to.

"I, myself, have sometimes felt that my contributions were not really appreciated—that I was not given my due, and though I tried to rise above the snub, the pain rankled." He sighed. "Surely you recall many times when you've been taken for granted or when your love and devotion has been overlooked. Perhaps the child—I know she has her charms—mistreated you? I've heard that she can be stubborn."

The woman maintained a steely silence where Matwyck expected an outpouring of tales and grievances. He listened to the fire crackle and the wheezes of the old dog.

"What I do know is you have labored hard here for many years, and I'm certain you've not been given your full due, either in recognition or remuneration. Please take these coins, with no obligation, merely as a token of *my* thanks for your years of devoted service."

He held out the gold, certain that the woman would be moved by his sympathy.

The nursemaid curled her lip at him and made no move to take the money.

"Oh Nana, Nana. You disappoint me." Matwyck returned the

coins to his belt purse. His tone grew harsher. "Let me ask you—what do you see in your own future?"

"That I will wait here for their return."

"As Lord Regent I now control the country and the palace. You may stay on one condition."

"What is it?"

"That you never work or speak against me. If you do, I will know, and I will have you thrown out on your broad arse. Or worse."

"Hmmpf," was all she replied.

Matwyck leaned over and grabbed her chin, his fingers pressing hard into her flesh, forcing her to look him in the eye.

"Hmmpf, my Lord Regent," he corrected her, and strode out of the room, humming again.

*Formidable, in her uncouth way. Best to keep her here under my eyes.*

# 16

## Wyndton

Wilim, the peacekeeper of Wyndton, got home late from his circuit of hamlets to the northeast. The last situation had been a dispute that tried his patience: he had ridden up there before their trip to Cascada and here he was, back once again. He had wanted to knock both the obstinate farmers' heads together, but his job was to keep the peace, so he kept cajoling until the two reached a compromise about grazing and watering rights. He would need to ride up soon to see if the truce held.

The rain had swept down in the afternoon, a cold driving sleet, more chilling than snow would have been. Though he was hungry and wet he took the time to rub Syrup dry and fork him some hay. This sorrel would win no races, but he did his best. Wilim gave him a pat on his rump as he left the stable.

Stahlia had already put Percia to bed, but she waited up for him with his supper still warm. She opened the door for him with their ritual greeting, "Home is the Rider!"

She hung up his oiled cloak. He took off his boots and stretched his damp stockings and trouser legs out to the fire, gratefully accepting a steaming bowl from his wife. After he finished a second portion, he would tell her all about the dispute—sometimes she knew that a present-day wrangle actually rehearsed an old grudge over a broken promise or a lovers' quarrel. He was pondering whether the pleasure of a pipe was worth the trouble of getting up and fetching his tobacco when Gili jumped up from the hearth and ran to the door, wagging her tail expectantly. Gili was no watchdog—more a companion for Percie—but obviously someone approached.

"Oh no," snapped Stahlia. "You just returned. I don't want you to go out again on this black night." Then she amended, "I hope there's no trouble, nor someone hurt."

Wilim grinned at his wife.

"What?" she asked.

"You," Wilim said. "You talk tough, but your heart is mush."

She was protesting, "Get along with you," when they heard a light rap on the door. Wilim motioned Stahlia aside. In his stocking feet, he crossed to open it. He saw a woman and child, both hooded from the rain. He didn't recognize their silhouettes, as he would most folk in his ward.

"Is this the home of Wilim the peacekeeper and Stahlia the weaver?" asked an unfamiliar female voice.

"Aye, you've found the right dwelling. Do come in out of the wet."

The travelers entered and stood just inside the doorway. Water dripped onto the floor, and the dog made a fool of herself trying to get attention. The woman looked closely at the householders. Then, with a sudden gesture of her left hand, she threw back her hood—revealing her blue hair and the glittering Royal Stone on her brow. Wilim and Stahlia froze, dumbstruck.

"Your Majesty!" breathed Stahlia; she attempted an awkward curtsey, almost tripping over her own feet, while Wilim fell to one knee.

"No. Please rise. Our showing up on your doorstep is not quite the chance miracle it seems," said Queen Cressa. "When you traveled to Cascada last week, do you recall that Percia had a pleasant time playing with an acquaintance on the edge of the palace grounds?"

Wilim and Stahlia exchanged confused looks.

"That acquaintance was the princella. You don't remember, because I fogged your memories of that afternoon."

Dumbfounded, Wilim started reviewing the day in Cascada in his mind. Stahlia recollected her manners more swiftly, "Whatever brings you to our home, Your Majesty, truly, you honor us beyond measure." Stahlia took their wet cloaks while Wilim offered their visitors their best chairs, but the little girl—the princella—sat on the hearth rug petting Gili, who rolled over showing her belly, her head lolling in bliss.

"Would you drink some hot tisane?" Stahlia asked.

"That would be most welcome," said Queen Cressa. "We have ridden far tonight, and the wet . . ."

While Stahlia set the kettle on the hearth, Wilim put his boots back on and rebuttoned his knee-length waistcoat. Wilim hardly knew what to say to royalty; he cleared his throat several times and ran his hands through his hair. He remained standing.

"We had the honor of meeting you in Cascada?" he finally asked.

"Yes, your daughter and Cerúlia played together all afternoon. They developed an exceptional bond. But you'll never recall this, so don't try."

"Where's Percia?" asked the princella.

"She's asleep. In the loft upstairs."

Not knowing what else to say, he addressed the child. "The dog's name is Gili." The princella nodded.

The queen bestirred herself to make conversation. "How long have you lived in Wyndton?"

"Since our wedding. The house belonged to Stahlia's family. My kin hail from the north."

"I see," said the queen.

Fortunately, Stahlia returned then carrying a tray with her fanciest, if mismatched, cups and a brew pot. As Stahlia poured, the queen addressed them both.

"I fogged your memories because you both impressed me, and Cerúlia developed a rare fondness for your little lass." The queen warmed her hands around the cup but did not drink. "I wanted to protect you from my enemies. But I could dimly foresee that there might come a time when we would need to flee Cascada, and I thought of your house as a possible refuge. Too quickly events have taken a dire turn. Our lives and the throne hang in jeopardy from treason at home and attack from abroad."

"Oh! Your Majesty! I'll ride to Duke Naven. I'm certain the duchy will rise to defend you." In confusion, Wilim knelt as if to pledge fealty, then rose and started to reach for his water-heavy cloak.

"No. Pray be still." The queen put up her palm. "I fail to explain myself. Duke Naven's guard isn't large or skilled enough to protect us, and at all costs I must avoid a civil war in which citizens kill one another."

The queen took a few shallow breaths. "I came to beg an enormous boon of both of you. I have battles to fight; I must be off. Yet I wish you to consider allowing Cerúlia to stay here, with you. In short, what I am asking is: Would you foster and hide the princella?"

The princella sat up straight and interrupted, "Mamma! Mamma! I told you on the ship—I've told and told you—"

"Hush now," said the queen, in a tone that brooked no opposition.

Wilim spoke into the awkward silence. "Foster—with us? Wouldn't a noble house be the better place for the princella? We don't have fare that's fit for her; we have no tutors nor ladies' maids nor guards. . . ."

The queen took a gulp of her tisane, which made Wilim realize that he held his cup so negligently it was bound to spill. He set the cup down on the mantel, out of harm's way.

"Ah, but they will look in all the noble houses. In fact, my enemies will scour the country for her. She would be safest in a modest home where no one would expect to find the heir to the Nargis Throne.

"I will return the moment I am able. However, the midst of battle is no place for a child. And the throne would be safer if we separate—I plan to draw the search away from here.

"I ask a heavy burden of you, and it brings dire peril. I hardly know how long this conflict will last. To speak frankly, it could be years." The child made a strangled noise, but the queen continued. "If the throne's enemies discovered her here, you could pay a heavy price." The queen paused. She took another sip of tisane, as if her throat was dry, and then a deep breath. "I should not ask this of you, yet I do. Please. I have spent the voyage over the Bay of Cinda pondering all the options. Master Wilim, Mistress Stahlia. Believe me: this is the best. I beg of you."

The girl was still sitting on the hearth, petting Gili. She looked up sharply when her mother finished speaking. "I don't want anything bad to happen to Percia. You didn't tell me Percia might be in danger!"

Wilim had devoted his life to keeping the duke's peace, which actually served as a proxy for the queen's peace. Stahlia was a self-taught scholar of Weir lore, weaving tapestries portraying scenes from Weirandale's history. Although they were stunned to have the queen appear on their doorstep, they felt honored to be asked to help the throne in any way.

Above all, they saw a little girl on their floor needing protection and yet putting Percia's safety above her own.

Wilim looked at Stahlia; she nodded her head decisively.

The queen exhaled a sigh of relief. "Can you devise a story that would explain the new presence in your home of a little girl? The better the tale, the safer you all will be."

"She couldn't be a relative, because the whole of Wyndton knows we now have none in the Eastern Duchies," said Stahlia. "Besides, she looks nothing like us."

Wilim agreed. "Best if we took in a foundling, connected somehow to my circuits."

"But if you had picked up a child," Stahlia said, "wouldn't you take her to the local village council? Wouldn't somebody take her in, a neighbor who would have known her and her parents for always?"

"Well, yes and no. Some queer folks live on their lonesome in hermit shacks in Anders Wood. Recollect, Stahlia, I found that old woman last year, dead some weeks? I buried her in that forlorn clearing." Wilim shivered. "No one even to bring the tidings of her death."

"So if you had ridden through Anders on your way home tonight . . ." said Stahlia.

"Yes, it lies between here and the farms I visited. . . ."

The queen broke in. "You need to know who her parents are. To have no kin would invite questions about her lineage."

"I understand." Wilim thought for a moment. "I swung by a shack I had stopped by last moon when I rode up thataway. The mother belonged to them Donigills." To the queen, "The Donigills are a vast clan of rather shiftless folk spread throughout the duchy; they don't even know one another, and they have little family feeling. Some of them turn to horse thieving. The woman was hiding in Anders Wood because . . . because—"

"—because her man was a sailor she had met in Gulltown who beat her."

"Good, Stahlia." Wilim smiled at his wife. "A moon ago she sickened. The child told me she joined the Waters in the night. I buried the mother and brought the girl back to foster here because we have been longing for a second child. Which is true, Your Majesty, though the Waters have not yet graced us with a living babe."

"What do Donigills look like?" asked the queen.

"They are small folk, kind of wiry, with curly, darkish hair," said Wilim. "Oft times they give their kiddies bird names: Robin, Finch, Lark, and such."

"Fortunate," said Queen Cressa. "This tale will have to serve." Turning to Stahlia, "Could I trouble you for a shears?"

"Out in my workshop. I'll fetch them."

As Stahlia ran for it, not even bothering to cover herself from the rain, the queen asked the princella to get up on a chair. Wilim watched as she caressed her daughter's river of long, blue hair.

Stahlia returned and made to hand the shears to the queen. Queen Cressa said, "I don't have the strength to do it. Would you oblige me?"

Stahlia asked, "How short?"

The queen gestured to the bottom of the girl's neck, just touching her back, a length favored by folk of small means, because it took less trouble to care for. Stahlia made a few cuts, and with horrid fascination and self-consciousness they all watched the locks slide to the floor.

"No," interrupted the queen. "This won't do. You cut too neatly. Perchance, Master Wilim—"

"Mamma, how can you do this? Mamma, my *hair*!"

The queen put her hand on her daughter's shoulder, and she quieted except for little tremors.

Wilim took the shears from Stahlia. He grabbed the girl's hair at the right length, twisted it all together, and hacked at the coil. In a thrice he cut through the hank. The girl sniffled several times. It felt like a dirty deed.

Wilim knelt to look at the child straight on. She had high cheekbones and liquid brown eyes. "I'm sorry I had to do that, Your Highness," he said. "I'm real sorry."

The queen gathered up one thick strand. "This will I keep, Cerúlia. I will make a braid to wear always around my wrist. Burn the rest of it, every bit." Wilim lit an extra lantern, and he and Stahlia scoured the floor and the girl's clothes with care, throwing handfuls of blue into the flames, where the hair sizzled away.

"Here I have something that will make all of you safer," said the queen. She pulled from a purse hung around her waist a little bottle. "You know that hair dye is outlawed everywhere, because the gentry hold such snobbish views about Old Colors. But no one would dream of fussing over a mixture that turns hair ordinary brown. This tincture is made of boiled acorns, coal tar, and bergamot oil. Without fail, Cerúlia, you must apply this to your head once a week. You will all think of it as a tonic for a skin condition. When this bottle runs out, you should be able to replenish it or mix your own."

Queen Cressa poured some of the liquid into her hands and rubbed it into the shorn hair. The blue immediately turned dark.

The queen added some more and smoothed it all around. Now the hair's hue was dark brown.

"Stand up, Cerúlia."

The girl rose. With her hair changed, her small features and her slight stature indeed made her resemble a Donigill. Wilim noticed for the first time that she wore torn and stained clothes. Nothing about her spoke royalty, except her proud bearing.

She surveyed the three adults with her chin jutted upward. "My name is Wren. I lived in Anders Wood. My mother said that my father was a sailor, but he was brutal to her, so she took me and ran away. Her soul left her body last night. This man brought me to this house."

"Very good, Wren!" Wilim praised. "People will surely ask you 'How many summers have you?' and 'What was your mama's name? Mayhap I knew her.'"

"My mama's name was—was Tana. I have eight summers now."

"Say nine, Wren," suggested Stahlia. "That way you'll be extra tiny for your age, like the Donigills."

"You speak like a princella, Cerúlia," said the queen. "You must talk little and listen to the village children. Watch, listen, and copy their ways. Never call attention to yourself. School your face to look dull. Try to be as quiet and inconspicuous as a little brown wren."

"Mamma," cried the girl, just holding back tears. *"I don't want to do this! I want to stay with you!"*

The queen then pulled her child into her arms. Wilim and Stahlia cleared the cups and brew pot to the larder area around the corner to give them a moment of semi-privacy.

"Should we go out to the stable or the workshop?" he whispered to Stahlia. She bit her lip but shook her head. The queen whispered to her daughter for several long moments.

The queen gave the girl a final embrace and the Queen's Blessing. Sobbing now, the child ran back to Gili, burying her face in the dog's soft fur. Gili pulled back, the better to lick her tearstained cheeks.

Stahlia knelt down by the hearth, one hand on the girl's boot, a gesture that seemed even more kindly in its awkwardness. "We'll be good to her, I swear," she told the queen.

Queen Cressa nodded. Her face looked haggard, and her lips had gone bloodless. She addressed the householders. "I can tarry no longer. I hid our horses just down the lane with a shield. I will take the princella's cloak with me because 'tis too fine for an orphan girl.

"I know you would never purposely give away this secret. Yet by accident you might say the wrong thing. Or you might treat Wren differently from your own daughter. Or you might spend your nights in fear of discovery. It will be much safer for you and much safer for her if you *believe* the story you have concocted, and if you have no memory of my ever having visited here. Thus, one time more, I ask you: let me enchant you."

Queen Cressa reached for both Wilim and Stahlia's hands.


Wren was sobbing and holding onto Gili.

"Stahlia, I will brew a sleeping tisane. Could you get Wren in her nightshift?"

"Did you think to fetch any of her things? She must have had some garments in that cottage."

"Oh, drought!" said Wilim, striking his forehead. "I didn't think of that. I just wanted to get her away."

"No matter. She can wear something of Percia's. I kept some clothing she has outgrown in the chest upstairs. Come here, little one; I'll not hurt you, I swear."

They gave her the tisane and put her in bed next to Percia. Gili jumped on the bed too. Wren did not speak to them, but her sobs quieted and soon she drifted off.

Wilim and Stahlia returned to the front room by the fire. "Wife, are you angry with me? For fetching back this gal? I didn't know what else to do with her."

"No, Wilim. 'Twas the right thing, the best thing, to do. We've hankered for another child. I thought we would have a wee one, but now Percia will have a playmate. The blessings of the Nargis Fountain work in mysterious ways."

# 17

## Wyndton

Wren woke up in a lumpy bed on a straw mattress in a strange room.

The honey-colored bird dog lay on the bed, and when she opened her eyes the dog's tail started thumping against the quilts. Gili scooted forward on her belly.

*Lick face? Lick face? Lick face?* This dog's mind opened to her completely.

*Hullo, Gili. Are you a sweetie? Will you be a comfort to me?* Wren allowed the dog to slobber her with kisses, and then she got up, discovering that the small room was situated under the eaves. A window covered only with oilcloth in the east wall let in midmorning light.

The garments she'd worn last night had gone missing. Wren rejoiced because the split skirt from Cascada had gotten hard wear during the six days on the ship, and the scratchy, smelly muslin shirt actually belonged to *Sprite*'s cabin boy. She saw on the foot of the bed a soft, worn white linen smock; a brown skirt; a pink shawl knit out of lamb's wool; hose; and her own boots. Mamma had asked Shield Seena to scuff up and worry the boots—now Wren knew why.

The shawl stretched long enough for Wren to wind it in a crisscross across her chest and then around her waist. It was warm and soft to the touch. She was much happier in clothes like these rather than the fussy silks and velvets Nana made her keep clean.

She walked down the steep staircase, placing each foot stealthily. But Percia stood on watch for her.

"Here she is!" Percia sang out to her mother. Then she ran up to Wren. "I'm Percia. Welcome to our home!"

Wren understood she was supposed to pretend that she'd never met Percia before, but how her heart lifted on seeing her! Percia's smile was just as bright as she remembered it, the laugh lines around her eyes just as crinkly.

She whispered in Percia's ear about her need to relieve herself. While the mother cooked some porridge, Percia showed her the jakes outside. Wren recoiled at a smelly, cold, outdoor privy, but she bit her tongue. Percia then gave her a tour of the whole house. The sizeable room on the first floor had a fireplace in the front, chairs, a table, and a bookshelf, and at the back, around a staircase, stood a small cooking area with dish shelves, a cast-iron stove, a sink, and a larder. Upstairs, Percia's room and her parents' room were tucked into the roof's slope. Wren noted colorful braided rugs on the wood floors and a few pieces of shiny porcelain. Small, vibrant tapestries hung on the walls. She found it all bright and cozy, rather like a slightly bigger playhouse.

"How do those clothes fit?" asked the mother. Wren showed her that the skirt sagged loose in the waist, and the mother promised to alter it. She was tall, with broad shoulders, a long neck, and large, rough hands.

Wren sat at the table with her fastbreak, tension making her swing her feet. Percia, bouncing in her seat, and the mother, pouring a cup of tisane for herself, kept her company and pelted her with questions: Did she sleep well? How long had she lived in Anders Wood? Was it horrible for her trying to nurse her mother? Was she frightened when Wilim rode up? Wren gave only one-word answers. She liked the tisane, which had more of a peppery tang than the brew at home, and the porridge tasted like porridge—though without cream, butter, or honey. After she ate, the mother said that the girls could go out to play for a bit before chores. Wren jumped up. But Percia whispered to her, "We wash our dishes here." Percia showed Wren how to do this in the kitchen buckets.

Then they ran outside. Percia identified the outbuildings: the stable for horses and chickens, the washhouse, and her mother's workshop.

"Yonder lies our vegetable patch in the spring. That tree is a chestnut; we get nuts from it. See the little lane? It's all muddy now. That leads to the road, and the road takes you to the center of Wyndton."

The workshop was a special place. Daylight flooded the room because one part of the roof had been cut out and replaced with mullioned glass. It had a wide hearth for warmth and a noticeably high ceiling. In the center stood a loom with a tapestry well underway. Pinned on the wall was a drawing as big as a bed quilt; Wren recognized the classic posture of ancient Queen Callindra the Faithful standing on SeaWidow Cliff. Diamond-shaped wall slots offered skeins of different-colored wool and silk. Percia showed Wren a small basket of cut ends. She called these "scraps." Wren and Percia dressed kindling dolls in different colors until the mother called for them to fetch firewood and water. Both felt awfully heavy to Wren, who had never done any chores, but she copied Percia as best she could.

The father came home for the noon midmeal "to check on all his womenfolk." Wren liked the way he looked like Percia, with laugh crinkles around his eyes. Before anyone ate, the mother led them in the traditional prayer to Nargis, "May Ye Never Know Thirst," after which they all took a swallow of cold water. Wren hated the soup with coarse, mealy vegetables in it, but she nibbled at it and hid her disgust. Wren had no idea what she should call the householders, so she just avoided addressing them, whispering any questions she had to Percia.

After the family finished eating, the father decided to show their new arrival the village of Wyndton. That Wren had no cloak caused some bother. They finally wrapped her up in a too-large fur hat and a small blanket, deciding their first stop would be to buy some fabric so that the mother could fashion her a cloak.

The horse whinnied with delight at Wren's presence, and Wren hugged his chest, savoring his horsey smell. She would have tried to touch him with her mind, but the father quickly lifted both girls up and then mounted behind them. Wren almost said something about her riding abilities, but held her tongue just in time.

A ride through woodlands on a narrow track brought them to the center of town. Wyndton turned out to be a village of stone and wood buildings of middling size, with four central roads intersecting one another, nestled in a small valley formed by Wyndton Creek.

"Nowhere near as big as Gulltown, of course, but over a hundred and fifty souls," said the father with satisfaction. Wren did not tell him that the palace employed that many cooks, gardeners, and maids. "We have our own inn, a smithy, a miller, two greengrocers, a dry goods, a feedstore, a healer, and yonder, a textile store. Here we be."

They dismounted at the mercer. The shop owner knew the father and greeted him with friendly words. While the grown-ups talked, the girls roamed through the small store, surveying the bolts. Percia admired a beautiful maroon wool and urged Wren to choose that. Wren loved it just as much but, remembering her mother's instructions, insisted on a humble russet. She was also worried about the cost; she hated that these people were spending their little coin on her.

The father did not act begrudging. With the girls clutching the new package, they rode down streets of frozen dirt proudly. They passed Wyndton's Church of the Waters, and the father hailed a Sister of Sorrow sweeping the steps. In fact, he had a cheery word for everyone they met, and he introduced most of the townspeople to Wren. She said little in reply to the numerous kindly questions, letting the villagers think her shy, stupid, or out of her senses with grief.

"She's not used to being around folk," the father excused Wren's behavior.

The father stopped at a sweetery and bought treats for "his" girls.

*You're not my father! My father is Ambrice, Lord of the Ships,* Wren thought, and then realized she was being rude, even if only in her mind. She should never forget that this family was putting their lives at risk to hide her. Even if they didn't know this—she did.

Last night, Mamma had told her, "Cerúlia, I could enchant you. I could take away some of the homesickness, or your longing for Nana, your pets, or your father and me. Yet I shall not do this. You must always know exactly who you are and where you come from. You must always remember that your country lies in the hands of usurpers who wish us ill. They are the ones who sent the assassins after us that night, and they will be constantly searching for you. Remember everything, but play your part all the time. Your foster family's fate depends upon it. The future of the Nargis Throne depends upon you staying safe and someday returning to Cascada."

The father took a side detour to show Wren the school she would be attending. The shabby building, which stood on a little hillcrest, served students not only from the village but also from all the neighboring farms and orchards. Wren had not even considered such a prospect.

"I've never been to school," she blurted out.

"Never fear, Birdie. I will take you tomorrow and talk to the masters myself. If you are behind the other children, you're not to worry. Both Stahlia and I have some learning; we'll help you at home, and soon you'll catch up."

Syrup plodded the leagues back to the tiny house. It started to snow, just sparse snowflakes, and Percia made a game of sticking out her tongue and trying to eat one. This distracted Wren from her new worry.

At the barn she offered to help the father with the horse. Although she couldn't reach very high, her offer of assistance pleased the father.

Before dinner, the mother proposed a bath. Percie protested, "Today isn't bath day!"

"Don't you want to be clean for your new sister?"

*Do they think I have fleas or lice?* Wren's upper teeth bit into her lower lip as she held in her anger.

In the washhouse the father filled the biggest laundry tub with water they had heated over coals. The mother washed Wren first; Wren was chagrined to see the water turn grayish with grime from the voyage and the mud-splashed ride. The mother finished by rubbing the hair lotion on Wren's shorn hair.

"Why did you do that?" asked Percia, grabbing the bottle and examining it.

"'Cause it keeps the skin on Wren's head healthy," said her mother.

"What happens if you don't?" she asked.

"My hair starts falling out," Wren said in an undertone, getting out of the tub and shivering. The mother tossed her a warmed towel.

Percie climbed into the tub that her mother had refreshed with warmer and clearer water and started unbraiding her tresses. "Now that Wren's with us, can she grow her hair long and wear plaits like me so we look more like sisters?"

Wren leaned over to whisper to Percia, "I'd rather keep my hair short."

"Mama, she says she wants to keep her hair like it is," Percia said, rubbing soap out of her eyes.

Her mother turned to look at Wren. "It looks as if someone took a hacksaw to you, Birdie. As soon as it grows out a bit, I'll even it up and you can grow it long. 'Tis more comely for a girl."

Soon enough the winter gray melted into black night. Wren allowed herself to be put in bed with Percia. But Percia fell asleep in a tick, and then Wren found herself all alone in the dark, without Nana, her dogs, or her mother in the next suite. Or even a candle. A hard lump rose up in her throat. She tried to swallow it down, but the more she tried, the bigger it got.

Then she was sobbing hard into the mattress.

Roughened hands turned her round and picked her up. The mother was so much stronger than either Mamma or Nana. She carried Wren into the parents' room, sat in a rocking chair, and placed

Wren on her lap. The father lit a lantern low, covered them both with a soft quilt, and left the room. The mother just rocked the chair and sang as if the girl in her lap weren't even there. The mother had a lovely voice; she sang all the verses of "The Lay of Queen Callindra." Warm, soothed, and distracted, Wren feel asleep just before Callindra's prince returned to her.

In the morning Wren had to wear that blanket outfit to school, which embarrassed her. She was not used to having anyone think her poor or pitiful. The father spoke to the masters, and they clucked over her and shook their heads sadly.

"I don't suppose you know your letters, dearie?" asked one master with bad breath.

Her pride rose at this, despite her resolve to play the rustic, untutored orphan.

"I do," said Wren.

"Oh!" said the master in surprise. "Good on your mama for teaching you. Can you read a little of this book? Just any words you recognize."

Wren could have read the whole page, but the master's surprise reminded her to keep to her disguise. She picked out the shortest words and stumbled over any that stretched longer.

"Very good, Wren. I shall tell Wilim how bright you are. I will put you in the second form."

Because she spotted Percia sitting in the front when he led her into a room with twenty-odd children, Wren thought she'd handled that hurdle well. Long, rough benches divided the chilly room in half, with girls on the right and boys on the left. The master found her a seat in the last bench of girls, next to a ragged child with stringy hair and chilblains on her fingers.

Never before had Wren been exposed to a room full of children, much less a room full of village and farming children. They all craned their necks, staring bluntly at the new student, giggling and pointing. "Who's that?" "Where'd *she* come from?" "Why's *she* got her nose up in the air?" She could smell their woolens and saw that many had grubby necks and patched clothing. She forced her features into a blank stare.

The master, a weak-chinned man who coughed, rapped for order. Whenever he turned his back, though, the boys began teasing, making faces, or throwing things. If one boy had acted the jokester, she might have found him amusing, but the shared disregard of all decorum emphasized how far away she was now from court. As the tutor droned on, drawing a map on the wall, Wren realized that his knowledge of geography was weak.

*Surely my mother didn't mean for me to be here!*

The master caught one of the boys in the act of stealing a classmate's quill and proceeded to cane him. At first, the punishment pleased Wren as justice meted out against a ruffian. Then she saw the welts the cane left and the boy's face twisted in pain.

The break for a midmeal in a cold, muddy yard became even more of a gauntlet for an erstwhile princella. The children ran wild. Some had no food and pretended not to care when their classmates unwrapped packages from home. Wren chewed her tough bread and clung to Percia, hoping to escape notice.

But it was not to be. A boy had the effrontery to snatch her fur cap off her head. Percia explained that he wanted her to chase after him, but when she didn't, he sullenly tossed it in the mud at her feet. Another boy threw a slush ball at her. The girls tortured her almost as much, teasing her about the blanket, "Kin I come under there with you?" or speaking with fake concern, "Ooo-oh. It must have been really awful to live in Anders. Weren't it fearful scary when your ma died?"

*I could have you all horse-whipped! You cannot treat a princella this way!*

One of the girls grabbed her left hand. "Why are your hands like this?" she asked.

"What do you mean?"

"Your skin—'tis so smooth and soft. . . ."

Wren snatched her hand away and hid it behind her back. "None of your business," she muttered, vowing to chafe up her hands that night.

Since she could not speak her feelings, Wren bit her lip and shrank herself smaller and smaller. The girls gave up on her and started playing a complicated game that involved claps and stamps to a rhyme.

Wren found it a new and thoroughly unpleasant experience to be ignored, as if she didn't count in the slightest.

When school finished for the day, Wren slumped from the emotional strain. But they still had a long trudge home in the cold on slippery paths. Wren had a shorter stride than some other children and was not as sure-footed; she flushed with shame that she couldn't keep pace and sighed with relief when Percia's and her path diverged from the main party.

When they reached home the mother had a surprise for her: she had finished the cloak. It hung soft and warm and excessively big (so she could grow into it). The concept of needing clothing to last for years surprised a princella.

"I thank you," said Wren, looking into the mother's face for the first time, realizing that her wide mouth held a soft smile, mirrored by her dove-gray eyes.

When the father rode home she put on her cloak and ran out to the barn to show him.

"Well now, don't you look grand!" he said, and his crinkles crinkled. She helped him brush the sorrel.

*Syrup, do you hear me?*

The horse snorted in surprise and started back a few steps.

"Whoa now, whoa now, fella! What's gotten into you?" said the father.

Wren grasped that she should talk to the horse when they were alone. She was following the father back into the house when she heard a voice in her head.

*Little princess! Little princess!* Wren looked around frantically, finally spotting a big horned owl on a branch.

"I—I need to use the jakes. I'll be in in a moment," she told the father.

*You recognize me. How?*

*Know thee.* The owl blinked and turned its head.

*I look different from other girls? Even dressed like this? Without my beautiful hair?*

*Thou art the princella.*

*Thank you, Owl. That's a comfort. I feel so lost here.* She regarded the big bird whose feathers formed a random pattern. *May I call you Speckles?*

*As pleases the princella. Dost thou realize one's feathers hide one from predators?*

*Yes. You're "camouflaged," like I have to be camouflaged in this country village.*

Wren turned to reenter the house, but stopped when a thought hit her.

*Speckles, have you ever talked to any other person?*

*Never.* His head rotated on his pliable neck.

*Do you know of other people who can talk to birds and beasts?*

He preened his chest feathers thoughtfully for a moment. *Nay.*

*If I can talk to you and my dogs and Gili here—if you all recognize me—then that chronicler was dumb. I can do something unusual! I told him, but he wouldn't listen.* She stamped her feet against the frozen ground. *Nargis gave me the Talent of talking to beasts. Mayhap it's a rare Talent, but it will be useful for me.*

The owl slowly blinked at her with his strange eyes. *One does nay follow thy meaning.*

*Never mind,* sent Wren, rubbing her cold hands together. *Just—I was worried about something really, really important, and now I'm not.*

"Wren?" called the mother.

"Here I am," she answered.

# 18

## Voyaging

On *Sea Sprite* Cressa fretted ceaselessly about her daughter and what Matwyck might be doing to hunt her. After they had cast off from the Eastern Duchies, she had enchanted all the souls on board to make them forget the ship's anchorage in the deserted bay close to Wyndton. So no one knew where her daughter hid now, except for herself and of course Cerúlia.

Also, she was plagued by a nagging fear that she had erred by fleeing from the conspiracies that surrounded her, rather than facing them. Had this been dishonorable?

Still, surrounded by the sea, Cressa could breathe more easily. The current seamaster, Bashkim—skinny, with a permanent squint—had once been Ambrice's second mate. And she recognized many of the sailors. On the ocean and among people she trusted, Cressa felt safer than she had in a long time.

So much of her youth had been spent voyaging. Cressa often stood at the rail, smelling the salt spray, enjoying the sunshine making the swells sparkle, relishing her freedom from confinement, sometimes turning the braid of Cerúlia's hair round and round. Cressa realized that while she often compared herself (unfavorably) to her stern mother, her father's seafaring blood also coursed through her.

She took her meals with Seamaster Bashkim and Captain Clemçon, men without guile who offered her their unvarnished opinions but followed her commands without demur. The three discussed the next course of action at length. Although the Nargis Throne had many allies, only two courses presented themselves as viable: east, to her father in Lortherrod, or south, to rendezvous with her husband. East would have been the obvious choice, because of both size and location. Lortherrod was a great and powerful realm, while Ambrice had only a few ships under his command. Moreover, Cressa had sent Ambrice to deal with the Pellish pirates marauding the Green Isles, but with more than five hundred Isles, no one knew exactly where *Sea Pearl* might be found.

Both Clemçon and Bashkim urged the prudent, easterly course. But her enemies would be expecting that choice. Might they waylay her one vessel at sea? Besides, what help would her father offer? He no longer ruled as king, having abdicated and placed his oldest son, her half-brother Rikil, on the Walrus Throne. Rikil was a cautious man. He would regret his half-sister's troubles; he would rue the internal turmoil in Weirandale. He would certainly offer her and her crew polite and comfortable sanctuary for all the years ahead. She would find safety there. But Rikil would not send his people to war for Weirandale.

Now if Mikil, her younger half-brother, had been king, she might have risked the voyage. When she was a child, Mikil, though still eight summers older, had spent much more time with her. Mikil and she had a closer bond, and Mikil had a more emotional and less judicious temperament. He would have taken the threat to her personally, as an affront to Lortherrod.

Overruling her advisors' advice, Cressa decided that the ship should head south toward the Isles and Ambrice. South, away from Androvale and Cerúlia's hiding place. It might take her some time to find *Sea Pearl*, but this decision would make it just as hard for any ship from Cascada to hunt *Sea Sprite*.

In general Cressa found relief in the easy comradeship of a small ship, as opposed to the formality of the palace. She joined with the Queen's Shield in mourning Bristle and congratulated Dariush and Yanath when Clemçon promoted them to sergeants. Clemçon assigned his female shields—Kinley, the stocky one with dark brown hair cut very short and a flat-bridged nose, and Seena, the tall, muscled one who had fought in Cerúlia's bedchamber—to wait upon the queen.

In her cabin, she attempted to get acquainted with her new attendants.

"I know you both signed up as soldiers. Are you content with these duties?"

"Sure, Your Majesty, ma'am," said Seena. "Precious little for shields to do on a ship anyway. And Captain Clemçon has excused us from mucking out the horse stalls in exchange."

"Well! That's the first time I've been told I am more interesting than horse manure," Cressa commented. "What was your life like before?" she asked. "How did you join the Shield?"

To her shock, Seena scowled darkly. "I'll tell you, if you so command, but do you need to know these things for me to fetch and carry for you?"

Cressa's mouth fell open at this rudeness to her friendly overture, and she glanced at Kinley.

"She doesn't know," Kinley said to the other guard.

"Right. I suppose she don't. She should, though."

"But who'd tell her?"

Seena shrugged.

Kinley turned to the queen. "You didn't know, Your Majesty, but the custom is that no one ever asks shields about their past."

"And why not?" puzzled Cressa.

"Because it might be something bad or worse if one joined the Shield to fight and die. And if you're a woman—well, it's bound to be something triple bad."

"I see," said Cressa slowly. "Please forget I asked."

Cressa changed the subject by holding out her ripped gray silk gown. "Do either of you know how to sew?"

"Nope," said Seena, and "Not I," said Kinley, and the three burst out laughing at their incompetence at a task that any village woman would have mastered.

"Hey, I've an idea. Give it here," said Kinley.

"Come back soon," called the queen. "I can't go on deck without my gown!"

As time slipped by, Cressa grew impatient. "I'm going to have to send you to scrounge clothing from the smaller men," she said to Seena, when at that moment Kinley returned, her grin showing her bad teeth.

"*Sailors* know how to sew!" said Kinley, demonstrating that the rent had been neatly patched with sailcloth.

When Cressa came out on deck in her patched gown, all the sailors clapped, and the queen played to the joke by twirling around.

"Excuse me, Your Majesty," said Seamaster Bashkim, breaking in on the levity. "We need to put in for provisions at the next trading port."

"Which is?"

"Yosta, a town on the coast of the Free State Wígat."

"And if Matwyck has agents there?"

"Yosta's a busy port. Probably twenty ships a day coming and going. With our name painted over and flying no flags, we'll be a ghost. Do your enemies have spies in every port checking every vessel?"

"Probably not yet, but soon. We must not dally. Get supplies and shove off. No shore leave for any of the men. And always be prepared for trouble."

"Very good, Your Majesty."

Cressa wanted to watch the provisioning from the deck, but Seena grabbed the back neck of her gown and yanked her inside the captain's mess hall. "Your hair! Your Royal Stone! Did you forget?"

Kinley agreed. "Even if we covered you up, 'twould look queer to have a delicate lady on board. Best keep out of sight."

"You're right," agreed Cressa. "Sometimes I forget my position, especially aboard the ship."

"Ah, Queenie," said Kinley in a mock scold, "good thing sensible folk stand by to remind and protect you."

Cressa laughed and accepted the informality, enjoying the new fellowship with her shields. *Sea Sprite* passed unquestioned at Yosta and—three weeks later—when they stopped at one of the northernmost Isles. They asked, discreetly, for any word of Ambrice's ship, but heard no tidings.

They headed deeper into the Green Isles, which poked out of the sea in clusters. Whether vast or small, most towered above the ship, showing their volcanic origins in steeply raked sides. Being covered by verdant foliage, all lived up to their name. Mist lingered on their peaks and fell in folds in the water passageways, so Bashkim picked their way with care until *Sea Sprite* broke out into open seas again.

Whenever the wake grew choppy, both Kinley and Seena became nauseous. Cressa cast around for subjects that might distract them and found that they were happy to talk about their recent sexual adventures. Kinley proved to have a fund of surprisingly funny dirty jokes, which she told with perfect timing.

"Does it cause problems amongst the guards if you dally with them?" asked Cressa. She was sitting idly on her bunk picking at loose embroidery threads on her gown; Seena sat on the floor sharpening the queen's dagger while Kinley, on the chair, polished the queen's salt-stained boots.

"It might, if you ever allowed it to get serious," answered Seena. "If you ever allowed a fella to feel as if he had a claim on you. So I make sure the man knows this roll-around is just a yen. And we both keep away from the Queen's Shield."

"Do you two ever think about marriage?" Cressa asked.

Seena and Kinley both hooted. "Marriage!" said Kinley. "Guards are rarely good candidates for marriage. They—we—drink too much, fuck around too much, die too often. They're dumb. We like to fight. And if you ain't noticed, they pick their noses and their feet."

"That's not fair," Cressa protested. "All the Queen's Shield is brave and well spoken."

"And there ain't a one of them that would make a good husband," said Seena. "Except maybe—" She exchanged a glance with Kinley.

"Who? Who?" pressed the queen.

"Sergeant Yanath, Your Majesty," Seena answered a bit reluctantly.

"Yanath? Really? Branwise is handsomer; Clemçon has authority—" She stopped, embarrassed to have revealed that she'd noticed her shields as men.

Kinley dropped the boot she was working on with a bawdy laugh. "And Pontole is so young he can't control that big bulge in his pants, can he? It ain't like we haven't noticed."

Seena chimed in on top of her, "How could you miss it?"

"But trust us, Queenie, you want a steady man, a smart man, a *good* man, Yanath's the one," Kinley enlightened her liege. "I mean—they're all the greatest chaps and we'd die for any of 'em. But marriage material? Only Yanath."

Cressa had never particularly paid attention to Yanath. He spoke less often than some of the men, and his physique did not stand out. "I'll have to figure out what you see in him," she said thoughtfully. "But just talking about men makes me miss my husband something fierce."

In return (though really it was a poor return), during empty hours Cressa taught her female shields to play Oblongs and Squares with Captain Bashkim's board. Kinley picked up the strategy quickly and crowed with delight when she slaughtered her opponent. Seena lost like a duck.

Although formality broke down on *Sea Sprite,* Cressa kept to one rule: she forbade any discussion of the princella.

When they put in at Slagos, one of the largest ports of the lush Green Isles, protected by high stone towers on both sides of the harbor, Bashkim's mate learned that *Sea Pearl* had herself stopped to reprovision not long ago. But when the drinking water merchant started asking questions of the mate, she thought it wisest to conclude her business and leave.

In the end, *Sprite* did not find *Sea Pearl;* the *Pearl* found her.

It happened this way: two weeks after leaving Slagos, crisscrossing the major sailing routes, *Sea Sprite* stumbled into the tail end of a typhoon. Cressa had experienced storms before, but she discovered that a tropical typhoon, fed by warm water, roared with rare fury. Rain fell in solid curtains, not in drops, and the sea rose in jagged peaks, not waves. The sea sucked one sailor overboard. Bashkim pulled in all sails. Even so, the wind raged so forcefully, the foremast snapped in two with an abrupt, terrifying crack.

Below deck, Cressa, watching Seena's and Kinley's vomiting, became seasick for the first time in her life and then, like the rest of the afflicted, suffered dehydration. Although she managed to anticipate the worst rolls and brace herself, some of her shipmates broke bones from being tossed about so violently. Cressa stumbled through the pitching passageway to find fresh water for everyone and help splint bones. She heard the horses thrashing about and screaming in terror.

When the storm finally died down, Seamaster Bashkim declared they needed to put to shore at the first possible harbor.

Later that day the lookout spotted a small island ahead in the fog, so tiny it wasn't even on their maps. Using their oars to circle it, they found a natural harbor. *Sprite* pulled in, anchoring as close as possible to a sandy shore that stretched as long as the Great Ballroom and offered almost as deep a white meadow of beach until the tree line closed in.

The sailors used the ship's rowboat to ferry scouts to survey the island's safety. Cressa rode in the second relay with the worst injured. She refused to be carried when the sailors disembarked, wading through the thigh-deep water impatiently, further taxing her already quite distressed gray silk gown. On land, she organized the care of the worst-off casualties. She had no particular skill at nursing, but most of the needs involved just commonsense measures such as splints, poultices, washing, food, and water.

After most of the people were ashore, her shields led the horses down the gangway and made them swim to the beach. Before the storm they had exercised the horses as much as possible by walking them back and forth in the hold, but the ten mounts had suffered greatly. One poor gelding was too weak to swim the distance. Despite their best efforts to hold up his heavy head, he slipped under the water's surface and didn't rise again.

The first day on land, caring for the most severely injured was all that the comparatively hale could stir to accomplish. When their dizziness abated on the second day, Seena and Kinley fashioned a private tent for the queen out of sailcloth, and Bashkim used the same material to make a canopy to keep the sun off their worst casualties. Sailors searched for the right size tree to cut down for a new mast, while shields groomed the salt off the horses and started to exercise them along the beach. The horses sampled the ample greenery near the shore, finding some of it to their liking.

The third day the queen and six of her shields mounted up to search the island. They had sweet water on board *Sprite,* but life would be easier if they found a source nearby. Also, any fresh food they could gather would be a welcome change.

The lush foliage on the island slowed the riders' passage, and away from the breeze on the beach insects swarmed. Cressa silently thanked Kinley for the foresight of forming her a makeshift head covering out of the tail of a sailor's shirt. She pulled her now-tattered sleeves closer around her and tried to swish the biters away from Nightmist, who flicked her tail at every step, huffed the bugs out of her nostrils, and shivered the skin on her neck. Her mare had handled the stresses better than most of their string, but she had lost weight, her muscle tone was poor, and the condition of her coat would have made the palace stablemen weep. Smoke was even worse off; fractious, he allowed only Pontole to care for or ride him. He would bite anyone else who came near, baring his teeth even at the queen.

Cressa on Nightmist, Shield Pontole on Smoke, Captain Clemçon (with a broken left wrist from being smashed against the deck), and four more guards stumbled onto a patch of small wild muskmelons. The soldiers sliced open a few and ate them on the spot, and then gathered as many as they could carry, awkwardly tucked inside their shirts, to take back to their companions. The queen undid her headpiece and turned it into an impromptu sack. Uphill from the melon patch the scouting party discovered a spring of fresh water. Men would need to come back with kegs, but the scouting party let the horses drink their fill and washed the itchy salt and melon juice off their own faces, necks, and forearms. Then the riders headed back to their companions on the beach.

However, when they emerged from the dense foliage, they were shocked to see a black-sailed galliot in the harbor and a sizeable group of disreputable-looking men climbing out of three skiffs pulled up on the sand. Sun-bleached rags covered their heads. They were barefoot, with breeches that ended above the knee. Their mostly black waistcoat skirts had a dull sheen to them, as if they had been oiled against the wet. Their arms were bare except most wore black forearm bracers, some of leather, some just of wrapped cloth.

"Who might you be?" Captain Clemçon moved forward to challenge the newcomers.

The leader of the landing party, who had two locks of pink hanging over his ears, looked at Clemçon with a dark scowl. If he recognized the significance of the men's silver breastplates, or the queen's untidy blue hair, he gave no sign.

"Not your business. I have business with that jewel on her forehead. It's a beaut. Hand it over, right quick."

Cressa could not hand over her Royal Stone even if she had wanted to. Royal Stones stayed on the queen's persons while they lived and melted away into Nargis Water once they died.

"I can't," she tried to explain. "It sticks to my skin."

"Then I'll cut it off," said the pirate, grabbing the handle of his cutlass.

With a clatter, Clemçon and the rest of the shield immediately pulled their own swords. So did all the pirates. Only Yanath and Branwise had their bows handy; they nocked arrows. *Sea Sprite*'s sailors, round-eyed with fear and surprise, dived for weapons, coming up with axes or rowboat oars.

While Cressa sat on her horse with her mouth open, the antagonists circled each other warily, sizing up each other's skill and ferocity. Pontole clucked his horse between her and their opponents. All at once, several of the pirates rushed in the direction of the canopy under which the most severely injured men lay, perhaps thinking to take the casualties hostage. Clemçon could not allow *this;* he kicked his horse and spurted between the pirates and their prey.

As a mêleé ensued, a pirate grabbed Cressa's stirrup; instinctively she stabbed at him with her dagger. When he jerked away, she lost her grasp of its hilt. Another pirate tried to yank her off her saddle. Cressa tried to summon her Talent, but she couldn't keep her hand on the man consistently. So instead, she smashed him in the head with the muskmelon bag, startling him into loosing his grip on her waist.

Desperate skirmishes broke out all around her. Pirates tried to unhorse the riders; riders used their height and speed advantage to cut down the pirates. Sailors fiercely swung their improvised weapons; more practiced pirates closed in with cutlasses and maces. Men cursed while startled horses reared and neighed. Cressa saw Clemçon lop off a man's head—watching the blood spurt from the empty neck, she was momentarily transfixed by shock. Kinley, with a wicked smile on her face, fought two-handed with a sword and buckler; she ducked low and used her surprising speed to bash knees or stab deep into groins. Sergeant Dariush already had a broken leg from an injury during the storm; he swung the rough crutch they had fashioned for him to keep the pirates away from his canopy-mates.

All at once, Smoke went berserk: biting, kicking, and bucking so ferociously that Pontole fell off. Pirates immediately swarmed around the shield lying prone in the sand. Cressa yanked Nightmist in a tight circle, intending to go to Pontole's aid.

At that moment an earsplitting whistle caused hostilities to pause.

"Back to the ship!" the leader of the Pellish pirates shouted. "Look yonder!"

Yonder all saw *Sea Pearl,* speeding into their harbor with sails belled taut in the wind and all twenty-four four-person oars stroking.

The Pellish tried to flee to their beached boats. But turning their backs on the shore combatants proved a mistake. Bashkim smote one man down with an oar to his head. Pontole, now afoot, skewered the pirate closest at hand and chased after another, swinging his sword with deadly intent. On his own accord Smoke ran down a Pellishman who had just reached the water's edge, kicking him with such force that Cressa heard bones crack—the man fell facedown in the shallows and did not rise again. Cressa urged Nightmist to collide with a pirate, sending him sprawling. The fleeing Pellish filled only one skiff and rowed it frantically toward their home ship.

Although her shields still fought with the left-behind remnants of their attackers, Cressa gazed transfixed by the drama in the harbor waters. The skiff almost made it to the Pellish vessel just as *Sea Pearl*'s keel bore down on it and crushed it like kindling. A rapid adjustment of sail and shouted commands then swung the carrack sharply starboard with a powerful lurch, and its pointed bowsprit punched a hole in the pirate galliot. The ship was hopelessly damaged.

Sergeant Yanath ran up to her, breaking her trance. "Your Majesty, are you all right? Drought-damn our stupidity; we should have raced you into the forest, away from all this."

"Aye. What about everyone else?" Cressa looked around her, then yelled across the beach, unable to keep panic out of her voice, "Seeena! Kinley!"

Seena waved her sword in the air so Cressa could spot her. Kinley knelt on the ground near the tree cover next to a prostrate sailor, but she roared out, "I'm over here, Queenie. No worries."

Yanath helped her dismount, and Cressa turned her attention

back to her men, to see what could be done for the wounded. The pirates had killed five: three sailors and two of the Queen's Shield, one of whom had busted his head against a bulwark during the typhoon and might not have survived anyway.

Nearly everyone else was wounded; the only question was how badly and who could be saved.

Cressa was concentrating on holding a ripped piece of gray silk on the third mate's gory upper arm, which had taken the points of a mace, when other hands, cleaner hands, came into her field of vision and a male voice said, "Let me do that; I can put more pressure on the wound."

She gave way and stood up, pushing her hair out of her way with her bloody, sandy hands. She noticed that *Sea Pearl* had sent several boats ashore and that healers with medical supplies were rushing to aid the combatants, while unfamiliar sailors dealt with the disarmed or injured pirates, and still more caught and soothed the horses that had bolted away from the smell of blood and death.

With the arrival of reinforcements, Cressa had time to realize—with no small degree of amazement—that she, *she* who had trembled before her councilors, had just been through a battle with Pellish pirates. She shook her head wonderingly, tried to control her panting, and gazed all around her again. There, on the beach, looking hale, fit, and disgustingly tidy stood Ambrice, Lord of the Ships, tall and broad of shoulder in his blue uniform with gold buttons, his coily brown hair, as always, neatly tied at the nape of his neck.

In the midst of all the chaos, Cressa felt the piercing desire that Ambrice habitually aroused in her. Their eyes locked. He went down on one knee in the formal bow of a loyal subject reporting to the queen of Weirandale. On wobbling legs, she ran into his arms—their embrace crushing between them the last, smallest muskmelon tucked inside the bodice of her gown.

"We've been looking for you everywhere!" Cressa cried to Ambrice, perched on his knee, arms around his neck.

"I've been looking for you! Well, not you exactly, but *Sprite*. We spotted her on the horizon just before the typhoon. I would recognize that silhouette anywhere. Why has her name been painted over?"

"That's all you care about? *Sprite?*"

"Well, I didn't know *you* were on it. I thought you had sent *Sea Sprite* after me with a message. Why *are* you on it? What in Water's name are you doing here?"

His hand came up from around the side of her waist covered red. "Wait. Is this your blood or someone else's?"

"No, of course not mine," said Cressa. "That is, I don't recall getting struck. That is, I hadn't realized . . ." And then her vision narrowed to a pinhole, and she lost consciousness.

When she came to she was lying on a pallet in her canvas tent. Her side hurt. It had been stitched up neatly, and she was now wearing a long white shirt free of both blood and melon pulp. Seena sat on a driftwood log close at hand, massaging her own bandaged knuckles and watching her intently through the tent's opening.

"Her Majesty wakes," she called to someone.

Ambrice appeared immediately. "How are you? Will you drink some wine?"

"I don't know how I am. What happened?"

He helped her raise her head and sip out of a cup. "Some villain stabbed you in the side, but the blade skidded off a lower rib."

"Why didn't I know I was hurt?" asked Cressa.

"It's not unusual, in the heat of battle, to miss a small wound. Your dander was up, and then you concentrated on helping your men. You only noticed it when I saw it."

"And then I fainted! How humiliating!"

"Nonsense! You fainted from blood loss, not hysterics. Your gown was quite wet. Here, drink some more. How does it feel?"

Cressa inventoried the fiery throb. "It hurts!"

"Aye, I'll wager it does. But my healers assure me you're going to be fine. The knife went deep through your skin and that luscious bit above your hip, but did no serious damage. I am the luckiest of men." He kissed her forehead.

Cressa gingerly tried to move about. Ambrice gently pushed her down.

"My healers counsel that, as the weather is fine, better not to shift any of you for a couple of days. We will make repairs and let your crew recover."

"How fare my men? Can Bashkim and Clemçon report to me?"

"Aye. Neither is too badly off. I'll have them fetched in a few moments." Ambrice urged her to drink a little more and held her slantwise against his warm and broad chest, gently stroking her hair.

Bashkim had lost only his right earlobe, but the bandage around his ear sagged low with blood. Clemçon displayed a long but not deep gash above his knee and half his face puffed with cuts and bruises.

"I didn't know you could fight like that, Your Majesty," said Clemçon.

"Nor did I," she answered him. "Muskmelons are not my usual weapon. Give the men my compliments; they fought so stoutly. Go rest, my captains." She exhaled, discovering that the motion of her chest caused her wound to hurt. "Tonight we lie in safe harbor."

As if from far away, Cressa heard Ambrice giving orders about posting watches, fetching food, carting water from the spring, and more juice of the poppy for the wounded. Just before she drifted off she realized that the wine he had urged her to drink had been drugged. Later, she felt him lie down beside her and gently draw close so that she was aware of his warmth against her back. The pain in her side receded a few more steps. She slept.

In the morning the passengers and crew of the *Sprite* awoke to the throbs of their wounds. The men and women gave the queen and her consort privacy to talk.

In the presence of her husband, Cressa felt whole, completed. Ambrice had been born the eldest son of a master shipwright in the coastal duchy Maritima. When he was a lad his father had fallen hard into his cups. His mother had left her drunkard husband, taking her infant children with her but leaving Ambrice behind. So Ambrice's grandmother had kept him in victuals and clothes while his father had slowly fought for his sobriety and even more slowly earned back the esteem of the Nishtar Shipyard's owners. From childhood, Ambrice knew all the inner sinews of a ship, but the sea called him rather than the carpentry shed. He enlisted in the Royal Navy at fifteen as an ordinary seaman. Since he exuded steadiness, calm, and a wry sense of humor, and since he never touched a dram of spirits, he rose quickly through the ranks. Now he wore leadership like a second skin and his men adored him.

Cressa told Ambrice all about the treachery of her councilors, the involvement of the Oros, and her hiding Cerúlia away.

"I had to protect Cerúlia, but it was cowardly for me to flee. Who knows what the councilors will do to the realm?"

"You were alone and in grave danger; you did the best you could." He shook his head. "My little rascal!" Ambrice rummaged in a leather purse and pulled out a small coral bracelet. "I bought this for her in Pilagos." He toyed with the beads as they talked. "I wonder if she's lonely or frightened. I grieve for her, but you did right to secret her away. No, don't tell me where. If ever I am captured, 'tis best that I don't know."

"Now that I have found you—or you have found me," Cressa said, "we have to plan how to reconquer the realm. Then we can fetch our rascal home."

"I propose," said Ambrice, "that in two days' time we sail for Pilagos. *Sea Wind* and *Sea Maiden* are to rendezvous with *Sea Pearl* there. I also hold the magistrar of Pilagos in high regard. We could hold a council to decide on the best course of action."

Cressa assented. Ambrice coaxed her to eat some melon and flatbread and reported that her wounded were recovering as well as could be expected.

By evening she felt strong enough to rise with the help of Ambrice's strong arm and make the rounds of her men. The severely injured slept in the oblivion of poppy juice. The merely hurt gathered around a bright fire of driftwood, scarfing down a hearty meal prepared by the cooks from *Sea Pearl*, swapping stories about the skirmish and telling the other crew about all their adventures. They cheered when they saw Queen Cressa and made room for her in their circle. Seena rushed to throw down a blanket for her to sit on while Kinley fetched her a bowl.

Cressa laughed with the group about Smoke the pirate-killer, Bashkim and his oar, wild man Dariush and his crutch, and even "the queen of the muskmelons." Clemçon made a little ceremony over returning her antique dagger with catamounts carved into each side of the handle.

*Is this the first time I've felt welcomed and admired amongst my people?*

Two more days passed while sailors replaced *Sprite*'s mast and restrung the rigging. Crew from *Sea Pearl* filled in the *Sea Sprite*'s roster. Cressa, her shields, the nonwalking wounded, and the horses loaded onto the larger and more comfortable carrack. Under a bright blue sky that brought out the ocean's clear turquoise hue, they set their course for Pilagos.

# 19

## Cascada

Nana found Teonora's funeral, three moons after the queen's midnight disappearance, a depressing affair. All of the servants who did not have essential duties attended, and a few of the administrators and gentry showed up. Nana noticed, however, that Duchess Latlie and Lord Retzel whispered and laughed together during the service in the palace Church of the Waters, and she found it hard to keep her fury in check.

Afterward, the new chamberlaine, Teonora's second, set up refreshments separated by station. The lower servants drank ale and ate cracked nuts in the servants' common room, a dim chamber near the pantries filled with scruffy wood tables and benches, though the floor shone brightly and the hearth drove away the cold.

Nana sat with Hiccuth on a bench, their shoulders and thighs touching.

"Better that they didn't come, than to behave like such boors. And these are supposed to be 'high-class' people," Nana said to Hiccuth.

Hiccuth just nodded and changed the subject. "Teonora was fair and steady and dignified," he said. "Hard shoes to fill. What do you know of the new 'un?"

"Martza gets flustered too easy," said Nana. "Gotta have nerves of steel to handle the gentry's whims, no matter how late at night or how silly. And also—you gotta admit—to keep us folks in line. There's some that would take advantage."

Hiccuth grunted.

"She's asked me to help her. Since Herself left I haven't had much to do. Martza comes to me all purty-like and says, 'Nana, I can't make you my official second, but you know the palace better than anyone. I'd like to assign you to where I need you most.'"

"What'd you think of that?" asked Hiccuth.

"I'd rather help Martza find where the biggest soup tureen has been stashed than go back to the scullery or scrubbing. I ain't leaving the palace, and that's *that*."

Hiccuth laid his rough hand on top of hers.

Besi, one of the cooks, brought her tankard and sat opposite them. "Hey," she said. "Sad day."

"That it is," said Nana.

"What's happening in the kitchens?" asked Hiccuth.

"A few burns. Lost my temper and slapped a mason who keeps coming in where he's got no business and pestering one of my gals. She should have told him off herself, but she's a bit of a ninny," said Besi.

"Before Teonora took ill, you could've just reported him," said Nana, "and he'd have been sent packing, his tail between his legs."

"Yeah, well. Felt awful good to slap someone," said Besi as she took a long pull. "Then I picked up my big carver and I told him that he ever come near one of my gals again I'd gut him like a pig. That felt awful good too.

"What's happening upstairs? Ain't seen you awhile."

"Geesilla got another job, I heard," said Nana. "Platsy returned to the roster of day maids. I dust the royal rooms; keep 'em ready."

"And your favorites—them ladies-in-waiting?"

"Duchette Aubrie went back to Maritima. She came to say good-bye to me, and she had real tears in her eyes. Nicest one of the lot. She slipped me a gold catamount."

"And the others?" asked Besi.

"The one who's kin to Latlie, she went to Latlie's manse in West Park. Guess it's too quiet for her here now. Fanyah and Dinista still float around, showing off their purty looks, purty hands, and purty gowns, making a general nuisance of themselves. Didn't come today to pay their respects, though I don't know what else they have to do. I suspect Dinista has designs on the queen's wardrobe, 'cause I caught her fingering some lace the other day."

"She'd steal from the queen!" Hiccuth was shocked.

"Not on my watch," said Nana, biting her words. "I keep the Passageway of Lost Babes open all the time now, so I can see into the queen's quarters."

"Ain't you scared of that dark passageway?" asked Besi.

"Not any longer. I figure the only ghost that haunts the place is Cressa's baby brother, poor little Prince Nikil. The moment the goody put that child in my arms, I knew he weren't long for this world. His lips were so blue." Nana unconsciously cradled the dying babe, lost in remembrance.

"Sorry to butt in," said Kiltti, who had diffidently approached while they were talking. "Nana, could you do me a service? Tiklok is taking the chamberlaine's death hard. He's acting real distressed."

Nana craned her head around the room until she located Tiklok standing in a dim corner with his face in his tankard.

"Weren't he waiting on her these last moons?" said Nana.

Kiltti nodded. "Made her tisane every day. Could you talk to him? I try, and it don't do no good."

Nana made a face. "Grief's grief, child. There's not much to be done." Kiltti's face fell with disappointment.

"Ach. Tell him to come to my room this evening. I'll trot out all the old sayings about time and keeping busy."

Kiltti brightened as she sped off.

Teonora had been popular because she almost never had servants whipped. Instead she gave them a wry tongue-lashing. A footman stood up to recount how once, bringing in guests' baggage, he had tracked in snowy boot prints. "And the chamberlaine, she says to me, '*If you must* leave icicles all over the freshly polished hallway, I wish you'd do so in the main entrance right before Duchess Latlie arrives, because I would find that *so* much more satisfying than watching one of the maids tumble.'" The servants hooted and banged their tankards on the tables.

"I was young in the stable and barely knew my arse from a hole in the ground," Hiccuth joined in. "One day we gets this order about ferrying a councilor to meet a ship. '*If you must* roll out a carriage that's dusty and littered with straw, Hiccuth'—I didn't even ken that Teonora knew my name then—'why don't you use it to transport the geese to market and we'll fetch the envoy in the goose cart instead.' I tell you, you could have wiped me off them cobblestones."

Others stood up with similar tales. Soon enough Martza came in and broke up the gathering, telling everyone it was time to get back to work.

As she filed out, Martza stopped Nana.

"Nana, the gentry had their repast in the Salon of Cinda, but they didn't linger long. Could you check that the room's in order?"

"Of course, Chamberlaine."

The footmen and servers who'd had to miss their own reception to attend to the gentry had finished sweeping when Nana reached the salon. The tables had been wiped spotless. Nana straightened some chairs and pried wax off some candlesticks, but nothing more serious caught her eye.

She paused her circuit of the room to look through the interior openings from the salon that faced into the third-story balcony of the Throne Room. She stared down, taking in the sight. Moonlight filtered in through the stained-glass ceiling. The catamounts lounging around the Fountain, Basin, and Pool paced and twitched their tails. The empty throne gave Nana a feeling she couldn't describe. More than sadness—a piercing kind of desolation.


One evening Nana was dozing in front of her fire when a tap on the princella's door startled her. She slipped on her clogs and clomped over to investigate.

"Oh Tiklok! I forgot you was coming to visit. Let's sit by my fire. Spring's threatening, but it ain't here yet. A warm fire's such a cozy thing."

Tiklok joined her in her small room, gently moving Zizi off the second chair.

"Where are her other cats and dogs?" he asked, looking around.

"The kennel master claimed the three big hounds," said Nana. "I cursed him for it, but he had his orders and wouldn't mind me. They put the old one down. Mayhap 'twas a mercy, 'cause he'd had sunk even lower after Herself left. The cats . . ." Nana twisted her head this way and that. "They's too smart for the men who came after them—they scattered. They're around the Royal Wing someplace, and they usually come find me at night. Ah-ha! Look there. Here comes the white one I call 'Pearl.'"

Pearl, a dirty-white short-haired cat, slunk into the room from the passageway, sniffed Tiklok's shoes and the hand he offered, and then jumped into Nana's lap and began purring.

Tiklok's mouth twitched into a half smile at the sight.

"I like having the cats to pet," said Nana, looking down. "I miss—I miss the touch of her little hand, you know."

Tiklok nodded.

"So, Tiklok. How're you faring?" asked Nana.

"I'm all right, Nana."

"Kiltti's worried that yer taking Teonora's death hard."

"Teonora was a great lady," he said solemnly, "but she's at peace on the Waters. She suffered a long time; I'm glad that's over."

"Aye," said Nana, "Teonora hired me, oh so many years ago. I shall miss her."

Companionably they watched the fire and listened to Pearl. Zizi circled about, indicating she too wanted up off the drafty floor. Evidently she decided that Nana's lap was full of cat, so instead she leapt up into Tiklok's lap in a swift bound, which made them both laugh.

"What should I do?" he asked, holding his arms out, obviously unused to sitting with a dog.

"If you don't mind her, you scratch her behind the ears. If she bothers you, brush her off."

He scratched her tentatively and the dog gazed up at his face a moment, then settled into a curl, tucking in her slender legs.

Tiklok cleared his throat and began to speak with intent. "Yester eve, I went into the city to tell a few people about the funeral today."

"Hmm. Did Martza send you?"

"No. I took it on myself. Martza had enough to deal with, but I wagered some folk would wanna know—tradesmen and such."

"Aye. I saw some at the service. You was taking a risk, leaving the grounds without permission. Could get whipped for that."

"Yeah. That's not the sticky point." He shifted his rump in the chair, holding Zizi stable. "Nana, I went to Tutor Ryton's lodgings."

"Ryton! I haven't seen him since—But he wasn't at the funeral. I would have noticed *him*."

"No. I didn't find him at his lodgings."

"Too bad. So mayhap he's found another position or moved?"

Tiklok shook his head. "His mother was there. She was all upset; she cried and clung to me. She told me—some weeks ago men in uniforms took Ryton away, and he hasn't come back. She's a frail old lady, so she sent her neighbor to the city watch post, and they told him they didn't know nothin' at all about it."

"*They* took him!"

Tiklok nodded. "Why? Why him?"

"I don't know. I don't think the queen ever confided in him; I don't recall her ever spending time with him outside the lesson chamber." Nana scrunched her forehead. "There's others she was closer to: Chronicler Sewel, for one. Why take Ryton?"

"Mayhap because he's educated?" Tiklok offered. "He helped me learn my letters."

"Could be. He could talk to people or write proclamations and be listened to and respected. While if you or me was to go around telling tales, well, we're just servants, but he would have to be taken serious."

"But Nana, Tutor Ryton don't know nothing. He's no threat to them."

"Since when has *that lot* cared about justice!" she replied with some heat. "Whether he's a threat or no, they'd want him out of the way."

"Is there naught we can do? To find him? To save him?"

"So *that*'s what's got you downhearted?" Nana chewed her forefinger. "We'd have to go to one of *them* and beg for his release. They ain't about to do me favors. I don't think they'd release him. And worse, they'd know that we know, and they might imprison *us*. I'm not a coward, but my first duty is to be here when Themselves return."

"I have duties too," said Tiklok reluctantly. "I'm not supposed to go to jail."

"Do you reckon his mother's in need?"

"Her neighbors was looking out for her," he said. "The man's a dockworker; the woman does some handwork."

"Some neighbors will stick forever and some will slack. Tell you what, next time you are sent into the city—don't go off without permission again—take Ryton's mother this." Nana got up, crossed to her bed, took a golden catamount out from under her pillow, and gave it to Tiklok.

Tiklok stood up and resettled Zizi back in the empty chair. He kicked a log deeper into the fire so it would burn more evenly. "Teonora, Ryton, the dogs—it's almost as if they're making sure that when Themselves do come back, they won't have any allies."

"That's why we've got to keep our heads down. I don't think we should even be seen talking together again. What do you tell Kiltti?"

"I don't tell her nothin'. I don't want Kiltti mixed up."

"That's good."

"Keep safe, Nana," said Tiklok. "I wanted to warn you." He left, gliding out, first looking both ways down the hallway.

Nana sank in her chair, and Pearl jumped back in her lap. A big thud startled Nana, but when she whirled around she saw only another cat, Plump-pot, who'd jumped down from where he'd been hiding on top of Chickadee's wardrobe. He slunk in to curl up on top of Nana's feet.

Nana addressed the cats, "Waters! How many will suffer before my Cressa returns to give them comeuppance?

"Tiklok wanted to warn me. I thought I was supposed to comfort *him*—but mayhap that was the real purpose of this visit? Hmm? What do you think, Pearl?"

She stroked the cat. "They've been gone so long. Chickadee's afraid of the dark. Who's looking after her?"

Sewel had returned to the Royal Library after the service for Teonora. He avoided both receptions because he didn't feel as if he fit in with the servants but equally didn't feel comfortable dallying with the aristocrats, most of whom he heartily disliked.

Besides, this morning he'd stumbled over the most interesting lead. He'd found a notation about a book entitled *The Nargis Ice Ornaments of the Early Queens*. Upon each queen's Dedication, Nargis fashioned a special jewel for her, a token of her Talent, which she pulled out of the Coronation Basin. Weir queens wore no crowns; instead they wore these emblems on their brow, in their hair, around their neck, etc. as the mark of their royalty. Some of these glittering jewels—particularly those for Enchanters—looked to the uninformed merely like geometric shapes, but often Nargis illustrated a Talent through visual symbolism. Clesidra the Kind wore a glittering tear, which, through the Spirit's power, stayed magically affixed to her cheek. The warrior queens lifted a small sword or shield out of the Coronation Basin. So this book about the ornaments of early queens might give Sewel information about Talents that had fallen into obscurity.

It took the chronicler until after midnight to find *The Nargis Ice Ornaments of the Early Queens* because the slender volume had been pushed deep behind larger books amongst the cluttered bookshelves of the Royal Library.

Sewel laid the book, which contained faded pen and ink sketches of the Royal Stones on vellum, out on his table and brought his lamp close. About ten pages in, Sewel came to a drawing that surprised him.

The unknown artist had sketched a figurative necklace. The bottom of the token had four hooved legs, like a horse, except the legs looked uncommonly short, and the trunk uncommonly round. The upper part presented the torso of a woman. The queen's name had faded; Sewel took out a magnifying glass and studied the illegible script until he could decipher "Queen Carlina."

The chronicler leapt to his feet and found his tallest ladder, reaching up to the top shelves, where the books of the early queens lay undisturbed.

*The Life of Queen Carlina* was at least three hundred years old. Carlina had no particular reputation amongst the Weir queens; she had ruled in the early days when recordkeeping was lax. Sewel didn't know her byname. The discolored vellum leaves needed to be turned with the utmost care so as not to damage them.

Sewel read aloud to himself. "Record of birth. Naming ceremony. Early years . . . Ah-ha! Here's her Definition."

I, Chronicler Lairthwina, did meet with the princella, now Seven Summers, and her Majestic mother, this Forenoon. Princella Carlina confessed that she could converse with her pet palm Pig.

I tested this assertion by having said Pig perform all manner of Unnatural Chores, things a Pig could not or would not do without Human Command. He carried my Quill across the table and placed it in my Hand! Satisfied that the princella was indeed communicating with the Creature, I Defined her as "Carlina the Gryphling."

I believe the term "Gryphling" to be my own Coinage: I desire the word to indicate the Talent of a Human Communicating with Animals.

Fascinated, Sewel read on through the night about Carlina's reign. Her Talent had become common knowledge. Country folk brought to the palace horses that wouldn't obey, milk cows that sickened, and temperamental oxen that balked at the plow, so the queen spent her days in the stables and paddocks diagnosing the physical ailments and personality quirks of beasts. Her efforts helped her people prosper.

Since Queen Carlina herself showed a particular fondness for pigs, the hills behind the palace gradually became a haven for all manner of swine. The habit of eating pork, ham, and bacon fell out of favor in Cascada, and even the catamounts obeyed Carlina and let the pigs roam their hillsides unmolested.

Sewel sat back in his chair, wondering if the close association of Carlina with such a humble animal had consequences for her later reputation. Undoubtedly, it was much more seemly to burnish the stories about Cayleethia the Artist or Charmana the Fighter than a queen who felt inordinately close to pigs.

Yet as Sewel read deeper into her story he discovered that the Talent Nargis gave Carlina proved invaluable later in her reign. An unusually cold winter created an ice bridge across the Ribbon, the ocean passage that separated Weirandale from Iga. The ice span was so sturdy that an army of Igalon intruders, mounted on bears, invaded. No earthly weapon could halt the magicked bears, created out of clay models by King Siga V through his Power of Transformation, but Queen Carlina enlisted flocks of herons carrying sacks filled with Nargis Water. When the herons dropped their bags on the bears, they melted back into clumps of clay. Then Weir soldiers, aided by platoons of enraged boars, fought off the intruders.

When Sewel closed the volume in the wee hours, guilt assailed him. Knowing about the Gryphling Talent could have helped his queen and princella. If he had hoisted the Queen's Flag, would events have unfolded as they did?

He could try to make up for this error by keeping knowledge of the Gryphling Talent secret. Knowledge provided power: the last thing he wanted was for Matwyck to obtain any clue that would help him find the royal heir, wherever she might be. What if she gathered pigs around her or healed animals like Carlina? All Matwyck would need to do was follow the gossip such a strange habit would inspire.

The chronicler climbed the ladder to rearrange the books so that no one could see that one volume had been extracted. Then he hid *The Life of Queen Carlina* under the floorboards. He closed and locked the door, then nervously reopened it to check that the floorboard did not look disturbed.

He would have to find a much safer place to hide this crucial chronicle. And someday, Nargis willing, he would make up for his ignorance and hubris.

# 20

## Androvale

Waiting by the crossroads that led to Duke Naven's manor house, Wilim fluffed his full sleeves and smoothed his stockings. He'd received a message yesterday from the duke instructing him to meet the carriage of a noblewoman driving north. She and her layabout retinue were probably taking their sweet time over the groaning tables at Buttermilk Inn. He might be hanging here half the day, so he hobbled Syrup and let him graze on the new spring shoots. Wilim used his cap to beat some dust off his clothes and ran his hands through his curly hair.

Then he sat, placing his back against a tree—scratching the itchy patch on his shoulder blade against the bark—and shielding his face from the sun with his hat. His head felt muzzy because he and Stahlia had stayed up later than their wont. Stahlia was fretting about Wren. Well, he couldn't blame her: the child acted strange, almost fey.

Although she'd been with them for several moons now, she barely talked to them and she would duck away from their glance. Waters forbid they should try to hug her! Wren's world revolved around Percie, and she used her foster sister as her mouthpiece to convey any wants or needs. She shrank away from villagers, no matter how kindly Sister Nellsapeta addressed her or how often people tried to win her heart. She wouldn't join in when Percie played with her little friends Dewva or Nettie.

"Was she raised by fairies?" Stahlia had griped. "She don't know how to do the simplest tasks—I had to show her how to peel potatoes!—and she drops her clothes as if magic hands are going to appear to pick them up. I have to stay on her to get her to do her chores."

"Well, we don't know how they lived in Anders Wood. Probably they didn't grow taters."

Stahlia had continued, unheeding. "She eats like a bird—sometimes I see that little mouth pull down as if my good food tastes like slops. She's such a puny little thing."

"She's helpful with Syrup and the chickens," Wilim had offered. "She does fine in her lessons. And Percie thinks the stars shine in her eyes."

"I know. Yesterday they didn't notice me and I overheard them playing some game while planting seeds. Wren spun some fanciful tale about ogres and giants in a prince's forest, and Percie sat back on her heels entranced. So Birdie *can* talk when she's comfortable—when she wants to. She's got imagination inside of her . . . mayhap from living all alone."

"Well, now they have each other, right?" Wilim had rubbed his hand through his hair. "What can we do? We just need to give her more time. She's still grieving, but she's young; she'll come round to us."

Wilim had fallen into a doze in the shade when vibrations woke him up. He stood up and readied Syrup as the dust cloud resolved.

He'd expected the coach and six, but not the twenty accompanying guards, all decked out in armor, their halberds held high.

An officer hailed him. "Are you the guide?"

"Yes, sir." Wilim doffed his cap and inclined his head. "Duke Naven asked me to show you to the manor. Are you expecting highwaymen?" He inclined his head toward the formidable troop with a smile.

The officer didn't deign to answer. "Lead on, then. And mind you set a good pace."

Wilim took the right fork and waited for the driver to turn the carriage. The manor house lay two leagues and two more turns away.

"*Now,* they're in a hurry? Come on, Syrup. This is when you gotta earn your corn." He cantered ahead, often turning to gaze over his shoulder at his charges as the coach and riders navigated the narrow road that ran between fields bordered by white poplar trunks, their bare branches just aching to pop their leaves. Occasionally, Wilim raised his hand to a farmer in the distance coaxing his plow through leftover winter clods and the sticky mud of spring, but the travelers ignored all the locals.

Duke Naven had ruled the duchy of Androvale for some three decades with genuine concern for both its people and his profits. He had a big chest, a hearty voice, and a warm manner. Duchess Naven was more reserved and preferred to have only such contact as necessary. Wilim wondered if she was generally shy, or whether her manner connoted upper-class snootiness.

The party rode in through the manor gatehouse, saluted by two of the duke's guardsmen, who were expecting them. In their brown ducal robes, the duke and duchess and all the little duchettes stood politely lined up outside the grand entry of the manor house just like a painting, waiting to greet this noblewoman.

The officer of the guards escorted the august passenger down the carriage steps. She turned out to be a portly older woman, with amber hair in ringlets; she wore a dress of black-and-gold brocade with elaborate sleeves and pink slashing.

"Duchess Latlie, what an honor to have you visit us!" said Duke Naven, coming forward with a bow.

"Thank you, Naven. You need to maintain your roads better; I do believe that was the most jolting trip I've ever had. Ah, Duchess, how fine to see you. Girls, you look very nice, very nice indeed. Your mother has turned you out quite prettily."

Wilim dismounted in the courtyard, intending to take Syrup around to the stables for the lads to care for. His task accomplished, his mind turned ahead to stopping round the kitchen door for a plate of whatever they had handy and a big tankard of ale or hard cider. Ofttimes Naven's baker would offer him a packet of ginger-bread or sweet cakes for his girls. Mayhap a treat like that would spark his new daughter's appetite.

"Won't you come in to Naven Manor?" he heard the duchess behind him invite her guest.

"I do believe I'll just have a stirrup cup out here a moment. There's a bit of business we must see to first."

"Orest," Naven called to his longtime chamberlain, "fetch Duch-ess Latlie a cup of wine and bring her a chair. But what kind of business is it, Latlie, that you must conduct out-of-doors?"

"Duke Naven," said the officer who accompanied the carriage, striding forward, accompanied by six of his guards, "I have orders from the Lord Regent to search your house, barn, outbuildings—indeed the entire hamlet. I request that you, your family, and your entire household remain outside, right here, under our watch, as we do so." Wilim halted his progress toward the rear of the manor and turned around in amazement to see strange guards surrounding the ducal family.

"What!" cried Duke Naven. "Sir, have you gone mad? Latlie—what kind of nonsense is this?"

Orest reappeared with a generous golden cup and a footman carrying a leather sling chair. Duchess Latlie let the silence build until she was settled in the seat and had gulped at the cup.

"The Lord Regent has sent me to make sure that no one is hid-ing the princella," she said, primly blotting her lips with a kerchief.

"Hiding the princella? *Why would I be hiding the princella?*" Duke Naven swayed on the balls of his feet.

"Well, someone's secreting her away, Naven! I do hope it's you, so I don't have to go jolting all around any farther. I do believe I'll never recover from this ride."

"Latlie, I'll not suffer the indignity of having my estate searched. You'll have to take my word that I've seen not a hair on her head. No," he snapped at a couple of guards who had started to walk toward the manor entrance, "you *do not* have my permission to enter my premises. This is folly—insulting folly!—and I'll not have it!"

"I regret, Duke Naven," said the officer, "that you don't have any choice."

Two of Naven's brown-sashed guards ran to the front door and crossed their halberds.

"Move!" ordered the officer.

"We take orders from our duke," one answered with a strained face.

"I take orders from the Lord Regent. Get out of the way or you'll regret it!" The officer pulled his sword.

The head of Naven's manor guard, Captain Walmunt, came bustling forward. "Sir," he said firmly, "do you have a writ to back up this egregious trespass?"

Duchess Latlie took a crumpled piece of paper out of a velvet bag. Bowing, Walmunt took it from her, scanned it, and passed it to the duke.

The duke scowled. "I don't care what it says. I simply cannot allow such an insult."

If ever a situation called for peacekeeping, this was it. Though it wasn't his place, Wilim felt duty bound to try. He took his cap off again and walked calmly into the circle of angry faces and threats.

"Steady now, gentlemen, fair ladies. Perchance we could talk about this situation before anyone gets hurt," said Wilim in his most coaxing manner. "Surely no one wants that, being as you are all intelligent, highborn, reasonable people. Surely if we listen to one another we can find some solution."

But the Cascadian officer turned out to be the unreasonable sort. Instantly, he bashed Wilim in the temple, just with his fist and sword grip, but the blow struck him hard enough to knock him off his feet. From the ground Wilim grasped that the officer's men had roughly shoved Naven's guards aside and started rampaging through the house. Duchess Naven and her daughters started screaming.

The second coachman, who had been holding the lead horses' heads, came over to grab Wilim's upper arm and help him regain his feet. He said nothing, but the apologetic look on his face spoke for him.

Wilim tried to clear his head, dimly aware of more bustle. Two guards brought down a big crate from the back of the carriage, opened it, and let loose three hunting dogs that immediately commenced yodeling.

The littlest duchette screamed with terror and tried to climb up her big sister's body.

"Now, missy, no fear. They won't hurt you. These here are the princella's dogs—they'll be sure to nose her out," said a man Wilim assumed served as a hunting master. He loosed the dogs' leashes.

All three dogs immediately set upon Wilim, nosing, licking, and fawning over him.

"The princella's *dogs*!" roared Duke Naven, even more wrathful. "THEN WHY ARE THEY JUMPING ON MY PEACEKEEPER?"

Wilim stroked the dogs to show the toddler they didn't bite. He found them quite friendly, though one bore the scar of a knife wound down its flank.

"Come on, you curs," shouted the hunting master, flicking a whip. "Into the house with you."

"Oh no! You're not taking those dirty *dogs* into my house. No! This is too much to bear. Latlie! The insult! Naven, stop them!" cried his wife.

"My dear," said the duke as guards and dogs streamed into his manor house and more offended servants started to gather outside in the courtyard, "I don't think we have any choice." But he did stride over to Duchess Latlie, rip the stirrup cup from her plump hands, take a great gulp, and then pass the rest to his wife.

An elderly woman, perchance a laundress—all Wilim knew was that her sleeves were pushed up and her hands soapy—came up to him. "Your brow's bleeding," she whispered, offering him her apron.

Wilim thanked her and dabbed at his cut. Six armed men stood guard over the assembled household with unfriendly faces. The youngest duchette, now held safely aloft by a servant, stopped crying.

"Excuse me," Wilim said to the guards. "I'm just going to water my horse at the trough over there." The man nodded. Syrup drank thirstily, and Wilim pumped some fresh water to splash on his own face and neck.

Everyone heard the noise of furniture being shoved aside inside the house. The duchess's face turned into a mask of fury. Duchess Latlie chattered to the duke, but from the jut of Naven's chin, nothing worked to mollify him. The servants eyed the foreign guards and threatening weapons with sullen fear.

Minutes dragged by uncomfortably. Guards' occasional shouts rang out: "No one in the barn!" "The cellars are clear." "We're checking the granary next!"

The officer returned to the front of the house after dispatching his underlings in the direction of the outlying cottages.

He noticed Wilim. "Ah, you, guide. I regret that." He motioned toward Wilim's temple. "You all right?"

"I'll be fine."

"Well then, no one needs you here now. On your way."

Wilim walked Syrup back to where the duke—his face stony, bouncing a little on his heels—stood.

Wilim doffed his cap. "Duke Naven—" he began.

"Peacekeeper, I'll not forget your stout heart. Nothing you can do here, and you've a fair ride ahead. But I'll never disregard those who do me a service, nor those who do me ill." He glared at the troop of Cascadian guards a moment and then offered Wilim his hand, saying with automatic politeness, "Off you go, Wilim. Give our regards to your missus."

Wilim bent his head and turned Syrup toward Wyndton, eager to be home and away from the quarrels of gentry.

# 21

## Cascada

Eyevie shuffled backward in the low-ceilinged basement room of the printing house, moving farther out of the light provided by torches. She had come reluctantly to this meeting at the Type and Ink at the urging of Sotteson, the dockworker she'd taken up with; he and his chums shared a political bent and an appetite for action.

Despite the lookouts she'd noticed at the business's windows, Eyevie worried the place would be raided. Even worse, she couldn't put away the fear that some of the other attendees might be spies for General Yurgn or Regent Matwyck.

She examined the faces close to her; they all looked innocent enough—working people, with desperation leaking from their wary eyes. Their clothes were coarse and patched (like hers) and their hands chafed (like hers). But then a spy would make sure he or she could fit in. Eyevie moved deeper into the shadows; Sotteson didn't notice that she'd strayed far from his side.

The conversation that eddied around her proceeded in low tones. Mostly people recounted stories about hard times; a dockworker holding up a stub told how his hand had gotten crushed when a crate fell on it and he'd lost his means of livelihood even though he had eight mouths to fill. A younger man to her left excitedly re-counted to everyone in earshot a long tale about being forced off his family farm by a noble who coveted access to his stream.

A woman with a babe in her arms pushed her way next to Eyevie; she wanted to lean her upper back against the rough plaster wall because the sleeping child was heavy.

"I wish they'd get started," the woman whispered to Eyevie.

"Me too," Eyevie responded without making eye contact, though she had vowed to herself that she wouldn't talk to anyone tonight. She stole a glance at the woman standing beside her, realizing that the mother sported red lash marks on the backs of her hands. Then Eyevie felt guilty for being unfriendly.

"Do you want me to hold her for a bit?" she offered.

"Nah, she might wake up if we shift her. But my hair's caught under her cheek—I'd take it kindly if you could sneak it out."

Eyevie carefully freed the loose strands that the babe's weight tugged on, and the woman sighed with a bit of relief. Standing close to her, Eyevie realized that the stranger wore too much rose water and her bodice was cut particularly low, even though—being so underfed—she didn't have much bosom to show off. Briefly, she shivered at the thought of one so young walking the streets and wondered what she did with her babe.

"Ah! Here he is now!" said the woman, and Eyevie returned her attention to the front of the room. Some men were bustling around; soon a tall, lean Brother of Sorrow in his long gray gown climbed up on a chair that had been placed there so that the two dozen people crowded into the small space could see and hear him.

"Good evening," said the man.

"And to you, Brother," said someone in front.

"I recognize some faces; others are new to me," said the man. "We are no better than beasts if we cannot trust one another, so I will give you our names. I am Brother Whitsury. The young lad who helped me up is Alix of Cascada. We've both been deeply in-volved with the Parity Party from its beginning a few years ago—us and a host of others.

"We two, we're not important people in the movement, which is probably why we're still at large. In the last moons, the leaders have been arrested or they've fled to faraway duchies or countries. Some have died in circumstances that look like accidents but probably weren't."

The crowd muttered at this news.

"Just a short time ago," the Brother continued, "we had great hopes. Queen Cressa was proving her goodwill and soft heart. She entertained petitions to extend suffrage and provide equality before the law—"

"—build sewers," called out someone in the crowd.

"—forbid confiscation!" called the young man who had lost his farm.

"My son was hanged for stealing a chicken!" called out an old woman. "One scrawny chicken. That's not fair; that's not right."

The Brother of Sorrow held out his hands. "Aye, my friends, you know I agree with you. You've seen our pamphlets urging that the courts offer justice and mercy, pamphlets her administration let us circulate freely. Many even printed by my dear friend here." The Brother gestured in someone's direction, but Eyevie couldn't see over the heads of the others.

"For a time we met openly and we spoke to people of influence, hoping to make them see reason.

"The queen had acted on only a few of our grievances, but we heard from her an eagerness to ameliorate hardship where she could. She warned us that some of our demands would be too expensive and others would run into opposition from powerful interests, but she committed herself to improving our lot and working for more equality between the high and the low.

"Now, she's gone, without explanation." The Brother sighed. "Regent Matwyck—Regent Matwyck is most certainly not our friend. Too many of us have already suffered under his decrees."

"Drought-damn the cad!" shouted someone in the crowd.

"I know that some of you are angry and ready to seize anything at hand and take to the streets," the speaker continued.

"Drought-damn right!" shouted a man up front, shaking his fist.

"Let's go now! People will pour out of their houses to follow us!" another voice urged.

"My friends." The Brother raised his voice, and his expression grew somber in the flickering light. "Hear me! You would be slaughtered without quarter. We have no reason to believe that a revolt would spread—the townsfolk are too frightened and confused.

"Thus, we, the remnants of the Parity Party—such as we are—urge a harder course. We tell you: we must disband for now. We must scatter; we must hide. Patiently, we must wait until Queen Cressa returns; surely she has not deserted her people.

"Even meetings such as this are too dangerous to keep holding. Like you, I fear that the regent will find ways to insert informers who will denounce us."

Dead silence followed this warning as everyone surreptitiously looked at the people around them, wondering, *Is he a spy? Is she on the payroll of the general?* The quiet gave way to muttering in the crowd and the scrape of boots on the hard floor.

Relieved that this would be the only meeting that Sotteson could drag her to, Eyevie relaxed her hunched shoulders.

Yet the woman beside her was not relieved—she grew bereft. She cried out, "But if the Parity Party won't help us, what are we to do?" and many curious faces turned in the direction of the back wall.

"I'm sorry," said Brother Whitsury. "I know this destroys the hope that a few of you harbored." The speaker deliberately turned his gaze so as not to be directly addressing the young mother. "If any of you find yourselves in desperate straits tonight, Alix and I have scrounged a small sack of coin that may help. Please—without shame—approach us at the end of this meeting. I wish we had more to offer."

Even with two little ones waiting for her in her flat (watched tonight by a neighboring widow), Eyevie didn't need their charity, but she suspected that the mother next to her would be forced to take alms.

"Before we disperse—and Alix and I will station ourselves by the front door and back doors to make sure you leave in staggered trickles, for safety—won't you join me in the Five Prayers to Nargis? Our Spirit will comfort our troubled hearts."

Sotteson, never a devout man, worked his way back to Eyevie once the praying began. He grabbed her upper arm and then pushed her lower back in the direction of the steep staircase.

"Let's get to the head of the line to get out of here, or we'll have to wait too long. I need a drink. Or two. Disbanding! Filthy cowards. Pah!" He spit in the corner.

Eyevie jerked her head back to exchange a farewell with the young mother, but the woman didn't see because she had bent her head over her sleeping child.

# 22

## Pilagos, The Green Isles

At Pilagos, Queen Cressa and Lord Ambrice found *Sea Wind* at anchor, but they had to wait several days for *Sea Maiden*.

Pilagos served as the capital of the Green Isles. It had the deepest and busiest harbor, through which many ships stopped to exchange trade goods or to reprovision. This archipelago of volcanic islands speckling the Turquoise Sea included many scattered communities, large and small.

While Ambrice set about supervising the provisioning of the ships, Cressa found a clothier that sold women's clothing ready-made. Green Isles citizens, men and women, generally wore a sashed, loose gown they called a craftan, but tailors were familiar with Weir styles of gowns and split skirts. She bought some items and through the shop engaged seamstresses to sew new outfits more befitting her position. She also hired two lady's maids to dress her hair and care for this elaborate wardrobe. One was named Arlettie; she was a Green Isles widow in her early twenties who was skilled with a needle. The other, Peketta, an older woman whose gentle hands worked her way through Cressa's neglected blue hair, reminded her of Nana.

So it came to pass that on Planting Day, Queen Cressa of

Weirandale called a council of Ambrice, Lord of the Ships; Captain Clemçon of the Queen's Shield; Seamaster Bashkim of *Sea Sprite;* Seamaster Wilamara of *Sea Wind;* Seamaster Gourdo of *Sea Maiden;* and Magistrar Destra of the Green Isles. The council convened in Pilagos's Magistrate Hall in the Old Quarter. The room was high-ceilinged and airy, with walls covered with large maps. As was the Green Isle custom, the participants sat in low-to-the-ground wicker chairs arranged to face one another; next to each stood an even lower side table holding a pitcher of fruit juice mixed with wine and a bowl of nuts.

Cressa recognized Seamaster Wilamara because she had offici-ated at her investiture in Cascada. She always marveled at the female seamaster because unlike Kinley or Seena, nothing about her be-spoke physical prowess—she was of normal height and build. Wila-mara could have been a schoolteacher or a shopkeeper rather than a captain of a crew of two hundred . . . until one noticed her perpetu-ally peeling red nose (which bespoke days spent out-of-doors) and her piercing metal gray eyes (which tolerated no fools). Gourdo was a new face to Cressa: he had been *Sea Maiden*'s first mate, assum-ing command only after his captain died in a clash with the Pellish. Magistrar Destra, their hostess, turned out to be a woman with high cheekbones, dressed in an unsashed craftan of white, with long coily brown hair streaked with several Old Colors worn in a single side plait that reached to her waist. It was impossible to guess her age; she could be thirty or fifty. She wore no adornment of any kind other than a bracelet of entwined leaves that symbolized the worship of Vertia, the Spirit of Growth. Cressa immediately understood why Ambrice wanted her included; Destra exuded an air of calm compe-tence, and her eyes reflected a kind smile.

Cressa explained the situation to the assembled group. Then Gourdo and Wilamara related their experiences since they sepa-rated from *Sea Pearl*. Both had seen scores of black-sailed Pellish ships that gave them wide berth. At ports of call they had heard many tales of the pirates' predations and cruelty.

A pox on these pirates! They had been plaguing the Turquoise Sea for twenty years or more. Cressa wanted to concentrate on plans to regain her throne. With the Weir army under the control of her enemies, what would it take to invade? Ten thousand infantry?

"Do you command an army of ten thousand?" asked Destra.

"Of course not," said Ambrice. He rose and restlessly began to walk around the room, intermittently studying the maps on the walls. "Our sailors excel at sea battles. The only land troops we can muster are some twenty shields, like those four presently standing in your entry hall."

"Then I fear you have no hope of regaining Weirandale through force. Nor, of course, of conquering Oromondo, which maintains the largest and fiercest standing army in Ennea Món. Their soldiers call themselves 'Protectors,' as if their role were purely defensive, but during the War of the Priests they invaded their neighbors as if their name was 'Conquerors.'"

Cressa could hardly gainsay this assessment, but its bleakness crushed her.

"I should never have left!"

Destra turned to face Cressa. "I met your mother, Queen Catreena the Strategist, once, many years ago. Catreena once wisely told me that one must know the past, but never spend a moment regretting it"—Destra held out her palms—"because only the future flows through our hands."

"But if I can't undo my flight and we can't recapture Cascada, our hands are empty!"

"I think not, Your Majesty," answered Destra. "One might wonder if you aim at the wrong target. I see before me a young queen who, like her father, is quite comfortable on the sea. Who married a seamaster. Who is followed by sea captains. Who is connected to Lortherrod, the greatest naval power of them all."

Ambrice broke in. "Ah! We should go with our strength, not our weakness. We have no cavalry and no infantry, but we have a navy, or at least the start of a navy."

Wilamara took up the thread, eagerly leaning forward. "The rest of our war galliots—*Sea Ghost, Sea Wolf, Sea Dog*—would surely gather round us if they were called to rendezvous."

"We have many friends and kin in the fleet. We know they are loyal to our queen and lord," put in Bashkim. "Fuck, if *Queen Carra* could slip out of Cascada's harbor she'd join up with us too."

"But what good would it do us to muster a larger navy?" asked Captain Clemçon, looking confused.

"You speak aright, Clemçon," said Cressa. "This discussion is not germane to the problem at hand." She glanced at Destra again and slowly spoke her thoughts out loud. "Unless . . . we don't declare war on Oromondo, nor storm Weirandale. We declare war on the Oros' ally, Pexlia."

"Indeed," said Destra. "The Pellish have been preying on many nations' ships and raiding every seacoast town. Every country in the world would send ships to join your fleet. One might hazard that given this target, Lortherrod, with the strongest navy in the world, would willingly send a large contingent."

"Forgive a landlubber's confusion," Clemçon broke in again, "but say we followed this course of action. Say we broke the back of the Pellish pirate fleet. How does that help get my queen back on the Nargis Throne?"

Destra did not answer directly, instead she looked down to her lap. "Queen Cressa, how are your enemies explaining your absence from Cascada? How long have you been gone?"

Cressa calculated. "Over three moons. I left well before Winter Solstice. They can't say I'm dead, because I might inconveniently appear alive somewhere. Besides, the Fountains flow on."

Seeing Destra's puzzled expression, Cressa explained, "The two Nargis Fountains—in the Throne Room and in the middle of the city of Cascada—are linked to the lives of Nargis queens. When a queen dies, they pause. If the line of queens breaks, they stop altogether. So every Weir citizen must know I live still. The councilors will have fabricated some story that hints at betrayal of the country."

"Indeed. You know that Pilagos attracts a large number of spies working for the Great Powers? Gossip has reached even my ears of an illicit relationship with a councilor. One 'Bilcazar,' I believe," remarked Destra, "or maybe it's 'Belcazar'? I'm afraid I'm not very good with foreign names."

"That's absurd! That's a lie! Tell me who told you that and I will challenge him!" fumed Clemçon, his hand reaching for his sword hilt.

Ambrice chortled and walked over behind Cressa's chair to lay his hands on her shoulders. "Do we need to discuss this in private, my heart?" Cressa laughed. To the room, Ambrice remarked, "This wild story does explain her absence and impugns her honor. But what about the princella?"

"Ah. They have bruited about that the heir visits with her kin in Lortherrod."

"And if my family in Lortherrod came forth and proclaimed that Cerúlia is not there, that she has been hidden away from would-be assassins?" Cressa patted Ambrice's hand.

"This would be a powerful counter-narrative that might disturb your citizens, would it not?" answered Destra. "Though you should know that they also spread a whisper campaign that Nargis has withdrawn her favor to the line of Nargis queens—that the princella has not been granted a Talent. On occasion, I'm told, these two slanders meet and twist together: the princella is devoid of magic because she is actually the offspring of this Bilthazar."

"Oh, for Water's sake!" Cressa snapped, more angry about disparagement of Cerúlia than she was about whispers about herself.

"But what if," said Seamaster Wilamara, warming to the theme, "our *noble* queen, with her *loving* husband at her side, emerged and publicly raised her banners against the pirates of the seas?"

Clemçon said thoughtfully, "That would make the councilors back in Cascada lose face; they would be shown up as uninformed or duplicitous."

"And what if," Ambrice added, "stories began to circulate about my lady's brave and stalwart actions fighting the pirates?" He resumed his seat again, rubbing his hands together.

"Ah, my lord," said Destra, pointing at him with her index finger, "one might suppose you have put your finger on the quick of it. The only way that Queen Cressa will win back her throne is if she wins the favor of the people of Weirandale. The councilors' power lies in their control of the populace. Let her defeat the Pellish, gain the acclaim of all nations, and prove her leadership, and even those who betrayed her will have to line the streets of Cascada with white roses."

Queen Cressa looked directly at Destra. "If we undertook to rid the Green Isles of the Pellish, we would also be helping your people."

Destra had a musical laugh. "Trust and shared interests form the best alliances, do they not?"

"How much would the Green Isles contribute to this alliance?" Cressa pressed.

"Let me be frank," replied Destra. "The Green Isles are but a loose confederation. One would think that as the highest governmental official I have broad authority, but actually many scattered islands pay no attention to the decrees from Pilagos: the inhabitants live in isolation and go their own ways. We have a sparse treasury and no armed forces. But I will contribute everything that is within my power to provide. Islanders don't like to boast, but you may find my counsel valuable."

Cressa pressed her lips together. "Yet fighting the Pellish might prove a long campaign—they have so many hideouts on so many isles. My people will think I have abandoned them."

*And my daughter. My daughter will think I have abandoned her.*

Ambrice read her thoughts. He said softly, "My heart, I don't see another option."

After a long pause Cressa turned to Destra, remarking, "I understand why the Oros would be in bed with the Pellish. They want to send their priests to proselytize and win converts. They also want to capture cargoes of foodstuffs. What I don't understand is why the Pellish lie abed with the Oros. I also don't understand why the Oros fixate on Weirandale as their nemesis."

"I agree we do not have answers to some key questions. As for the Pellish, did you ask any of the pirates you captured?"

"Ask the pirates?" Clemçon grew outraged at the suggestion. "They attacked my queen; they didn't survive the battle."

"Pity. Well, we'll see if we can locate a specimen to question. In the meantime, perhaps you might make arrangements for your 'Grand Mustering of the Fleet'? Tomorrow might suit, in Pilagos's Central Square?"

"Tomorrow?" said Cressa, stunned at the sudden speed of events.

"Aye," said Ambrice. "No profit in delay. Let's strike immediately."

"If you will excuse me," said Destra, "I need to make arrangements for something simpler—our midmeal."

The five Weirs warmed to their task, each coming up with better ideas of how to reveal Queen Cressa's whereabouts, declare war on Pexlia, and inspire other mariners to join their cause.

The luncheon, served in a nearby room where one wall opened to a colorful garden, consisted of fish and fruit in a delicate sauce. The tasty fare turned the conversation in a lighter direction. Gourdo teased Wilamara about which of her many suitors she would favor. Bashkim, for the first time, spoke longingly of his family back home. Destra revealed that she was not a Green Islander by birth but a former citizen of the Free States. "Of course the Islanders couldn't agree on one of their own as magistrar. They chose me precisely because I'm an outsider with no favored birth isle."

Her Free States background accounted for the glint of gold in Destra's hair. In the light of the dining hall, which had a thatched roof but walls open to the breezes, Cressa saw it clearly. She'd been taught, however, that all of Iga's Old Color and all its Magic had been wiped out centuries ago. Could Destra wield any of Iga's ancient Power of Transformation?

After the meal had been cleared, Destra brought three Islanders into the hall to meet the Weirs. "I'd like to present Donna Simonetta, and her kin, Don Jaret and Don Laret," she said.

"We are pleased to meet you," said Cressa. "Please rise. How can we be of service?"

"We think we might be able to be of service to you, Your Majesty," said Simonetta. She looked close to Cressa's age, but years in the sun had made her skin darker brown and leathery. Her hair, pulled up in a horsetail on the top of her head, shone full shimmering green—the green of fresh-hatched leaves. Her craftan's fabric was deep turquoise with green stripes. "We three hail from a tiny isle, Saltera, way way south. The Pellish overran it two years ago and destroyed our kin and our village."

"You have my condolences, Donna," said Lord Ambrice. "I've heard this sort of story much too often."

Simonetta nodded and stayed silent for a moment. "The Isles, you know, they are all unique and oddly formed. Some harbors any fool could see; some *you'll* never find."

"But *you* can find the harbors?" Wilamara had heard the unstated claim. "Most Islanders only fish their own waters. How have you gained such expertise?"

"Saltera has a natural chain of ponds, perfect for salt pools. For decades we have produced the most and—though Islanders don't like to boast—the tastiest salt in the Isles. And then our boats traded, north, west, everywhere."

The young men both wore their darker green-and-brown hair in a bowl cut with bangs, and had on deep blue craftans with white waist sashes. "The reason we survived the Pellish raid," said one of them, "was we were away on deliveries. Laret and me, we have sailed throughout the Isles since we were but the size of sea urchins. Simonetta handled the money and drove the bargains; we handled the boats."

"Islanders don't like to boast," said Laret, with an easy smile, "but we know more harbors than Vertia has forgotten."

"What price for your unique pilot services?" asked Wilamara.

"Aye, indeed, Seamaster, we ask for a price beyond treasure," answered Donna Simonetta. "At the end of this war, we want Saltera back. We three—we share one dream. We wish to sit on our porches, and sprinkle our roasted muttonfish with our salt, watch the sun go down, and feel the shades of our kinfolk at ease."

"Done," said Ambrice, and he jumped up to clasp wrists with all three Islanders.

The Weir seamasters returned to their ships to make preparations, but Magistrar Destra asked Queen Cressa and Lord Ambrice to tarry with her a moment.

"Actually, we happen to have a Pellish mariner enjoying the hospitality of our cells right now. I thought we should hold on to him, in case we ever need to ransom a citizen." Looking at Cressa she asked, "One might wonder if you'd care to question him?"

Cressa was not surprised that Destra sensed her Talent; she was just grateful that her hostess had approached her privately. Ambrice, however, found the suggestion offensive. "Why bring the queen into such business? If he need be questioned, let me send Clemçon and some shields."

"No, my lord. I am the one to do it. Come. I'll show you," said Cressa.

Destra led them across the street to Pilagos's central jail, and through the building to a dank underground cell of stone with a tiny portal for an entrance. Cressa requested that the jailers chain the captive to the wall. Then she entered with Ambrice, who kept his hand on his dagger, and Destra, who carried a lantern. Though dirty and wild-eyed, this prisoner was of higher rank than the pirates who had attacked *Sea Sprite*—his black waistcoat's skirt and his wrist bracers were made of real sealskin and studded with silver buttons. Bright pink tufts of hair stood out from a brown background all around his head, and his expression showed that he recognized the queen's Old Color. As Cressa approached he pulled as far away as his chains would allow and heaped curses on her in Ancient Pellish.

Until she placed her hand on his shoulder and ordered, "Stop that."

He quieted instantly.

"Tell us your name and rank," she commanded.

"I am Admiralini Heptex. I control the Southern Quadrant."

"Southern Quadrant of what?" Cressa asked, puzzled.

"Of the Green Isles."

"So you are not striking spontaneously; you are organized?"

"Naturally," he grinned. "We communicate over distance by means of trained petrels."

She had the prisoner in her power—she no longer needed to maintain physical contact—so she stepped back the better to watch his face. "And what do you want?"

"Plunder and slaves for us—slaves to row our galleys. Foodstuffs for our allies, the Oromondians."

"Why do you feel you have the right to take from others?" Cressa's tone grew censorious.

"The *right*?" The captive laughed. "How naive you are! We have the *need*. You must be very ignorant about Pexlia: our soil is exhausted and we have no mines, no marble quarries, and no fat fisheries. Once we had tall groves of teak, but these now lie depleted. No Spirit looks out for *us*—we call ourselves 'Pexlia the Abandoned.' *Need* provides right."

"Your king or queen should treat with other nations. . . ."

Again he laughed without mirth. "Which one? In my years we've had five, each murdered by the next greedy idiot avid for the Teak Throne."

Cressa paced a few steps in the tiny room. "Why did you ally yourselves with the Oros?"

"They pay extremely well. And they treat us properly. Other nations call us 'dirty Pellish.' Or say we stink. The Oromondians call us 'Lords of the Sea.' If we find a light-haired child for them to raise, they praise us as beloved brethren."

*Revenge. Respect. Like all peoples, the Pellish want respect. And a way to feed their families. And to spit in the faces of those who have more. What would Weirandale be without Nargis's favor?*

"Do you worship the Oros' Magi?"

"Their Magi wield fearsome powers; they deserve a man's worship. But unlike our cousins the Zellish, we have never been a particularly devout people. When the Oromondians come around, we worship. When they aren't by . . ." He shrugged.

"Why do the Oros focus their wrath on Weirandale?" the queen pressed.

"This comes from their Magi. *I'm* not privy to their wisdom."

Cressa turned to Ambrice, who had been standing with his mouth open behind her. "What else do you want to know?"

"Your Talent! *Now?*" he exclaimed.

"Yes," said Cressa, with a sigh, "when I really needed it—when the realm really needed it—I found it."

"Can you ask him about the location and strength of their entire fleet? And the ports of call where they provision? And their spies and allies: where are they placed and what are their names? And who and where is their admiral? Can you get all that?"

"I can make him tell me everything he knows. And make him forget afterward that he ever saw us."

Turning to their host Ambrice said, "Magistrar Destra, might I have some paper, ink, and quills? Would a small writing table fit in here?"

The next day, at midmorning, Pilagos saw pageantry the likes of which had never before graced that island.

A blare of trumpets and the beat of drums started the procession. Two hundred sailors, dressed sharply in official uniforms of blue with white sashes, paraded through the streets and under the stone arch leading to the Old Quarter. After them came Queen Cressa, garbed magnificently in blue, with jewels adorning her blue hair, mounted on Nightmist (whose coat now gleamed), with her husband, Ambrice, Lord of the Ships, riding a black horse half a length behind.

*During my Dedication, I moved in a trance, still shocked and mourning my mother. This feels more like a true coronation than the earlier ceremony. Or is it that I have finally become a true queen?*

The members of the Queen's Shield, four ahorse and another sixteen on foot, flanked the royals. The Queen's Shield carried an enormous Weir flag, the blue river and green banks on a white background, borrowed from *Sea Pearl*'s mast for the occasion. After the flag came another two hundred sailors (the crews from all four ships). As crowds gathered, the procession circled Pilagos's Green Square, a garden boasting a statue of Vertia, surrounded by low plantings. Then the queen and lord dismounted and climbed to the top steps of the Magistrate Hall that fronted the square's north side. Destra came out of the door and knelt in greeting. Cressa took her hand and bid her rise. The trumpets blew another fanfare.

"We have chosen your fair city as the place to announce matters of consequence to all nations," proclaimed Cressa in her loudest, proudest voice. "For too long, the Pellish pirates have disrupted trade, stolen goods, terrorized citizens, killed the innocent, and enslaved your kin. I have left the comforts of my home country of Weirandale because this plague can no longer be countenanced. With my beloved husband, Ambrice, Lord of the Ships, at my side and at the helm, I intend to forge an alliance of navies and lead it in driving the Pellish out of the Isles—indeed out of the seas of the civilized nations!"

Applause and shouts rang from all sides.

"Your wise magistrar has blessed this endeavor. We will always be thankful to her and to you, brave citizens. Thus it is in Pilagos that we, the rightful rulers of Weirandale, pledge our undying efforts to defeat such piracy once and for all. So that a merchant might trust his goods, a sailor might sail these seas, a fisherwoman might catch her dinner, and towns might live in peace without fear of the depredations that for too long have been tolerated as if they were part of nature, like the rain.

"The Pellish pirates do not have to be tolerated. They must be STOPPED. With your help, and by the grace of Nargis and the blessing of your Spirit, Vertia, that is what Ambrice and I intend to do."

At a sign from Cressa, two captains carried a generous offering of fruit and greens to the feet of the grand marble statue of Vertia in the middle of the square.

Magistrar Destra stepped forward. She appeared without retinue, still garbed only in white. Her simplicity spoke of her confidence. Holding her arms outstretched, Destra called out in a ringing voice, "As our friends the Rorthers say, 'Be it thus and ever so.' Vertia the Bountiful, let us grow fruitful."

Cressa strove to use her Talent to persuade the minds of the throng of onlookers. "People of Pilagos, I plead for your help. We need seamen to join our ranks. We need shipmasters to ferry messages. And we need all of you to spread this news far and wide across the Isles and beyond. Will you join with us?"

Her sailors broke out into wild cheering. The two thousand or more Green Isles citizens who had turned out to see the pageantry joined in. As Cressa and Ambrice shared a public kiss, the Queen's Shield started yelling her name: "Cres-sa! Cres-sa! Cres-sa!" The crowd picked up the cry until the stones of the Old Quarter echoed with it.

The procession wound back to the docks, where the queen and her husband boarded *Sea Pearl*. A great cheer went up when they reappeared on deck waving to the onlookers, and another when sailors rehoisted the Weirandale flag to the top of the mainsail.

By the score, Islanders came up to talk to the Weir mates who had set up stations on the dock. Years of pirate raids had traumatized them so severely that many just wanted to share their scarring tales of how the Pellish had stolen their cargo, burned their seacoast village, or killed their kin. Others wanted to hire on as sailors; several offered their vessels as message carriers.

On the evening's tide, the first wave of fishing and trading boats carrying crucial missives and instructions left for all the major cities of the Green Isles, for Lortherrod, Rortherrod, the Free States, Gulltown, the coastal city of the duchy of Androvale, and even for Cascada, the capital city of Weirandale.

# 23

## Wyndton

Wren hated the village school. She found the slow instruction tedious and had to bite back her desire to correct or prod her blundering instructors. She missed Tutor Ryton's gentle manner and vast store of knowledge and now regretted that she had teased him so often.

The only thing she enjoyed at Wyndton Under School was when the class sang in unison. In song Wren felt a sense of connection with her classmates that otherwise escaped her. Otherwise, she often grew impatient with the slower children; she cloaked her own abilities and tried to hide her disdain, but they caught the outline of her attitude. They knew that Wren didn't care for them, and they shunned her in return. Only Percia's fellowship and protectiveness saved her from ill treatment.

Thus, school's closing down for the summer season delighted Wren. The girls had the freedom to roam the neighboring farms, woodlands, and meadows with Gili bounding about them, vainly chasing swallows. Wren stretched her Talent, touching the minds of cows and geese, woodpeckers and rabbits. Of course, the girls also had endless, boring chores to do around the cottage, such as caring for the chickens and tending the vegetable garden, but Wren found these tasks less burdensome than the hard bench in the school-room.

As the grain ripened in fields around the village, Wren learned that everyone was expected to help with harvesting because only a short window existed between when the wheat, rye, and barley matured and when the stalks would drop their precious kernels on the ground to be stolen away by birds and rodents.

At first Wren was excited and curious about this break in routine. The community gathered, early one morning, on the biggest plot of tilled land near Wyndton, a long series of meadows on the side of a gentle slope, with a forested swatch at the bottom where a rivulet gathered. Everyone showed up—from the shop owners to the blacksmith's apprentices, from the babes to the elderly—and everybody already knew their duties. The men wielded the scythes; the women raked and tied the sheaves; and the older children lugged these sheaves to the farmer and his workers, who stacked them up to dry in upright haystacks or loaded them into wagons to store in barns. The younger children gleaned the fields. Even the invalids and the elderly sharpened scythes or dandled the babes who had been set in the shade under the wagons.

Working alongside Percia, Wren started ferrying bundles. The first hour passed and the novelty wore off. As the midsummer sun grew hotter, Wren flagged. Her arm muscles ached from carrying, her back from stooping over, her feet from so much treading through the stubbly fields, and somehow the plot's incline grew noticeably steeper as the morning progressed. Her sweat made holding the sheaves more difficult, and more than once she dropped them or let them come untied. Even though Stahlia had wrapped her hands in the morning, the stalks scratched her hands and forearms. Creepy insects crawled out of the wheat onto her arms, but she couldn't brush them off without fumbling the precious sheaf.

Wren fell behind on her side of the furrows, and Percia had to take her bundles while the other sets of children moved farther ahead.

"Aren't you hot, Percie? When do we take a break?"

"We break at midmeal. Sure, I'm hot. I just don't pay it no mind."

Wren tried to match Percie's steady rhythm, but it eluded her.

Older men fetched covered water buckets to the edge of the fields and children carefully carried skippers when called by the thirsty. Wren took a long drink, which refreshed her for a few minutes. But she and Percia finished gathering their row last of all the teams; all the other kids had moved into freshly scythed areas and the newer haystacks stood farther away.

"Sit and rest for a spell," said Percia. "I'll do the next bit alone."

Wren flopped down, wiping her dripping face on her shirtsleeve and her sweaty hands on her apron. She felt exhausted—and this was only the first morning of the first day. She looked around at everyone else working without complaint and felt deeply lonely.

"Water!" she called to one of Dewva's little brothers.

He detoured to bring her his cup, and she drank deeply.

His mother stood up from tying a bundle to call unsolicited advice. "Best not drink so much. 'Twill make you sick."

*What does this stupid countrywoman know?*

Wren drank more both to quench her thirst and to prove that she wouldn't be bossed around. She went back to Percia.

"Percie, I really need to pee," she muttered.

"There's trees over that way," Percia said, pointing.

Wren left the field to relieve herself. The cooler air smelled of spruce and moss, so Wren dallied. By the time she got back Percia had joined forces with Dewva and Nettie rather than work alone. Wren labored alongside for a while, but whereas the village girls made every stoop and lift count and moved steadily, Wren stumbled and struggled, falling behind again.

The boys from her school noticed and Ferl made some jibe about "worthless Donigills never learn to work." Wren's ears burned, and even more heat rushed into her face. She stumbled on a rock, bruising her toes. She snatched at the slipping sheaf awkwardly—a stalk penetrated her finger underneath her nail, which hurt worse than all her other aches combined.

"Watch it now, gal!" reproved a woman Wren didn't know. "We

ain't raked and tied them for the likes of *you* to let them fall!" So much contempt was packed into that one little "you."

Misery beat Wren down by the time the harvesters stopped for midmeal. She scanned the deep blue sky, finding it devoid of clouds that might provide relief from the bright sun. She was too nauseous to eat the coarse bread, ham, and cheese, though she drank a lot of water. Stahlia chatted with neighbors; she didn't notice Wren's food strike, and she barely glanced at Wren's hands when her foster daughter asked her to rewrap them.

When they finished eating, they all started again. The only concession others made to the heat was to wash their faces and tie wet kerchiefs around their necks. Wren couldn't understand how everyone else could continue at this pace with the sun beating down on them. Gnats tried to feast on the sweat around her eyes. She felt weak and dizzy, humiliated and inadequate. No one paid any attention to her uniquely awful suffering.

*No Weir princella should be expected to work in the fields like a common laborer.*

Without warning, Wren's stomach heaved and she vomited up all the water she had been drinking. Nettie made a noise of disgust; Percia and Dewva—facing away—either didn't notice or pretended not to. Alat, another one of the boys from school, said something loud about "Pukeface," making a whole group of boys laugh.

Wren broke. She ran off the field of torture into the woods, going deep into the cool, dim copse, far enough so that she couldn't see the wheat field—but not so far that she was lost. She sat down, curled up her knees, and cried out her misery, loneliness, and self-pity. She was too far from the cottage to walk home, and besides, her feet hurt. So she dozed and rested in the shade, counting each bug bite and scrape, waiting for someone to care about her.

A red fox nonchalantly trod past on silent feet.

*Hullo,* sent Wren.

The fox kept pursuing her own business, though Wren was certain the animal had heard her.

*Hullo, I said.*

The fox stopped, regarding her.

*One has never conversed with humankine before. How dost thou speak in one's mind?*

*I just think what I want to say.*

*Dost thou have a thing of import to tell one?*

*No. I'm just lonely. I think Nargis gave me this Talent so I'd always be surrounded by creatures who honor me. Why don't you keep me company?*

*One is busy hunting for dinner, human kit. Thou needst to learn manners,* the fox sent, and summarily disappeared into the underbrush.

*My manners are better than yours!*

Bored and forlorn, Wren watched the sun slant through the upper story of the trees and the squirrels scurry about their business.

As the sun started to wane, Wren heard Syrup approaching. Wilim had not been scything—he'd been negotiating with the other farms the order of their harvesting—so he hadn't witnessed her poor showing nor her flight. She stood up so her foster father could spot her.

"Ah, there you are," said Wilim. "What're you doing, Birdie, hiding in the woods?"

"I felt sick," she said, settling on a half-truth.

"Did you now?" said Wilim neutrally. "I'll take you home to Stahlia for some dosing." They rode silently; Wilim didn't ask about her illness. Since he often tolerated her "whims" or odd behavior better than Stahlia, Wren grew uneasy.

When Wren saw how sunburnt, begrimed, and weary Percia and Stahlia were, she felt both defensive and guilty about her malingering.

Stahlia felt Wren's cool forehead, pulled down her normal lower lids, and peered down her healthy throat.

"A touch of the sun, mayhap. I should whip you for running away, but I'm too tired," said her foster mother. "Wash and get to bed."

When Percie shook her awake the next morning, Wren left the bed reluctantly. She considered hiding before the wagon came to pick them up, but she couldn't think of any place where her family couldn't find her. Besides, Stahlia kept eying her as if she could read her thoughts.

At the new field Stahlia put a firm hand on Wren's shoulder and guided her away from Percia and her other age-mates.

"You're about the size of the six-summers younglings and, like them, this is your first harvest. You'll work alongside them gleaning. See if you can keep pace without slowing anybody down." Her tone of voice was brisk and matter-of-fact; if she knew how much she had humiliated her foster daughter she gave no sign in tone or expression.

The second day offered much the same agony as the first: Wren tolerated her protesting muscles for the first hour, but as the day got hotter she flagged, worn out less by heavy lifting and more by the constant stooping down. The difference now lay in the fact that some of her fellow gleaners also faded, so the whole group's pace slowed. By biting her lip, fighting back tears, and willing her cut and swollen hands to keep opening and closing, Wren continued gathering the leftover stalks into small sheaves and picking up spilled kernels without falling behind the rest of the youngsters.

Wren sulked behind a wagon wheel with her food at midmeal, too ashamed to seek out Percia, but no one noticed. Nettie's little sister, sucking a gash on her own little finger, tugged Wren's apron string.

"I heard tell you're a good one at telling stories. Can you give us one now?"

Absently, Wren began throwing out wild ideas about flying horses and dogs that could sing, and other grubby gleaners gathered round her, rapt. The story grew to include warrior rabbits as big as people. It buoyed the gleaners all through the remainder of the break and into the afternoon, when the farmer's wife decided the "plucky little tykes had worked long enough" (how her condescension grated on Wren!) and treated them to cider and poppy seed cakes (which Wren savored as much as anyone).

Throughout the rest of harvest Wren worked alongside the younger children. Though she felt her own weakness and mortification keenly, the boys from her school soon lost any energy for taunting. On the third day she realized that everyone was just pushing themselves to keep going; no one was paying attention to *her*. On the fourth day she discovered she actually enjoyed assuming the role of leader of the younger band.

On the sixth day, when they relocated yet again to a different field, Wren started to worry whether two of her favorite youngsters— Dewva's little brother, whose legs bent queerly from rickets, and Istorie, who wheezed all the time—were strong enough to survive village life. Though they never complained, the harsh physical labor took an obvious toll on them.

Wren offered to give the crippled boy a ride on her back when their group moved to the next field. He glowered at her, his pride stung to the quick.

Her next attempt was more successful. Stahlia had carefully covered her daughters' heads with both cotton kerchiefs to soak up the sweat and straw hats to shield them from the sun; Wren shared her hat with bareheaded Istorie, whose wheezing left her lips blue.

Wren had learned that village life had a hard and pitiless streak. The frail had to survive as best they could.

# 24

## The Green Isles

Weir ships were the first to join Cressa's fleet that initial summer. Her captains' predictions proved true: the sailors were loyal to their queen and deeply attached to Lord Ambrice, one of their own. Matwyck's hold did not extend to the navy.

*Sea Ghost, Sea Wolf, Sea Dog,* and *Sea Gull*—one by one the ships rendezvoused in Pilagos. Provisioning all these ships did not prove too much of a burden because Green Isles merchants wanted to be rid of the Pellish so much that they sold the quartermasters their goods at cost or even contributed them free. And Clemçon still had a sack full of Oro gems.

After taking stock of his fleet, Ambrice met with all the captains and outlined strategy, assigning ships to various quadrants of the Turquoise Sea based on their capabilities for maritime combat; the shallow-keeled galliots were best for direct encounters with the Pellish vessels, while the deeper-hulled cogs carried men and provisions. Green Isles fishing boats could not participate in battles, but they scouted ahead, ferried messages, or brought captives to *Sea Pearl* for the queen to question. Jaret and Laret of Saltera would move between quadrants, providing navigational expertise as needed.

The campaign began quietly. The ships slipped away from Pilagos one by one, as soon as their officers were briefed and their holds provisioned.

One dawn in the fall, as *Sea Pearl* herself was headed back to Pilagos after supervising the engagements in the northeast section of the Isles, Shield Seena knocked on the queen's stateroom door.

"Your Majesty, Lord Ambrice says 'tis something you need to see."

Cressa climbed out onto the deck. A fog hugged the waves this morning, but by squinting her eyes, she made out the outline of a great flotilla of oared warships also sailing in the direction of Pilagos. As the wind blew gaps in the fog she saw they flew the gray, white, and purple colors of her father's realm: the Lorthers had arrived.

"Look, my heart," said Ambrice, coming over to her with his spyglass. He helped her aim it. "Look at the grand dromon in the center. See the lettering, *Shark Racer*? See the flag?"

"Oh, Ambrice, my brother has come at last!"

Because she was queen and Mikil merely the brother of a king, protocol dictated that he come to her, but Cressa wanted to sail to him directly. To her, the hours until both ships docked at Pilagos stretched achingly long. She drove Peketta to distraction by trying three different hairstyles and sent Seena and Kinley running with contradictory instructions to the ship's cooks.

Cressa had always been closer to Mikil than Rikil. Unlike Rikil, who was proper and polite, Mikil had been actively kind to his young half-sister. He sometimes took her riding or sightseeing around her foster country. At court events such as balls, held in the echoing Hall decorated with trophies of narwhal horns and walrus tusks, he watched out for her, making sure that she was both treated with the respect befitting her station and having a decent time. More than once he cut in on a clumsy dance partner or told a drunken lord who was boring her that King Nithanil begged a word with him.

Learning swordplay from Mikil, however, had been a mixed blessing, because he was strong in Anticipation. Anticipation was the ancient gift of the Spirit Lautan to the Lorthers; it helped them sense what the wind or sea (or a person) was going to do just moments before it did it. This Talent served them well as a seagoing nation. Most Lorthers showed some degree of Anticipation—cocking their spear the instant before their quarry came into view or putting their hands out to catch a jug before it slipped off a shelf. No one could explain exactly what alerted a Lorther; they possessed a special ability to sense movement and direction. In Mikil, and the other storied seamasters of Lorther lore, Anticipation ran strong. This meant, of course, that no matter how much Cressa tried to surprise Mikil, he inevitably knew where her sword would end up, even before she moved it.

He always beat her at Oblongs and Squares too.

But she didn't care much about winning; the important thing was that Mikil provided companionship and made sure the kitchens offered her something besides fish stew. He also bolstered Nana's authority whenever she had difficulty getting the foreign servants to follow her instructions.

Otherwise, her life in Lortherrod, in that cold stone keep on a high sea cliff, was austere. Her father remained an enigma to her. On one level she knew he treasured her because his face would brighten like the sun piercing through a clouded sky whenever she entered the room. And each year he would be waiting to meet her ship at the pier, wearing the same beaming smile. But once she had settled in her suite and he had ascertained that the fires were hot enough for her thin blood, Nithanil had little to say to his daughter. He would visit her rooms each evening before High Table and inquire after her health, compulsively tying knots on a piece of sailing rope he habitually carried about with him. King Nithanil looked so uncomfortable during these conversations that even at an early age Cressa felt sorry for him.

She could not recall him spending relaxed time with her except for one special day. That day (she had been maybe ten summers old) had broken with rare bright sunshine and a steady, small wind. Her father had sent for her and ordered Nana and his guards to stay behind. Alone, they had ridden down to a small sheltered bay with tiny waves like gleaming ripples of silk. An extraordinarily cunning, two-person sailboat, bearing her name in elaborate decorative lettering, had sat beached on the sand. Nithanil had spent the whole day patiently teaching his only daughter how to sail it. When the sun had made the air unseasonably warm for Lortherrod, he had smiled like a small boy up to mischief.

"Watch out!" he'd cautioned, and then he deliberately sprang to the bow and jumped on the sprit until the craft capsized.

Cressa had shrieked with laughter, pulled her soggy hair out of her face, and clung to the overturned boat.

"Now what, Papa?"

"Now, I'll show you how to right a boat. You may not have the weight yet, but you must learn never to be afraid of the sea. Let go. You're perfectly safe. Lautan has you in its embrace."

They had practiced flipping the craft again and again, until he was certain she had internalized the skills. Then she had sailed in to shore and her father told her this *Princella Cressa* was her very own, to sail in this bay, whenever she wished. He had covered her with a dry blanket, handed her some seal jerky, flatbread, and a small jug of mead. When they had finished their repast he escorted her back to Tidewater Keep. His daughter had noticed that with each of the horses' strides his face lost its softness and resumed its customary glower.

He never again spent a full day with her. Often, though, a servant would bring a gift to her suite of interconnecting rooms. A carved toy wooden boat. Or a doll's bed made out of abalone shells. When she grew old enough to wear jewelry, she would receive a necklace of sea pearls or a broach in the shape of a seahorse. Her father never sent a note, but if he observed her playing with his gift or wearing it, the same smile would break through his stern face.

With a father so distant, Cressa felt especially grateful to her half-brother and his joking ways.

And now, at last, here came Mikil himself, dressed in gray silks with a dashing purple cravat, asking permission to come aboard *Sea Pearl*. He had come alone, without any retinue.

Cressa rushed to meet him at the top of the gangplank. "Well met, Mikil!" she cried, raising him from his bent knee and clasping both hands in hers. Many years had elapsed since she had last seen him. He wore his steel-gray hair in the Lorther fashion: short on the sides and top, with a plait extending a hand's length down from the back of his head. He had a smallish, neat build; he was still trim and his sea-gray eyes still bright.

"Well, Little Shrimp," he said, using his old dear name for her. "You didn't think you could host a naval jamboree and not have us participate, did you?"

"What took you so long?" Cressa asked.

"Oh, you know, the old man, and the young old man with his butt on the throne. Cautious. But what be the point of having the best navy in the world if you never let it out to play? Did you really think I'd let the Weirs win all the glory?

"How fare you, Little Shrimp?"

"I am delighted now that you are here. Mikil, prince of Lorther-rod, may I present my husband, Ambrice, Lord of the Weir ships."

Ambrice and Mikil clasped forearms, taking each other's measure and smiling.

"I hear I have a few thousands teases to pay back to you, Prince," said Ambrice good-humoredly.

"Ah, no need. I gave them away freely," replied Mikil airily. More seriously he added, "I hear I have years of love and care to thank you for."

"No need," Ambrice answered, his gaze moving to his wife. "I've had my reward and then some."

Cressa had ordered a royal meal prepared to welcome Mikil, and she led him to the canopied dining area that the sailors had fixed on the top of the forecastle. She asked after her kinfolk. Rikil's wife had delivered of another healthy son. Her father appeared restless since his abdication, spending much of his time fiddling with dioramas of sea battles. Mikil thought that Nithanil's taking a bed wife, to warm his bed at night, had somewhat improved his disposition.

Mikil had inherited from their father the same propensity for gifts. But her brother would seek out the most unlikely presents he could find. After the many tasty courses, while they sipped brandy (and Ambrice, as usual, abstained), Mikil presented her with a box.

Cressa opened it expectantly and then held up hair ornaments made of preserved herring skeletons.

"You don't like them?" Mikil asked, playing crestfallen.

"Oh, but they're lovely," said Cressa. "Just the perfect accent for my ball gown!"

"Oh, if it's formal you crave, then you'd better open this too." Mikil passed her another box, this one from her father, which contained a hair band studded with tiny purple amethysts. It reminded Cressa of a broach her mother had worn long ago.

"Father has been working on that band for more than a year, so you had better like it," said Mikil.

"What? He crafted it himself?"

"Of a certainty, lackwit. He always makes all the gifts he gives. When you are king, and can afford anything of any cost, gifts have no value unless the value arises from your time and craft.

"By the by, what news of the Shrimpella? As you requested, we've proclaimed often and loudly that she isn't visiting with us."

Cressa's happy face turned grave. "She is far from this conflict. Pray the Waters she is safe."

"When you see her, give her this." Mikil produced another fancy box. Inside lay a walrus tusk, intricately carved and polished into the shape of dolphin. Cressa understood that Mikil had carved this himself, taking great pains.

"She gets a lovely present while I get herring skeletons?"

"Ah, but I put weeks into searching for those herring bones!" Mikil twinkled. Besides, you have already received the best presents: my ships, my men, and me."

"Indeed," Cressa acknowledged.

Eventually, they settled down to talk strategy. The Pellish pirates were more dug in than anyone had realized. Over twenty years they had built a network of safe harbors, and they paid a vast network of spies and collaborators to warn them of incipient attacks. Their shipmasters excelled at slipping away in the night or in battle confusion.

Even with the additional ships that had flocked to the queen's banner, Ambrice could not blockade or cordon off five hundred islands, and their adversaries knew of slender straits not on any maps, so that when Ambrice thought he had them surrounded, they melted away into the fog.

Thus, Mikil's additions to the fleet were thrice welcome. Mikil proposed a plan he labeled as "Hounds, Rabbit, Snap." Ambrice's ships would chase the pirate galliots; they would flee, thinking themselves safe in their bewildering maze of straits; Lorther ships would greet them at the end of their bolt-holes. All of his captains had some degree of Anticipation, if not as strong a power as Mikil himself, and he felt confident that they could position their ships so as to cut off the pirates' escape.

They would all try to preserve captives—especially high-ranking ones—to be questioned by Cressa.

"So," said Mikil, "you finally can do something useful with your Talent, Little Shrimp?"

"Yes. Just in time."

Her brother rose, grabbing a carafe. "Will you join me in a libation to Lautan, to look favorably upon this campaign?"

Cressa had learned her kinfolk's practices during her many visits; this ritual was practiced every time her ship set out for Weirandale. "Gladly, Brother."

Putting aside his typical joking demeanor, Mikil strode to the bow of *Sea Pearl*. He poured a quantity of the wine over the deck rail and into the sea, intoning the prayer in Ancient Lorther. Cressa knew the proper responses. They entreated Lautan, so Powerful, so Cruel, and so Munificent, to forgive their trespasses upon the Spirit's territories, to hold their ships in a protective hand, and to accept this wine as a token of their enduring reverence and gratitude.

After a short stay in port, the combined navy put their new strategy into practice. Mikil's unerring sense of which direction the Pellish would scurry helped counter their enemy's expertise at evading engagements. When rammed and boarded, the Pellish fought back stoutly. Cressa's heart broke when Bashkim, the seamaster of her own *Sea Sprite,* led one of the boarding sallies, only to die on a Pellish cutlass.

Once the Pellish realized that the Weirs had some means of making captives talk, they started to employ suicide attacks. It became common for a lone pirate to set his craft on fire and aim it to collide with an Allied ship.

A different stratagem had disastrous consequences. A Weir ship patrolling near *Sea Pearl* gave chase and caught an enemy vessel in its grappling hooks. Before they could board, however, the Pellish used a catapult to launch a straw basket onto the Weir deck. Unafraid of straw, the Weirs just gaped at this missile in confusion. The impact ruptured the container—angry black-headed vipers, tongues darting, slithered out at lightning speed in multiple directions.

Shield Seena, eager to be in the forefront of the boarding party, stood near where the basket landed. Before she could behead it, a viper sank its fangs into her left calf. Twice.

By the time rescuers brought her back to *Sea Pearl,* her leg had swelled three times its size. Someone had already cut open her pant leg to relieve its constriction, but the internal pressure made the skin on her leg fissure in a dozen places, weeping a clear liquid. Seena screamed hoarsely with each breath.

"Cut off her leg if you have to!" Kinley shouted at a healer jittering about the mess table where they had lain her.

"It won't help," he shouted in reply. "The venom already travels in her blood, spreading through her body. Look! See, her fingers puff too."

Kinley turned her fury on her friend. "Fuck you, Seena! Why'd you have to be so brave? Why'd you always have to be first?"

Seena's tongue swelled up and turned black. The venom had reached her brain, so Cressa couldn't connect with her mind to enchant her. When Seena couldn't draw in enough air to scream anymore, she still made pitiful, unbearable moans.

"Damn you, Cap! Stop her agony or *I will,*" Kinley shouted.

Captain Clemçon pulled Cressa out onto the deck.

"I'm going to end this," he said, his hand on his dagger's hilt. "She would do the same for any one of us. You should remain out here, Your Majesty."

"I want to be with her at the end," said Cressa, reaching for strength she didn't think she really possessed.

Cressa laid her hands on both of Seena's temples while Kinley held Seena's right hand and right arm. Clemçon, with scrunched-up cheeks but steady hands, struck her heart on his first blow. After all the overlapping frenzy, the silence throbbed in their ears. Everyone in the room stared at the knotted floorboards, speechless, as blood dripped down the table.

*This is too much to bear. Can't I do something?*

Cressa crossed to Captain Clemçon, reaching for brown-and-bloody hands still rigid around his dagger's hilt. "You will not re-member what happened here," she said. "Seena was wounded in a raid. We surrounded her at the end, and she died peacefully and with little pain, knowing she was cherished. Now, leave the room."

Then she turned next to Kinley. "She smiled at you and told you you were right, as usual—she shouldn't have tried to go first. You told a joke and she laughed. You comforted her, and she slipped away holding your hand on her heart. She told you to take her sword and kill scores of Pellish for her." Cressa proceeded to the other wit-nesses and similarly replaced each person's memory of the scene that had just ensued.

Left alone in the mess, she swayed for a moment, considering whether she could now safely faint. But the dizziness passed, and eventually she had to open her eyes to face the sad sight. She closed Seena's bulging eyes and smoothed the hair plastered on her sweaty face. Since she had hired the two maids, Arlettie and Peketta, Cressa hadn't spent as much time with Seena and Kinley. But she still trea-sured the connection the three of them had formed on *Sea Sprite*. Cressa covered the wracked body with a blanket and wiped the tears off her own face.

She couldn't erase the sight of her friend's swollen and distorted body from her own mind. Nor could she stop Seena's wrapped form—like so many other fatalities—being slipped from the deck of *Sea Pearl* into the night waters as her men gathered on deck and a piper played "Lament for the Lost."

The hide-and-seek strategy continued over long moons. Rortherrod sent ships to bolster their forces, and the Free States contributed shiploads of foodstuffs and weapons. Each night Cressa prayed that the next battle would prove decisive enough to allow her to return home and reclaim her daughter.

After the Battle of the Muskmelons, the queen was never allowed close enough to directly observe the fray, but Ambrice would return to *Sea Pearl* with tales of the Allies' successes. Sometimes he'd be so flushed with victory that he'd entice his wife to their cabin for fevered lovemaking, after which he would narrate a tale of flight and pursuit, hulls rammed and grappling hooks thrown, arrows and swords cutting through the air. Other times he'd sorrow over good men lost, and Cressa would talk softly to him, rubbing his shoulder, trying to share his burden.

Two years into the campaign the pirates grew more desperate and changed tactics.

The Isles banned hair dye—just like all other countries—but the Pellish improvised a way to tint their hair green with plant extracts and disappear into the population. After one sortie, Ambrice returned to *Sea Pearl,* the muscles around his jaw tight with anger.

"What is it?" Cressa asked in alarm.

"We've figured out how the Pellish disappear," he replied. "They've bought off *whole islands.* When we close in, they scurry to their rat holes. We beach and question the Islanders: they swear they've 'seen nothing, know naught, no Pellish anywhere about these parts.' But a Rorther search party found two swift boats pulled up into a river mouth and camouflaged with branches. We burned the boats but never found the men. For all we know they stood right there among the villagers, lying through their teeth about how much they wished they could help us."

"Let me come with you," pleaded Cressa. "I could talk to the Islanders. I could discover who's been bribed and who's innocent."

"And be the target for scores of Pellish arrows! No, my heart. We'll bring prisoners to you after they've been thoroughly searched and restrained."

A few days later they brought her a handful of new Pellish to interrogate.

"Are Islanders helping you?" she asked a trussed-up captive, her fingers lightly touching the back of his hand.

"Aye. Those that can be swayed by money."

"And those that can't be bribed?"

"We take their kin. We tell the Greenies that they'd better cooperate or their family will become fish meal."

"You keep kinfolk for leverage?"

"Aye."

"Where do you hold them? On your ships?"

"Nah, we don't want these mewling Greenies in our way. We have holding pens."

"Show me where, on this map." The Pellish mariner pointed out the two prison islands, separated only by a narrow causeway.

A week later, when a low cloud cover dimmed slivered moons, Don Jaret, the Green Isles pilot, guided *Walrus Racer* while his cousin, Don Laret, led the *Sea Wind* to Jade and Jadeling Isles. The Allies caught the bored Pellish jailers by surprise, so Lorther arrows took down their sentries in the opening minutes of the attack. After a brief skirmish, the Allies freed hundreds of starving hostages from the miserable water pens where they had been kept.

The prisoners were in sad condition. The Allies did what they could to succor them and slowly fetched them aboard. The two ships and *Sea Pearl* ferried the freed men and women to Pilagos to access healing centers and reunite them with loved ones.

When they reached the harbor, Ambrice and Cressa stayed

on board, letting the erstwhile captives disembark first. Watching their kin and countrymen welcome the former prisoners as they came back from the dead provided an unforgettable sight.

That night, heaps of flowers left by grateful Islanders on the wharf where *Sea Pearl* tied up turned the wooden pier into a riot of color and scent. From her perch on the foredeck, Cressa could see that Weir, Lorther, Rorther, and Island sailors clapped one another on the back with pride over the rescue mission. Locals accosted all the mariners with hugs and cheers and offered to stand them to drinks.

Shield Kinley stood behind Cressa regarding the starlight on the water and listening to the happy clamor from shore.

"*This* is a good night," she said.

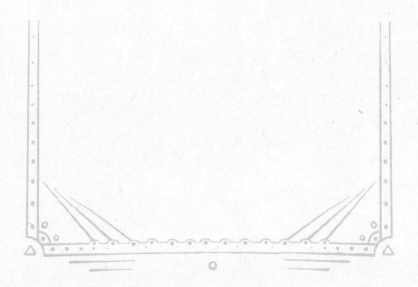

# PART
# THREE

*Reign of Regent Matwyck,*
*Year 3*

# 25

## Femturan, Oromondo

Sumroth pulled his wife, Zea, closer to him in the dark, relishing the warmth of her skin and the way her body fit so perfectly next to his own. He rested his chin in the soft pillow of her hair. Because he was off duty tonight, they luxuriated in the rare privilege of a night together.

His quarters were situated in the enormous army base and barracks outside the capital city of Femturan; its official name was "Iron Valley Protectors' Headquarters," but everyone called it "the Forge," because this was where raw recruits were forged into disciplined soldiers. The small rooms barely stretched four paces in width, but they provided privacy, a perk that Sumroth had earned by rising in the ranks four levels, from a lowly ember to a midlevel fire tender.

Along with barracks and administrative offices, the Forge featured practice fields and a stadium that hosted the Combats, massive ceremonies during which Oro soldiers competed against each other for prizes and glory. Combats took place at eight-year intervals, and all soldiers and civilians anticipated them keenly. When Sumroth was younger he'd dreamed of winning laurels for his fencing prowess; he'd even dreamed of challenging the reigning champion,

Tulsham, who was famous for besting all comers with his two-handed great sword. But like other normal activities, the Combats had been suspended since the coming of the plagues.

Zea worked inside the city gates at the Office of Reverence, filling orders that came in from all districts of Oromondo for holy pamphlets. The Office of Reverence had bookbinders and book distributors stationed in many locations to supply materials for worship citadels. Official decree encouraged keeping husbands and wives together because babies these days so rarely survived; thus the Office of Reverence diligently allowed Zea to work close to Sumroth's postings. When Sumroth had been transferred here, the Office obligingly reassigned her to Femturan.

Unfortunately, neither Sumroth nor Zea favored city life.

The capital, filled with huge buildings, dominated by the Magi's Octagon, now jutted up against a salt marsh. Long ago, Femturan had been a port, allowing Oromondo to ship its precious minerals to the rest of Ennea Món. But centuries of silt buildup from the Iron River and a shift in ocean currents had turned the once-thriving harbor into a vast, unnavigable, and fetid bog.

Zea complained that Femturan's streets thronged with desperate-eyed refugees from failed farming villages. The constant smoke and cacophony from the metalworking concerns gave her headaches. She disliked her lodgings in a hostel along with scores of other women and children. Mostly, she hated the marsh's smell, which was pungent whenever the wind blew in from the east, and so unlike the bracing mountain air where they used to live.

Sumroth appreciated the honor of being brought to the center of government. But then his battalion often patrolled the border or escorted ore shipments down from the mountains, and he didn't have to tolerate Femturan unceasingly. If Zea didn't adjust, he would ask for a transfer; he could not be content if she was unhappy.

Sumroth caressed Zea's full body—muscular but also womanly soft, lit up in the soft reflected glow of his fireplace. Proudly his index finger traced the jewels affixed to the rims of her ears—the fire agate in her right ear from her own career, and the row of four red garnets denoting his rank in her left. But right now he felt sated. What he really wanted was to talk.

"Zea, yesterday Three and Six addressed the high officers in the Stadium."

"Hmm?" replied Zea drowsily.

He nudged her. "Don't fall asleep yet. I want to tell you about it. Something worries me."

Zea made an effort, propping herself up on her elbow. "What? Magi have addressed you many times; you get used to their burning eyes and the bats that perch on their shoulders. Terror converts to pride. They make it a practice to keep up morale amongst important people like you: miners or metalworkers, priests or Protectors."

"Aye. But something felt different. Something was . . . amiss."

"What?"

"Three looks very, very ill," he temporized. "Six spoke most of the time, but her speech didn't make sense. Rambling even."

"If Three has been infected by a plague, if he passes to the Eternal Flames, the others will name a successor for him. We always have eight: Pozhar has decreed that the role is bigger than the person who holds it."

"I know, but it makes me nervous to see a Magi so weak." Sumroth traced the line of Zea's jaw with his thumb. "Six worried me even more. She called out enemies everywhere: Unbelievers, of course, and Weirandale, as usual, but then a list that included most of the other nations in the world. And she named groups of people we must keep a watch on, including healers, farmers, midwives, animal tenders, teachers, importers, and exporters. The list went on and on. I almost expected her to list the Protectors. Or the Office of Reverence."

"You make terrible jests," said Zea, punching him lightly in his ribs.

"Nay, I jest not. Also, she exhorted us not just to kill the enemies and traitors but to dismember and burn them." Sumroth winced at the memory.

"That's hard." A little shudder passed through her body. "Did any of the other officers get upset?"

Sumroth took a breath. "When Six pressed us to kill animal healers someone *laughed*. I don't know why—maybe in surprise. Six lifted up her hands and demanded silence. It got so deathly quiet; no one dared even sneeze. The Magi looked out at the crowd. . . . It felt as if she could see into our hearts and discover the slightest bit of doubt or rebellion. Then she pointed with her finger—like this—and an officer near the front burst into flame! Was he even the one who laughed? Who knows? He paid the price."

Zea grabbed his pointing hand, pulled it down, and interlaced her fingers with his. "Then what happened?" she whispered.

"What could happen? We never question; we always maintain order. We just moved away from the charred remains and started cheering. She whipped us all to a fine frenzy." He rubbed his wife's white hair. Like most of his countrywomen she wore her hair cropped the length of a finger and brushed up; his own cut was similar but shorter. "I felt so isolated, Zea. But then, I banged my fist on my armor and shouted too. I didn't want to be the only one in the arena standing still."

"I've not seen a backslider pay the final price, but I've felt that way betimes," Zea said. "I mean, I've pretended more spirit for a while. But by the end of the Magi's speech or the priest's oration, what was pretend became real, and I was filled with the Fire, the Passion of the blood that is our birthright."

"Aye—but yesterday I never truly felt the Fire. I felt . . . lost. I feared that Six is weak in her mind. I couldn't shake the feeling that—that we are being led by priest-rulers who are weak in their minds."

"Fie, fie, Sumroth!" She put her hand over his mouth. "Don't say that. You'll put yourself in danger. You put us in danger. If anyone overheard you, no one could save you. Not your superiors nor my director."

"I know." He turned over in the small, hard bed.

He heard the cries still reverberating, *Duty! Strength! The Eight!*

*The Power of the Eight! Long will Their Flames burn and conquer.* He smelled the odor of charred flesh. He'd feared that Magi Six would read his heart and would next send a fireball to incinerate him. He'd felt shaky with relief when she continued her oration.

When had he become a coward, a sham? Though he'd fulfilled every duty conscientiously, perchance he hadn't truly earned the rank of tender. He felt the ridged tattoo above his left brow, still slightly new and sore. He couldn't fulfill his duty as Protector with honor if he didn't believe.

This morning he had practiced his swordplay in the yard with a fury, battering all opponents, hoping exhaustion would quiet his doubts. His arms and hamstrings already ached from the exertion. The officers he'd bested might hold grudges; he'd apologize if he knew who to speak to, but he had no idea who his sparring partners had been.

Zea pulled at his muscled shoulder so that he rolled back toward her. She traced the new tattoo above his left brow that denoted his promotion. "Husband, hush. You'll make yourself sick in your mind. Come, I will make you forget about these phantom worries. I know what you need."

She kissed him deeply, then pushed him on his back and rolled her naked body on top of his.

He gave himself over to her touch, hoping in the sweet succor of her warmth to find relief from his nagging doubts.

# 26

## Cascada

Heathclaw, Matwyck's secretary, sent Tiklok into Cascada to seek a special blend of tobacco for the Lord Regent.

Tiklok stopped at several shops, enduring the stares of numerous strangers unaccustomed to his disfigured face. The shopkeepers had sold out of their stores of this fashionable tobacco, but Tiklok persevered, fearing that if he returned empty-handed, he'd be whipped.

Finally, at a store near the quay, the clerk admitted that he had reserved a small stash.

"I need to buy it," said Tiklok.

"I can't sell it to *you*," said the man, shaking his head. "My best customers, rich folk, duchesses and lords, expect this shipment."

"I'm not shopping for myself. The palace sent me. The Lord Regent desires this tobacco."

"The Lord Regent himself? Why didn't you say so?" The man bustled about with an effusiveness even more embarrassing than his earlier disdain.

Finally completing this commission, Tiklok detoured to the North Downs neighborhood to undertake an errand of his own: he wanted to check on Tutor Ryton's mother; he hadn't been able to see her for half a year, and the old woman had become increasingly frail.

The North Downs wasn't quite as poor as the slum where Tiklok had grown up, but litter and leavings dotted the streets, and the inhabitants' clothes had shiny elbows and ragged cuffs. He climbed the flimsy stair treads to knock on Mistress Rysta's door in the modest lodging house. No answer. He knocked harder, recalling that the old woman was hard of hearing. The door across the dim and dingy hallway opened.

"Oh, it's you," said the neighbor lady, a trim woman with a smart face, as she wiped her hands on her apron. "She ain't there. Come in for a moment, why don't you?"

Tiklok had met the neighbors several times in his visits to Mistress Rysta, but he'd never been inside their flat. Their place fronted the street and sported big windows, and it looked cheerful and tidy except for a clutter of something being assembled on a big oak table. Two little boys, giggling and making animal noises, chased one another through the two rooms; they both wore hand puppets—one a blue dragon and one a green sea monster. Tiklok then realized that the table was covered with sewing tools and pieces of fabric, yarn, and stuffing to make more toys.

"I was hoping I'd see you one more time," said the woman. "Would you like a cup of tisane?"

"Thankee, I've been running around the streets and I'm quite thirsty." The dragon collided with his knees, bounced off, and continued pursuing the sea creature with an increase in shouts and squeals.

"Here, it's brewed," she said, handing him a mug.

"Where is—?"

"Mistress Rysta died. A fortnight ago. Peaceful, I hope; at any rate, in her sleep. I'd brought her some supper, but she said she weren't hungry, and when I checked on her in the morn, she was gone."

Tiklok digested the news. "May she sleep forever on the Eternal Waters."

"Not to worry! I had her buried, right and proper. Kind of sad that only six of us attended the service—me and the boys, a Brother of Sorrow, a local under schoolteacher and the teacher's sister. A life drained dry, and only *six* folk to say goodbye, and not one of us true kin. I would've sent for you, being you're a friend of her son's, you know, but I don't know where you live. In fact, I'm embarrassed to admit I don't know your name."

"I'm Tiklok," he said, holding out his big hand.

"And I'm Eyevie," said the woman, placing her smaller hand in his. "I suppose my man, Sotteson, knew your particulars, but," she lowered her voice to a whisper, "he left us two, three moons ago." The boys' noisy chase covered up her whisper.

"I'm sorry," said Tiklok, not knowing what else to say, and wondering if now he needed to worry about Eyevie.

"Never mind *him*. He ain't the boys' father, and he ain't hardly worth spit. I want to show you something."

Eyevie got up and rummaged around through a cupboard, pulling out a thick book. Inside the cover were two letters protected by the book's leather binding.

"I was hoping to see you, Master Tiklok, because I've got some news worth telling. Ryton was able to smuggle a letter out to his mother, see?"

"Oh! He's alive!" Tiklok grinned with relief, and then he puzzled through all the ramifications of the news. "And—and his mother knew that before she passed!"

"Yep. Do you want to read the letter?" She held out the creased paper.

Tiklok looked at the tiny handwriting, a little daunted.

"Would you like me to read it to you?" asked Mistress Eyevie. "Boys! A little quieter, please."

She read aloud:

Mother,
One of the jailers here has promised to try to deliver this.
If he does, my prayers will have been answered.

*I am hale. No one mistreats me, though often I long for the comforts of home and your companionship. Boredom and loneliness are my biggest vexations. I have taken to writing poetry in my head to pass the time. If this jailer indulges me with more paper I will write down my verses. .*

*I think of you often, Mother, and I worry about you more than you should concern yourself about me. With Nargis's grace we will be together again, either on this side, or the other, of the Eternal Waters.*

*Your loving and devoted son, R.*

Tiklok was quiet a long moment, thinking. Then he remarked, "He doesn't say anything about where he is being held."

"No," said the neighbor. "I imagine the jailer wouldn't let him."

"Still, it must have been a terrible comfort to Mistress Rysta to get this."

"Aye. I've never seen anyone weep from happiness before. When I think about what it might be like to not be able to see your son . . ." She *tsk*ed a few times, and her eyes rested on the children bouncing on a mattress in the other room. "Quite a blessing that this arrived before she died."

She took a swallow from her own mug on the sewing table. "I want to show you something else. This other paper I've got."

Eyevie handed it to Tiklok and he unfolded it. It wasn't a letter, but rather some type of legal document. It had seals and signatures.

"What is it?"

"This is the deed to their farm. Ryton and his mother—they had to come from someplace, right? Well, they come from a little holding in Riverine not far west of here. Mistress Rysta told me they used to grow mostly cabbages. I can hardly imagine that fragile lady or her educated son digging cabbages in the mud. Anyhow, about five moons ago she sent me for an advocate, and she signed the property over to me upon her passing." She looked Tiklok in the face, eager for him to believe that she hadn't taken advantage of an ailing old lady. "I didn't have anything to do with this—I didn't even know she owned anything."

"She felt grateful to you," said Tiklok. "You looked after her, faithfully, all these years."

"Yeah, well, I would have done that for pea pods. She was a sweet soul and sympathetic; she would listen to my troubles with my man. She acted sort of like a grandmother to the boys. I think they miss her."

"What are you going to do? With the farm, that is?"

"Well, at first I thought I would sell it and use the money for school fees. But lately, I've been thinking it might be a good idea to leave Cascada." Mistress Eyevie glanced meaningfully out the front windows.

"Really?" Tiklok said, for want of anything smarter to say.

"More tisane?" she offered.

Tiklok shook his head. The tisane had been weak and not very flavorful.

"Tell me, that getup you wear, does that mean you work in the palace?"

"Aye. This is a worker's uniform. Not as fancy as a footman's." He gestured to his own doublet. "It doesn't have the braid—"

"So do you know the Lord Regent? Lord . . . Matwyck."

"Umm." Tiklok raised his eyes over his mug. "A little."

"Tell me, what sort of man is he?" Eyevie looked down at her hands.

"I don't know what you mean."

"Is he kind and gentle—like Ryton and Rysta—or is he conniving?"

"Ma! Ma!" called one of the boys from the other room. "A dragon should win, shouldn't he? Ma?"

Tiklok didn't know what to say; he didn't know what he *could* say.

Eyevie grabbed his forearm tightly. "Tell me, Tiklok. Please. I've heard some things, and I knew him long ago, and I need to know how he's turned out."

"Once when I bumped into him, he threatened to cut up the rest of my face," he blurted out.

"I thought as much," said Eyevie, as if this little anecdote decided something. "I think I'll take my boys out of the capital, live quietly in the country, where we'll be unnoticed and safe. We'll learn how to farm, and keep the house up, in case Tutor Ryton ever gets released and needs a cozy hearth for his last years."

The sea monster chased the dragon through the front room again, filling the space with improbable, lion-like growls. "Boys! I can't hear myself talk!" The roars fell down a notch.

"Mistress Rysta didn't say anything about her personal things," Mistress Eyevie continued. "Her clothes were more than worn—mostly I've been using them as fabric. Found a few of his books I'd like to keep, if no one minds, to school my sons. But I unearthed one pretty thing; I'm thinking mayhap it was a present someone gave her."

Eyevie moved into the bedroom and came back with a flat package wrapped in many layers of paper. "It's old silk, and it's got a lovely feel to it. It's got nary a spot on it. I've been wondering if you'd like to have it. You've been looking in on her for years too. Give it to your mother or sister as a shawl."

"I don't have a mother or a sister," said Tiklok. "But I do have a sweetheart."

"Really?" said the neighbor with mild surprise. Then she smiled, showing all her teeth, and commented, "Now ain't she a lucky gal."

And Tiklok decided that he liked her.

# 27

## The Green Isles

When ships needed repairs or bad weather raged, *Sea Pearl* would berth in Pilagos. Cressa might have relished these respites from shipboard confinement; she might have strolled the marketplaces or taken Nightmist (who now lived full time in Magistrar Destra's stable) out for a long, restorative gallop along the beach or up and down the jagged green peaks. But the magistrar warned the Allies that the Green Isles swarmed with spies and agents of all the Great Powers. The Shield doubled and tripled layers of security, essentially keeping Cressa prisoner in the guesthouse that Destra graciously offered. Her shields hovered around the queen, suspicious that she would make a break for freedom.

But Cressa held her guards in too high regard to cause them extra worry. Fortunately, this high-ceilinged guesthouse, filled with colorful pillows and luxurious rugs, offered more space and comfort than her shipboard cabin and boasted a full-size bathtub. Cressa sent her maids out shopping for things she craved, such as broadsheets and books, paper and pens, skin salves and boiled sweets.

Evenings might be lively affairs: Destra would provide a banquet from her kitchens and join Ambrice and Cressa for counsel and conversation. The best nights ensued if Mikil also berthed in port; then these dinners turned frolicsome. He never turned up without some offering that cheered them all. Once he brought bells they had to wear on their toes; another time he showed up with parrots he'd taught to mangle bawdy Lorther songs. For a few hours they would drink fruit liquors, argue over who cheated at Oblongs and Squares, and set aside the grim work of war.

Such breaks occurred rarely; most of the time the ships cruised the Turquoise Sea pursuing their quarry. Each island, each town, each harbor presented unpredictable dangers.

Cressa took the death of each member of her Shield hard. From the original twenty-two who had sailed away from Cascada, the squad now numbered less than ten. After Seena's death, she decided that she would no longer allow them to participate in raids, but instead insist they fulfill their primary purpose of serving as her personal protectors. Watching her was surely the safest of all posts, since Ambrice kept whichever ship she stayed on away from all dangers.

If the shields regretted missing major battles, they complained to Clemçon, not to Queen Cressa. She saw only their attentive regard as they staked out her cabin, shadowed her movements, or supervised her interrogation of captives.

Kinley often found excuses to linger, and occasionally Cressa invited her for a game of Oblongs and Squares. They drank wine and shared memories of Seena. Kinley even told Cressa about her relations with *Sea Pearl*'s sailors: apparently she'd found some solace with the young bosun's mate, who had prodigious stamina in a hammock.

During the third summer after she left Cascada, Cressa discovered that despite her efforts, she still couldn't protect her people. A tropical fever raged over *Sea Pearl*, striking down several sailors and three of the Queen's Shield. For days they sweated and trembled while their friends bathed them and healers brewed fever-reducing draughts. Slowly, reluctantly, the illness ebbed, and the afflicted began to regain their strength.

Then Kinley caught the same fever. Cressa took shifts at her side, wiping off the sweat and spooning in broth. Kinley appeared to have turned a corner, but that night the fever returned, hungry for prey.

As dawn threatened, a knock made the queen's cabin door vibrate. Arlettie crossed to answer. From her bed Cressa overheard Clemçon's voice, "Fetch Her Majesty. Shield Kinley's started seizing."

"I'm coming," she called out, pulling a skirt on over her nightshift and following Clemçon's slumped shadow. They'd brought Kinley out on deck to catch the slightest of breezes and laid her on a pallet on top of a closed hatch. Two of her fellows continually waved fans, trying to make the air around her cooling. A shaded lantern glowed dully, revealing that Kinley wore a stained undershift. Recently so stocky and strong, her body appeared shrunken and her skin loose. Her lips looked white with chapping; her short dark hair glistened; and her black eyes darted randomly above newly visible cheekbones.

The people gathered round made space for the queen. Cressa took Kinley's hand: it pulsed with the heat of her fever.

"She's just come out of a fever fit," explained the attending healer. "She was thrashing about something terrible."

"Kinley, Kinley, do you know me?" Cressa spoke softly.

The shield turned her head in her direction. "I can't see you. But I know your voice, Queenie."

"It's still dark. That's why you can't see. I'm here with you," said Cressa.

"You won't leave me?"

"No. Lie back; I'm here."

Everyone waited silently.

Cressa reached for a normal, reassuring tone of voice. "I'm here, Kinley. Feel my hand. This will pass like a bad nightmare. When you're better we'll play Oblongs and Squares like we used to and you'll beat me, just as you used to."

"Drought-damn these Isles—their fuckin' pirates—their fuckin' fevers," Kinley muttered.

Cressa gathered her wits and reached for her Talent. "Kinley, I'm going to cool you down. Now imagine you float in a cold stream back at home. It's pure and clean, and it numbs your fingers and toes—"

"Drought-damn fuck!" Kinley interrupted, just before her body arched and shook like a loose-limbed doll.

"Make it stop!" Cressa implored the healer, but all he could do was restrain her wild gyrations by pushing down on her shoulders. The fit continued for long minutes while Kinley's head snapped wildly on her neck. Then just as abruptly as the seizure started, it abated and she collapsed back on the mattress. She'd bitten through her tongue; blood rushed down her chin; the smell of urine rose from the pallet.

"I'm here, Kinley," Cressa said loudly, stroking her face. "I'm here." But Kinley lay unresponsive, occasionally twitching a limb or an eye.

The healer swabbed at the blood.

Shortly after daybreak, Kinley died. Clemçon, Sergeant Dariush, and Cressa stood beside her while the sky brightened, the sailors quietly drifted back to their tasks, and the waves rolled ceaselessly.

Cressa held her hand until it began to lose its abnormal heat. She had no words of comfort for Captain Clemçon, and he had none for her. Finally, she wiped the tears from her cheeks and left the body to the sailors who would sew a shroud.

The moons dragged on. The Allies killed more pirates, uncovered more collaborators, burned more ships, weathered storms and doldrums. They suspected that Pexlia had sent in reinforcements. Their provisioning funds grew lean, so Clemçon took one of the queen's necklaces to Pilagos to sell. Donna Simonetta, the salt trader, fumed when she heard the price: "You got rooked, man! Islanders don't like to boast, but I can get you a much better deal." So in the future they put her in charge of such bargaining.

The islands all came to look the same to Cressa, and she tired of the sea that had once offered such freedom from palace constraints. She missed her home, her palace, and—especially—her daughter.

Time and again Cressa woke up in the middle of the night crying out for Cerúlia. In those nighttime hours she argued vehemently with Ambrice.

"You and Mikil have the naval strategy in hand. I would take a ship and sail to where I've hidden Cerúlia. I must see her! It has been too long."

"My heart, 'tis too dangerous. One ship could be prey to weather or attack—"

"I must see her. I could sneak in at night—I could just check that she is well cared for. I must be sure she knows how we love her, how much we think of her, that we haven't forgotten her. Or I could fetch her away with me; she would be safe now with us, on the command ship, or with Magistrar Destra in Pilagos—"

"Cressa. You could not sail without a large escort, an escort that would divide our strength from this fight. And we need you here: the information you obtain saves lives. Besides, Cerúlia is most secure if no one knows where she is; the minute she reappears all of the might of the Oros and the councilors would descend on her. The Green Isles harbor more spies than mosquitos."

"I want her near me; I crave her presence. Stop telling me what I cannot do! I am the queen!"

"It is because you are queen that you must sacrifice your own desires to protect her. The throne is safer if you live separate. You know this. We've been over and over this."

"Why do I have to choose between my daughter and my duty? I am not strong enough for this!"

"None of us can choose our time; the times choose us. You *are* strong enough; look what you've endured. Only a little longer now. A few more seasons, a year at most." Ambrice stroked her hair. "Hush, hush, now, don't weep, or you'll break my heart."

# 28

## Cascada

Matwyck leaned forward in his box in the Peacock Theater, his arm on the railing, his eyes drinking in the spectacle, his ears catching every word.

*So this is what pity feels like? What? Are these real tears on my cheeks? It provides a certain ennobling glow!*

Plays gave Matwyck a rare taste of the emotional palette that people around him claimed to experience. Watching from his special "Regent's Box," Matwyck not only recognized the character's sentiments; he came close to actually *experiencing* them. He attended most productions several times, finding that familiarity with the story enhanced rather than detracted from his delight. This was the third time he had seen *The Maiden's Plight*.

Its dramatic action stirred him. He responded especially to the middle of Act Two, when the mother fainted from bad news (*poor soul, taxed beyond what she could bear*) and the end of Act Three, when the maiden's brother swore to avenge her (*Yes! I would do that too!*), and the climax when the woebegone heroine had sunk to her knees and rent her dress in anguish (*oh, the picture of innocence persecuted*).

"She *should* rip off that dress—it's so-oo out of fashion," commented Lady Dinista.

"Shut up!" Matwyck hissed at her, annoyed that she had interrupted his trance.

He turned back to the stage, where the dashing hero—so what if his belly hung low, he had a great voice that throbbed with feeling—now vowed to give up his throne for her.

*Is this selflessness? Does love actually inspire selflessness?*

Matwyck had become a devotee of the theater. Because Cascada was a magnet for all the artists in the land he'd heard concerts by court musicians and watched performances by the Royal Dancers. But it was the plays at the Aqueduct and the Peacock that had caught his fancy with their fencing, twirling silks, tension-filled stories, rousing music, and firecrackers set off at the finale. For the space of a few hours his heart beat faster with concern and suspense. Better still, he knew that all the other spectators shared his feelings. At the theater he felt most fully alive and almost . . . normal.

Matwyck always found it deflating to leave the magic of the theater and return to real life. Especially tonight when he was obliged to host a late-night supper party. His new chamberlaine pulled it off quite well, but then it wasn't a grand event, merely a token engagement celebration for Lady Dinista and Lord Retzel's second son. Matwyck rejoiced in getting Dinista—that grasping schemer!—out of Cascada. The Retzel family should be able to afford to keep her in the height of fashion.

Due to the queen's prolonged absence the custom that stewards serve no more than one ten-year term had, naturally, been suspended. In the years Cressa had been gone Matwyck had consolidated his hold over the Western Duchies, the army, and the court. As Lord Regent and Lord Steward he dominated Weirandale.

Last night's banquet had been part of his ongoing campaign to keep the nobles from getting restless. They appreciated that he had put down the Parity Party troublemakers with their demands for suffrage, property rights, religious freedom, and the like. Matwyck recognized the irony of himself (born a commoner) becoming the champion of the aristocracy, but he decided that his birth had been an accident. Surely his mind, his skills promoted him to the natural nobility. Surely his rare intelligence and capabilities entitled him to rule: he was the only one competent to do so.

However, much as he tried to censor the news, the continual successes of the Allied Fleet against the Pellish made some of the gentry wish they were winning these laurels, or at least had them pining to gain the favor of this dashing and heroic queen. Amongst the dukes and lords Matwyck carefully employed just a little sarcasm or raised an eyebrow—undercutting her accomplishments, reminding them of the scandal with Belcazar—all the while exuding complete confidence that this monarch would never be returning to reclaim her throne. Keeping his influence amongst the rich aristocrats required constant wining, soothing, flattery, financial inducements, and—occasionally—a veiled (or even naked) threat.

Matwyck enjoyed all of this because he felt himself at the height of his powers. He would look about the supper table at all the people of such noble lineage. Their insecurities, ambition, or greed blazed nakedly to a watcher as skilled as he. He could play them like the keys of a harpsichord.

Amongst the little people, Matwyck also performed a tricky balancing act. Publicly he proclaimed himself to be Queen Cressa's most ardent admirer and her most devoted servant. An early decision designed to demonstrate this loyalty had been to promote Lady Fanyah, one of the queen's hand-selected ladies-in-waiting, her trusted advisor and friend, to the Circle Council to take the place of Belcazar (who had left because of a regrettable illness in his family). Fanyah's elevation had turned out to be more than a symbolic gesture: it was she who had the inspiration of forging communiqués to the Lord Regent in Queen Cressa's name, communiqués that urged the people to obey the regent in all matters.

But while Matwyck tried to persuade the people of the legitimacy of his rule, he also inexorably squashed the least hint of discontent with his administration. A new proclamation made it a crime to disparage the Lord Regent. People who couldn't hold their tongues got ten lashes or a day in the stocks.

This morning Matwyck studied the paper in front of him: the duke of Crenovale reported so disciplining twenty-seven scoundrels. Matwyck compared the reports from other duchies, realizing that the duke of Maritima had not sent one in.

*Is trouble brewing in Maritima? The last time I saw the duke and duchess they pestered me about the princella. But then everyone pesters me about her. If she isn't in Lortherrod, where is she? Behind this perpetual question lies an insinuation: "You're not holding her captive, are you?"*

A knock on the door interrupted Matwyck's headache.

"Lord Regent, we have the men you seek," announced Heathclaw.

When three of the Queen's Shield, escorting four horses, returned to Cascada, they tried to slip back on the sly. Fortunately, Matwyck's spies reported their arrival immediately. Since the horses returned to the Royal Stables, he would have found out eventually . . . though he had doubts about the loyalty of all the stablehands.

Matwyck came forward to greet his guests, noticing that their uniforms were faded and salt-stained and their skin had taken on even darker shades of brown. Heathclaw made introductions: the one with a white-and-red slash across his lips and chin and knocked-out front teeth was named Pontole; the man with his arm in a sling was Branwise; and the oldest, the man who must have been Matwyck's age or more, who looked hollowed out by illness but had a cunning look in his eyes, was their leader, Sergeant Yanath.

"Would you care for wine, rum, or mead? The castle cellars are at the disposal of the men in blue!"

"No, thankee, milord," answered Yanath, standing straight in the middle of his office, a man on each side.

"Come, come, men, you are off duty!" Matwyck scoffed. "We must celebrate your return!"

"A bit early in the day for us, milord."

"To each his own," said Matwyck, pouring himself a small glass of wine from the decanter on his table. "Your health and prosperity!" he said, downing his glass and hoping it would alleviate his headache.

*Shields declining to drink? They must be watching their tongues.*

"When did you last see our noble queen?"

"Close to three moons ago; the winds did not favor us," answered Sergeant Yanath. Apparently, he was to be the spokesman.

"Where was this?"

"In Pilagos."

No surprise. Matwyck's spies had kept him informed that Pilagos was the base of Cressa's operations. They had also informed him that repeated attempts to penetrate the guesthouse she stayed in had needed to be called off.

"Was she healthy?"

"Very hale, Lord Regent."

"Ah, how it gladdens my heart to hear this! And she is well supported? How many ships now follow her banner?"

"Dunno exactly, Lord Regent. Dozens. We're shields; we're not privy to the navy's discussions or ledgers."

"Of course, of course. But we heard that the Rorthers and the Lorthers have joined the fray and that our heroic Cressa wins great victories."

"I guess," said Yanath shortly.

"You know, men, it was the Circle Council that sent the rest of the Weir fleet to join the fray. We support the queen wholeheartedly. Nightly we entreat Nargis for her victory."

Yanath said nothing.

"How goes the fight against the Pellish? Decidedly tough combatants, I hear."

"Aye, milord. Plenty of Weir and Allied blood to testify to that."

"You've lost friends and companions?" said Matwyck, trying sympathy. "You've suffered, I see."

"Oh, we're all right," said Yanath.

"Such modesty! Shall I ring for palace healers to examine you?

Is there anything you need? Nothing is too good for our fighting men!"

"Thank you, milord. We'll do well enough."

"How does the princella fare? Is she affrighted, the precious thing?"

"The princella, sir?" echoed Yanath.

"Yes, the princella. Has your illness affected your hearing?"

"I hear well enough, Lord Regent. But we haven't seen the princella since we left the palace, I guess three years ago. Pray the Waters she be thriving."

"Do you expect me to believe that in all this time, the queen has not visited with her only daughter? Come, come! Everyone knows she dotes on the lass, as we all do."

"Lord Regent, our job has been to protect Her Majesty. We have seen nothing of the princella."

Matwyck placed his hands together in a prayerlike position and smiled broadly. "I was testing you, men. We know the princella is safely away from the fray—awaiting her mother's triumphant return, as are we all."

Yanath said nothing. Pontole and Branwise stared at him warily and shifted their weight.

*Truculent. I won't tolerate it.*

"Why have you left your posts?"

The men stirred at this sudden thrust, and Pontole folded his arms across his chest. Yanath kept his cool. "Queen Cressa herself sent us back to Cascada, Lord. She said she was tired of losing good men; she wants some of the Shield to survive. And she wanted the horses to come home."

"So you say." The regent tapped each matching finger together. "Did she send you back with written orders?"

"No, sir."

"So I have only your word you are not . . . deserters." Matwyck lifted an eyebrow and let the word hang.

The guards compressed their lips but did not respond.

"What's this about horses?"

"A ship is no place for a fine animal," answered Pontole, gesturing with his hands. "And they weren't no use on island skirmishes. Nightmist and Smoke, they be the best stock in Weirandale. Nightmist and Dariush's mare, Bucket, they should be bred; they are both still in their prime. . . ." His voice trailed off as Matwyck stared him down.

Matwyck abruptly changed topic, hoping to catch the men off-balance.

"What letters has the queen received?"

"Lord Regent, such is hardly our bailiwick," responded Yanath, glancing at his fellows. Branwise's face had turned even darker. Yanath continued with some heat in his voice, "And if we did know, we wouldn't speak of it, not to you nor anyone else."

"I much dislike your tone. You mistake me. My concern for the queen, the princella, and the realm makes me anxious."

Matwyck tapped his fingers together while he considered the situation. *I could have them questioned professionally, but I doubt they know much or Cressa would not have sent them back. This is a waste of my time.*

"Very good, men. I welcome you back to your homeland. What are your plans for the future?"

"We are sworn to the queen. We will wait in attendance for her return."

Matwyck allowed himself a short laugh. "Wait *here*? In the palace? I think not. With no queen in residence your company in the palace would be neither appropriate nor appreciated. You will have to find yourselves other employment." He enjoyed the look of shock Branwise covered up slowly. "But let me congratulate you on your safe return." Matwyck called out for Heathclaw.

"Lord Regent?" he asked as he opened the door.

"Reward each of these men with two golden catamounts for their fine service and see them out." The three guards marched out, their backs stiff at being summarily ejected.

Matwyck sent for Prigent.

"What do you hear from your contacts?"

"I informed you, milord, the last time a bird arrived. The Pellish fight craftily, but lose territory. The fleet has driven them out of more than half of their former sites. They can mount fewer raiding parties, and their supplies dwindle."

"Did you send more funds?"

"Yes, but by ship, not by bird. The thought of diamonds slipping off of leg bands into the sea appalls me. We are going to have to review the budget soon; costs have escalated. If harvests ever come in scant we'll be in real trouble."

Matwyck waved this consideration away. "Have you increased the bounty?"

"I believe the bounty is sufficiently high now, my lord. On their own account the Pellish would be delighted to be rid of the queen and her consort, but they haven't had an opportunity, neither on land nor sea. That Lorther Anticipation—it may help them escape all our nets."

"I would like to speak to Envoy Thum. Make arrangements." Matwyck dismissed Prigent.

*Could it be that after all my efforts, Cressa will indeed defeat the Pellish and return home triumphant? I must not allow this to happen.*

*And where is the princella? Why has Yurgn's network failed to find her out?*

*I'll need to enlist Thum's Magi in both causes—defeating the armada and finding the girl.*

# PART
# FOUR

*Reign of Regent Matwyck,*
*Years 4 to 6*

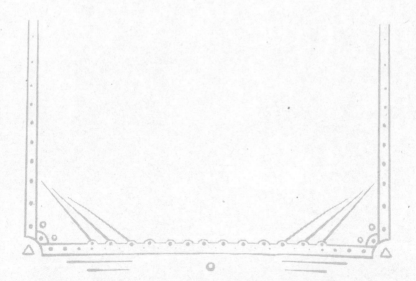

# 29

## Sutterdam, The Free States

Norling caught Thalen's eye and nodded her head at him, urging him to speak up. It *was* a good moment. The family relaxed around the table, having just finished a fine midmeal of roast fowl, topped off by one of Norling's berry pastries. His pater and mater had both enjoyed tall glasses of mead. Hake stared out the window, hoping to catch a glimpse of the pretty candlemaker who walked down Lantern Lane on the way to her shop. Even Harthen lounged, sated and momentarily at peace, wetting his finger to cadge the last crumbs of pastry crust in the dish.

"Pater, Mater," said Thalen. He stopped to clear his throat. "I would like your permission to enroll in the Scoláiríum in Fígat."

His mother sniffed and looked at Norling reproachfully. "You've been encouraging him."

"Fetch my pipe, Youngest," Hartling said to Harthen. Then they all had to wait while the pipe was packed and lit and Hartling got it to draw. After he blew out a mouthful of smoke, Hartling said to Thalen, "Why do you want to go to the Scoláiríum? You just graduated from the upper academy. Proud of you, we are. Isn't that enough learning?"

With quiet firmness Thalen said, "The Scoláiríum has the

greatest teachers. It has a library of ten thousand books. I thirst to know so many things. The answers lie with the books and scholars in Fígat."

"I know how bright you are," said Hake. "I know you could be a good calculator if you'd just put your mind to it."

Thalen understood that his brother had just paid him a compliment and that he meant well, so he tried to keep the frustration out of his voice. "But I am not interested in how many casks of wine or reams of wool sell in a week or for how much profit. I yearn to know where the stars go during the day. Why salt and sugar dissolve in water but sand does not. Why did Oromondo start the War of the Priests? Does any of Iga's Power of Transformation survive? There is so much I long to understand."

"Would you leave those who love you, Middle?" said Mater, with pain in her voice.

"Latham is not so far. I would visit. You would probably see me as often as you will see Harthen. When he joins the cavalry, he'll have to live in the barracks."

"But what about the fees, Middle?" his mother argued. "The Scoláiríum enrolls the rich, those who don't need to work to make a living and can spend their time pondering such impractical things."

Pater blew a smoke ring. "Now, Indy, I catch the boy's craving. I recall when I was hungry to learn new glazes and to try new patterns. You're such a good manager. And business has been so brisk. I'm sure we could afford these fees."

"I *have* been saving for the lads' futures," Mater admitted. "But I doubt we have enough, and what would be left for the boy thereafter, to start his real life?"

"I've solved this problem," said Teta Norling. "I sold the inn. I want to spend my profit on Thalen's education."

"Wait! No! Don't you want to save that? With that windfall you'd be a great catch for a handsome new man." His father was joshing his sister, but he was serious too.

"What I want is to spend it on Thalen," his aunt replied. "I want to ensure his future."

"But what kind of future is in it?" asked Hake, who was always so practical. "Once you've studied at the Scoláiríum, how do you make a living? Do people pay you to find out about stars, birds, sand, or wars?"

"Would you become a councilor?" asked Mater. "Or a government minister?"

"I doubt it." Thalen shook his head. "I think councilors get selected for their riches and influence, not their expert knowledge. Tutors are the only people chosen for their learning."

"What's a tutor?" asked Harthen.

"A scholar, a teacher for those who go on to study after upper school."

"Would *you* become a teacher?" said Mater, considering. "It might be nice to have a teacher in the family—we could save on school fees."

"Who needs to pay school fees now?" asked Harthen.

"For the brats you'll sire someday," said Hake, and Harthen wrinkled his nose at the thought.

"Now, Eldest, you're the one most likely to start a family in the near future," said Mater.

"Right!" said Harthen. "You're the one always mooning over that girl."

Hake threw his napkin at his youngest brother.

"Mater," said Thalen, annoyed that at the moment when his whole life was at stake his brothers were clowning around, "Teta says she'll pay for it, and there's nothing else in the whole of Ennea Món that would satisfy my craving."

"Indy," said his aunt Norling, "let the boy follow his dreams."

The room fell silent for a moment. Even Harthen kept still and held his breath.

"We-ll, I can't see that trying out this Scoláiríum place would do Middle any actual harm," said Thalen's mother.

Pater tapped his pipe against the table edge to make it draw better. "But Thalen, you must not disappoint us now. We expect you home for every fest."

The next few weeks overflowed with the preparations, but his mother and brother managed all the details so the arrangements went smoothly. His teachers at the upper academy sent a letter to commend him, and a reply came that Thalen was allowed to sit for the entrance exam in a moon. Thalen had outgrown his clothes, so new ones had to be tailored. He packed and repacked one of Norling's old travel cases and a rucksack.

The night before he left, his brothers gave him leave-taking presents. Hake had bought him his first neck drape, the long scarf that was a sign of maturity amongst Free States men. Neck drapes had started as useful articles of clothing amongst laborers, who still wore long white strips of muslin to wipe sweat, cover their mouths against dust, or knot into impromptu bags. But Free State weavers had turned the garment into a key and stylish accessory.

"Do you like it?" asked Hake. "I want you to know that you're the equal of any nobleman's son."

"It's so handsome," said Thalen, rubbing the gauzy fabric.

"The shop had a nice brown one too, but Mater said to get the blue to match your eyes, and I think she was right," said Hake, pleased.

Harthen handed Thalen a small box. Inside sat a pipe Harthen had carved out of maple. On one side of the bowl he had etched a perfect bird and on the other a cluster of stars. Thalen didn't smoke, but he was touched to know that Harthen had been listening to his questions about natural phenomena. Pater bristled when he examined the fine craftsmanship; he started fuming again that Harthen's real talents would be wasted in the cavalry.

One more present remained to be unwrapped. Norling gave him the flute they had played together for many years. Speechless, Thalen hugged her close.

Pater invited just Thalen to accompany him to the local tavern, the Weighted Scale. After the server had brought them their mugs of hard cider, he passed several coins across the scarred tabletop.

"I want you to have some spending money, Middle."

"Thank you, Pater," answered Thalen, putting the coins away carefully.

"Having money in your purse makes a man feel secure and stand tall. The only other thing I can give you, Son, is a bit of advice my father gave me when I was starting out with my pots: always look people in the eye. You learn who to trust and who is shifty. And the people you are in business with will learn to trust you. Course I'm talking about suppliers and customers and workers, not an upper, upper academy, but I imagine people are people the world over."

"I don't know what purse to put that advice in, but I will keep it safe," Thalen replied.

Hartling nodded with a grin, and they finished their cider in companionable silence.

On the day of the journey, Thalen woke up even before his mater. Norling gave them a packet of food wrapped in paper and tied in string for the journey. Mater dressed in her fancy gown and a hat with cloth flowers around the brim. Thalen thought she looked young and pretty. They took a Long Roads Cart from Sutterdam to Trout Landing, the station for the ferry that crossed the broad Clear Lake. The trip across the lake lasted half a day, so they relaxed in the sun and fed breadcrumbs to the lake's fish. Jerinda chatted with other travelers while Thalen studied the patterns of the water ripples.

*Why do some fish live in salt water and others in fresh water? Why is Clear Lake so clear? What stone lies on the bottom of it? Why do some ripples flow one way and some another? How long has Clear Lake been here?*

About midway across the lake, seasoned passengers pointed out a special sight: on a hilltop dominating the northwest shore one could just make out a jumble of pillars and rocks.

"What is that?" Mother asked.

One of the ferrymen responded, "That there's where the Castle of the Kings stood. Long ago, them Kings and their followers lived up there, with the lake as their view from their front balcony. During the Bloody Revolution, ya know, it was sacked."

On the far shore, coaches waited to take passengers to various destinations. Mater and Thalen found the right vehicle for Latham.

By the time they arrived, they were bone-weary and the streets beyond the carriage stop yawned pitch-dark. With a pickiness that exasperated and embarrassed her son, Jerinda declined the inn the coachman recommended because she thought it wasn't clean enough, but after stumbling over rough cobblestones and waking up cranky landlords, she eventually found a lodging that suited her.

In the morning Thalen set off to find his exam site. His mother decided she would visit merchants and chat with them about Sutterdam Pottery's wares.

The Scoláiríum itself was easy to find, and no one challenged Thalen as he walked through the gate onto tidy grounds where stone buildings stood arranged in a circle. Thalen found it odd that their rooftops were painted in a pattern of alternating black and white. An old porter led Thalen to a room where four other would-be entrants also gathered—two other young men and two young women, all more fashionably garbed than he, even though he wore his blue neck drape. Thalen, overcome with shyness, could hardly summon up polite words of greeting.

Thalen found the exams on Logic, Geography, Nature, and History quite easy. He struggled with the one on the Arts of Beauty (and silently blessed Norling for teaching him music and his father for what he had picked up about ceramics). Ancient Languages Thalen knew nothing whatsoever about; it made sense that different countries had developed their own distinctive speech before trade and travel had led to the development of the shared tongue, but his academy had not exposed him to this topic. Thalen left that part of the exam blank, wondering if that might preclude his entrance as he snuck out of the room where the other candidates were still furiously writing away.

When he joined his mother at the Quill and Ink Inn for a hearty supper of pigeon pie, however, he assured her he had found the test manageable. She was in a good mood because she had enjoyed her day in Latham.

"It's just a small town, Thalen, mostly set up to serve the Scoláiríum," she said. "There's one wineshop that wants jugs, and the inns ordered ewers and bowls. But I had fine chats with friendly people." She had already spent the money that these commissions would bring in by picking up little presents for his brothers and a fine comb for Norling.

*If I've failed the exam, I will work at the Scoláiríum or here in town as a servant while I study up on these languages.*

The next morning Thalen told her she could safely leave him, which she did, after filling him with warnings and advice.

Thalen didn't know whether to go out or stay in his inn. Finding a book, *Historic Sites of the Free States and What Transpired Therein,* on a shelf in the parlor, he sat down with his long legs stretched out across a braided rag rug. The next thing he knew it was midmeal time, and Thalen took his book into the tavern area to keep him company. In the early afternoon, the porter came to find him.

"Rector wants to see ya," the man said, jerking his head in the direction of the Scoláiríum.

Thalen followed him to Scholars' House, a grand marble building. The porter led him to a hard bench outside a chamber and told him to sit. One of the girls from yesterday—the thin, pretty one with multiple silver rings and bracelets—sat there too. They acknowledged one another warily.

The girl had brought a book in her bag. Thalen wished he had been so foresighted. After an anxious wait long enough for Thalen to count the white marble tiles in every direction and study the gray-and-tan striations in each of them, the door opened.

The rector turned out to be a woman of middle age, with dark ringlets, dressed in an orange-and-white-striped skirt under a black doublet. She also wore colorful earbobs of starfish painted orange. Her jolly smile warmed a rotund face.

"We'll start with you, Thalen. Come in, come in," she said. "I am Rector Meakey." He entered her spacious chambers and sat across from her cluttered desk.

"Umm, umm," she said, looking at papers in front of her. "Thalen of Sut-ter-dam. Son of a potter. Did you know that you got perfect scores on four of our exams?"

Thalen did not know that and had no idea what to say to this surprising information, so he kept silent.

"Sutterdam Academy is not really first-class," she continued confidingly. "Hasn't been for years. So do you mind telling me how you did it?"

"I don't know, Madam Rector. I just knew the answers?"

"But *how* did you know the answers?"

"Well, for Geography, I just see the map in my mind and draw in the names of the cities and countries."

"So you memorized maps of the known world. And for History?"

"I've read as many books as I could find on history. So for each of the questions I consulted the relevant book."

"Consulted?" Meakey frowned at him. "And for Logic?"

"Well, the questions were pretty simple, don't you think? I mean, there was only one rational way to consider each problem."

"I do not know that, Thalen. *Logic* would tell me that an artisan's son with middling schooling should not perform so well on our Scoláiríum exams. But you can't have cheated, because we drew up the tests just the night before! Hmm. Let's try a little experiment on you, shall we?" She started madly sorting through her books.

Thalen had bristled at the suggestion of cheating and the slurs on his background, but he gathered she was not trying to give offense, but rather studying him as if he were an unusual specimen.

"Help me find Systium's *Whale Migration Routes,* won't you?" she asked. "It has a gray cover."

Thalen spotted it under a jawbone as big as his arm.

"Ah, good. Now you cannot possibly have seen this before, because I have the only copy." She stared off into space absently. "Systium was one of *my* tutors, so many years ago. Rather nasty man, prone to making students cry, myself included I'm afraid, but what a magnificent work of scholarship! Does that make up for his personal deficits? Now *there's* a question to ponder, but not right now.

"Right now, I would like you to look at this map of the whales' journeys for a moment." She opened the book to a page and allowed Thalen to gaze at it for half a minute. Then she took the book back and paged to a list of the 187 known bones in a narwhal specimen. She let Thalen look at that page for half a minute too. Then she asked him to write down what he remembered from both pages. Thalen did as he was bid.

"Ah-ha! A perfect memory!" said Rector Meakey. "That *is* useful for a scholar. That's how you 'consulted' history books."

"May I ask a question, Rector? Why do the whales follow that exact route? And how do narwhals' anatomy differ from that of other whales?"

"You've asked three questions," she replied, and they were off on the subject of whales, pulling out more books and drawing pictures on the floor with chalk. From whales somehow they moved on to porpoises.

After a while Thalen heard a rap on the door. "Madam Rector," said a new servant in the tone of a parent chiding a wayward child, "another applicant has been waiting in the hallway all afternoon. Shall I send her home for the night?"

"Oh dear me. How very, very rude of us! Thalen, you never should have let this happen. Send her in; send her in. What's her name?" Rector Meakey clapped a chalky hand to her forehead. "Ah, um. That's right—Gustie."

Gustie walked in as Thalen was attempting to rub away the chalk drawings with a rag. Her expression conveyed both annoyance and amusement.

"Ah, Gustie of Weaverton! How wonderfully gracious of you to wait for us! Really, you've been most kind. Now don't you ask me about porpoises, or we will all miss our dinner! You two have been accepted. You start tomorrow. One of our older students will fill you in about the library, student lodgings, and so on and so forth."

Thalen almost asked the rector about his poor showing on Ancient Languages, but thought better of it.

The rector walked to the door to call out to the servant, "Whom should we assign to be their mentor?"

The servant answered, "Quinith, Madam. You have said that 'Quinith is simply a genius at acclimating new students.'"

"So right. I did. Now." She clapped her hand to her head again, leaving more chalk dust fingerprints. "I really must dash away. I just remembered that I have a whole gaggle of students running an experiment, and if I don't supervise, the whole thing will go awry.

"Welcome, Gustie; welcome, Thalen! Here. Our students each get these wristbands. I promise we will talk about seals another day." She ran off.

Thalen joyously fastened on a wristband of braided white-and-black leather, but he felt terrible about Gustie's long wait.

"I'm sorry," he said. "We got to talking, and she knows so many things, and I forgot about you. May I buy your supper to apologize?"

"I'm not sure it's *your* fault," she said. "The rector seems somewhat . . . addlepated."

"She's rather enthusiastic, that's for sure," said Thalen, marveling that this brand-new student would be so blunt about a rector.

"Waiting around always makes me hungry," replied Gustie. "Dinner would be lovely."

So they walked back together toward Latham's taverns. Thalen asked polite questions: Gustie turned out to be a wealthy silversmith's eldest daughter, obviously accustomed to speaking her mind, which was evident when she complained to Thalen, a very recent acquaintance, about her stepmother's ability to "pop out a baby every year." Thalen liked her best when she spoke about her fascination with Ancient Languages; then her face softened and her manner became more patient. Thalen asked her to explain her interest to him; she complied over a celebration dinner of ham and stewed greens at the Readers Tavern that ate up most of Thalen's pocket coin.

"But all the Ancient Languages have now been replaced by the Common Tongue, right?" asked Thalen.

"Not completely. If you know where to look, you will find that we still use some words. Take the term 'Ennea Món'—what does it signify?

"Ennea Món is what we call our known world."

"Yes, but the term comes from Ancient Lorther and Ancient Rorther: literally it translates as 'the World of the Nine.'"

"You mean eight, don't you? Religious people count *eight* Spirits."

"Well, maybe long ago people confused 'ennea' and 'eight.' But you're missing the point—terms you think stem from the Common Tongue actually have older roots."

The next morning, a young man inquired for Thalen. Quinith was slightly pudgy, but his well-tailored clothes downplayed those pounds. His manner was so friendly and organized, he reminded Thalen of his brother Hake. They picked up Gustie on the way to campus. Quinith explained that at the Scoláiríum pupils did not attend classes; instead they chose subjects they wanted to read and scholars to guide them.

"You are interested in sea life, I hear," Quinith said to Thalen, trying to control the smile that tugged at his lips.

"Not particularly. Or not exclusively—we just got to talking."

"The tutors here are so absorbed in their fields they tend to sweep students along in their wake," Quinith replied. He counseled the newcomers to think hard about their own interests; he himself studied music. He showed them their dormitories and arranged for their trunks to be fetched. He guided them to the refectory where they would take their meals.

"Tell me, Quinith," Gustie said, "why do we wear these wrist-bands?"

"White stands for emptiness, for ignorance, and black symbol-izes fullness and knowledge. We braid the strands together and wear them on our wrists as a constant reminder: 'The more you learn, the more you discover your infinite ignorance.' The tutors wear them too."

He led them to the middle of the grounds, where a marble build-ing stood. "And that's why the scholars named this the 'Library of Humility,' so that we all keep our lack of knowledge in mind."

Inside, shelves filled with books of all sizes and bindings reached from floor to ceiling. Students were permitted in the building at all hours. Lanterns, chairs, and tables had been placed in various nooks. Students were reading, surrounded by piles of books, with quills behind their ears or on the tables. Thalen pulled out volumes at random. *Rortherrod Stories and Legends. The Magic of the Rortherrod Kings.* He rubbed the book covers reverently.

"You've got it bad," said Gustie.

"Got what?" Thalen asked.

"Epistemophilia," she answered, drawing out each syllable. "Love of learning. It comes from Ancient Dorian."

"There's a word for this yearning?" Thalen grinned. He turned to Quinith, "How do you decide which field to concentrate in?"

"Most students browse for a while," Quinith answered. "Then you find that you keep coming back to the same stacks, that those books call to you in a special way. I've heard it said that students don't choose their subjects; the subjects choose us."

# 30

*Oromondo*

The first time Sumroth had a man dismembered and burned, he almost vomited.

His corps of Protectors patrolled the Obsidian Mountains between Sixcaster and Sevencaster, watching for infiltrators and securing the camps where the miners pulled lead, zinc, gold, and gems out of seams of rock.

A shepherd from Alpetar, the country on their southern flank, had chased a wayward billy goat at least a league into Oromondo by the time Sumroth's patrol captured him.

"Sir," said the ember holding the man's arm. "What should we do with this prisoner?"

"Please," the Alpie begged. "Please. I'll be more careful in the future. I meant no harm. He's one of my prize goats, and I didn't want to lose him. But if you let me go, I'll never cross the border again!" He looked from one captor to another and to Sumroth. "I have a family! You can't blame me! You can't harm them too!"

The man, weaponless, with a slim build and the white-yellow hair that was common along the border of the two countries, obviously posed no threat. Yet Sumroth felt his soldiers regarding him, weighing his steadfastness and intestinal fortitude.

"We have a penalty for invaders," said Sumroth. "And to be a Protector is to follow orders." He motioned to his men.

His men cut off the man's arms and then his legs. (The terrified screams stopped after the arms—either from blood loss or shock.) The crumpled figure lay on the ground; Sumroth himself severed the head with his great sword. They built a fire around the bloody chunks, though they had difficulty getting it to catch. The smell of burning flesh clogged his nose and raised his bile so Sumroth had to stride in the direction of fresher air.

But he noticed that his men's salutes became crisper and they jumped faster when he gave an order. They feared him now, in a way they hadn't before.

Sumroth found it a horror to kill citizens; in his heart he knew the Magi were paranoid and dangerous. But to protect himself he tried to grow a callus over his conscience. When his corps rode through a village, if the cattle breeders told him that their cattle sickened, he dismembered the local animal tender. If a teacher was denounced for questioning the Magi, Sumroth hid his disgust at the townsfolk's bloodlust. He had made his choices; now he had to see them through. His men followed his lead without demur.

"Duty! Strength! The Eight! The Power of the Eight! Long will Their Flames burn and conquer. Duty! Strength! The Eight! The Power of the Eight! Long will Their Flames burn and conquer." He joined the chants loudly. The louder he chanted, the more he could partition to the side any internal doubts.

But after he had proven his brutality and obedience to the Magi, he found that he had room to make exceptions.

One town in a valley below a mine had suffered a rash of plagues. The people's fears eventually clustered on a widow woman, for no discernible reason other than because she and her children had remained healthy.

"She must be a witch! A traitor to the Land!" shouted a group of frenzied villagers one day as they dragged the trussed woman in front of him in the town square that held the village well.

"Sistern, how do you explain that your neighbors sicken but you and yours do not?" Sumroth asked in front of the hushed mob.

"Protector, sir, I hardly know. I pray nightly to the Eight, but so do my pious neighbors. Our farm sits a little away from the village, on the rise over that way. Could it be that the vision of FireMount in the distance sends a blessed aura?"

"Kill the witch!" shouted someone from the crowd.

"My cows have all died!" yelled someone else.

The woman looked up at him pleadingly. "I have three healthy children dependent upon my care."

Sumroth made a decision. "Citizens, in your fear you have chosen the wrong target," he called out. "This woman is innocent of any wrongdoing. You will leave her and her family in peace, or *you* will pay the penalty."

The woman fell to her knees and tried to kiss his hand. He put his hand on her head briefly, feeling the self-satisfaction of mercy. He had his men cut her bonds and escort her home. And he told the mayor—in graphic terms—what would happen to her if the woman met with harm.

The reaction of his men interested Sumroth more than the sensibilities of the hamlet. He had made no friendships or bonds among his underlings because he continually worried a friend would sniff out his hidden disability—his inability to distinguish faces and tell people apart. So he made it a practice in his commands always to refer to his soldiers by rank: "Ember," "First-Flamer," "Second-Flamer," and so on, not because he inherently craved formality, but because he was able to count tattoos. Since he felt isolated from his men, he was continually preoccupied by any indications about morale.

The night he pardoned the young mother, when he entered the officers' meal tent to partake of their frugal rations the men stood as usual, and then they broke into sustained cheering and applause. His men had grown accustomed to fear; what they yearned for most was clemency. Sumroth wondered if some of the other soldiers harbored secret doubts about these executions, but of course it was impossible for him to probe their feelings.

A messenger from Femturan caught up to his company outside the village. Sumroth opened the dispatch anxiously, fearing that somehow his superiors had already heard of his using his discretion and pardoning the woman.

But the message relayed that his company had been given the honor of escorting four Magi on a visit to Pexlia. Of course they would go overland: an ocean voyage might have been quicker, but—even setting aside the unnavigability of Femturan harbor— the Magi never put themselves in the care of Lautan, Spirit of the Sea. Sumroth's orders instructed him to rendezvous at the pass near Sevencaster. The message did not tell him why the Magi were leaving the Land, and it was not his place to ask. His task was to lead the caravan safely south through the Trade Corridor crossing Alpetar to Pexlia and back again. The messenger also brought news that the Octagon had promoted Sumroth another level.

He sent the messenger back to Femturan with a long letter for his wife and turned toward the garrison town. The caravan of four Magi in palanquins, plus numerous servants and supplies, appeared after a wait of six days.

*Four Magi entrusted to my care!* They wore tabards of golden silk with their numbers encrusted with jewels. They each traveled in a black palanquin, carried by porters who were fed triple rations.

Because horses had proven particularly sensitive to the blights that affected the Land, Sumroth personally surveyed all the horses in the caravan. He didn't want the trip to get bogged down because of sick animals.

Each morning of the journey started with a Magi leading the entire caravan in prayer. Eyes glowing red with ardor, Magi Three spoke with particular fervor. He usually led the worship, though sometimes Four, Seven, or Eight ascended the traveling podium. The prayers inspired devotion; Sumroth's soul burned in their warmth. And he made damn sure that his soldiers cheered their throats hoarse and slammed their fists red.

The Trade Corridor, created as part of the settlement of the War of the Priests, stretched two leagues wide; it led through Alpetar to the port city, Ixtulpus, in Pexlia, which Oromondo now used as its primary nexus for trade. As they traveled they glimpsed no Alpies; those weak herders kept their distance from Sumroth's soldiers.

The sun shone bright, but not too hot. The Alpetar foothills resembled the foothills on the Oromondian side, rocky and steep, but once the caravan reached lower, flatter terrain, Sumroth inspected his surroundings with interest. The land rolled into the distance a lush green; the trees and foliage looked healthier. In the distance he could see fields of crops and hear the lowing of cattle. Sumroth envied the fecund surroundings.

*Someday soon we will take this bounty to feed our hungry people.*

A runner summoned Sumroth to the palanquin of Magi Eight. Like all of the Magi, her black palanquin glittered with gems. When he took off his helmet and bowed his head, she pushed aside the red curtains to converse.

"Your Divinity, you sent for me?" She sat in the dark shadow of the conveyance. All Sumroth could see were her eyes, a hint of red. Feathers of fear ran up and down his spine, but he forced himself to hide his trepidation.

"I did. We need to arrive at Ixtulpus in two moons. Are we traveling quickly enough?"

"In that case, we need to pick up the pace. And spend fewer morning hours in prayer." Sumroth cursed himself for the last sentence, which he had blurted out without thinking. It might be his death sentence. But this morning the group had prayed for nearly two hours before breaking camp, hours that could have been used to cover ground.

"I will see to it," was all Eight replied.

"And I will see to the pace, Your Divinity."

"Fire-starter, if our mission succeeds, you will be raised to the rank of fire-stormer. You will be given six flames."

"I am not worthy of such a distinction."

"We'll see," replied the Magi.

"What I would like most," Sumroth heard himself say, "is extra time with my wife."

"We'll see," said the Magi again.

Sumroth pulled his whip out and lashed her porters. "Double time."

# 31

## Wyndton

In the rural valley in the middle of Androvale, life followed the seasons without being affected by outside disruptions. News of distant places was accepted on par with a thunderstorm seen off in the distance—a far-off disturbance that would blow over before it touched them.

A coarse paper broadsheet was printed in Gulltown, the most populous city of the duchy, and whenever townsfolk visited they would return with a copy to share out amongst their neighbors. Wilim felt that as a peacekeeper he was duty bound to keep up with events. Stahlia was especially interested in anything having to do with royal history or court because these themes filled her tapestries. Thus, their household usually got its turn with a sheet before it got smudged or tattered by too many hands.

Through broadsheets they had learned of Queen Cressa's mustering the Allied Fleet; of the other Weir boats being sent by her loyal regent to join the fight; of King Rikil of Lortherrod lending his brother and major warships, and King Kentros of Rortherrod sending an admiral and twelve more ships. The paper reported on Duke Naven's trip to Gulltown to see off their own *Sea Gull,* a small vessel crewed by local boys. The whole family eagerly awaited more news of the adventures of *Sea Gull* and the Allied Fleet's victories against the Pellish.

By the time Wren had twelve summers (and Percia thirteen), she found herself relatively settled in the routine of home life with Teta Stahlia and Teto Wilim. Her role-playing appeared to have fooled the community; privately Wren thought she had considerable acting talent, and sometimes she toyed with the fancy of running away to join a troupe of players.

The only person who regarded Wren with anything approaching suspicion was Stahlia. Wren insisted both on keeping her hair short and on wearing split skirts (suitable for jumping on a horse at any moment), and her foster mother found such choices odd and unbefitting a young woman. After a few heated occasions when she'd defied Stahlia and yelled, "You're not my real mother!" Wren learned to bridle her tongue. Once Wilim had sent her to fetch Stahlia in the Church of the Waters, and she'd overheard Sister Nellsapeta and Stahlia conversing.

"I imagine Nargis brought you Wren," said Nellsapeta, "because she knew you would be a good mother to a difficult child. I've seen her over these years; she's a strange child—what with her shyness yet those eyes that see everything. I can't think of another mother who would do a better job with her. Those Donigills, they're queer folk."

Stahlia's voice answered. "When I try to talk to Wilim he says something like, 'You have to remember she grew up all alone in Anders Wood; she's a timid, wild creature.' Except ofttimes she's not timid; underneath that shyness you hit steel."

Nellsapeta laughed. "You've got steel in you, Stahlia; that's why you recognize it in her."

Wren tiptoed away, vowing to stay more on her guard with her foster mother.

Fortunately, the whole family was distracted: before Winter Fest Stahlia gave birth to a healthy baby boy, Tilim. Tilim shared Stahlia's large eyes and light brown hair, though his locks stood up every

which way, as if licked by several extremely persistent cows. As dot-
ing older sisters, Percia and Wren cared for him whenever Stahlia
worked at her loom.

Wren now understood that Stahlia's craft kept the family comparatively well-off for Wyndton. Duke Naven believed in paying in
compliments rather than coin, so Wilim's salary barely covered their
food. Farmers' children fared poorly during the years when harvests
fell scant; many days they had only biscuits made of ground acorns
to eat, and then they had a hard time concentrating on their lessons.
And the town's merchants depended on the farming families having
coin to spend. Stahlia's tapestries, which pleased the nobles and rich
merchants in the Eastern Duchies, brought in commissions that
spared the family from the scarcity so many of their neighbors endured.

Wren learned little from the teachers in her school, but a lot
about aspects of rural life. To supplement her schooling Wren read
her teta's books on Weir lore.

The books taught her that the duchy system had been established
in the era of Crylinda the Fertile. Most Weir queens gave birth to
only one child: the daughter and heir. But Crylinda had borne not
only an heir, but also seven sons. This was during a time when the
central government struggled to keep order throughout the length
and breadth of the realm. So when the boys came of age, Crylinda
named them dukes and gave them all territories to administer. Over
hundreds of years, four sons of later queens had joined the original
seven to make eleven duchies, eight in the west and three across the
Bay of Cinda.

This history also explained the small tapestry hanging in her
teta's bedroom, picturing a queen, a young blue-haired princella,
and seven naked amber-haired baby boys crawling around their feet.
Wren pointed out to Stahlia that the seven boys could not all have
been babies at the same time. Stahlia, snuggling her own precious
newling, laughed and answered, "Artistic license."

Wren asked Wilim to borrow books from Duke Naven's library
but made him swear to say his wife asked for them, not his adopted

daughter. Wren never wanted to call attention to herself, especially not with any of the nobility. Wilim complied without questioning her whim.

· Wren worked alone on another part of her education—her Talent. Whenever she found solitude she sought to discover its possibilities and limits. So far, she could only talk to one beast at a time, and the connection became stronger if she could touch the animal. However, she didn't need physical contact with birds, and many seemed eager to converse if she approached. Most animals "recognized" her, but some refused to acknowledge her as royalty, and these wouldn't mind her. For instance, the raccoons wouldn't leave the cottage's chickens alone just on her say-so; she had had to threaten she'd lead Wilim to their tree hollow. And so far she couldn't converse with anything that lived in water.

Meanwhile, Percia had developed her own magical ability. Ever since the Nargis Fountain had healed her leg, Percia had fallen in love with dancing. She loved the music; she loved to make her skirts twirl around; she loved to learn the steps; and she loved the excitement. She relished her own natural grace and skill. The local dancing master asked Percie to train with the older children she was teaching to perform in festivals. The whole family traveled over to Glynton for Summer Solstice Fest to watch Percie perform. As a jewel shines in a setting, so she shone in the midst of her fellow dancers.

A dancing master from Gulltown recognized Percia's grace and skill. She approached Teta Stahlia about having Percia come to study with the Gulltown Dancers. Wilim and Stahlia promised to consider the opportunity.

Percia begged to go, though her parents felt loath for her to leave their care. Over several days, they worked out an arrangement: Percia would travel to Gulltown on the milk wagon at the beginning of the week, board with the family of a peacekeeper Wilim knew, and return on the post wagon four days later. Wilim would take her to the city after Harvest Fest.

Percia's upcoming absences would affect them all, but Wren would suffer the most. Wren still used Percia as her emotional mainstay and her mouthpiece for most of her requests. When Percia left, Wren would be both lonely and more exposed. Syrup and Gili had little to offer her other than love. And Speckles provided scant comfort; when she moped about the arrangement, he responded unsympathetically, *All fledglings must fly.*

Fortunately, a newcomer showed up in Wyndton that summer. Like Wren, Lemle was an outsider; his parents had died the previous year of the pox, and he came to live with his uncle, a veteran of the War of the Priests, on the outskirts of Anders Wood. He was a slender boy with a pretty face, and the other children shunned him, jeering that he acted like a girl.

Wren had seen him around the small village, but their friendship started one hot summer afternoon when she took Tilim to splash in Wyndton Creek.

Wren rolled her breeches up to mid-thigh, took off all the babe's clothes, and sat him chest-deep in the transparent water in the shallow nook where the stream was warm and smooth sand created a tiny beach. Tilim cooed and splashed while Wren talked baby talk to him and trickled drops onto his head. Light filtered through the trees and gleamed off the creek. Several ducks that had originally been startled by human interlopers went back to bobbing upside down. Wren dripped a handful of water over her own head and down her neck, relishing the relief from the muggy heat.

"Hullo," called Lemle, coming down the twisting path.

"Hey." Wren darted a quick glance in his direction, relieved that it was him and not someone else from the village.

"Do you mind if I sit here too?"

"We don't mind, do we, Tilim?"

On the bank, Lemle took off his shoes. He looked around himself and gathered and arranged a few small pieces of debris.

"What're you doing?" asked Wren.

"Making a toy for the babe. Look." He was clever with his long fingers: he had fashioned a little rattle out of a stick, a nutshell, some reeds, and some gravel. He shook it for Tilim, who crowed with delight.

"Thanks," said Wren. As Tilim smashed the rattle into the water, startled when the splash hit him in the face, she asked, "Do you have brothers and sisters?"

"Not anymore," he answered.

Wren let the silence alone. And in a moment, Lemle explained, "My aunt in Barston took them in."

Wren heard the unsaid completion of the sentence: *And she wouldn't take me.*

"I'm sorry," said Wren. "That stinks. That stinks so much."

"You're the one who's also lost her real family?" asked Lem, rolling up his trousers.

"Aye," said Wren, again addressing the baby, "and I was lucky to end up where I am, here with Tilly-dilly."

"And I was lucky to end up with my uncle. Though sometimes I have to remind myself." Lemle slipped into the creek, letting out a sigh of relief at the cool water.

"Me too," said Wren, with a crooked smile, daring to meet his face. "Living somewhere new—it takes time to adjust. Because in the new place you have to be someone new too."

"I hadn't thought of it that way." Lemle waded deeper for a few moments and then came back to play with Tilim with her. The baby shrieked with delight when Lemle pretended he was a fish, come to eat little baby toes.

"In the long evenings, the village boys play Water Sprout. Are you going to play with them?" Wren asked.

Lemle shook his head decisively.

After a while Wren asked, "Do you think Tilim's getting cold?"

"Could be."

"I'm going to take him out," she decided.

They sat together on the grassy bank, letting the sunshine dry the baby's tawny skin and the hems of their sleeves and rolled-up trousers. Tilim kept rubbing his face, so Wren picked him up against her chest and patted him the way she'd seen Stahlia soothe him. Lemle and she talked quietly over the drowsing babe—Wren found herself confessing to Lemle her dread of Percie leaving for Gulltown and realized he was a much more sympathetic listener than Speckles. She could tell that his hands were busy again, but he was keeping his handiwork, whatever it was, on the side away from her.

When they heard the shouts of other Wyndton children rushing to the creek after chores, without open acknowledgment they both knew they wanted to leave. As Wren rose to take the baby home, Lemle offered her a scrap of sacking on which he'd sketched a likeness of the wild iris blooming by the bank.

Wren relished the way Lem accepted her just as she was without asking prying questions about her quirks. When they had free time the two would often take long hikes to spots that became their special places, including a hilltop that provided a grand view of the valley; a meadow filled with wildflowers; and a hidden turn where Wyndton Creek pooled deep and green. Often they would share confidences, such as Lemle's worry about a gang of village toughs that called him names and gave him a shove whenever they crossed paths, or Wren's confused complaints about her family or town life. Sometimes they wouldn't talk at all, just tramp in silence, smelling the pines and listening to the birdcalls. If she needed to bring Tilim along, Lem was unfailingly patient and would offer to strap the babe around himself, even before Wren felt his weight as a burden.

School began again once grain harvesting concluded. Lem was in the same class as Wren and Percia, the last their under school offered. By age twelve or thirteen, village boys and girls went out to labor or apprentice, or—if their families were rich and had ambitions for their child to become a healer or a merchant—they might be sent to upper academy in a bigger town, like Glynton.

One afternoon in mid-autumn, a week before Percia was to leave, Lem was walking with the girls on the path toward their cottage, which was a tolerable way out of his own route, when six village boys, led by Ferl, accosted them.

"Scuttle on home, wenches, we need to have a chat with Lem here," said Ferl.

"I have no business with you," replied Lem, stretching his hands out.

"Ah, but we have business with you," said Alat, a big, dull boy with bad skin. "We saw you eying Ferl. We're gonna teach you a lesson. Percia, Wren, scoot along now!"

"No," said Wren. She didn't have to search for this courage; it was unthinkable that she would abandon her friend in this situation.

"We've warned you," said Ferl.

"Now hold on, boys," said Percia, assuming her father's reasonable manner. "You don't want to cause any trouble. Such a nice day; there's no need to be cross or unfriendly."

The boys paid no attention to Percia; Ferl spat on the ground and muttered dark curses under his breath. Wren whispered to her, "You've got to get help."

"I'll stay."

"No. You must go. Go now!" Moved by the note of command in Wren's voice, Percia sped off.

Wren pulled the small dagger she always wore on her belt. Lem picked up a long stick. By instinct they placed themselves back-to-back. The boys started by shouting insults at Lem. Then they picked up cow plops and earth clods and began throwing them. Wren and Lemle stuck together, moving slowly down the path, and dodged the missiles as they could.

"Score!" shouted one of the boys when he hit Lemle on the forehead with a cow plop.

*When I'm queen won't I teach you manners!*

Then the gang moved on to pebbles. When Nowltin struck Lem on the forehead with a large pebble, breaking the skin, the sight of the blood spurred them to closer contact. The ruffians began pushing and shoving.

"Beg pardon and mayhap we'll leave you alone," said Ferl. But instead of giving in, Lem lashed out with the bit of a branch in his hand, giving one of the crew a resounding whack.

"We'll teach you!" shouted someone, and the shoves became fists and kicks. Lem fought wildly until his stick broke. Wren used her knife with icy control: she did not want to kill anyone, so she poked fleshy places like buttocks and thighs.

Someone got behind her and wrapped his hands about her neck. Another boy grabbed her wrist and kept banging it against his knee until she dropped the dagger. The boy choking her let go once she opened her hand. So Wren whirled around and butted him in the belly as hard as could with her head tucked and felt triumph when he fell down with the wind knocked out of him. Then she jumped on another boy's back and bit his ear.

Despite their aggressive defense, neither Wren nor Lemle equaled their attackers in size or brawn, and six-to-two was a ratio they could not overcome. Soon, Lem rolled up in a ball on the ground, protecting himself from kicks, while Wren kept inserting herself between her friend and his attackers. The village boys repeatedly threw her off to the side, where she skidded on the rough ground on her hands and knees.

Out of nowhere, Gili dashed into the mêleé. Old Gili could not quite bring herself to bite anyone, but she barked up a storm and made angry little rushes, disrupting the attack.

Stahlia, right behind the dog, had torn down a hazel branch and began raining blows down on the boys. "Corburret, Alat, Ferl"—*switch, switch*—"you lay off that boy this minute"—*switch*—"do you mind me? If there is anything in this duchy"—*switch, switch*—"I cannot abide"—*switch, switch, switch*—"'tis a bully!"

Such was Stahlia's rage and authority that the boys broke and ran, leaving Lem moaning on the ground.

Stahlia took one look at him and turned to Percia, who stood a few paces behind her gaping and holding her side from a stitch.

"Percie, run to town and fetch Healer Goddard," said her mother, breathing hard. Then she put her arm under Lem's back and started walking him to their cottage. Wren followed behind, coughing, dizzy, and hurting, spitting blood from a cut lip and picking bits of cow dung off her face and out of her hair.

It seemed to take forever to reach their lane. Gili walked by her side.

*Little princess, one loves thee. Stand still and let one lick thy hurts.*

Stahlia seated Lem in a chair and hurried back to help Wren

the last thirty paces to the cottage. She pumped water and held rags to their various wounds. Lem's eyes looked unfocused, and he still made pitiful sounds.

After what seemed like forever, Goddard arrived on horseback, with Percia clinging on behind. He said nothing consoling or sympathetic, but he crossed straight to Lemle.

"His shoulder is out of place. Missus, stand behind him and hold your arms across his chest. Don't let him move now!" Goddard jerked Lemle's arm straight and to the side. With an audible pop it snapped back into its socket. Lem's moans ceased, and he gave Wren a weak nod. Peremptorily issuing orders about basins of water or getting him more light, Goddard sewed up the boy's deeper cuts and splinted his broken fingers.

"Your turn. Show me that wrist." Goddard's hands probing Wren's swelling wrist were not particularly gentle. "This is just a greenstick break; I'll splint it."

He also fixed a cooling poultice for the darkening bruises around her neck.

"Here, missus," he said to Stahlia, "this is tincture of willow bark. Put drops in their tisane. If you need me, I'll be at home or at the Arms. So far, you owe me three silvers."

"Wilim has our purse on him; he'll settle up when he comes home."

"See that he does," said Goddard as he departed.

Percia, who had watched all the doctoring with concern, asked, "Mama, where's Tilim?"

"Oh sweet Nargis! I forgot all about him! I left him in his cradle in the workshop. Lamb, will you get him while I see to these two?"

Stahlia washed the rest of the dirt and manure off Lem and Wren with hands as gentle as Goddard's had been brusque. She gave Wren something to bite on to make the cut on her lip clot and brewed her some willow bark tisane, but she encouraged Lem to down two stiff shots of brandy.

After creating a bed of quilts and cloaks on the floor of the front room, Stahlia helped Lem lie down. He drifted off into a half doze, though he called out and twitched as if he were still fighting. Percia cooked everyone porridge, changed and fed Tilim, and put the babe to bed. No one spoke much. Percia was struck dumb by the gravity of events; Wren's cut lip made speaking painful; Stahlia's mouth was tightened with temper.

Her foster daughter had never seen her so angry. Wren ached so, and now she was frightened of the consequences of the fight. Would one of the boys die? Would Lem be all right? Would the duke have to be informed? Would this lead to her secrets being discovered?

Too worried and uncomfortable to sit still, Wren fidgeted around the little room until Stahlia, sitting in a rocking chair, reached out her long arms to draw her into her lap. Since the first weeks of her arrival Wren always avoided physical touch from her foster parents; this evening, in her need, she allowed herself to relax. Stahlia gently stroked her forehead, rocked the chair, and sang a few of the stanzas from songs about Weir queens. Wren felt . . . comforted.

Night fell, yet Wilim had not returned from his ride (though he often traveled far and stayed out late). Speckles circled outside; these days Wren could hear him even when he flew farther away. The owl sent to her, *Man coming*. Soon they all heard a knock on the door, and Percie rushed to open it—there stood Lem's uncle. Though shrunken with age, Rooks held his body straight, like the soldier he once had been.

"My Lem has not come back from school, and I've started to worry. Have you seen him?"

Stahlia apologized for neglecting to send word, invited him in, and told him about what had happened. Lem slept on fitfully; his uncle sat down cross-legged on the floor beside him. All her teta had to offer him to eat was cold porridge and cold tisane, which must have shamed her and made her even angrier. They spoke together in low whispers.

Speckles sent, *Horse and man*. Rooks and Stahlia heard Syrup's hoofbeats and rushed outside to talk to Wilim. With a meaningful glance at her sister, Percia opened the front shutters so that she and Wren could eavesdrop on the angry conversation in the yard.

*—beaten to a bloody pulp!—brought up to be ruffians—thumbprints on her neck!—does no one any harm!—shoulder dislocated—Now, now, calm down!—What are you going to do?—teach those bastards a lesson they will never forget—calm down—let me do my job—this is my job.*

As the adults entered the cottage, the girls scampered away from the window. Teto Wilim came over to Wren and knelt down to her eye level. "Some ruckus today, I hear. Birdie, can I take a look at you?"

Stahlia handed him a lantern. Wilim pulled the poultice away from her neck and looked at her wrist. She showed him her lip and also pulled up her split skirt to display her triple-scraped knees, which were not her most serious injuries but the only body parts that were bloody and dramatic-looking. Wilim's face grew grave, but he ruffled her hair casually. Then he moved the lantern over to peer at Lem. He turned to Percia. "You weren't hurt? Who did this to them?" Percie told him the names of all the boys. He rose, walked out the door, and whipped plodding old Syrup into an actual gallop.

Teta decided that Percia and Wren must be off to bed now.

*Fat lot of help you were,* Wren told Gili when the dog jumped on the bed and tried to lick her scrapes again.

*Oh but one loves thee,* answered Gili. *Let one lick thy legs. Thy blood tastes so sweet, and one's tongue will heal thee.*

In the morning, Percia had already risen and Wren slept late. She crept painfully down the stairs, the dog breathing on her ankles. A fresh loaf of brown bread cooled on the table, and Teta was stirring a huge mash-up of eggs, cheese, leeks, and potatoes with herbs, which smelled so good.

Lem sat up against the window wall; he looked battered but himself. With his good arm he held Tilim in his lap; most of the babe's chubby fingers were in his mouth, and drool dripped down his hand to his wrist. Wilim was cheerfully talking to Rooks as they both drank out of mugs.

Rooks stood up when he saw Wren. "I wants to thank you,

missy. There's not many would have stayed and fought for my nev-vie. Much less a wee missy. Took a lot of guts. In your debt."

Wren was embarrassed. She lowered her glance and sidled over to Wilim.

"Teto, what happened last night?"

"I rode to each of them six houses. Got sass from Alat's father—that Halat's a mean son of a bitch—but the rest had the sense to look shamefaced. Though I am not sure if they were ashamed because of what their sons did, or because their lads got tore up so bad by Lem and you and that hazel switch." He grinned at Stahlia. "Some welts you raised there, Wife. Glad you never took a switch to me."

Stahlia flashed him a smile and snorted. "See that you mind me, then."

Wren asked, "Are they going to live?"

"Live? *Live?* Of course. Though most of them are going to have trouble sitting down for weeks! Nice sticking, Birdie! And they all owe fees to Goddard."

Wilim used two hands to pull her gently by the waist until she was directly in front of him, and then he raised her chin so he could look right in her face. "See here, Wren. I have dealt with gangs of rough lads before. This is how it works: they need to pay recom-pense. One will weed our vegetable patch for two moons. Another will cut firewood for us. Two families will bring Rooks produce and cut his firewood. They will pay the healer's bills for caring for you two. And apologies will be delivered all round. None of this wipes the slate clean, but recompense restores the balance in the commu-nity, and we can keep the neighborhood peaceful-like.

"*You're* not to fret about any of this. You just concentrate on heal-ing up. *I'll* make sure the debts get paid. That's my job."

Wren sidled over to Lem. "How are you?" she whispered.

"Not too bad. My shoulder pains me some though. You?"

"All my hurts trouble me too."

"You was brave to stick with me. You could have run away," Lem said.

Wren didn't understand the stress on her courage—it had felt instinctive to protect her pack.

"Wanna see my knees?" she asked, and Lemle *tsk*ed over her gory-looking scrapes.

After the delicious fastbreak they heard a knock on the door. Ferl, walking stiffly and with a stripe across his face, appeared in their doorway with his mother. He had two overflowing bouquets of mums from his mother's cutting garden. His mother pushed him forward. He gave one to Wren and one to Lem, muttering, "Please, forgive me," but he didn't really sound regretful.

The next knock came from Alat's older sister. She had brought sacks of barley candy and a curious, impudent look. And so it went all day—a steady stream of forced apologies awkwardly delivered and received.

Though he stayed with them gathering his strength for two days, Lemle healed without complications. Then his uncle took him home and Wren dared to hope that this trouble had passed without consequences.

Two weeks later, as she walked home from the village market with salt, a pork bone, and some rye flour she heard hoofbeats.

"Hold up there, gal," said a man who rode up behind Wren and passed her on the path, blocking her way with his horse. The man dismounted in front of her. His face looked familiar.

"I have to hurry home." Wren tried to brush by him, but he grabbed her by the shoulder in a tight grip.

"Why're you bothering me?" Wren asked, with a defiant jut of her chin.

"*You're* the Donigill brat Wilim's raising."

"*Peacekeeper* Wilim won't like you disturbing me. And he's the duke's man."

"Here's what I wants to know," said the man, drawing her close enough that she could smell his unwashed body and liquor breath. "Who are ya?"

"Look, you're Alat's father, aren't you? Haven't we had enough trouble? Just let me go, and I promise—"

"Shut up, brat." Halat shook her vigorously. "I gotta think. You came to the village as a lass. There's something not right about *you*."

"There's nothing not right about me."

"So say you. But fighting boys with a dagger; sticking up for that pervert! That's not right. Whatcha hiding?" He grabbed her by both arms and shook her until she bit her own still-sore lip.

Wren couldn't think of a story that would get her out of this fix; in fact she couldn't think at all. Her hands clenched tight. She had her little knife in her waistband, but with one arm in a splint and the other holding the market bag, it might as well have been on Daughter Moon.

"Here's what I think," Halat continued. "I take *you*. I take ya down to Gulltown and ask some fellas there some questions. I know people who knows people, people who work for that General Yurgn 'crost the bay. Mayhap they'll be happy to see ya. Mayhap they'll make it worth me while. At any rate, 'twill cause that arsehole Wilim a whole mess of fret."

When Wren remained silent, his face got darker. "You think I'm dumb! Wilim thinks he can lord it over me! I don't have the coin for those healer's fees! I'll snatch his little brat right from under his nose and he'll see. You could be the by-blow of some lord or duke. Tell me your secrets now, gal, or you'll feel the weight of my hand!"

"No wonder Alat turned out to be such a bully," she shouted, "with such a muck wit drunk for a father!" She started to wriggle and kick, trying to slip out of his clasp.

He swatted at her a few times; his backhands boxed her ears. As he dragged her toward his horse, Halat used one iron handhold to straighten her up before he landed a solid punch to her cheek that sent her sprawling into the dirt, losing both her market bag and her dagger. The blow sapped all the fight out of her. He hoisted her limp form into the saddle like a sack of grain and mounted behind her.

He turned the horse southwest. Wren gradually regained her senses, but she pretended she was still only semiconscious.

*Tell one how to help thee, little princess,* said Halat's mare, breaking into her thoughts.

*Oh horse! Would you help me? Can you throw him off?*

*He is cruel. One hates him. Now?*

*No, wait a bit. Let me pick the spot.*

"You dead, girl?" Halat said, poking her waist with a hard index finger. "I thought not," he said, when she recoiled. "You mind me now, or you'll get more of a licking."

Halat guided the old and swaybacked horse to skirt any dwellings. She couldn't let him get too far from home. They were coming up on Wyndton Creek, which gave Wren an idea.

"Please, can I put some water on my face? It pains me so. Can I get a drink?" She made her voice meek and frightened.

Halat halted, and Wren slipped off the mare. Her abductor threw down a water bag so it hit her in the chest. "Fill that too."

Wren soaked her cheek in the cold creek water and took a long drink. Halat sat relaxed in his seat, one hand slack on the pommel as he watched his captive and the other thoughtfully picking his teeth with his fingernail. Wren filled the water bag, praying to Nargis.

As she threw the water bag toward Halat, hoping he would reach for it with two hands, she sent to the mare, *Rear and dump him in the creek. Now!*

The horse reared up on her hind legs so abruptly that she threw Halat violently onto the rocks of the creek bed.

Wren didn't stop to watch; she was already running as fast as she could down the bank. Only when she realized that no footsteps or hooves pursued her and she stopped to catch her breath did she realize that just escaping from Halat wouldn't keep her safe.

*What about when he talks about something being wrong about me?*

She could easily imagine gossip and rumors spreading among Halat's drinking cronies.

*Do I have to go back? What if his legs are broken? What if his back is broken? I could push his face under the water, but he would see me— he would reach out and grab me—*

She compromised by deciding just to go back and check on his condition.

With great dread she circled around to the spot where the horse had thrown her rider. The mare munched the grass nearby; Halat lay on his back with his knees and boots out of the water and the rest of his body submerged. It didn't look as if he'd moved since the fall.

Wren approached with the wariness of a rabbit that suspects a snare is about to snap. Under a palm's depth of the clear stream water Halat's open eyes stared blankly. A dragonfly zoomed over his face and tiny fish nibbled at his hands. Waves of terror, nausea, and then elation buffeted Wren. She found a long stick and jabbed him with it. He didn't move. She poked him hard in the stomach.

*I think his neck broke,* she told the horse. *Or he drowned.*

*Good,* answered the mare, who had tufts of greenery sticking around her bit and caught in the sides of her bridle.

*What will you do?*

*One will feed here then head back to the stable. The woman does nay beat one.*

*Thank you for saving me.* Wren folded herself into the horse's chest and stroked her neck until she could stop shaking. *I thought that Nargis gave me this Talent so I would always be surrounded by those who knew me, but maybe she gave me this so animals would protect me.*

Then, marching quickly, she set off back toward the cottage. She'd have to find her market bag, and she'd have to think of what story to tell. As she walked she felt her cheek puffing up so big her eye closed. No fib about tripping was going to explain this injury.

By the time she got home it was so dark she stumbled on the familiar path.

"What happened to you? Where've you been? We was just about to go searching," Teta Stahlia started chastising before Wren got fully over the threshold.

Wren described Halat accosting her on the road, letting them believe that this attack was all spitefulness about the healer's fees.

"He hit me real hard, here on my cheek, and then rode off. Southward. It took me a long time to get up and get myself home."

Wilim smacked his hand on the table. "The bastard! As soon as it's light, I'm going to get Rooks to track him. That man has just been looking for trouble. Attacking a girl, a peacekeeper's daughter! This will earn him a spot in the duchy jail."

Stahlia pulled Wren over to the firelight to look closely at her shiner. "You'll be all right, my Birdie. Bet it hurts, but your teeth and eye are undamaged. Many a person's felt the weight of that idiot's fist." She made a warm compress for Wren's eye and tore up bread into her soup to make it easier to chew.

After school the next day Wren was cleaning the chickens' roosts in the stable when Wilim rode in the yard. She ducked out of sight so she could hear his conversation with Stahlia.

"Found the bastard in Wyndton Creek, south of Ackerty's fallow pasture. Dead. We can't figure out how he ended up in the water, but he must have been drunk to the gills. Broke his back and drowned. Thank the Waters we're shut of him and we don't have to worry about him coming after anyone."

The lasting consequence of the fight with the ruffians was that Wren was always welcome in Sergeant Rooks's dark shack with its dirt floor. Rooks and Lem didn't farm; they didn't even keep a vegetable garden. They didn't actually own their plot but rather squatted on it, trusting that no one would turn them in. They satisfied most of their needs by hunting and traded game and pelts for the rest.

Wren mulled over her situation for weeks. One day, visiting with Lem, when her wrist was healed and her eye socket only faintly black and green, she burst out to his uncle, "You were a scout in the army, weren't you?"

"Yeah," replied Sergeant Rooks.

"Would you teach me?"

"Teach you what?"

"How to be safe in the woods. How to track an enemy. How to hunt. How to fight," said Wren.

"Got a taste for it, have ya?" asked the old soldier.

"No! Well," Wren considered, "a little. But more I realized that sometimes fighting can be necessary."

"You don't cozen me, missy," said Rooks.

Wren's lungs forgot how to draw in air.

"'Wren,' my arse. 'Hawk' more likely."

Wren breathed again. "And would you do this for me without telling my teta and teto?"

"Our secret, you want?"

"Will you?" she pressed.

"No one has laid a hand on my Lem since that fight. And you took the brunt of Halat's wrath. Reckon I owe you.

"You're naught but a scrawny thing," he pronounced as he reached over and squeezed her arm muscle, "and you'd best have no dreams of becoming a fierce soldier. But I can show you a thing or two. Mind me now: no complaints and no tears allowed.

"And Lemle, you're going to join the gal. Easier to work with two sparring partners. You are who you are, so you need to know how to defend yourself."

# 32

## On the Gray Ocean

*Pray the Waters, I am so sick of war; Nargis, make war sick of us.*

*Sea Pearl,* with most of the Allied Fleet, pursued the remnants of the Pellish flotilla back toward Pexlia.

A captive had told Cressa two co-admirals commanded and controlled the Pellish fleet from two sister warships that served as headquarters. Ambrice had been searching for these for many moons, but they moved so often and hid so effectively that each lead evaporated into mist.

Finally, one midnight Don Jaret climbed aboard *Sea Pearl* with news: "Lord Ambrice! Lord Ambrice! We've found the Pellish admirals."

"Show me where!" Ambrice rushed Jaret into the chart room, as Cressa followed at their heels.

"Here, in the West Quadrant. What a sweet secret bay on the leeward side of Little Fern Isle! But Laret and I—we know it well. Laret led *Shark Racer* right to them! Instead of standing to fight, the Pellish turned tail. Prince Mikil says you're to follow at once! He's in pursuit!"

Ambrice weighed anchor and sent word to the rest of his fleet. If they could catch up with these vessels and sink them, the Allies would break the last might of the Pellish navy.

Now Ambrice joined Cressa on the forecastle, spyglass in hand. He stared at the dots in the distance a while.

"You are enjoying this," she accused her Lord of the Ships.

"Yes," he admitted. "Their admirals will want to get to harbor before we catch them. Now comes the test of seamanship: who can ride the winds and currents better? Who can put on the most sail without damaging the masts, hold the wheel in exactly the best line, and work his oarsmen so as to get the most out of vessel and men? This is a race. Not a game of cat and mouse, but a match of sailing skill."

"They're so far away I can hardly see them," said Cressa. "Aren't they winning?"

Her husband put down his glass and moved behind her, wrapping his arms around her waist and holding her back against his chest. "Ah, my heart. Early days. Nothing but open ocean and weather between here and Pexlia. The only thing I worry about is that under cover of a storm they might try to double back on us. Watch and wait."

"Waiting is hard. I have been waiting for years. Our daughter won't know us anymore."

"What a wonder it will be to see her; she'll be a young woman," mused Ambrice. "Though I doubt she's keen on frippery and needlepoint. She was my royal rascal before; she can't have changed that much. Surely her Talent has manifested by now. I wonder what Nargis has in store for her."

"If this is really the end, our next destination will be back to Cascada," said Cressa, pursuing her own train of thought. "I'll sail into harbor with all these Allies as escorts, with you and Mikil at my side, leading two thousand mariners, with news of a conclusive victory. We will be welcomed and I will clean house. A long-fought triumph—a costly triumph—but a triumph nevertheless. Only when I sit again on the Nargis Throne will I forgive myself for abandoning my country and our daughter."

Little by little the Weir ship gained on their foes. Now Cressa could see the warships clearly, even without a telescope. No other seamaster could equal Ambrice's skill, so the other ships of the Allied Fleet fell behind. Only Mikil's dromon, *Shark Racer,* kept neck and neck with *Sea Pearl*. Often her brother mouthed teasing words at Cressa, but she couldn't hear him over the seas and wind, no matter how much he mimed.

A middling gale blew up from the south. Ambrice worried so that the Pellish vessels might change course in the night that he sent a lookout aloft, even in the worst of the weather. Cressa thought he took risky chances with the lives of his men, but she held her tongue. This whole war had been a desperate gamble, and they had to win out.

The storm left the Allied ships scattered farther behind, nearly out of sight on the sparkling waters, but Ambrice had made the wind work for him and had gained ground on his competition. The only thing about the storm that disquieted him was that he had planned to transfer Cressa and her maids to a noncombatant vessel when they drew closer; now that option was foreclosed.

On the sixth week of the chase their lookouts spotted land: the coast of Pexlia stretched like an indistinct cloud on the water in the distance. First with a spyglass and then with her naked eyes, Cressa could read their quarries' names painted on their wooden bows, *Pexlia's Pride* and *Pexlia Unconquered*. She could see their sailors as little figures on deck. She wondered if they looked back at *Sea Pearl* and recognized their doom.

Ambrice spoke to each watch in turn and sent signals to *Shark Racer*. "Prepare for battle."

The wind shifted to spur them on. After so many weeks of waiting, the last hours thrilled and terrified the queen. She went inside to her stateroom.

"Arlettie, I need to change out of this dress. Peketta, fetch my sword and scabbard. And my dagger."

"You don't intend to fight yourself!" said Arlettie.

"Certainly not. I'm hapless with a sword. But it heartens the men to see their queen girded for battle."

Peketta pinned Cressa's hair up and out of the way. Cressa checked herself in a looking glass, satisfied that she conveyed a martial air. But she was loath to go back on deck for more anxious waiting.

"Fetch me something to eat, Peketta. Just anything. And get enough for you and Arlettie too."

The *Pearl*'s stores were low because it hadn't stopped to reprovision for a long time. Peketta came back with dry biscuits slathered with jam. Cressa forced herself to eat two pieces to keep up her strength. Arlettie, who had grown increasingly tense, couldn't eat a bite. Although Cressa had confidence in Ambrice's and Mikil's superior abilities, she too found herself wishing there had been a method of removing her women from the sight of a battle.

"Sit down, Arlettie, and try to eat," she coaxed her wardrobe maid.

"Oh Your Majesty," said Arlettie, "are you certain our soldiers will win the day?"

"Absolutely!"

"But what if Pellish board the ship? What if they break in here, looking for you?"

"Bar the door."

Arlettie examined the door bar and whispered to Peketta.

"What?" asked the queen.

"The door bar is not very thick. What if they kick it in?"

"Oh Arlettie, my dear. You are dwelling on things that will never happen. Here, take some brandy to settle your nerves."

"I wish I could hide somewhere," said Arlettie, wringing her hands.

Cressa looked around the stateroom, her gaze alighting on a trunk of clothes.

"Here, see if you fit inside here."

Arlettie climbed in. If she curled up like a frightened child, Peketta could close the lid.

"But you'll smother in there!" said Cressa. "Here, get out a moment while I cut some air holes." She used her dagger to chip away at the wood, glad that no soldier saw her misusing a fine weapon in such a manner, and glad that Nana didn't see her defacing a fine chest.

When she was certain that Arlettie would be able to breathe, she turned to her older maid. "What about you, Peketta? Are you all right?"

"Yes, Your Majesty. But perchance I could have just one more swig of brandy?"

"Of course. Drink as much as you like—then give the flask to Arlettie in her nest. Maybe she'll drink herself to sleep, and when she wakes, it'll all be over." Cressa squeezed Peketta's hands and patted Arlettie. "Time for me to go on deck to watch our great victory!"

Outside, she saw that through his own magic, Ambrice had closed the gap even more. The Pellish ships foundered in the waves, tantalizingly close, almost within arrow range. A few overeager men-at-arms on *Shark Racer* loosed their bows, but the pitch of the swell threw the shots too high or too low. Ambrice wouldn't let his archers loose; he ordered the mates to hold the men back. Ambrice's eyes shone with excitement.

The black-sailed ships threaded a narrow channel through rocky shallows and then resumed their southern route, paralleling the coastline. Cressa looked with interest at the high limestone cliffs of Pexlia—cliffs the maps indicated eventually gave way to the bowl-like harbor of Ixtulpus, a large city famed for shipbuilding. Fighting in the harbor would be bloody and costly of life. They needed to catch up with *Pride* and *Unconquered* before they could berth.

An arrow shot from an enemy vessel whizzed by her. Captain Clemçon and Sergeant Dariush, her constant shadows, yanked her behind the cover of the forecastle, pulling out the swords they kept so carefully oiled and sharpened.

Now Weir mariners took careful aim; skilled at compensating for the ship's movement, they hit their targets on the enemy's deck.

The battle had started.

Arrows struck flesh on both ships. *Sea Pearl* aimed for *Pride,* leaving *Unconquered* for Mikil. They closed distance every second, skimming the waves with sails so taut and oars pulling so hard that

Cressa feared that cloth or muscles would rip at any moment. Ambrice shouted orders; his sailors jumped to adjust. *Pearl* pulled even closer. Would Ambrice ram the ship's stern, or heel to for boarding? Cressa saw his sailors warming their arms up, twirling the ropes tied to grappling hooks.

A prickle of Anticipation—she often forgot that she too had Lorther blood—prompted Cressa to glance up. On the cliff top she noticed a large gathering of people. She had just time to murmur, "That's odd."

All of a sudden, *whoosh*! A fireball the size of an ox flew from the cliffs, striking *Shark Racer*. The missile tore through the ship as a dagger smashes through custard, crashing through the decks with a noise like thunder, setting the ship ablaze throughout its path.

Frozen in shock with her hands over her mouth, Cressa saw more fireballs rain down on the Lorther ship and then on her own, catching the vessels in a deadly barrage.

"It's a trap!!!" she screamed, but no one could hear her over the fearsome noise of impact, the roar of the fire, the cracks of big sails torn loose in a high wind, and the screams of terror.

With an incredible tearing, grinding sound, the *Pearl*'s high ram crashed into the stern of the Pellish vessel. The collision knocked everybody off their feet. The upward pitch of the deck made Dariush slide from her side, helplessly slipping into a jagged hole created by a fireball. With a shriek he vanished from sight.

Another fireball hit the prow of *Sea Pearl,* and the fire spread to the entangled *Pexlia's Pride.* Fighting now was out of the question, as men could not board either vessel through the wall of flames. Both ships listed to starboard, while the untended helm whirled wildly and untethered sails snapped in every direction in ragged freedom.

Face rigid in shock, Ambrice regained his feet and started to work his way back to her, yelling "Cressa! Cres-sa!" All of a sudden an arrowhead poked out of his chest; it had pierced him through from behind. In horror, she saw Ambrice fall to his knees, waver half a second, and then pitch forward onto his face. In that instant, Cressa knew for certain her husband was dead.

"No!" she screamed, her hands braced on her knees. "No! No! No!" The rending pain in her own heart engulfed her.

Despite the chaos, Clemçon had managed to stay beside her. Now he pulled at her arm, jabbering about boarding the ship's boat, yanking her back to a modicum of consciousness of her own peril.

Queen Cressa tried to stand straight on the listing, burning deck, finding it hard to balance. All around her casks and people—alive or dead—slithered on the slantwise surface like dishes on an up-ended table, crashing against obstacles in their path. A line from a sail hung near her; she reached up to clutch it for support.

"Your Majesty—Your Majesty!" Clemçon urged. "Come with me, this—"

The line she tugged on hung from a massive mainsail in flames; all of a sudden the fabric tore free from its upper spar, landing directly on top of her.

Cressa was enveloped inside a dirty white covering. Instantly, the air inside became unbearably hot. "Clemçon!" she shrieked. "Clemçon!!" But opening her mouth was a mistake, because the hot air seared her lungs. Her faithful captain did not—could not?—come to her aid. Frantically, she clawed at the cloth, but she couldn't dislodge it. Sparks spread from the sail to her clothing and her hair—*she was burning*—and she could not see for the swirling smoke. She sank to her knees, trying to crawl her way out from under the flaming blanket, banging into a piece of wood much too heavy for her to lift that held the material tight against the decking. Finally, she thought to pull her dagger and slice wildly, letting in cooler air; with a few more wild slashes she managed to make an opening wide enough to free herself of the engulfing sail.

Stumbling on the deck, she batted at her smoldering clothing; her legs, her upper chest, her back, and her hair were on fire. The ship listed at an even steeper angle. She could no longer see Clemçon—or anyone—in the cloud of black smoke. Were her clothes still burning? She had to quench the fire. She had no choice, no choice at all: she took a running leap off the deck, jumping for the sea, now lapping only a few paces below her.

*Lautan, the Munificent . . .*

She hit feetfirst. The impact, the salt water up her nose and sinuses, and the friction against her burns caused an explosion of agony that turned her vision black with jagged edges.

Cressa almost passed out. She reached for that oblivion—she longed for oblivion. But traitorously, her body broke the surface and she gasped for air in the cold seawater. At last, all the flames had been quenched, but they had done their damage.

*Lautan, show mercy; take me. I have nothing left.*

Waves dashed her face, and she spit out salt water. She'd dropped her dagger during the fall. Far-off, she heard a young sailor screaming in high-pitched terror, "Mama! Save me!"

*My mother would have recognized that this was a trap. I failed.*

"Here! Here!" shouted a male voice close by. "Swim to me!" A short distance in front of her a wooden debris field—and a man's wet head—bobbed up and down. Could it be Clemçon?

With the last of her strength, Cressa kicked the short distance to the caller, buffeted by disorganized waves splashing her in the face.

"Who is it?" she asked. The smoke, the water, her shock—her vision blurred.

"Prince Mikil," he said, and she recognized her brother's voice. "Who are *you*?"

He reached for her arm, and a layer of burned fabric and skin sloughed off, turning the water around them red.

"You're so burned! Where—where can I grab you?"

Kicking to hold herself upright, Cressa held her hands out of the water to show their conversion into black char.

"Don't. Touch," she croaked.

"The Royal Stone! *Shrimp,* is it you? *Cres-sa!*"

"Mikil—"

"Here, I'm passing you this bit of oar; use it for support," said Mikil. "Lean on it wherever you can."

"No." She ignored the debris and spit seawater out of her mouth.

"Or I'll grab your clothes. Tell me the best place. What about your waist?"

"No," she breathed.

"*Cres-sa!* Through the grace of Lautan, I'll save you. I swear it."

"Mikil. I'm in torment: body and heart. Every second."

A large splash hit them both in the face. Mikil dashed the water out of his eyes and met her pleading look.

"End me," she said, her voice hoarse. "Lautan won't let me drown."

"I can't do that. Of course you won't drown, and your injuries . . . We'll tend to them."

"You can't undo my failure. You can't bring Ambrice back—"

"No, but—"

"I am *queen;* don't make me beg." She put her last strength into her voice to make it audible over the noise of surf, the crackle of fire, and the far-off screams of dying men. "Mikil, I am your sister; don't make me suffer any longer."

A long moment elapsed as a wave lifted them both high and then dropped them both down.

*Will I have to use my Talent on my brother?*

"Forgive me," he muttered.

"Nothing to forgive." She raised what was left of her hand to her mouth in the opening of the Queen's Blessing and then felt his firm grip on the nape of her neck and the merciful, clean touch of metal at her throat.

# 33

## Cascada

The most unearthly, painful noise shattered a normal day in the palace.

Matwyck had just given his valet his orders; the man froze, asking, "What's that?"

But the Lord Regent was already sprinting toward the Throne Room, joining a stream of servants, guards, and gentry all headed in the same direction. They crowded into the lower level while still other palace residents appeared on the inner balconies that faced the Throne Room.

The catamounts were yowling. Their voices ranged from high-pitched screeches to low growls, varying without pattern in pitch and volume. Inside the cavernous hall the noise reverberated so deafeningly no one could talk. But everyone looked to the Dedication Fountain, because the Waters had *ceased flowing*. Only on the death of a queen did a Fountain break from its comforting, constant flow. In the city center, in the Courtyard of the Star, the Nargis Fountain must have stopped too.

Matwyck watched the Dedication Fountain in agony. This cessation had to be for Cressa. If the Waters stopped entirely, then the princella was dead too. With anxious hope he bit the inside of his cheek bloody staring at the dais. The Waters began to flow again, and the catamounts ceased their awful caterwauling.

Matwyck recollected himself enough to fall to one knee in a show of piety toward the old and new queens, a gesture all in the room followed. As he bent his head he pulled himself together.

*The important thing is that Cressa is dead. Tidings of her triumphs have become insufferable; even some of my confederates looked forward to her return. Now I can grieve her. The role of mourner-in-chief suits me. And my hands are completely clean of this deed.*

*As for the princella, she must be only . . . twelve. If I could only locate her, my original plan could be put into play.*

Matwyck rose and climbed onto the step to address the assembled multitude. He might have climbed higher, but he suspected that the mountain lions would not allow this trespass.

"What a wretched day this is for all of Weirandale! Our courageous Queen Cressa, taken from us after such a short reign! After all her bravery in lifting the scourge of the Pellish from the seas. I warned her; I told her that joining the fight would put her personhood in danger, but she was ever a touch stubborn. That trait gave her strength, but now has brought us everlasting sorrow.

"I will immediately commission the composition of a great lay about her heroic deeds. While we do not yet know the circumstances of her death, we can be certain that her ending has to have been as stirring as her life.

"The funerary feast will be one week from today.

"That is all I can say to you right now, my friends. I am quite . . . overcome."

A portly older woman (*Ah yes, the nursemaid!*) sobbed uncontrollably, and the freakish servant with a hole in his cheek had a hard time holding her up. Matwyck strode out of the Throne Room. He plumbed his feelings and found to his surprise that not all his grief was feigned. He remembered Cressa as a fresh-faced young woman, so eager to do well, so cowed by Catreena's long shadow. She had looked to him for guidance and been so keen to learn. He had felt touched by her trust and stirred into something like loyalty.

*When did my loyalty evaporate? Well, she grew stronger, that pliable sapling. As she took firmer hold of the reins of government, she came closer to sniffing out my various side deals and secrets.*

*And at the end, I just spotted my opportunity.*

Matwyck returned to his chambers and poured himself a full glass of wine. He raised it to Cressa's memory in salute and drank it down.

*I do so hope I will not have to kill your daughter.*

Prigent was the first of his associates to seek him out. Of course, Latlie's and Yurgn's age made it hard to stir themselves quickly, and Tenny would be paralyzed, wrestling with her conscience.

"Now what, Lord Regent?" asked Prigent. He was shaking, just a little.

"Now it becomes even more imperative that we find the princella. Folk—little people or gentry—like stability. Nothing breaks up stability like the death of a monarch. We need to find the girl, get her Dedicated, and put her on the throne while she is still easy to control."

"We have searched everywhere," said Prigent.

"Well, she lives," commented General Yurgn as he entered, "or the Fountains would have stopped completely, and if she is alive we can find her."

Latlie and Retzel showed up, waddling slowly together. How Matwyck wished they would die, so that he could surround himself with sharper young minds!

"Oh my poor queen," sobbed Latlie. "My poor Cressa. To die at thirty-six! I was a friend of her mother, you know. I do believe that Catreena would be so grieved to learn what has happened to her daughter. And she never even met her grandbabe." Latlie was putting on quite a show of grief. Though perhaps the sentimental fool truly believed her own stories.

"Yes, yes," said Yurgn. His usually mild blue eyes had a shrewd look today. "Do you have any fresh ideas, Lord Regent? For finding the princella?"

Lord Retzel broke in. "I had a thought."

Matwyck did not let the surprise show on his face. "Pray enlighten us, Lord."

"Remember that shield, that man, Pontille or something, eh? You questioned him closely when he returned with the horses, eh?"

"Yes."

"And he knew nothing of the princella's whereabouts, eh? And he knew nothing of where she had been hidden? Mayhap now that Cressa is dead, her Enchantment would weaken, eh?" Lord Retzel raised his eyebrows, pleased with himself.

That *was* an interesting idea. Matwyck sent for the royal chronicler immediately. While they waited, he offered his guests wine and ordered oysters from the kitchens.

The royal chronicler, Sewel, arrived after a short delay.

"My lord regent," he said with a sidelong glance at the wine and oysters, as if disapproving of their comforts. "A terrible day for Weirandale. I have a crush of ceremonies to arrange with the Sisters and Brothers of Sorrow. How may I serve you?"

Matwyck and Sewel did not get on. By every measurement Matwyck held more power and stature, yet he intuited that Sewel scorned him. Matwyck bristled at the man's imperviousness and impertinence.

"Then I will get right to the point," Matwyck said icily. "Cressa's Talent was Enchantment, correct?"

Sewel blinked at the fact that this secret was not actually secret. Given that she had perished, though, he no longer felt duty bound to keep her Talent quiet. In fact one of his obligations was to publish her name for history: "Cressa the Enchanter."

"Yes," he confirmed, but he had already dropped the honorific "milord."

"Will her Enchantments fade away now she is gone? That is, will those she Enchanted now regain their memories or knowledge?"

"No. When she Enchanted them, she changed them. It would

be impossible for anyone to reverse the magic. They might gain new knowledge at odds with what they previously believed, but holding two contradictory ideas would cause them unbearable strain."

"Not even under strong inducement?"

"No," said Sewel, his nostrils flared from this mere suggestion of torture.

"Very well. You may leave us."

"Ah . . . wait one moment," broke in General Yurgn. "When I was a lad I learnt a ditty. I recall only the last line, 'A talent for the times.'"

"Yes," replied Sewel. "Children sing a play song, 'The Water's Choice.'"

> *When danger through the Realm may reach*
> *The Nargis Nymph allots to each*
> *A Talent for the Times.*

"Exactly!" said Yurgn, slapping his knee. "The song indicates the Spirit knows the gravest challenges facing the nation in advance and gives the queens Talents accordingly. But since Cressa is— alas!—no more, shouldn't the Lord Regent be equipped with the information you possess about the princella, so that he may safely guide the realm in her absence?"

"I never had the opportunity to Define the princella," said Sewel primly. "And you know that seeking to ferret out Talents constitutes high treason."

"Never Defined the princella? What, with the child being so grown before she left us? You never raised the flag, but it is impossible that you don't know something about her abilities." Matwyck's tone of voice conveyed his distrust of the chronicler's veracity.

"Her lack of Definition caused both the queen and daughter distress."

"How very peculiar," said Matwyck, "but let's not bandy about the word 'treason,' Sewel. You never know to whom the word might stick."

Sewel departed, and while his guests fed their sorrow, Matwyck tapped his right middle finger against the soft hollows of his left fist. "There was still something in what you said, Lord Retzel. We know when *Sea Sprite* left here and that it turned up in Yosta for provisions weeks later. Shield Pontole didn't recall exactly how long they had been at sea." Matwyck thoughtfully held up his hands, his fingers opposing one another, and tapped them together, first the index fingers, then the middle ones, and so on. "Prigent, I am going to send you to Yosta. You will go through all the paperwork of all the merchants four years ago until you find the ones that provisioned *Sea Sprite*."

"But how will that help us, Matwyck?" asked Retzel.

"When we know the exact amount of time *Sea Sprite* spent at sea, we will have mariners calculate what possible ports of call she could have put into. That will narrow our search considerably."

"I thought along these lines some years ago, Matwyck," Yurgn said, "but other variables include the weather and how long the ship may have tarried in port. And the girl may well have moved on from her first hideaway."

Matwyck was annoyed that Yurgn had already dismissed his breakthrough. "My esteemed general, I hear your quibbles, but have you anything else to suggest?"

"Well, I had hoped that Cressa would lead us to her kitten. Since that no longer appears possible . . ."

"Prigent, pack your bags," ordered Matwyck. "And pack up that curvy little mistress too. You may be going through dusty papers in Yosta for a long time." Turning to his valet he said, "Send word of these events to my wife in the country." Then, since the other councilors looked so comfortable and settled in his chambers, Matwyck left the room, eager to get away from his closest advisors.

He walked through the palace with no particular goal, just observing the activity and the people. The corridors and the halls remained as polished as ever, but most of the servants he passed were in shock or grieving. Matwyck may not have actually liked individuals, but he always found being in the presence of other people soothing.

He patted a young page on the head and offered a crying cook his kerchief. He felt useful and needed. This was his palace; these were his people; they counted on him to keep the realm under control. He spent too much time with the scheming nobles and gentry. The simple folk held the real power; as regent he needed to be loved by the people so that he had an alternate power base—that could indeed prove handy.

He would speak to the city tomorrow from the balcony of City Hall in the Courtyard of the Star, offering reassurance and stability. A steady hand in a trying tempest.

Really, he should change into a black outfit. He might even have a new one made out of silk. And a simple mourning circlet. Severe and simple, but the finest silver. Silk for the funerary feast would be most fitting. And mayhap just a smidge of rouge to redden the eyelids.

# 34

## Wyndton

Gili could no longer keep up with the family when walking to the town center. Her hips or back hurt too much to climb the steep staircase. Her once-silky coat fell out in patches, and sores multiplied on her broken skin. She no longer stirred to chase squirrels or greet home-comers. Ofttimes the dog staggered into a corner, growling at nothing; finally she refused to eat. As much as possible Wren lingered by Gili's side, stroking her and whispering in her ears.

Coming down the stairs early one morning Wren saw that the dog was absent from the bed of blankets they had made for her comfort in front of the hearth. Wren could not connect with the dog through her Talent. The family searched the property, eventually finding Gili hiding as far away from her pain as she could, in the darkness under the chicken roosts. Lifeless.

Wilim dug a grave in the meadow and he, Stahlia, and Wren buried their longtime companion. Wren sobbed for hours. Although she had known that Gili was failing and she'd tried to prepare herself, the snapped connection left her bereft.

That night, Wren dallied over getting into her bed. The house felt so empty and quiet that she went out to the stable to lean into Syrup's warmth and comfort. As she was reluctantly returning to the cottage, Speckles sent, *Canine sorrow, Your Majesty.* Wren nodded, a rock-hard lump in her throat.

A fortnight after Gili's death, Wilim insisted that she accompany him to Duke Naven's manor. The ducal family had traveled to one of their other estates, and Wilim had business with Naven's chamberlain, Orest. "Do you good, Birdie. Get out a bit."

Wren did not have the energy to protest, so she agreed, hoping for a chance to peek into the library that tempted her. Indeed, the duke's servants allowed her to wait in there for Wilim, and the cook plied her with a plate of sweet cakes. Though she didn't dare touch any of the volumes, Wren enjoyed looking at the titles of the books and deciding in what order "Missus Stahlia" would ask to borrow them. A book with a black leather binding, entitled *Weirandale and Oromondo through the Years,* pulled at her. She decided this would be the one Stahlia would request first.

A commotion from outside startled her. A side window gaped wide enough for a slim girl to climb through, so she slid out and ran in the direction of the noise to a nearby paddock. There, a stableman with a replacement front gold tooth cursed and whipped a horse, a young chestnut gelding with white stockings, while the horse screamed in protest.

"Stop that! Stop that!" she shouted at the man, forgetting herself, ordering him around as if she had the prerogatives of royalty. Completely astonished, he did halt for the moment.

"Missy, this be a bad-tempered horse. I must break him of his evil habits before the duke returns. Besides, where do the likes of *you* get off telling me my business?"

*I can't order this man about, but Wilim could reason with him.*

Wren ran to find her foster father, who was conferring with Orest in his office near the kitchens. Wilim accompanied her back to the paddock. She wanted to hurry, but her teto insisted, "Slow down. In tense situations, don't add your own anxiety." In a few moments they turned the corner and approached the paddock, where the man had stopped laying on the whip but held the horse's cheek piece in a tight grip. The horse's eyes rolled in fear.

"Nice day, is it not?" Wilim asked the stableman companionably, leaning against the top fence rail.

"We-ell, not so nice. Look at this bite that damned critter took out of me shoulder." With his free hand the man yanked his shirt down from his neck and showed the teeth marks and broken skin.

"Nasty, that," Wilim commiserated. "How long have you owned the horse?"

"A week. Bought him off a passing tradesman cheap. Thought he would do for the oldest duchette, being kind of nimble and pretty. Now I'm afeard I spent coin on a horse that's mean and bad-tempered."

While the men conversed, Wren slipped between the fence posts.

"He isn't bad-tempered, are you, boy?" said Wren, stroking the horse. "Fine for the duchette—if you treat him kindly."

"Hey, gal! If'n he hurts you, I's not responsible."

Wilim ignored Wren's unauthorized presence in the paddock. "Rather a pretty horse, as you say. I see why you bought him, you being a wise judge of horseflesh. You couldn't have known he'd be a biter. That tradesman better make himself scarce in my ward." Wilim rubbed his hands through his hair, making a show of considering. "Hold on, now. I might take him off your hands, and I'd swear never to complain about him to the duke. But I don't have much free coin.

"As you see, my daughter is taken with him. Awful fine lines," Wilim smiled as he said, "and we've seen his good teeth." Wilim rubbed his hands through his hair again, as if struggling with a problem.

Her foster father addressed Chamberlain Orest, who had ambled over to join them, "Perchance we could parley about the gelding over another mug of your cider?"

The three men strolled away to make a deal. Wren stroked the horse's neck, reflecting on how her teto had handled the conversation—how he sympathized, rather than accused or ordered.

Wren addressed the horse, *Won't you talk to me?*

The horse's mind opened only a suspicious chink. *Thirsty.*

She opened the gate and took him to a full watering trough. He drank his fill. She used her cupped hands to wash the places she could reach where the whip had cut him. He broke wind in noisy gusts, which made Wren chuckle. His long-lashed orbs looked her over more carefully and he snuffled up her scent, now paying more attention to the small human. With each touch he opened his mind a little wider. By the time the men came back, shaking hands, he stood outside the stable yard, grazing placidly on the duke's green a few paces from the duchess's winter flower bed.

On the way home to Wyndton, Wren tried to thank Wilim. He brushed her comments aside.

"We've needed a second horse for a long time, Birdie. I just never found one I liked enough or at a price we could afford. Because the horse put on such a show of being so ill-tempered, we got him for pea pods, and they threw in the tack too. How'd you know he'd respond to kindness? I see how he behaves with you; but will he act up on Percia or your teta?"

"Oh no. He won't. He will be as gentle as Syrup."

"How do you know?"

"He told me so." Wren remembered her old playacting. "I said 'Horse, will you be safe with my family?' and he said, 'Of course, because they would never whip or starve me.'"

When they got home, Stahlia exclaimed over their purchase. The horse lipped a carrot from her and bunked in the stall beside Syrup as if this was where he had always belonged.

"What with my new commission from Duchess Pattengale, we can afford the horse, his oats, and more besides," Stahlia said. "Isn't he a looker—almost the color of a field of barleycorn.

"Oh, but 'tis the day for beasts," she continued. "Since morn a strange dog has been hanging out near the house. I've shooed him away, but he always comes back."

Wilim and Wren knew all the dogs around Wyndton, so they

strode over to have a look. Thirty paces from the cottage stood a dog they'd never seen before. He had a thick head, a big jaw, and a squat body with a broad chest; in truth, he was quite ugly, boasting scars from dogfights or kicks. And he was so underweight that sandbars of bone rippled under his black-and-brown coat. He stood defiantly braced on all four legs—neither advancing nor retreating as the strangers approached and looked him over.

"A stray. Ignore him. He'll move on," Wilim concluded, and entered the cottage. Wren heard Tilim's delighted laughter as Wilim tossed him up in the air.

In the gloomy twilight Wren knelt to look in the dog's round eyes. *Why are you here?*

*Your Majesty needs a new dog. One came. Walked many suns. The queen must have a strong protector. One is thy shield.*

*I do need a new dog, but I intended to pick him, not allow the dog to pick me! Where are you from?*

*Barston.*

*Did you run off from your master?*

*No master. One finds one's own food.*

*Barston is leagues and leagues away. How did you get here?*

*One walked. The queen needs a new dog. One came.*

*You are mighty forward, aren't you? Hey! What did you call me?*

*The queen.*

*No, I am only the princella. Stay here. Spec-kles! Spec-kles, are you nearby?*

The owl flew to a branch above the stray dog's head. Wren asked him, *Didn't you call me "Your Majesty" the other day?*

Blinking slowly Speckles replied that he had.

*But why? I am the princella. My mother is the queen.*

*See thee.* Speckles rotated his head on his neck one way and then the opposite. *Know thee. Thou art queen.*

*The only way I could be queen is if my mother has died.*

*Mother sorrow, Your Majesty,* replied Speckles.

Wren glared at the owl. *I don't believe you.* She ran into the barn and asked the horses, *Who am I?*

Syrup and Barley blinked drowsily at her. *Does one need to leave the warm stable, Your Majesty?*

Wren entered the house apprehensive and confused but far from convinced. *What do they know? How could they know? My mother is on a ship hundreds of leagues from here. Animals have no way of knowing what is happening so many leagues away.*

But the following day Percia returned from Gulltown on the post cart. "I bring awful tidings," she said, pulling out a broadsheet. The headline blared, "Queen Cressa Dead. Weirandale in Mourning." The broadsheet told the story of the Nargis Fountains and described the sorrow and shock in Cascada.

The ground beneath Wren's feet turned both shaky and soupy—as if she could no longer trust that the earth was solid enough to stand upon. She staggered and had to step forward a pace. Her family and other townsfolk were crowding around Percia and the broadsheet, so no one noticed.

Throughout an anguished night Wren kept hoping against reason that the broadsheet was wrong, mistaken somehow. Her mother had promised to return for her someday. This house, this family—they weren't where she belonged; this was just a temporary haven. Her mother was going to come get her and take her back to the palace. She would show Mamma her new skills, and her mother would praise her for how careful and secretive she had been. On solitary walks, Wren had often imagined how grand it would be to shock all her Wyndton classmates, or the pleasures of rewarding her foster family with lavish gifts. How surprised they'd be and grateful! And she would be the bestower, rather than the foster waif, a recipient of their charity.

Memories of her mother's voice, her face, her touch made Wren's eyes sting. No one could replace her mother. How could she be gone?

The next day the Wyndton Church of the Waters planned rites for Queen Cressa. Beforehand the townsfolk gathered in little knots in the street.

"What will happen to us now without our queen?" asked the owner of the Wyndton Arms.

"May the Waters save us," said Goody Gintie, "'cause that Regent Matwyck surely won't. His lot only cares about power and riches. My brother joined the Parity Party: it was our best hope. Now they've all gone into hiding or been killed. Cruelty reigns."

Wren, standing close enough to overhear this conversation, flinched.

"We will endure, by the Grace of the Waters," said Teta Stahlia. "What else? We have no choice."

"Don't feel right at all," said Sergeant Rooks. "Feels like—it feels like a pond that's gone scummy. We've always had a queen. I fought for that Queen Catreena. What've they gone and done to the young princella?"

"If the mum's dead, she's the queen now," put in Goody Gintie.

"From what I've read, it's not quite that simple," said Teta Stahlia. "To become queen a princella must be Dedicated in the Throne Room and Nargis must create her Royal Stone."

"Her what?" asked Rooks.

"It's a piece of Nargis Ice designed just for her," said Stahlia. "You see one in all the paintings. A different one for each queen."

With the whole community unsettled, Wren's personal grief passed unnoticed. She was free to cry or not, without needing to explain her distress to anyone. When everyone reentered the church she sat on a bench as close as she could get to the small Fountain, her arms wrapped tight around herself, hoping to be soothed by the Waters, but her thoughts tumbled about, wheat chaff in a wind.

*Mamma, come back. You said you would. You promised you would. I thought you were coming for me soon. Mamma, I need you!*

Sister Nellsapeta spoke quietly about the death of the ruler and about honoring her memory. The town folk sang the hymns of mourning; Teta Stahlia, as usual, led them through the songs. When the churchgoers moved on to prayers for the princella, Wren slipped outside.

*Where was Father? How could this have happened? Where were your shields? If you, who were so protected, can die, what's to save me? Have you left me here all alone and forever?*

She approached the ugly dog who had followed her into town and who currently loitered around the corner of the produce market.

*How did you know? Why you?*

The dog couldn't provide clear answers. Days ago (maybe the exact time her mother died), he had just felt an overwhelming urge to leave the streets of Barston, where he foraged through garbage as a stray, to seek her out. He knew nothing of Queen Cressa or ships or the Pellish. Wren herself had drawn him like a cord. His life's purpose from now on was to protect her from any threat. He assured her he was fierce and vigilant.

Wren wondered if her scent had changed when her mother perished.

After they returned to the cottage, Wren addressed Stahlia as she started to prepare supper. "Would it vex you if we took in that stray? He isn't as sweet as Gili, but he may be an alert watchdog." When her foster mother made a face, Wren appealed to her compassion. "He looks so lonely and hungry."

"Oh Wren, right now I care not a scrap about mangy dogs." Maybe she saw a shadow of desperation in her foster daughter's eyes, because in the next instant Stahlia's face softened. "If you insist, we'll give him a try. But the first sign he's trouble, out he goes."

Wren washed the dog thoroughly in the laundry tub. He did not look any handsomer clean, but he smelled better. She treated his worn paws, removed all his ticks, and soothed his fleabites. His short coat felt surprisingly silky, rather than bristly, to her touch. She named him Baki, brought him inside, and fed him.

Percia scowled at Gili's unsightly replacement. But Tilim, who now could just stand on his chubby legs, eagerly patted Baki's broad back and steadied himself against the patient pillar the dog provided by remaining stock-still. Baki gave Tilim's chin a lightning-quick lick, making the babe giggle.

When Wren and Percia went to bed, Baki did not follow up the steep staircase. He lay in the front room, eyes and nose directed at the doorway.

*I have no one to teach me. But I now have a canine shield to protect me.*

In the dark of their bedroom, after Percia breathed rhythmically, Wren felt even more angry, bewildered, and forlorn. Her chest hurt, as if her heart had literally been shattered into pieces. She longed for just one more day, one more hour with her mother.

Speckles rustled at her windowsill to get her attention. *Your Majesty!*

*Stop calling me that! I don't want to be queen,* Wren sent to him. *I don't know how to be queen. Mamma would have taught me how so I would be ready when my time came. But she should be with me, to guide me.*

*Thou hast some time in this nest,* sent Speckles. *And a good nest it be. Learn what thou can. This one and the canine will protect thee whilst thou stretchest thy wings.*

*I will try,* thought Wren. *I must try. The harm an evil ruler inflicts is unmeasurable. The future of the Nargis Throne now lies on my shoulders.*

She reached up to squeeze her own twelve summers' shoulders, so scrawny they were barely capable of carrying two buckets of water.

# 35

## Sutterdam

Thalen, his brothers, and father lounged in the small and patchy green space behind the house, where they had been exiled by Jerinda and Norling. His mother and aunt were toiling over a Planting Day dinner. When Harthen and Thalen had begun hovering over the preparation, stealing little bites, Mater had smacked their hands with a spoon and shooed all the men out of the cooks' way.

Pater had fetched his pipe, and Hake had brought out a bench they could sit on in the cool spring sunshine. Harthen used their one scraggly shrub as a target, idly throwing whatever pebbles he could find at its trunk.

Thalen stretched out his long legs and relaxed from his trip home. He had fairly faithfully returned to Sutterdam during holidays, partly because the Scoláiríum refectory cut down to half staff then and the meals suffered. He always looked forward to these homecomings—but they rarely turned out just as he hoped or imagined. Every moon he lived away at school seemed to distance him from his family.

"Pater," said Hake, "what do you think about the tidings of the Weir queen's death and the burning of two of her ships?"

"From what I've heard"—their father took his pipe out of his mouth—"the Allied Fleet had already destroyed the Pellish pirates. So a sad business, but it won't affect our ability to ship goods."

"I'm glad I fight on solid ground," said Harthen. "Sea battles don't allow soldiers much freedom of movement. And there's precious little chance to distinguish yourself."

"Well, none of the Free States supports a navy, so it's not as if you had a choice," Hake pointed out. He turned to Thalen. "What are they saying about these events at that school of yours?"

"Many readers and tutors submerge so deep in their studies they pay no attention to what is happening in the wider world," he replied.

"Cloud-heads," Hake snorted with mild derision. "Merchants have to pay attention because conflicts affect trade. The pottery has lost several shipments to the Pellish."

"I wonder if the pirates use the pieces they hijack or if they just smash them up," Pater mused. "That shipment three years ago, it had my yellow series on it. How I labored to get the glaze just right. So tricky. I had it once, but I've never been able to duplicate it again— the color comes either too orange or too green."

Thalen resumed as if he'd never been interrupted, "*A few* of the readers and tutors, however, pay close attention to the balance of power. The death of the queen has more consequences than a thousand yellow pots tumbling into the sea. Oromondo will grow stronger and its Magi bolder without the counterforce of a Weir queen. We may be entering dangerous times."

Harthen had not missed the tree trunk in his last ten attempts. "Don't be pompous, Thalen. Will there be war?" he asked eagerly.

"Don't be so keen," Pater reproved his youngest son. "War is nothing to get excited about."

Thalen felt wounded by Harthen's casual snub, and for his part, Harthen did not take Pater's scolding well.

"It's boring back here," Harthen said as he stood up with a scowl. "Let's go to the Weighted Scale while waiting for dinner. I'll stand you all a round."

"Where'd *you* get any money?" Hake asked Harthen. "Been stealing from my purse again?"

Harthen ignored him and turned to Thalen, "Come on, Middle. A pint of ale, a game of darts? You haven't been home in a while."

"No, I'm kind of tired," said Thalen, "I think I'll just sit still."

"You guys are the laziest, the most boring—"

"All right, all right, I'll come," grumbled Hake. "But you're paying. No weaseling out of it this time."

His brothers left, and Thalen tried to enjoy the smell of his father's tobacco mixing with the aromas wafting from the kitchen.

"Do you really think there'll be a war?" Pater asked, briefly taking off his wig and scratching his scalp beneath.

"I'm worried," admitted Thalen. "I heard two tutors talking. The Magi's strategy and abilities frighten them. And the tutors kept wondering about the Weir princella. Is she a captive someplace? Even if she appeared to claim the throne, is she old enough or powerful enough to hold back the Magi? Does she possess a mighty battle Talent? One tutor said he'd read that if an heir is not Dedicated within ten years of a queen's death, Nargis will withdraw its favor."

"Your hotheaded brother—I can't abide his joining the cavalry." His father puffed his pipe furiously. "He'll be putting himself in danger. You watch: he's going to break his mother's heart."

"Harthen will be Harthen no matter how much you fume. He's addicted to excitement, and he'd never be content as an artisan. His head is full of dreams of glory."

"I know, Middle, but sometimes I just have to fume. Not a word of this war talk to your mother and aunt. No need to make them fret this holiday. Their joy in having us all together must not be spoilt by worrying about Harthen."

"Of course. Besides, the tutors may be wise in their subjects, but they don't know the future. And you needn't worry about *me* joining the cavalry since I lust for books, not battles."

Pater wasn't listening; he still muttered about "that willful boy." Thalen sought some way of turning his father's attention his way.

Thalen gently tugged his sleeve. "You know, I've been studying ores, everything about their properties and colors. Tell me about what you put in your glazes to tint them. When I return to the Scoláiríum I can experiment with finding a true yellow."

"Ah, now that would be a useful thing to come from your useless education!" exclaimed Hartling.

# 36

## The Scoláirium

"Tutor Granilton, pray, may I speak with you?" Nine moons later Thalen stopped the tutor on the path between the library and Scholars' House. Thalen had tried to work himself up to approach the elderly man for weeks. Now he felt his pulse throbbing in his ears.

"You are—"

"I'm Thalen of Sutterdam, sir."

"I've heard of you. You are studying Earth and Water with Tutor Irinia."

"Yes, sir."

"Well, I know nothing whatsoever about mountains, rocks, riverbeds, and whatever else it is she analyzes, so I am afraid I cannot help you. If you will excuse me, the cold chills my toes."

"May I walk alongside you, sir? I wanted to ask you something that lies within your compass. I wanted to ask you about the War of the Priests and the treaty that ended it."

"So? Been reading the broadsheets in the common rooms, young man?" His tone was dismissive, even acerbic. "There is much more to know about history and diplomacy than the latest gossip, mangled by scribblers."

"Yes, sir, I realize that." Thalen pressed on in a rush, "I wanted to ask you which theory has more merit: that relations between states should be regulated by the rule of law, or that all countries have a duty to protect their own self-interests through force if necessary."

Granilton stopped on the path and peered over his spectacles at Thalen. "You *have* been reading, I see. Here, carry these for me." Abruptly he handed Thalen four heavy volumes, which freed his own hands to pull his fur-lined cloak around him closer. "Both have merit."

Thalen's mouth gaped. "Sir, how can that be so?"

"Ah, rocks and lakes are comparatively simple things. People, however, are complicated. Nations of people compound the complications, and history's effects on groups of people—an endless, fascinating enigma."

Thalen followed Granilton into the building and slowly up the stairs into his chambers. "Put those books there," the tutor ordered. "Sit down, young man."

Thalen had to discreetly move more books off the only chair to do so.

The old man peered at him over the top of his spectacles. "You're the one with the memory, are you not?"

"Yes, sir," said Thalen. He continued in a rush, "But memorizing facts is nothing. It comes easily for me, but other students can do this too with a little more effort. The real excitement, I think, lies not in the information, but in the *whys*. *Why* are some lakes clear and others full of algae? It has to do with the temperature of the water, the depth of the lake, and the lake's sources."

"Well, then. You got your *why*. You should be happy."

"But . . . I find I am not, sir. I need—I need to understand why the Oros broke the Treaty by invading Alpetar."

"Oh, that's even easier than your algae question," said the old man impatiently. "They are hungry, and Alpetar has a modicum of food. The more complicated question is this: What are the other four nations that signed the treaty going to do about this incursion?" Granilton rubbed the bridge of his nose where the wire had pinched a red indentation. "If you have been doing some reading, how do we define a Great Power?"

"It's not an issue of the nation's size or riches or how massive an army it can raise," answered Thalen. "Historians say that Great Powers wield armies *and* Magic, either through many citizens or through a select class of priests or royals. Iga and Rortherrod were once Great Powers, but no longer, since we believe they have lost their Magic."

"Correct. Which leaves Oromondo, Weirandale, Lortherrod, and, across the Gray Ocean, Wyeland." Tutor Granilton leaned back in his chair, taking on a lecturing tone. "Alpetar did not sign the Treaty and it has no strong alliances with Great Powers. We don't have any conclusive evidence about Magic within Alpetar itself—for all we know it is a country of shepherds living in isolated hamlets. I would have hazarded that the Spirit Saulé guarded its people, but apparently not—or not in any way we can determine—so the country lay unprotected: a goose plump for the plucking. Though if the Oros were more clever and farsighted, they would have preserved Alpetar as a colony, rather than just raiding it and disrupting all its agricultural resources."

Eagerly absorbing this information, Thalen blurted out, "Sir, would you consider taking me on as a reader?"

"Young man"—Granilton leaned forward—"students generally stick with their studies. You've been concentrating on Earth and Water for many years. To switch at this late moment would be highly unusual. Irinia might accuse me of poaching one of her students, and that would be most unpleasant for me."

"I realize this is irregular, sir," Thalen replied, straightening his stance and meeting the tutor's gaze.

"Hmm. I know that Irinia works her students hard, but you can't have heard that I'm an easier taskmaster. Tell me, *why* do you want to switch fields of a sudden?"

"Sir, my brother joined the cavalry back in Sutterdam. When I went home at Summer Solstice Fest he said the cavalry doubled its training and started seeking recruits."

"A wise precaution. Cavalry officers can usually read maps," commented Granilton dryly.

"Yes, sir. But so can I. If the Oros didn't gather enough food in Alpetar, they might look northward toward Melladrin. And after Melladrin, I keep thinking, all they have to do is cross the Causeway of Stones to breach the Free States."

"And so, nowadays you are thinking that while knowing why lakes are clear or full of algae is all well and good, knowing history and diplomacy may be a matter of life and death for countries and for people. Indeed—for the Free States."

Thalen's eyes widened with surprise that Granilton had read his mind so clearly. "Yes, sir. Have other students been approaching you with this same request?"

"No, no." The elderly man's voice carried more than a touch of bitterness. "Most readers think of history as dry, dusty, and dead. They would rather chase seals, filter water, or compose music. They do not realize that knowing history is the only way to make educated guesses about present quandaries.

"Well. Humph. If you are going to read with me, you have got much work to do, and precious little time in which to do it."

Granilton held up his hand and ticked off his fingers. "First, however, you will need to visit Tutor Irinia and the rector and get their permission.

"Secondly, for tomorrow I assign *The War of the Priests: Its Causes and Consequences* by Tordwell, Tiomkin's *Ghost Walkers on the Steppes: The Melladrini,* and Gummury's *The Benefits of War.*"

"Yes, sir." Recognizing that he had been dismissed, Thalen stood up and approached the door.

"Oh, young man," the tutor called after him. "Thirdly, get yourself a bow and a sword and start practicing."

Since Thalen was already in Scholars' House, he decided to approach Tutor Irinia before he lost his nerve. Tall and bony, she stood in her meticulous office labeling soil samples in her precise hand. The only thing ever out of place about Irinia was her hair, which, thin and wispy, always dripped down from her pinned-up style.

She looked hurt when he broke the news, and he fumbled awkwardly in trying to explain it to her. He didn't want her to believe that he had tired of working with her, so he stressed the dire consequences of the Oro threat. Tutor Irinia gave her permission for him to leave her tutelage, but as he was exiting the room she remarked, "But Thalen, the clarity of a lake can also be a matter of life and death. Don't you understand *that*?"

In her chamber, Rector Meakey gazed at him with great curiosity. "Thalen, Thalen, Thalen of Sutterdam. What *are* we going to do with you? You are a most unique specimen! Truly, most unique."

Thalen thought she was going to prod him or dissect him to try to find out what made him different. However, though she stared at him intently, she did not bar him from switching subjects.

After these interviews, Thalen trudged across the snow-covered grounds to the library. He had already read one of the books Granilton assigned, so he had only two to study for the morrow. These, however, weighed him down like a potter's wheel, and he felt apprehensive as to what he had gotten himself into.

At the refectory, Thalen found Quinith and Gustie sitting side by side, lingering over their plates at a long trestle under a chandelier brimming with candles. He slid on the bench across from them and explained about his change of focus, hoping they would support him.

"I wish you had consulted me before this rash move," said Quinith. "Granilton has almost no readers because he's so cross and difficult. And he has been fixated on Oromondo for decades, long before these events in Alpetar."

"Leave Thalen alone," said Gustie. "He's allowed to change his mind. Change can be good."

"You just say that because *you're* fickle," answered Quinith. "One day you say you'll marry me tomorrow, and the next day you say 'never.'"

"Ask me today," said Gustie, licking her lips.

"I asked you this morning and you said, 'Ask me later.'"

"Poor Quinith," Gustie teased, "you're having trouble getting the timing right, aren't you?"

"Stop flirting in public, you two," said Thalen. "It makes me uncomfortable. Granilton also told me I need to learn basic weaponry. He spoke of archery and fencing."

"Really? How peculiar," said Gustie. "Oromondo is hundreds of leagues from here. But if you're truly eager to learn archery, I'm happy to teach you. I'm a crack shot, and I brought my gear."

"When did *you* learn archery, my gentle dove?" asked Quinith, with an ironic twist on the last words.

"My father taught me."

"You never cease to amaze me," said Quinith before turning to Thalen. "I might be able to teach you how to handle a sword. My father wasted money on a fencing master for years. My grandfather was in the military, you know—always prattling on about winning glory for the family name."

"Doesn't sound as if you're really keen," Thalen commented.

"No, I hate fencing. But I need some exercise if I am going to be trim enough for my bride-to-be."

"Isn't it too cold now?" Thalen glanced out the high window, where the wind shook the bare trees in the early winter twilight.

"Nonsense. Do you think enemies wait for perfect weather? Besides, we'd warm up soon enough if we're active."

The next morning Thalen reluctantly pulled himself out of bed and met his friends on the Games Field, a flat meadow ringed with trees behind the library. Gustie demonstrated how to stand, hold the bow, and nock the arrow. Aiming for the elm they used as a target looked simple when she did it, but Thalen's arrow slipped out of his grasp and caromed off to the left. It took him ten tries to even touch the bark.

When it was Quinith's turn to instruct him with a sword and dagger, Thalen felt even more awkward. He kept slipping in the snow. And he discovered fencing entailed too many things to think about simultaneously—his feet, his weight, his grip, and his gaze, not to mention his strikes.

"I'm going about this all wrong," Quinith graciously concluded. "What a lackwit! I need to get a set of wooden practice swords. That's what I learned on. Then you can bang away without fear of hurting anyone much."

Later, at the library, other students saw them carrying weapons and inquired about why. Two students Thalen knew from Tutor Irinia's laboratory asked if they could join.

Accidentally, Thalen had started a movement.

As word spread of their early gatherings, about a dozen readers—and even a couple of the staff—decided to participate, either for the physical exertion or because, like Thalen, they had never before had the opportunity to learn weaponry. Soon Quinith set about organizing everyone into rotations, with equipment, drills, and sparring partners.

Thalen grimly stuck with the discipline, gradually seeing small tokens of progress. His mood rose when he spied Deganah, a young woman whose brown hair had streaks of Rorther red, joining the burgeoning group. Thalen had long been eager to spend more time with Deganah, but she studied Comparative Magic, so he rarely had occasion to run into her. Other students (and his brothers at home) navigated romance adroitly, but Thalen felt as clumsy and self-conscious about courtship as he did with archery. On the practice field, however, he could find excuses to talk to Deganah, and he made the most of these.

She didn't seem to mind. In fact, by the end of a week Thalen could have sworn she sought him out for jokes about who was more fumble-fingered. By the end of two weeks they found excuses to touch one another ever so casually: Thalen reached over to pull her hair out of her eyes, and later that session, Deganah adjusted his grip on the bow. Thalen relished the feeling of her hands on his.

After they collected all the strewn-about practice gear, Thalen, Gustie, and Quinith strode together back toward the buildings. Gustie and Quinith kept whispering to each other.

"Stop it, you two," snapped Thalen. "You're acting like children."

"Your stance is improving," said Quinith, instantly sobering up. "You're remembering to keep your knees loose."

"That is, when you aren't staring across the field like a besotted yearling," added Gustie.

"It's none of your business," snapped Thalen.

"I don't like her," said Gustie, never one to hide her feelings.

"What Gustie means to say—" said Quinith.

Thalen glowered. "I heard her. And, again, it's none of your business. Either of you."

Gustie persisted, "I lodged with Deganah the first year. I know her well. She's too much like you: she's stubborn and closed-minded."

"As am I, Mistress Sharp Tongue?" Thalen challenged her.

Gustie squinted at Thalen as if she could weigh all his strengths and faults. "Well, you can't deny that you're quite focused once you make a decision. After all, who has thrown himself wholeheartedly into worrying about the Oros?"

"Come, let's not argue," said Quinith. "We had a good practice; Hyllidore says he's got some materials we can make padding out of, which will save us a lot of bruises; and that innkeeper I mentioned to you who used to be a brawler, Wrillier, has agreed to come later in the week to show us some blocking moves."

"And Thalen's working on a particularly tricky series of thrusts and parries," added Gustie, with a wicked smile.

Thalen stomped the rest of the way in furious silence.

# PART

# FIVE

*Reign of Regent Matwyck,
Years 8 to 11*

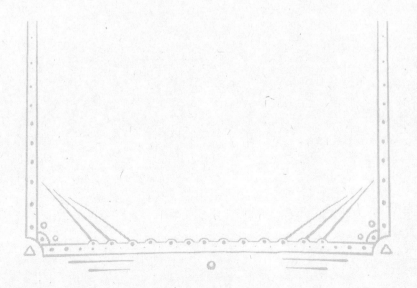

# 37

## Wyndton

Wilim, who was the only one still downstairs, crossed the room to answer the quiet knock on the cabin's door. Raynr, the peacekeeper from the ward south of Wyndton, stood in the nighttime air.

"Ah! Good to see you, Wilim."

"And you, Raynr. What brings you up here? Won't you come in, take a weight off, and have something to eat?"

"Thankee, Wilim, but I'm in a hurry. I just wanted to pass some news: there's some strangers heading north. They've got a large wagon, and they take all the byroads so that they don't go straight, but this way and that."

"Are they selling something?"

"No. My people got pretty suspicious of them. Don't have nothing to sell, don't want to talk to nobody, just driving queer-like. Foreigners, I'm fairly certain. And my people didn't trust them."

"Do you know what's in the wagon?"

"Nah. But one farmer offered it must be livestock, 'cause it has air holes in it."

"Did you question them?"

"I never caught up with them. Thought I saw them once, far off in the distance. One of them is very tall."

"Huh. Well, first light, I'll ride out and have a look."

"Thought you'd want to know. Give my greetings to Missus Stahlia and tell her next time I'll stop for a proper visit. How old is your babe now?"

"He's three and a handful. Safe home, Raynr. Thanks for the warning."

Wilim latched the door, banked the cook fire, and climbed the stairs to his bedroom with a candle. Stahlia sat up in bed.

"Who was it? Trouble?" she asked. "I thought I heard Raynr's voice."

"You did. He came to tell me about some travelers I need to look into. Go to sleep—I've got to ride out early."

In the morning, Wilim headed Syrup on the paths of his southeast circuit. No one he hailed reported anyone out of the ordinary until he stopped in Glynton. People there jumped over one another describing the wagon (weathered wood, with no paint on it), the horses (hard-mouthed, a hired team), and the drivers (unfriendly, silent men). Wilim pushed Syrup along the route the Glynton folk indicated but didn't catch sight of the wagon.

The next day he tried again. Midmorning, he crested a rise and spotted the wagon jostling straight at him on a stretch of dirt road that ran between cow pastures.

"Come on, Syrup. Let's see what these men are up to that's got everyone in such a lather."

He rode leisurely down the hill, with a hand up and a big smile. Two men sat grim-faced in the wagon seat; initially the driver looked as if he'd refuse to rein in, but at the last moment he yanked back on the leads.

"Hey there, strangers." Wilim halted on the left side of the wagon. "I'm the peacekeeper in this ward. Wilim of Wyndton, at your service."

The driver nodded but did not doff his cap. "What can I do for you?" Tall and broad, he spoke with a foreign accent. The man next

to him couldn't compare in build, but his expression radiated menace. Both wore hats pulled tight over their heads so that you couldn't
see their hair, and both wore swords.

"You are?"

"Cupist," said the driver. "Johin," said the man next to him.

"Where're you folks from?" Wilim asked, because neither had
identified his home.

"Not from hereabouts." Johin spoke as if he expected to be paid
for every word.

"What's your business? Are you lost or something? Can I help
you out?"

"No. We know where we're headed," Cupist answered.

"What's in the back of the wagon?"

"Some goods," said the taller man.

Wilim broadened his smile to mitigate any offense. "I'd like to
have a look, if you don't mind."

"But we do mind," said Johin, ostentatiously flexing his sword hand.

"Now hold on a moment," said Wilim, patting Syrup's neck
because the gelding had started to fidget. "Why would you? I'm sorry
to delay you or put you out. I shan't keep you long, nor disturb any
of your merchandise. Surely you are reasonable men; you can understand I just got a duty to see that everything is on the up-and-up."

When no one replied, Wilim continued, "Don't you think it's too
nice a day to quarrel over such a modest request?"

Cupist snorted through his nose. "Best show this peacekeeper
our writ."

His companion pulled a piece of vellum from a leather envelope
and thrust it roughly toward Wilim. Wilim clucked Syrup closer so
he could reach it.

The bearers serve by commission of the Cascada Insti-
tute of Natural Inquiry. I expect them to be granted all
courtesies.

                          General Yurgn

"Well this is quite a document!" said Wilim. "It prompts more questions than it answers! Who, exactly, are the bearers, and what is your commission?"

"*Look,* you country cock, at the signature and seal," said Johin. "Himself General Yurgn!"

"You don't say! How special! Of course, since I've never seen General Yurgn's signature before, this could be my father-in-marriage's curlicues, or your father-in-marriage's, for all I'd know."

"I'm not married," said Johin, humorless.

"Well, you take my meaning, I'm sure."

"Obstinate fellow," Johin said to Cupist. "Won't listen to reason."

"Yeah," said Cupist, with a big huff through his nose. "Well, we don't want no fuss."

Slowly he passed the reins to his fellow and climbed down off the seat and paced to the back of the wagon. Wilim slid off Syrup to follow him. The tall man unlocked the door with a key that hung around his neck. Wilim saw an immense wire cage. Clustered all over the wire ceiling he saw hundreds of black, rustling wings.

Seeing Wilim's puzzled squint, Cupist explained, "Bats."

"*Bats?* Why, pray tell, are you riding around Androvale with a wagonful of bats?"

"Orders from the Nature Commission. Bats in this ass-end of Ennea Món have been dying from some kind of illness. Can't have that—your people'd have all sorts of problems with bugs and such. They bred these bats to resist the blight. So we're setting a breeding pair or two free all around your precious duchy."

During this longer speech Wilim could hear the man's foreign accent more clearly, but he was distracted by the bats' cage, now noticing the water trough and something set out to feed them. He also noticed that the floor was splattered with their droppings.

Cupist closed and locked the door.

"Huh," said Wilim, considering. "Have you cleared this project with Duke Naven?"

"Don't need to. The Cascada Commission trumps his authority."

Wilim shook his head. "In Naven's duchy, courtesy demands you talk to the duke."

"Actually," said John, coming round to join them, his hand on his sword belt. "We're on our way right now to the duchy manor."

"The manor lies pretty far east of here," said Wilim, leaving unspoken that the wagon faced west.

"Yeah, well, we're saving time by releasing a few pairs on our way," said Cupist with a wink, which might have been an attempt at chumminess.

"Why did this Cascada Commission hire you two? You're not Weir, are you? Why not hire locals?"

Cupist shrugged. "We took the job."

"Are you just driving through Androvale?"

"No, a few other duchies too," said John. "But how's that business of yourn?"

If there was going to be violence, Wilim knew John was the man who would start it.

"Look, Peacekeeper," Cupist interrupted, "we don't want any trouble. You got your job to do. We got our job to do. Why not just let us go on our way? We'll be out of your ward soon, without any ruckus. Won't touch a hair of your precious womenfolk, won't start any fights."

Wilim didn't like these two at all. Obviously they wouldn't have told him about the bats if he hadn't insisted, and he doubted that they would stop at the manor house. If their business was on the up-and-up, why had they behaved so secretively?

However, he couldn't figure out any harm in distributing bats. And no one had lodged a complaint against the men for theft or any other wrongdoing. He had no right to detain them, other than that the whole setup stunk, and probably no means of doing so—what with two against one, and his sword (which he almost never used) hanging out of reach on Syrup.

"Well, gentlemen," Wilim said reluctantly, taking off his cap and rubbing his hands through his hair. "I'll wish you good day, and good fortune with your duties."

He remounted, silently vowing to keep eyes and ears on the pair while they traversed his ward, notify the peacekeeper in the next ward north, and send a note to Duke Naven.

The duke didn't respond, but he could have been traveling to one of his other estates. The wagon and the men moved on their way without incident, and Wilim had other problems to keep him busy, such as Donigills stealing chickens and a vicious quarrel between neighbors that led to serious injuries and threatened to blow up into a retaliatory feud.

The strange travelers and their cargo receded from his memory.

# 38

## The Scolárium

Though Thalen would never admit it, Gustie had been right about Deganah. Thalen's affair with her intoxicated and maddened him. Their lovemaking was a joy; the bed became a haven of discovery and transport. But on mundane matters they rubbed one another like whetstones, without polishing off their sharp edges.

They fought and dramatically broke up; then they reunited. At times they created trivial reasons to be jealous of one another. Often they quarreled about their studies.

"You think you can understand history just by studying *people*. What about the will of the Spirits to protect their elements and domains?" Deganah challenged him as she dressed for the day while he still lounged in her warm and rumpled blankets.

"What Spirits? I don't see any Spirits. I see people, pursuing human aims."

"Don't be deliberately dense, Thalen."

"You can call the wind 'Ghibli' or call the ocean 'Lautan,' if you like the names, but what's the point?"

"What's the point of calling you 'Thalen' as opposed to 'man'?" countered Deganah.

"'Thalen' refers to one individual. But the wind I feel today is not the same wind that blew yesterday or that blows in Sutterdam or across the sea."

"All air, all over the world moves by the will of Ghibli, just as the sunshine comes from Saulė," she reproved him. "And Ghibli will blow down any structure that displeases it, just as Lautan will wreck any ship that trespasses without permission. Tutor Hilbus says that the Spirits choose human agents to speak for them in human affairs. We have sacred texts, such as *The Story of Adikron, Once a Simple Carver, Later Eyewitness to Works of Wonder as the Agent of 'Chamen, Spirit of the Stone.*"

"Any madman can claim to be connected to the Spirits," grumbled Thalen. "And any gullible fool, looking for solace from a world of hurts, can follow madmen."

"Every indication points to Adikron being sane and rational. More sane and rational than a potter's son who makes judgments about things he knows nothing about! Adikron's book and other texts explain magic and how each Spirit favors its chosen people. You're slandering my whole field of study just to be provoking."

"I don't like the idea of bowing and scraping to unseen elements," said Thalen. "Free Staters no longer tolerate a monarchy, even if Rorthers do. And you always ignore the influence of time and social circumstances. Besides, even according to your system, some countries don't have hovering, loving Spirits. That's just plain unfair—why should one people be chosen and another abandoned? That's just as unfair as one country having rich soil and another having poor."

"Not all of the Spirits demand or even appreciate human reverence," Deganah replied, overlooking his point about equity. "Nargis merely wants people to keep its sweet water pure. Saulė asks for nothing at all. Lautan expects libations. Only Pozhar expects that sacrifices be thrown into volcanoes."

"I hope they choose religious fools as sacrifice."

In anger Deganah threw her hairbrush at him and slammed the door on her way out. Since she landed her blow Thalen earned himself a bit of a bruise. He felt ill-used. A few minutes later when he tossed his cloak over his shoulders, he accidentally knocked over Deganah's bottle of scent. The aroma—the smell of her neck, elbow, and bosom—induced a rush of desire. But telling himself he had to hurry to the refectory for fastbreak before it stopped serving, Thalen neither made up the bed nor straightened the things he'd disarranged.

After eating he felt ashamed of his petty behavior, so he stopped back by Deganah's room to place the scent bottle upright, mop up the spill, pick up her scattered hairpins, and refill her vase with an offering of lilies of the valley.

That afternoon he met with Tutor Granilton in his book-strewn, second-floor office. These meetings had grown longer and more intense as Thalen finished preliminary readings. He had to use all his wits to keep up with his tutor's expectations.

"No country has stepped forward to punish Oromondo for its invasion of Alpetar," said his tutor. "Why is that?"

"Weirandale is without a queen. Lortherrod would be capable, but her current king does not believe it in his country's interests to engage in foreign battles. This now leaves Melladrin unsupported and unprotected."

"What could be done to forestall an invasion of Melladrin?" Granilton tapped his folded spectacles against his desk.

"If Oromondo threatens its neighbors out of scarcity, countries could sell Oromondo the food it needs."

"And why are they not offering such wares, young man?"

"Not enough transportation?" Thalen guessed.

Granilton looked sour. "Did you learn naught from *Wars of the Magi*?"

"Ah, yes." Grateful for the hint, Thalen leaned back in his chair. "Even before the War of the Priests, Oromondo threatened the peace. For centuries its Magi have believed it their right, their duty really, to convert the peoples of the world to their faith. They will do this by persuasion or by force. They believe that Pozhar granted them Passion."

"What do they mean by 'Passion'?"

"They define it primarily in a religious sense—a passionate faith—but also in terms of love or other strong emotions."

"So the food scarcity may be genuine now, but it ties into a longer history of religious expansion," said Granilton. "Religious expansionism will never win a country allies.

"Moreover, states hold long grudges. No realm would step forward to help the Oromondians. They would sooner let them starve. Shortsighted, really. When you drive a country into desperate straits, you shouldn't be surprised how it reacts."

"Tutor, I have been thinking about the food scarcity and the blights that affect Oromondo. The reports of illness, dying animals, and ruined crops are so varied and so widespread."

"So?" Granilton was gazing down at some papers, only half listening.

"I don't know of anything quite like this. Usually a crop disease affects only crops; an animal disease affects only animals, and only certain animals at that, not all of them."

"True. This is why the Oros charge the Weirs with deliberate sabotage."

Thalen stood up and began to pace, conscious that the theory he had been forming would sound preposterous. "But crops, animals, people—there is one thing they all share in common. You know I studied Earth and Water first; I've been thinking about something that Tutor Irinia said, something about the clarity of a lake also being a matter of life and death. What if—what if all the water in Oromondo is tainted?

"Well, maybe not *all*," Thalen rushed to qualify, "maybe *half*. Maybe *most*. You could see where the water was worst by tracing the progress of the blights over the years. That is, if we had maps and good records."

"Tainted—but how?" Thalen now had Granilton's full attention. "What could taint half the waters of an enormous country? Surely not poison. Magic?"

"I don't know," said Thalen, wincing. "Still ponds grow scum that sours the water, but that couldn't be true of all of Oromondo, with the rivers that rush down from the high, snowy mountains."

"This is an interesting theory." Granilton paused, considering. "Humph! As soon as you have a chance, go back to Irinia, who knows about such things, and talk to her about it."

Inwardly, Thalen quailed, because having left Tutor Irinia's tutelage, he felt it to be rude and awkward to go back to her and beg her for help.

"Sit down, young man, and let's continue reviewing your reading. What, historically, has kept the Magi from achieving their goals?"

Thalen knew this answer. "Somehow, the Weir queens have always possessed an appropriate 'Talent' that forced at least a stalemate."

"Yes," said Granilton. "A wide array of Talents, each uniquely suited to the threat at hand."

Thalen interrupted the thread of their discussion. "Tutor, in *History of the Weirs* there's an oblique reference to the 'Initial Crime,' but no explanation."

"Ah. Yes, the Weirs have a bad conscience about that, and they have tried to scrub references from the literature. Here's the version I know: about four hundred years ago, a ship from Oromondo landed in Queen's Harbor in Weirandale, full of refugees who sought asylum from a despotic regime. The immigrants pledged to be faithful to their adopted realm, as long as the Weirs permitted them religious freedom.

"The queen of the time—I think it was Cinda the Conqueror—initially welcomed the fugitives and granted them sanctuary. But some years later she heard complaints that the Oros were sacrificing animals as part of their rituals. This upset her, so she had the Oro asylum seekers rounded up and slaughtered. Babes, children, women—everyone. *That* is the 'Initial Crime.'"

"Harsh," said Thalen, wrinkling his nose. "If you promise religious liberty you may have to tolerate practices you dislike. Or at least not kill people for them—give them a chance to emigrate elsewhere or adapt their practices."

"Indeed," agreed his tutor. "Oh, the Weirs tried to excuse their massacre by claiming that the Oros threw the offal in their river, and no one knows the true facts anymore. And Cinda issued a strange proclamation about her grandmother's close connection with animals. Many years later one of the queens—I don't recall her blasted name, but her sobriquet was 'the Just'—officially apologized for this barbarity, but the seeds of enduring enmity had been sown."

"And since then Oromondo has sought vengeance, but been held in check by each queen's Talent?" asked Thalen.

"Right," said Granilton. "So, returning to the present day, we might partially ascribe this current invasion of Alpetar to the death of Queen Cressa and the mysterious absence of her heir.

"Now then, for tomorrow: one, read this new work, *The Limitations of Diplomacy* by Tenny." He handed Thalen a manuscript. Granilton held up another finger. "And two, attend the concert of lays tonight, put on by the music students."

"Sir, I was planning to go, because one of my friends studies music. But I would think that lays present distortions of history; these songs offer history with all the complications and ugly bits left out."

"Young man, that's where you're wrong. Lays fascinate historians, because they reduce everything to the actions of key individuals, neglecting larger forces such as drought or epidemics or"—he inclined his head toward his pupil—"poisoned water.

"You should have already read *my* humble contribution, *The Songs of Rortherrod, Examined.* Moreover, by studying lays we can understand how countries *desire* to understand their pasts. And yet, interspersed with all the fiction, because songwriters compose them close to the time of events, lays often give historians specific details. We use them as primary source material, especially about Magic."

Thalen leaned forward in his chair. "Sir, I don't know what to think about Magic. Could we discuss 'The Lay of Queen Cressa'? The Weir composers talked with seamen on the ships that trailed behind. Certain stanzas have been running through my mind. The lines about '*a rain of boulders of fire*'—I cannot think of any natural phenomenon on the seacoast so distant from the volcanoes that would—"

A knock on the door interrupted their lesson, and a servant entered with a letter for Granilton. Thalen felt awkwardly in the way so he pretended to scan his notes while his tutor tore it open.

"That is all for today. In fact, you will have to work on your own this week, young man. Finally they have paid attention to my entreaties. I have been summoned to an audience with the Assembly of Electors. I hope to persuade the electors to mass our armies at the Causeway of Stones, to block the Oros from even entering the Free States.

"While I am away I want you to write an essay on why Rortherrod has fallen from its former status as a Great Power." Granilton waggled three fingers in the air. "I'll expect you to cite the lays from the concert, my modest contribution, and Mariah's *The Fall of Rortherrod*. Mariah of Feldspar has no great analytical powers, but she was an eyewitness to the later events."

# 39

## Wyndton

Wren was lost in Anders Wood. Well, not precisely lost—she just couldn't find her way back to Sergeant Rooks's shack.

Never before had Rooks taken her so far into the forest. He had blindfolded her securely as he led her on an indirect route. Then he had made her turn around six times to lose her sense of direction while he slipped away. Even with his limp from his stiffening old wounds, Rooks crept stealthily. She needed to retrace their path, reading only the signs of the trail they had left. But Rooks had made her wade through streams three times and led her over rock ledges. And he would certainly have erased any obvious footprints.

If she didn't return by morning, probably Rooks would come rescue her. Or maybe not. After all, since Baki refused to be parted from her (he had gnawed through the rope Lem tied him up with), she should be in no real danger from man or beast, especially now in midsummer when animals had plenty of forage. Wren looked at her dog, who was scratching his ear with his hind leg. If she asked him, he would lead her straight to Rooks. Yet the point of these lessons was for her to learn woodcraft herself, so relying on her Talent would be cheating.

Wren sighed, scratched some insect bites of her own, and bent again to study the ground for a broken twig or a spot that had been smoothed by a pine needle broom.

Woodcraft remained the most challenging of her lessons. Not that she actually distinguished herself in swordplay or archery, but when she and Lem practiced those skills Rooks stood right there, berating them, in his cranky, nasal voice. Learning to follow a trail or survive on one's own in the wilderness involved a degree of solitude and self-sufficiency that came hard for a former royal, born into pampering. Even now, she almost never had to fend for herself; although Percia had relocated to Gulltown to dance full time (now that she had become a lead dancer), Stahlia, so strong and capable, came to Wren's aid if she had trouble working the mangle or gutting a fish.

Rooks was forever harping on her that she needed to sharpen her senses. "Feel the sun, you lackwit!" he would chide her. "Any idiot can tell the difference between maple and elm leaves underfoot!" "Pine smells completely different from cedar!"

She surveyed the half glen where she had paused, but the thick spruce trees filtered the light, making it hard to see clearly, especially in the humid air. She heard insects whining as they tried to feast on her and a woodpecker pounding away. Jays kept pestering her for her attention, and she had to block them out of her mind. It had rained hard some nights ago, leaving the ground a little spongy, which might help her, as the damp ground would hold marks.

Eventually, Wren spotted the subtle impressions of the needle broom, a clue that allowed her to move confidently for about twenty paces before she had to search again. Wren looked closely at the log and noticed a compressed chunk of bark. One pace onward she spotted a smidgen of her own footprint, so she struck out on the faintest trace of a trail, confident about her direction again.

Since Rooks had not allowed her to pack water or food, Wren had gradually been growing thirsty. She stood still, listening with all her might, and in the distance she detected the splash of a stream. She angled in the water's direction, climbing over obstacles, for about half an hour, until she struck its bank.

She lay down to cup water to her mouth, savoring it, as Baki lapped beside her. Wren considered the stream carefully. This had to be the stream Rooks had used on the way into the depths of Anders Wood. In which case she didn't need to literally retrace Rooks's twisted path, but rather just follow the water. The stream would find the easiest and most direct route and save her from getting lost. She set off with renewed speed.

When it got so dark she smashed her toes on roots and rocks, Wren chose a level stretch of bank, neither damp nor rocky, to halt for two hours of rest, smearing mud on her skin as protection from the biters, waiting for the moons to rise high enough so she could continue. Baki circled around, tramping down some ferns to make a soft bed, as she leaned against a black oak trunk and watched the water swirl by, white crests glowing faintly.

Lulled by the hum of the cicadas and the periodic hoot of owls, her thoughts roamed randomly. It disturbed her how Wyndton folk shunned Rooks and Lemle, as if the villagers needed to set certain people beyond its pale. She'd noticed how tightly neighbors clung to subtle status distinctions, even when they all faced poverty, hunger, and backbreaking labor. Heartwarming kindness might be extended to one of their own, but cruelty was directed toward anyone who threatened traditional ways.

And when trouble bit too close to the bone—like when a lightning strike took one barn and not another—people eyed each other and dark rumors sprang up like mushrooms. Many turned to superstitions such as amulets and fortune-telling. Even Wilim threw nutshells over his shoulder if he saw a buzzard.

Despite town disapproval, Wren kept up her friendship with Rooks and Lemle, and no one openly chided her. But she knew that if these good people even suspected her Talent, she herself might be in danger. Extraordinary abilities were heralded in legend and song, but having them manifest in your own valley would be highly unsettling.

She could just imagine the gossip: "If Wren could talk to animals, perchance *she* was responsible for the coyotes that carried off four of Wyndton's prize geese."

Her mind turned to her Talent, and she realized that now, at full dark, forest creatures called to her. While most mammals and birds recognized her, not all were cooperative; she constantly needed to reevaluate her abilities with different species and individual animals.

She made Baki keep still and silent while she communed with the deer.

*Come on. Come here; I won't hurt you. I'd like to stroke your fur.*

*Oooo, that feels so nice,* sent the fawn when Wren scratched it behind the ears. *A little like when mother licks one, only different.* She bent her head lower and took two hesitant steps closer.

*Your coat is very soft,* replied Wren.

*She is a perfect fawn,* said the doe proudly. *See her pretty markings? And she follows attentively.*

Baki lifted his head and growled a warning. The startled doe and fawn skittered off, their white tails receding in the gloom.

Wren peered through the darkness. The nearly full moons had risen and hung in the tree branches.

*What do you smell?* she asked the dog.

*Don't know.* He wrinkled his nose again. *Something strange.*

*Baki, look. See the tiny little red sparkles? Two sets of two, there in that maple. And they fly!*

*Bats,* he answered. *Ah. They smell.*

Wren had lived with bats all her life, but never before seen eyes like these. She tried to speak to them, but their minds remained shut to her; the only impression she received back hinted at fierce determination, as if their will had been bent to one task, which was unnerving. Mother Moon and Daughter Moon had risen high enough to throw pale light on her route, so she resumed her trek.

The red-eyed bats followed her, flapping from one branch to the next. Then they began to flutter in circles around and around.

The bank was uneven, sometimes rocky, sometimes littered with downed trunks. For speed, Wren stepped into the stream itself;

at first she tried to stay in the shallow edge, but soon enough she slipped and slid into the middle of its flow, where she encountered the fewest obstacles. She splashed up to mid-thigh, heedless about getting wet, eager to get away from these strange pursuers. Baki caught her fear and jumped upward, snapping his jaws, but the two bats soared above his reach.

*Speckles! Speckles, where are you? I need you.*

Wren feared her call for assistance would be futile. Owls stick close to their home nests; she had no idea how far her Talent would reach these days. When she looked up from her slick footing the bats pursuing had grown in number to six or more. Because they flew in swirls and swoops, Wren couldn't really keep count. Their eyes glowed, their wings rustled, and she heard strange chirps. Her pulse started pounding.

A bat made a dive at her head. She uttered a little screech and waved her hands around herself frantically as she splashed faster. Her wild movements seemed to scare it off for a moment, but she slipped and fell heavily in the water. When she rose, dripping, she grabbed a floating stick as a weapon.

Two bats circled closer and closer, even though she swung at them with the stick. The creatures didn't appear put off by the stick itself, but her erratic movements also shook many drops of water into the air. Baki barked, but he was helpless to protect her from a threat coming from overhead.

*Help! Help me!* Wren called to the woodland around her in general.

She left the stream only when the slight rise on the right-hand bank looked familiar. Leaves that had not decomposed crunched under her sodden boots; these must be the oaks where Rooks had brought her for her first lessons in woodcraft. When she came up over the rise, she could smell woodsmoke from Rooks's supper fire, and in the sky she caught the pale glint of the high branches of the two tall white-barked sycamores behind his hut. She was close to safety now. On dry ground she moved faster.

When she was one hundred paces from the cabin, all of a sudden hands came out from behind a spruce: one clamped over her mouth and the other grabbed her around the neck.

Terror overwhelmed Wren. But in the next half second she realized that Baki had not growled and that the hands smelled like the scented soap Lemle favored. She elbowed him forcefully in the belly, and he let go.

"Oh! Oh! Oh! You got me good! Did I scare you?" Lemle said. "I've been waiting for ages. Rooks made me do it, you know. He said you would drop your guard when you thought you were safe home."

"You scared me out of my boots, Lem! Did I hurt you?"

"Only a little. I held my breath as you came up the hill so you wouldn't hear me breathing. I thought that Baki would give me away; I wonder why he didn't."

"Let's hurry inside," Wren urged Lemle.

As they jogged up the hillside, one bat settled on her shoulder while another lit on her head. Wren jerked her body violently and threw up her hands to brush them off before they could bite her. Almost simultaneously she heard the hoots and rustle of several wood owls.

*One comes to thy summons, Your Majesty,* said these new allies.

*Get these bats away from me!*

*One will hunt the creatures that trouble thee.*

She risked a quick glance upward, where she spied the owls chasing and the bats fleeing. Lem and she burst into the cabin, disturbing Rooks, who lay covered up in his bunk. Wren was aghast: he had been *sleeping* while she was out alone in the woods? A second glance revealed that her instructor was still fully dressed and booted—so his casualness was feigned.

He wanted a report about her trek back. She told him everything about her decision to follow the stream home—except her fear of the strange bats. Had she been childish? Inside the familiar cabin with Lem, Rooks, Baki, and a lantern, it was hard to fathom the fear they had raised in her.

Rooks chortled about the trick he had played on her with Lem and then grew serious.

"Too many scouts have died because they let down their guard when they imagined they was safe. When you're on patrol, you stay on patrol. Balls, even when you're off patrol, you never let your guard down like that. My Lem huffs like a bear and smells like a posy; he should *never* have been able to get within six paces of you, let alone grab you. *Do you get me?*"

Wren swore she had learned her lesson. She did not tarry for any words of praise from Rooks about her speed in returning from the drop-off point. If he had not cursed her, he was pleased enough.

Barley dozed in the glen behind the cabin. As she mounted up, she saw Speckles soar in from the south, settling gently on a nearby sycamore.

*The bats! Did the other owls get them?*

*One finished off the last straggler.*

*What are they? Why are they following me?*

*Smelling thee.*

*Why?*

Speckles had no answer, which alarmed Wren even more.

*Take me home, Barley, quickly.*

*Home, Your Majesty.*

*On watch, Baki?*

*One is thy shield.*

*Speckles?*

*One flies above.*

Sighing out her relief, Wren could relax a little: regardless of Rooks's warning, the animals had much sharper senses than she did. Famished and exhausted, she yearned for the cottage.

She didn't know whether these forestry lessons would be of any use to a queen, but she could concoct no instruction in commanding subjects or choosing councilors, and she needed to do something to prepare herself.

Someday she would have to leave this remote hamlet and find a way of claiming the throne. When should she leave? How would she proceed? She had no plan and no one to advise her.

Thinking about her isolation, Wren's thoughts moved on to her foster parents. Though they may have wondered why she spent so much time with Lemle in Anders Wood, they knew courting was not an issue. If they asked, Wren had an answer ready: she would say she was searching for her birth mother's shack—though she expected this ruse would wound them.

Knowing that her foster parents loved her while she *used* them, she always walked a tightrope between accepting their affection and pulling away. Often she would relax and find herself confiding some little worry to Stahlia or enjoying Wilim's gentle teasing. The next moment she would remind herself that every minute of her life with them was a lie and one day she would be leaving them.

A few days later, while gulping down his tisane, tucking some bread and cheese in his waist purse, and pulling down his hat, Wilim said, "Syrup threw a shoe last night right afore I got home. Take him to Carneigh."

Wilim rode off on Barley to meet up with Duke Naven's taxman and guards; the villagers would be less bitter about the tithing when they recognized a familiar face. Since it was market day Wren checked whether her teta needed anything else from town. Then she and Tilim led Syrup into Wyndton with Baki roaming before and behind them, startling a flock of wild turkeys. They found Carneigh busily repairing a farmer's cartwheel.

"Can you leave Syrup with me for a spell, Wren? I'll get to him as soon as I can."

Wren left the horse and stopped at the market stalls, where she filled her bag, and then proceeded to the apothecary because they needed more coal tar for her hair tonic and more liniment for Stahlia's aches. She paused outside the door.

"As soon as we're done in here, Tilim, I'm treating you to whatever you fancy from the sweetery," she said.

Then she walked in, hoping that old man was behind the counter today, and not his youngest son, Volthain. Wren still tried not to attract attention, but at sixteen summers she could not overdo her performance of shyness. She had rounded out and grown to her full height, which she guessed was a tad taller than her mother had been. She didn't think of herself as comely, certainly not as pretty as Percia, but she must be at least moderately appealing, because a few of the local lads signaled interest. Corburret she put off with frost, but she found it harder to be rude to Volthain. He had an eager way about him, a soft curl in the middle of his forehead, and he asked with genuine friendliness, "And what can we get for our Wren this day?"

*Our Wren.* Wren sometimes felt as if she actually belonged here. Though she found her endless round of chores arduous and boring, her life in Wyndton felt precious, perhaps because she knew she was only biding her time, waiting for some unknown signal, listening for an inaudible call.

She told him what she needed. As Volthain poured out the mixtures, he said, "Say, Wren, I heard that there's going to be a new fiddler at the Solstice Fest dance, and I was wondering—"

"I'm sorry," she said, tucking the bottles in her basket and trying to mitigate her rudeness with a half smile. "I promised Tilim a treat and he's been so patient; we really must dash."

Tilim, with the pokiness of a four-summers boy, took forever to decide what he wanted from the sweetery; then he ate his fudge ever so slowly. Afterward, they stopped at the Church of the Waters. Since no one was about, Wren cupped her hands under the small Fountain's trickle and drank. Then she offered a gulp of Water to Tilim.

They headed back to the blacksmith's yard to find Carneigh refitting the repaired wheel rim on a cart while his apprentice, Alat, shoed Syrup. Alat concentrated on the task and did not look up.

He pounded in the last nail and straightened.

"My thanks," Wren said, as casually as she could manage.

"Wilim can settle up with me when he's next in town," Carneigh called over.

"Right. I'll tell him." Wren led Syrup to the mounting block, tied her market bag on, helped Tilim into the saddle, and climbed up herself. As she clucked to the horse, without warning, Alat grabbed Syrup's cheek strap.

"Don't think I've forgotten, you Donigill bitch. One day I'll find a way to get back at you."

Without a command from Wren, Syrup yanked his head out of Alat's grasp and picked up his pace.

*Rooks is right. I mustn't let down my guard. Even here, in Wyndton, I am surrounded by those who wish me harm.*

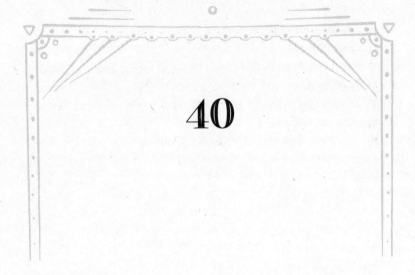

# 40

## Oromondo

The years passed quickly for Sumroth. His sixth flame, which had been awarded for his successful leadership during an incursion force into Alpetar to strip the country clean of foodstuffs, faded into his skin; a newly tattooed seventh flame now sat on his brow in recognition of his able work forging new Protectors over these last years. He had attained the rank of fire maker, but he used the common term, "general."

He built up a disciplined force. (Better food would have allowed him to improve the men's physical strength, but the Alpetar spoils were not limitless.) Amongst the men he had a reputation as business-like and aloof, insistent on obedience.

His army of twenty thousand currently massed on a high plateau situated outside of Twocaster. Magi Two had lost all her hair except for a few white strands she allowed to straggle around her bald head. Her pupils glowed red, while the whites now looked egg yellow. She wore a loose gown of white, and over it a thick tabard with flames etched in rubies.

"Protectors!" she hailed his troops. Sumroth, standing close to her, could have sworn she whispered, yet by Magic craft her voice carried to the multitude of waiting soldiers.

"You are the pride of Oromondo. You represent the hope of Oromondo. On you rests the safety of the Land. The Mellies are not the simple goatherds that awaited you to the south in Alpetar. They are brave fighters, prepared for our invasion. You should anticipate stiff resistance.

"But no matter how much they struggle against our righteousness, you *must* prevail today. Years of training have honed you into the best warriors of Ennea Món. And you know that the Land needs and expects this victory. We Magi demand this victory."

A loud chorus of "Duty! Strength! The Eight! The Power of the Eight! Long will Their Flames burn and conquer!" interrupted her speech. She held up her hands to quiet the crowd.

"Save your breath, Protectors. We know how loyal you are. We praise you among the men of the Land, second dearest to Our hearts only after Our sacred priests. Our strength is your strength; your strength is Ours. Pozhar's flames course through you. Smite Our enemies on Our behalf! Let Mellie blood water their prairies! Should you fall, the flames of Oromondo will sing your names into the Everafter."

She let her ropy arms drop, and a deep hush pervaded the field. A moment later the sound of thousands of soldiers tapping their breastplates with their dagger pommels arose. She stepped down from the hastily constructed stage, Sumroth following behind.

Magi Two wheeled to grab Sumroth's forearm. "We will help you in the pass, but We will not journey into heathen countries, leaving the Land. Win Us this victory, General, or your life will be forfeit. We *will* see you burned alive."

"Divinity, I would expect no less," he replied. His arm felt scorched from where she touched it, but he would not allow himself to look at the burn.

Sumroth surveyed his troops. He had no complex battle plan to employ here. One pass, one pass only—the Mouth of the Mountains—

stretched wide enough for his army; it led through the high peaks and onto the steppes of Melladrin. Their soldiers knew his were coming; he knew theirs waited. This day would hinge on force and will.

Magi Two spoke truly; the Mellies fought well. Even though their style differed completely from that adopted in Oromondo, they had proven this in the War of the Priests. Mellies wore no armor, only thick leathers, relying instead upon their fleetness of foot. They favored archery, using recurved bows made out of lacquered wood, rather than the sword or pike, and they shot these bows unerringly even when running or seated atop their sparse herd of small and shaggy horses.

But these arrows, which did not fly with as much force as those shot from long bows, should bounce off the Protectors' steel armor. While on patrol on the steep borders Protectors wore only helm and breastplate to lighten their load for their arduous climbs, but for this battle they would add shoulder greaves and thigh protectors.

Sumroth had no bowmen. Two generations ago, when by some witch's curse the soldiers' eyesight would no longer allow them to hit their targets, all archery units had been disbanded. The general planned to bull through the Mellie defense of the pass with five thousand men, then bring the rest of his regiment—fifteen thousand troops and supply wagons!—along tomorrow after clearing the way. All reports agreed: Melladrin was a sparsely populated country. Sumroth estimated that he'd be facing one thousand defenders, at the most. Though his enemy would hold the high ground, Sumroth counted on the Protectors' armor, their numbers, and their discipline to win the day. Not to mention Magi Two's Powers.

Sumroth looked about, checking that the flag bearers (their banner a black mountain profile spitting out eight flames), trumpeters, and his underlings stood at readiness. He did not want to tarry under the sun; even on this early spring day this much armor felt stifling.

The Mouth of the Mountains stretched about a league in length, and its span was broad enough for twenty cavalrymen to ride abreast. His cavalry rode aurochs, nasty oxen-like beasts. Though they moved ponderously and their bony spines made riding uncomfortable, aurochs had proven more resistant to the plagues than horses. Among their other deficits, however, these creatures could not be trained in battle tactics. They served only as crude conveyances.

Sumroth gave the signal to move forward, and the horns commenced their signals. His army set off with a roar and the tramp of thousands of feet. Magi Two, carried in a palanquin, took a position near the front.

Halfway through the Mouth lay the border marker where one left the Land and passed into territory held by Unbelievers.

As her palanquin neared the boundary, Magi Two stepped out of her conveyance. She held up both arms and pointed her index fingers. Fire broke out on the ridgelines, consuming all the trees, brush, and low growth. The flames raced in straight lines bordering the pass, pushing the Mellie archers lying in wait back from their positions, obscuring their sight and compromising their air.

Even with this barrier, when Sumroth's first battalion (commanded by an eager fifth-flamer) reached the boundary line, enemies perched on high braved the flames and smoke to push down boulders about the size of goats. These bounced against the cliff faces and hit the ground with formidable crashes. These projectiles killed, injured, or disrupted whole squads of men and aurochs.

"Keep moving!" Sumroth ordered, knowing that the Mellies' supply of boulders had to be limited. Sure enough, rocks followed boulders; unless these fell directly on a soldier's head these killed fewer, but they still maddened the aurochs into running amok. Many of Sumroth's foot soldiers were killed or injured by their own mounts rather than the enemy.

The general, who entered in the middle of the column, looked behind him. The last of his troops had moved from the assembly point to enter the Mouth of the Mountains. Magi Two's palanquin, however, had done an about-face and returned to the Land. All at once a wall of flame as tall as the Octagon rose behind them, cutting off any retreat. Magi Two had used her Power to state, *Forward or burn.*

Sumroth took out his whip, laying it into aurochs and men alike. "Forward. Don't lag! Move forward! Quicker! Go! Go! Go!" His officers copied his actions, whipping buttocks and backs of legs. "Forward!" they yelled. "Forward lies safety! Tarry and you die!"

After the Mellies had used up all the rocks they'd fetched to the top of the cliff they turned to their arrows. Because the brush fires obscured their vision, instead of aiming, the enemy let their arrows sail in massed flights, cutting the air with a whirring noise. When an arrow hit armor it bounced off with a loud clang, but often enough the barbs bit flesh, and the pass echoed with his men's cries and curses.

A fourth-flamer, using his whip liberally, pushed back through the press to report to Sumroth. "Sir! They've dug a ditch at the opening. It's too wide to cross! Archers on high and standing on the opposite side are cutting us down!"

Sumroth had expected some sort of barrier; the Mellies would want to slow them down to reap more casualties.

"Deploy the plates to cover the frontline companies. Fill in the ditch with the casualties. We *must* keep moving forward."

Although Oros normally carried no shields because they were too heavy and cumbersome for patrolling mountain trails, Sumroth had ordered metalsmiths to forge gigantic shield-like plates for protection against Mellie arrows; these he had placed in aurochs carts just behind the vanguard. Holding these plates both in front of them and overhead as protection, his soldiers dragged dead men and animals into the shallow trench. If a Mellie managed to shoot a Protector during this dangerous duty, well, his body contributed more fill.

Finally, his front battalion strode over this unstable, yielding obstacle onto the high steppes of Melladrin. Aurochs and carts that followed the first brigade bogged down among the corpses until a clever third-flamer had the idea of laying the metal plates down on top to make a more solid surface. If any of the men in the ditch still had a spark of life in them, they were smothered under the crushing weight.

When Sumroth's front line succeeded in pushing past this trap, the standing archers turned and ran. But behind them appeared a troop of Mellie cavalry directly massed in front of the opening of the pass. Like waving a flag in front of a bull, the sight of the enemy on flat ground, nasty bows notched to shoot their cursed arrows—*right in front of them*—caused his vanguard officers to charge pell-mell.

The Mellie cavalry immediately galloped off.

"A ruse!" Sumroth shouted to junior officers surrounding him. Sumroth mentally complimented the Mellie battle commander (whomever he was) for enticing his men forward without a backward glance. As soon became apparent, the enemy had moved the main force of their archers from the top of the pass to the cover along the slopes of the foothills on either side of the Mouth's opening. These archers began picking off Protectors *from behind:* a bare arm here, a naked leg there, a neck, or an aurochs' haunch.

"We must flank them!" Sumroth yelled, dispatching battalions to climb above the hidden archers. Slowly, inexorably, scrambling sideways on the foothills' incline, his troops flushed the Mellie bowmen down onto the plain.

Now, his troops could engage their foes directly.

Sumroth himself rode out of the Mouth. He drew his great sword and kicked his stinking aurochs into running over a fleeing Mellie. Hungry for more, he sawed on the reins until the cursed animal obeyed and turned right, where he could slash off the arm of another enemy trying to escape.

Controlling his own battle lust, Sumroth rode to the top of a tiny hillock to survey the terrain. He motioned for his aide to bring him water, and he took off his red-plumed helmet for a moment to wipe the sweat off his head.

*The tide has turned!* Though some Mellies halted to shoot, and the damned enemy cavalry wreaked havoc in small rushes, his men outnumbered their foes. And the Mellies were running out of their barbarous arrows. Some Protectors even began singing their battle hymn, "Cleansing Flames," as they brought down the Unfaithful.

Sumroth roared with pride for his men's discipline and bravery. "Yes! Make them pay!"

Within moments the battle became a rout. When the enemy broke, hundreds of Mellies swiftly scattered in every direction.

"Don't let them get away!" Sumroth shouted, his trumpeters and signalmen relaying this order to his officers. "No mercy, no quarter!!!"

When his men could catch up with their fleeing foes they hacked them down with pikes, halberds, and swords. Sumroth watched as three pikemen surrounding one enemy played a game by prodding him this way and that, each soldier keeping his weapon from making a killing thrust. Then the tricky Mellie bastard feinted left and quickly rolled on the ground to the right, breaking out of the circle of spears. He might have escaped too, but for a fourth-flamer watching the sport, who thrust his sword into the devil's gut.

By the time the sun went down, bodies—Oro and Mellie—covered the treeless steppe.

Many of his men had injuries; everyone swayed with exhaustion.

Hunger and thirst assailed them. They had carried almost no provisions into battle so as not to be weighed down. They combed the bodies of their enemies, scavenging a few water bags and a sparse quantity of some kind of meat jerky.

Sumroth dismounted to examine a few of the corpses. He noticed that Mellie men wore their hair cut neatly just below their ears on the sides, and shaved close above the back of the neck to reveal the point of their skulls. But some of the smaller bodies had long plaits with strands of dark plum intermixed with their light brown. He turned a few of these over with his boots, surprised to discover that they were women.

*If their population is so low they send their women into battle, we have little more to fear from them.*

The Mellie didn't herd or farm. Mostly they lived by hunting small wild game, and they roamed the Melladrin steppes, stopping only at temporary villages. Sumroth knew, but had not told his men, they would find nothing in the way of supplies here. Even the first sizeable river stretched a half a day's march away. This country was merely a desert to cross.

After the desert, a slick, three-league causeway of boulders traversed the sea.

On the other side of the causeway, however, stood the rich and densely populated Free States, hubs of commerce with vast warehouses of grain, and ships that could fetch stores home to the Land.

Sumroth moved his forces away from the carrion and, after posting lookouts, let the Protectors drop to the ground to sleep. In the middle of the night a volley of arrows came arching into the camp from the featureless black, but when his men rushed that direction, the scum had faded away. He posted more guards. "I will personally gut any man who sleeps on guard duty," he warned.

No sooner had his army gone back to sleep than another assault came in from another direction. By the third time, his forces did not even rush out; they just let the arrows reap their harvest. If Pozhar chose not to protect you, you might as well die while you slept.

At first light Sumroth's officers reported on casualties.

"General, twelve hundred and eleven men are dead. As you see, we have started the pyres. Fourteen hundred and seven are wounded. We lost more than three hundred aurochs."

"Of the wounded, how many will live with all limbs after moderate patching up?"

His officers conferred. "About half. These took an arrow in the calf, a concussion, a smashed elbow—"

"I don't care to hear the details. Send those back through the Mouth to Twocaster. They can still be useful to the Land."

"And the more seriously injured, sir?"

"Put them down. We have no resources to spare."

Sumroth justified this to himself as a mercy; they were putting the brave souls out of their anguish and sending them to Pozhar. But in truth, he didn't agonize about this decision—he just followed customary practice. If the priests who had accompanied his forces wished to say prayers, that was up to them.

Moreover, like his men, Sumroth's powerful thirst crowded out almost every thought.

After reorganizing brigades, they set out for the river. In three leagues they saw the glitter ahead of them. The aurochs stampeded to get to water, and Sumroth's men showed even less discipline. While they drank water of surpassing sweetness, however, Mellie archers picked off soldiers on one flank. While they forded the river, arrows flew from another unexpected direction.

These random sneak attacks maddened his men. When a company did capture a group of three Mellies (two of them female!), they flayed them alive. Sumroth hoped that their screams would scare off other attackers. Perhaps their opponents kept a warier distance, but the harrying did not cease.

Soon enough, his main force of fifteen thousand men, with supply wagons pulled by aurochs, caught up with Sumroth; Umrat, the sixth-flamer in command, had encountered little resistance as his troops crossed the blood-soaked fields. Showing initiative and common sense, Umrat had left behind butchering crews to carve up the dead aurochs. After hours of stewing, the meat, while full of gristle, would be almost edible. Softer aurochs tongue would be served to officers.

After two days' march they came to a small village of thatched buildings. The place sat completely deserted. His soldiers tore down the huts, but found not a single grain of foodstuffs nor a single useful implement. Since his troops had looked forward to pillaging, they were furious, and they set the shelters alight. The fire moved into the surrounding grasslands, and a swell of small game rushed away from the flames.

Subsequently, to supplement the supplies they had ferried from the Land and the aurochs meat, they learned to set up a line of soldiers and set a field alight. When the pheasants, rabbits, and other game tried to escape, the pikemen bashed their heads in.

In this way, they were able to get enough food to continue their march northward, ever northward, day after day. When the army reached the correct latitude, Sumroth sent one of his more reliable officers, Sixth-Flamer Chumelle, with several companies of Protectors to take and hold the harbor of Drintoolia. That was where he intended to ship back foodstuffs.

Sumroth kept up his stern demeanor, but inside he nurtured high hopes. He would go down in Oromondo history as the general who conquered all the northern countries, laying them prostrate at the Magi's feet. Zea would never go hungry again. His people would never go hungry again, and the Unfaithful would serve the Faithful, as Pozhar decreed.

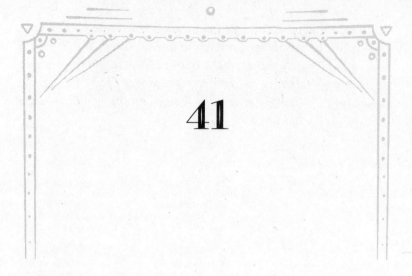

# 41

## Cascada

Matwyck, wearing a hat and a cloak though the summer night held the day's heat, walked carefully in the direction of the Sea Wench Tavern, situated on a crowded, boisterous street near the quay. He hated that he had to handle this purchase himself. However, the wealth in jewels in his purse was just too enormous to trust to anyone else. And if what he was buying was genuine, well, that also was too valuable to trust to anyone else.

The Sea Wench announced itself boldly with a sign of a comely woman in a low dress winking her eye. The open door spilled light onto the pavement, and he pushed into the crowded tavern, smoky with badly trimmed lanterns and pipes. He didn't look unusual next to the regular clientele, and in a dim tavern, wearing a hat, no one would recognize him. He shoved his way to the tavernkeeper, ordering a private stall along the back wall, a carafe of their best wine, and a serving of clams.

The Lord Regent slid onto the bench. The server was much too busy to take a close look at his customer; he plunked the carafe and bowl down with a graceless thud and sped off. The Sea Wench's best wine tasted like vinegar, but Matwyck sipped from his flagon to give himself something to do while he waited.

A few minutes after the appointed time, a man in ordinary seaman's clothing slid across from him. He stood mid-height and was slightly past mid-age, but carried himself straight as a guard. His eyes were gray and his hair flecked with red, with a close-shaven blaze pattern stretching back from each temple, as was typical of Rorthers. He poured himself a flagon of wine and helped himself to a clam. Instead of using the knife provided by the tavern, he pulled out his own wicked dagger to open it.

Matwyck nodded toward the sharp dagger. "You don't trust me."

The man smiled, a thin smile. "Nor you, me."

"Ah, in this world, how sad it is that man cannot trust his fellow," Matwyck declaimed in sarcastic, orotund tones. Then, urgently, "Show me the Rorther Stone."

"I'll put it on the table when you show me the payment."

Matwyck pulled out his purse and yanked the strings loose enough so the seller caught a glimpse of the jewels within. He left it on the sticky table, but close to his own hand.

The Rorther reached inside his jacket and pulled out something wrapped in a cloth. He loosened the cloth and lay the Stone, uncovered, beside the jewel pouch, hidden from the rest of the room by the bowl of clams and the wine carafe.

Matwyck eyed it warily. It looked . . . just like an ordinary stone. About the size of a hand, and flat, with rounded edges. It had no markings of any sort. It did not look as if it had been chiseled, more as if it had been worn smooth.

"How do I know that this is really it?" he asked, disappointed. "How do I know that you're not trying to sell me a river stone?"

"Try it," said the man. "Place your hand on top of it."

Matwyck followed his suggestion. He noticed nothing but the silky smoothness and coolness of the stone.

The man leaned over slightly and grabbed Matwyck's wrist, firmly, making sure his hand stayed in direct contact.

"How many jewels did you bring?" he asked.

Matwyck replied, truthfully, "They are worth four hundred golden catamounts."

"Do you plan to rob me after the deal?"

"No," Matwyck replied. The truth again.

"What are you going to use the Truth Stone for?"

"To find the princella," answered Matwyck, and then gasped. For although this was indeed his plan, he had had no intention of telling the seller, or anyone, this fact.

The seller smiled when Matwyck gasped. He pressed home his demonstration. "Why do you want to find her? The main reason."

Matwyck tried to pull his hand away; he sputtered a little, and then he spoke the truth, "To stay in power."

The Rorther released Matwyck's wrist. "Do you still doubt that I've brought the Truth Stone of Rortherrod?"

Matwyck shook his head and then used his forefinger to push the purse toward the seller. The Rorther pocketed it. "Aren't you going to count it?" Matwyck asked.

"No," said the seller. "You and I both know you told the truth, and that I will leave this place unmolested." He drained down his bitter wine, ate a couple of clams, touched his cap in salute to Matwyck, and casually sauntered out of the Sea Wench.

Matwyck nodded at Captain Murgn, Yurgn's nephew, sitting unobtrusively across the room. He and his men would dispatch the seller on a dark street. How fortunate the Rorther guard had just asked him about stealing back the jewels, not about whether he would live to spend his new fortune.

Matwyck sipped from his flagon to recover his nerves. Having the truth pried out of him by the Stone—regardless of his will—unsettled him.

He wrapped the Stone back in its coverings, carefully stowed it under his cloak, left coin for the barkeep, then pushed his way back out of the smoky rooms into the damp and slightly salty air.

He walked through the cobbled streets of Cascada slowly and hailed a carriage at a busy intersection. Inside the conveyance he recalled that when Yurgn had come to him with this proposition, he had barely believed him.

Once, Rortherrod had had its own Magic. While Weirandale's Powers came from the Nargis River, and the Magi of Oromondo controlled Pozhar's Fire, Rortherrod's Trinity of Gaia had worked through Stones: the Truth Stone, the Protection Stone, and the Repair Stone. Eons ago, when civil war broke the kingdom and the two brothers fought over the Marble Throne, legend had it that the Protection Stone was thrown off the castle battlements and shattered in two. After this blasphemy, the Repair Stone no longer worked its Magic; it no longer healed rock sundered by quakes. Nothing was publicly recorded about the Truth Stone. Matwyck now suspected that it had been held in a treasure chamber, unused, because the Rorthers were afraid to wield it—afraid of the truths it would reveal, afraid to confirm it too had lost its Powers, or afraid to reveal to Ennea Món that they still had it.

Probably the guard had substituted an ordinary look-alike. King Kentros would be wroth indeed if he knew he had lost his last Stone. Fool! Not to better secure such a treasure. And not to use whatever Power lay at his hand.

Matwyck thought it was a pity that no one would ever know he saved Weirandale from a similar fate. He let his confederates believe that Envoy Thum had bargained for the queen's death, when actually the Oros had angled for a shipload of Nargis Water, hoping it would cure their plagues. In the end, Matwyck hadn't been able to bring himself to barter a drop of Weir Power. (Not to mention such a sale would not have eliminated Cressa.)

*How unfair, that I will never receive the proper honor for my loyalty to my country!*

Well, now that he had it and it had proven its ability, he could use this Stone to achieve his group's goals. Matwyck could place the nursemaid's hand on the Stone to see if she knew anything. But he doubted that the servant held vital information.

Besides, Matwyck recently had received his strongest lead yet as to the princella's whereabouts: Prigent's labors in the Green Isles had narrowed down the search area to the Eastern Duchies.

But whom should he send out with the Stone? Lady Tenny, of course. The rest were bunglers. Yurgn hated clever women, finding them presumptuous (well he hated dumb women too, finding them tiresome), but Matwyck always respected ability wherever he found it, and Tenny had always been the smartest councilor.

Though Tenny had pulled further and further away from the council over the years, even she would understand that now with Oromondo ascendant and on the march, they simply had to find Cerúlia. The girl wandering loose in the world put the realm itself at risk. Tenny would see the danger that if the girl should die without issue, the Fountains would fail, and Weirandale would lose its Magic, becoming, like Rortherrod, a lesser power.

The Oros might be pleased by such an outcome, but Matwyck's first choice would be to enhance, not diminish, power.

And he could persuade Tenny that she, above all others, would be the gentlest one to unmask the girl and fetch her safely to Cascada. Sending one of the others would be preposterous. Of course since Tenny's loyalty remained tenuous, he would have to send escorts he could trust to accompany her.

Matwyck had the carriage let him off a few streets from the Arrival Gate. There, he identified himself to the palace guard. He took one of their horses to ride down the long avenue in style—it would not do for the Lord Regent to approach the palace like a beggar.

He reached his own chambers, which had been still and empty when he left. Now, lamps shone out brightly; while he was out, his wife, Tirinella, had returned from one of her frequent stays at their country estate. He had married her when he was young for her beauty, luscious body, soft lips, sweet disposition, and for the fact that she was the grandniece of a duke. But he had not chosen wisely for his future career; Tirinella turned out to be annoyingly highminded. She instinctively shrank away from any taint of court intrigue, and she refused to listen to the gossip of women and report back to him. She found an excuse to leave the room when his councilors entered; in particular she found Retzel and Latlie unbearably greedy and gauche. She snubbed Prigent's strumpet completely.

Matwyck rather enjoyed her snootiness, and he still found her attractive. They did not confide in one another, but they were both too proud to engage in either open or covert hostilities. Tirinella spent a great deal of time in the country, but returned to the palace often enough for appearances. In return, he treated her with respect and never took a regular mistress (though naturally, he took his pleasure with serving wenches or called for a prostitute when the urge moved him). In fact, he found his wife's slight air of reserve and disapproval a powerful aphrodisiac.

He had two major complaints against Tirinella. The first was that she had not borne him any more children after Marcot, who arrived at the end of their first year of marriage. It was just like her, to turn barren and deprive him of more heirs! Matwyck held no sentimental regard for babies or children, but he would have liked to surround himself with dutiful offspring.

The second arose from how she had raised the one son she had deigned to provide him. Oh, she had been an attentive mother, and Marcot had been well instructed. Matwyck trusted she had never actually complained to Marcot about his father, but the boy had imbibed from her an air of distance and judgment. And Matwyck wanted more from his son. Loyalty. Respect. Mayhap even affection. Every time the boy gazed fondly at his mother Matwyck had to fight down bitterness.

Marcot and Tirinella both sat in his sitting room. They rose to greet him. "Lady Wife," said Matwyck, kissing her cheek, "how lovely you look in that gown!" She wore the amber earbobs he had sent as a gift; he gave one a tiny tap to show he noticed. "Marcot, my son, how fare you?"

"Quite well, Father," he replied. At nineteen summers, he had reached his full height. The country life had given him good color and a manly physique, though Matwyck always regretted that he shared his mother's soft doe eyes.

"You have been out late tonight, Lord Husband. Have you dined? Marcot and I have just completed our meal. Shall I order for you?" offered Tirinella.

"Pray, do so." While Matwyck gave his cloak and hat to his valet, he overheard his wife ordering dishes with meticulous instructions about how rare he liked his meat. Of course the kitchens knew these details by now, but this was one way she publicly demonstrated her loyalty.

His little family joined him at the table; Marcot even ate again lightly, while Tirinella toyed with the spoons. Matwyck inquired about their interests, such as her patronage of a local under school and the boy's riding and hunting. Marcot politely thanked him for the new saddle he had sent.

Matwyck felt moved by the events of this strange evening to speak up about a decision he'd made long ago, but had delayed voicing.

"Marcot," Matwyck said. "'Tis time you relocated permanently into the palace. You need to learn the details of administration. You've grown to manhood now and can no longer put off taking up the duties of maturity."

Tirinella started. Matwyck took her hand and kissed her palm, adding just the briefest lick of his tongue. "I am not taking him away from you, my dear. With Marcot here, possibly I will see you more often.

"Well, Marcot?" he pressed.

"As you wish, Father," he replied. "I will do my best."

This was not the answer Matwyck had hoped for. He felt the Truth Stone as a hard lump against his waist. He longed to pull it out and ask his son, "Do you love me? How can I make you love me?" But of course, Matwyck did not do so.

He feared the answers. Perhaps this was why King Kentros had never used the Stone.

## 42

## Cascada

After the queen's flight, Tiklok continued to perform all manner of tasks as Nargis instructed. He checked the Dedication Pool daily to keep it free of even the most negligible impurity, such as a cata-mount hair. Sometimes he warned people to flee Cascada before that band of cutthroats and bullies paid by the Lord Regent, which folk had named "Matwyck's Marauders," arrested them. Once he helped Chronicler Sewel hide heavy books in the root cellar. On sev-eral occasions he stole royal jewels back from the people the regent had bribed and smuggled them to Nana for safekeeping.

And in his sleep he represented Nargis at the Agents' Moot Table.

He wasn't sure how he knew this tiny, flat, barren island with its wave-pounded, rocky coastline was named Moot Table. He also un-derstood that Restaurà, the Spirit of Sleep and Healing, had conjured this place for all the Agents to meet whenever one of the Spirits called for a Judgment. He'd been called to this magical place several times, and he found the experience terrifying both in a good way (because it inspired awe) and in a painful way (because he felt so inadequate).

Tonight, when he fell asleep in Kiltti's narrow bed, a vivid dream possessed him. Seven figures stood with him in a circle on the Moot

Table itself, a perfect oval in the center of the island, but lots of vague reflections thronged just beyond the oval's edge. Thinking about the shadowy figures after his first visit, Tiklok had guessed that these belonged to Agents-in-waiting, those whom the Spirits had chosen to take over when their current mortal representatives (though certain Spirits could extend lives past the usual span allotted to humans) passed on. Perhaps these shadowy, someday replacements also dreamed this dream, but in confused snatches like the dreams he himself had had before being anointed.

He relished one particular thing about the Moot Table—in these dreams the hole in his cheek vanished. Possibly because of the magic of Restaurà's Agent, Healer. Otherwise, Tiklok felt terribly out of place in front of the other Agents, all of whom looked so grand in the robes and insignia of their Spirits. He never got used to the fact that when he appeared there he wore a robe of blue silk, and in his hands he found a golden bowl of water that spilled rainbows if he jostled it.

Healer called the meeting to order. Mason, the Agent of 'Chamen, Spirit of Stone, had called this moot with a grievance. He strode into the center of the oval, his cloak of stone dust shimmering.

"One of the Sacred Stones of Rortherrod has been stolen," he said, solemn with heavy anger.

"Do you know who would dare commit such a crime?" asked Healer.

Mason turned slowly around and pointed his stone chisel at Tiklok. "One of Water Bearer's countrymen. The man who rules Weirandale."

Tiklok almost collapsed at being called out. "Lord Matwyck? I-I-I didn't know. I'm sure that Nargis doesn't know. Of course, I-I-I vow we will work to return it. Your Stone. Your treasure."

Hunter yawned, bored and disinterested. "You called us here for a *stolen rock*?" The impossibly long feather in her hat stretched out in the air, even though Tiklok didn't feel a breeze.

Mason said, "It is one of Rortherrod's Sacred Stones. Water Bearer has pledged to return it. You are all witnesses."

"If this rock is so precious, the Rorthers should have taken better care of it," sniped Hunter.

"Oh, but the Weirs are always double-dealing," said Smithy, a gigantic man in chain mail whose very presence frightened Tiklok.

Healer, as usual, tried to make peace. "I believe Water Bearer has heard the complaint. Do we have any other business this morn?" asked Healer.

"No, Healer. Dismiss us," said Hunter. "It was stupid enough to be called out for this."

"Very well," said Healer, and she moved her arm, palm forward, in an enormous arc, starting at her left shoulder, reaching high into the sky, and finishing with her arm outstretched to the right, palm up. Moot Table faded away into ordinary dreams.

The very next day, Tiklok set out to find this magic rock. He would have done so anyway, out of a need to defend Nargis's honor, though the minor earthquake that shook Weirandale in the morning spurred him to take action immediately.

As a lackey fetching messages and letters, he found excuses to be in Matwyck's offices. Tiklok would linger casually to snatch fleeting moments when the rooms emptied to hunt through drawers. No stones there. On a second occasion, he had fumbled around the bookshelves and chair cushions, finding nothing. Heathclaw abruptly entered, and Tiklok stammered that he was checking on the firewood. Fortunately, the secretary accepted this explanation.

Matwyck's personal chambers presented a little more difficulty. Tiklok grabbed an ash pan as an excuse. He swept out all the fireplaces on the same hallway, watching. He had to wait a long time for Matwyck's valet to leave, carrying some pairs of boots.

Tiklok ducked inside, hastily peering inside cabinets and sliding his hands under cushions in the sitting room. He heard footsteps in the hallway. He grabbed his bucket and left the suite as casually as he could. The noise he'd heard turned out to be maids just walking down the hall, but by then Tiklok had lost his nerve.

A week after his Moot Table dream, Tiklok reentered the Lord Regent's rooms with a canister of lamp oil. Though his hands trembled and he spilled some drops, he filled the lanterns in the sitting room. He wiped the oil up with a rag. Then, heart pounding, he slipped into Matwyck's bedchamber. He'd looked under the bed pillows and squatted on the floor, peering under the bed itself, when the Lord Regent unexpectedly burst in, pulling at the neck of a shirt.

"What are *you* doing in here?" asked the Lord Regent icily. "What are you looking for?"

Tiklok made no reply, though somehow he now knew that the lord carried the Stone on his person, in fact in a purse under his vest.

"Cat got your tongue?" asked Lord Matwyck. "Or did a rat climb in through that disgusting hole?" Matwyck crossed the sitting room to the outer door. "Soldiers! On the double. Take this thief downstairs to the cells."

The first in command of Matwyck's Marauders, Captain Murgn, thought he was an expert at inflicting pain. He punched Tiklok in the belly until Tiklok started spitting up blood. He broke Tiklok's fingers, one by one. He stripped off his uniform and held matches to his private parts. He kept asking, "What were you doing in the Lord Regent's chamber? Who are you working for? What were you trying to steal?"

Tiklok suffered, but he wasn't shocked or frightened by the pain or degradation; he had endured much worse at the hands of his own father. Murgn's efforts hurt his body, but not his heart.

Besides, Nargis never left him to bear agony alone. He constantly heard the Spirit in his mind, fortifying him and promising him succor in the Eternal Waters.

Real voices brought him back to consciousness in a cramped room with thick stone walls.

"Thank you, guard. I'll only be a few minutes. No, I'm sure I don't need assistance; Murgn says the thief is close to all in, and he should know."

Lord Matwyck entered his cell, stepping carefully around blood and vomit. He shook his head over Tiklok's injuries, as if the sight displeased him.

"Tik-lok, Tik-lok. What a shame you've brought such consequences on yourself. A young, strong man with many years of work left in that big body. Here, let me give you a sip of water." He held a cup to Tiklok's lips, and Tiklok drank gratefully.

Matwyck wiped some blood off of Tiklok's face and stared into his face. "I'm not going to hurt you, I promise," he said, loosening the binding on his right forearm. "I just need to borrow your hand for a moment, and then all of this unpleasantness will be over."

Very gently, Matwyck placed his crushed right hand on a smooth stone. He held it there firmly, but with almost tender care.

"Who do you work for, Tiklok?"

"Nargis," he answered.

Matwyck recoiled in surprise and then continued his interrogation.

"What do you do for Nargis?"

"Whatever the Spirit requests."

"Have you been spying on me?"

"No."

"How long have you thought you've been working for Nargis?"

"Since I was a boy."

"Ahh, I see. And a pitiful little boy, you were, beaten by—your father was it? You must have gotten solace from thinking the Spirit chose you."

Tiklok made no reply. Just breathing took all his will.

"Why were you in my chamber?"

"I was searching for this."

"This? What do you mean?"

"This Stone. The Rorthers want it back."

"I would imagine so," said Matwyck with a smile of pleasure, "look how well it works! You have provided me with a great demonstration!"

"I guess."

"Are you working with anyone else? Any other *people,* I mean?"

"No. Nargis chooses only one Agent at a time." Tiklok coughed a few times.

"So no one else knows about the Stone?"

"'Chamen knows, and his Agent . . . And Healer and Hunter were listening too, and—"

"But no one here in Weirandale."

"I guess not." He found it hard to breathe and talking took too much air.

"Here, have more water, my man. You're doing splendidly, splendidly. I'm so proud of you. And what fortitude—to last so long against Murgn's treatment! Really, you have hidden depths. You know, I myself don't come from a noble background, but rather from a poor family, maybe a little like yours."

Tiklok, in his battered state, gratefully accepted any scrap of comfort, but he still didn't care whether or not Matwyck was proud of him.

"One more time, Tiklok, I don't understand: Who told you I had the Stone?"

"'Chamen's Agent. He's called Mason."

"How very apt. And where did he tell you this?"

"In my dream."

"I see."

Tiklok's throat constricted. He tried to clear it and coughed up more blood. Matwyck jumped several paces away; then he came close and repossessed the Stone. He pounded on the inside of the door.

Tiklok barely made out the conversation of two men talking.

"I'm done here, guard."

"Yes, sir. Do you have any special instructions?"

"Tell Murgn he'll get nothing out of this man except gibberish. Dispose of this mess, right away."


The next day a rare but serious earthquake shook Cascada, destroying several poorly constructed buildings and burying a few dozen people in the rubble.

And thereafter, tremors shook the realm with uncommon frequency, even in areas where no such activity had ever been known to exist.

# PART
# SIX

Reign of Regent Matwyck,
Year 12

SPRING AND
SUMMER

# 43

## Gulltown

Lady Tenny lodged at Duke Naven's manor in Gulltown to recover from her voyage over the bay from Cascada. The Bay of Cinda had been quite rough during this crossing, and her stomach was hardly seaworthy under the best of conditions. This morning her legs still shook and her head pounded.

Naven's servants crept around her timidly. One had already felt the lash of her tongue for waking her by knocking over andirons in the room next to hers. Tenny felt shame about losing her temper so; after she had another cup of tisane she would have to find the parlor maid she had abused and slip her a coin.

When she was younger a rough crossing had not laid her so low. Was it the seasickness or her errand that vexed her so? When Matwyck had shown her the Stone and explained why he was sending her, she had recoiled from the mission, but she could not fault his logic. He was right: better she than one of the others.

And yet, if Cerúlia desired to remain hidden, Tenny wished her to do so. She did not trust Matwyck—he had already proven himself capable of sending assassins after one queen. Really, the thought of the princella in his clutches made her stomach heave again.

*Why, why did I ever become a party to that treachery? Why did I allow his veiled blackmail and his specious arguments to persuade me? How could I have been so gullible and disloyal?*

She tried to take herself in hand. No good came of these self-recriminations. She had told herself this one thousand times, yet she couldn't forgive herself for her complicity in the treason against Cressa. And Matwyck exploited this self-torment, offering this mission as the unique opportunity to earn back her self-respect; by finding Cerúlia, guiding her, seeing her safely Dedicated, Tenny could do a great service to Queen Cressa and the Nargis Throne. She had a chance to undo her earlier disloyalty. And she had no doubt that the two guards sent with her "for her protection" had orders to see that she scrupulously followed Matwyck's instructions.

Tenny finished her tisane and rang for Naven's housekeeper, who would help her dress. The long black skirt presented no difficulties, but the elderly woman fumbled so with the laces on the back of her beige silk overdress that Tenny snapped, "Gracious woman, do you have the hands of a gravedigger?" Tenny scandalized herself with her words; she whirled around, grabbed those arthritic hands in both her own, and murmured, "Pardon, pardon, I pray you, pardon me." The old woman, confused and frightened by her guest, excused herself as soon as she could. Tenny pinned up her amber hair herself and covered it with a black-and-beige turban before she could terrify any more servants.

Duke Burdis, Duke Naven, and Duchess Pattengale, the gentry of the three Eastern Duchies, awaited her in the library, which was decorated with all kind of memorabilia from when Duke Naven's father was a soldier—swords, pikes, and torn banners hung on the wall. Tenny, the diplomat, found the martial look distasteful, but she warmed to her friends from former, better days. After a little light chatter and more serious speculation about what the Oros would do once they tore through Melladrin, she got to the point of her visit.

"I have traveled here on a most important matter of state. The Lord Regent has reason to believe the princella might be living in the Eastern Duchies in a disguise. Androvale is most likely, though neither of the other Eastern Duchies can be ruled out."

Naven chuckled and smoothed the impressive amber mustache he'd grown as his face aged. "Oh, I assure you, Tenny, I am not hiding her. That Latlie came here on this same mission more than ten years ago. She couldn't find her then, and you won't find her now." He shifted his bulk in his chair. "Once and for all, Tenny, she is not in my root cellar!" He laughed heartily at his own witticism.

"I heard she has sought refuge in Lortherrod. Is that not the case?" said Duchess Pattengale, examining her wine in the shafts of light that came through the windows.

"Could be, could be, my dear duchess, though the Lorthers deny it. Yet the Lord Regent insists we hunt again, and we are all his servants in this matter."

"This time I am to run a systematic inquiry," Tenny continued. "In the past, he deemed secrecy vital, but now we must put that aside and enlist the people of the duchy."

Naven frowned. "What do you mean to do?"

"I would like to question three categories of people. I'd start with the village midwives, since Cerúlia would have been eight summers when she arrived. The midwives would know if a young woman lives in their hamlet whose birth they did not attend. Then, your peacekeepers. They should know if a new family moved into their ward with a young daughter. If those folks don't lead us to the princella, I am prepared to offer a reward to any person who comes forth with information about a young woman of twenty summers who can't prove her parentage."

"Rewards are rarely a good idea, Tenny," said jowly Duke Burdis. "You get folk all riled up and greedy-like, coming in with all sorts of tales. There's drunkards—men and, yes, women too—who would disavow their own kin at the thought of a few golden catamounts."

"I can well imagine," said Tenny. "Which is why I would like to start with the midwives and the peacekeepers first. Also, the fewer

people who initially know about the search, the less likely the princella would hear of it and flee."

The duchess leaned forward. "Tenny, my dear, be frank with
old friends. What I do not understand is why the princella would be
*hiding* or *fleeing* in the first place. I feel certain that if she resided in
Weirandale she would have come forward and claimed the Nargis
Throne once her brave mother had passed on."

Tenny had come prepared for sticky questions of this nature.
"We surmise that the night the Oro assassins nearly killed Queen
Cressa, she took fright for the safety of her child and heir. We believe
that she hid dear Cerúlia where she thought she would be safe, and
she Enchanted her to keep hidden. Lord Matwyck has the means to
break such an Enchantment so she can assume her rightful place."

Her friends looked skeptical, but they had trusted Tenny for decades.

"I suppose this is *possible,* Tenny," said Duke Naven. "But I side
with Pattengale—I believe she thrives in Lortherrod or another far-
off place. That she is still alive, we know. I suggest that we just wait
until she appears in her own good time."

Tenny sighed and replied sincerely, "I would that we could,
Naven. I would that we could. But during these perilous times we
need her on the Nargis Throne."

"I have said my peace. Since you can't be dissuaded, how do you
wish to proceed?" asked Naven.

"Burdis and Pattengale, at this juncture all I ask of you is that
you redouble your border watch to make sure that no young woman
crosses back and forth. Naven, since Matwyck has some evidence
pointing to Androvale, we will start here."

"You mean *here,* in Gulltown? Bad place to start, I'm sure. Too
many people move in and out of a big city like Gulltown. Midwives
don't know the folk like they do in villages. Same with the peacekeepers. No, best to start in the north, refine your method, and work
your way south to Gulltown."

"And 'tis smart you are, my dear old Naven. I take your point.
But I would like at least to keep a lookout on passengers sailing away

from here. Any young lady passengers trying to board a ship need to be questioned. Couldn't be too many of those for your harbor watch to round up for me."

"No-oo. Not so many. But if we stop families, couples, and solitary travelers, we'll have to hold a lot of angry people."

"True," said Lady Tenny, considering. "But I would imagine that your watch can see a family resemblance; if the young woman has true blood siblings, they'd look like one another and the soldiers could let them proceed."

Naven pouted. "But answer me this, Tenny. If my watch holds a young lady for you, or if a midwife or a peacekeeper brings us a lass, how are you going to recognize Cerúlia?"

"Ah. I knew Queen Cressa at this age. That is why Lord Matwyck sent me. I can hardly fail to know her."

Again, the gentry's faces looked grudging and doubtful, but they bit back any further protest.

After a fine midmeal with some local rich merchants, with a little sparkling wine that helped settle her stomach, Tenny felt recovered enough to wander the house. The guards—she had already deliberately forgotten their real names and called them "Stare" and "Twitch"—scrutinized her movements. She explained she sought the parlor maid she had chided earlier in the day.

Tenny finally located the maid outside on her knees, scrubbing the front stairs to the street, her knuckles red from the harsh soap, her face equally red from the exertion. When she saw Tenny, she pulled the wooden bucket out of the great lady's way and shrank against the balustrade.

"No, I don't intend to go down. I was looking for *you*. I must apologize for my temper this morn. I have not been well, but that doesn't excuse my rude behavior." She offered the girl a gold catamount coin.

The girl turned spooked eyes to her. She looked at the coin but did not dare take it. Tenny wondered how old the girl was. She might have been ten, which seemed awfully young to labor so hard.

"Go on," said Tenny. "Giving you this is the only way I have to make myself square with you."

The girl still hesitated. "Do ya feel better now, my lady?"

This brought a wide smile to Tenny's lined face. "Yes, indeed I do. Yet I will feel even better if you accept the coin."

The parlor maid took the catamount, glancing at it wonderingly.

Because bending over hurt her back, Tenny sat down in the sunshine, on the clean—and now only slightly damp—top step. "What will you do with the money, child?" she asked.

"Give it to my ma," said the girl unhesitatingly. "She has four littler ones to feed. And one already died of the flux."

"That is right and proper. And yet I wanted you to buy something nice, just for yourself." Tenny reached in her purse and pulled out a silver tear. "Here, if I give you this too, will you buy a hair ribbon, or a sweet, or both? Go on; take it."

"My lady, 'tis too much. I can't take money for naught. Would ya like to swear at me again? Or can I do an extra chore for you? Ya traveled without a maid. Perchance there's somethin' I could fetch for ya?"

Tenny smiled at the girl's sweet nature. Then she recognized an unplanned and precious opportunity. Stare and Twitch had remained inside the manor; they might be watching out a window, but they certainly stood out of earshot. "Now you mention it, there is one little thing you could fetch for me. It costs nothing, but finding exactly the right one might take patient searching."

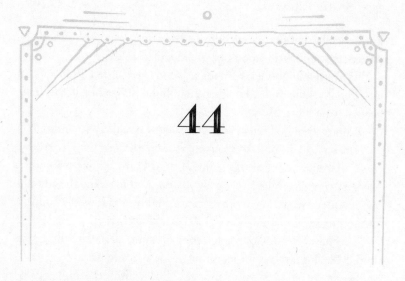

# 44

## Latham/Jutterdam/Latham

To Thalen's relief, when he approached Tutor Irinia with his question about the water in Oromondo she was willing, even eager, to share her expertise and work with him again.

"I think you're right, Thalen, that the only thing that would harm crops, animals, and humans would be bad water. But what would cause such a taint and spread it so widely?"

"Some people assume Magic," said Thalen.

"Claiming 'Magic' just means they don't understand it," sniffed Irinia. "Let's go into the laboratory; maybe looking at my collections will spark some ideas. Or perhaps"—her eyes lit up—"we'll run some experiments!"

"Poison water, drink it, and see if we get sick?" Thalen asked with a smile.

"No, lackwit! But we could add substances to water and use it to water plants. Or pour some in Rector Meakey's fishbowls!"

Thalen chuckled at Irinia's conspiratorial glee.

So late at night for a week, when other students weren't using the lab, Tutor Irinia and he would mix concoctions and pour them over carefully labeled grass samples. In the case of lye, the grass wilted so immediately that no one could miss the effect, and with other substances the stalks still stood upright like little soldiers.

"We're going about this wrong," Irinia concluded after another long night. "Do you know when the blights started or if they have been getting worse?"

"I don't know," Thalen admitted, "but I could try to find out."

Irinia nodded, and she looked around the lab with narrowed eyes. "Moreover, a lot of things we've tried I now realize were just a waste of time. Lemons don't grow there, do they? And, besides, no one is squeezing them into the streams all over the whole country. What does grow there—some type of noxious berry?"

"I've never read about Oro crops or flora." Thalen rubbed his tired eyes. "It's famous for its mining of jewels and ores."

"Right, of course," agreed Irinia. She continued thinking out loud. "Jewels don't dissolve in water. But in volcanic rock one might also find other metals. . . ." She ran across the lab to a drawer and pulled it open, revealing rock samples, each with a white paper tag.

"Ah-ha! I have nothing from Oromondo. But I do have specimens from the Green Isles. The isles are volcanic too, though they've been dormant for centuries."

"Do you want to try these?" he asked. "How do you get rocks to dissolve in water?"

"You'd need to chip them or drill them as you would if you were mining," she said almost dreamily. "But you also want to control the concentration and how many times you water the grass samples."

She came out of her thoughts and looked up. "Go away, Thalen; you look exhausted. You go back to your studying with Granilton. Now *I'm* intrigued with this question—I'll pursue this on my own. But find out whatever you can about the timeline of the plagues."

It took Thalen days to figure out how to research this timeline, but ultimately *Trade amongst the Nations: A Tally* provided sufficient information about when Oromondo began importing foodstuffs in quantity and how these shipments had grown steadily over the past seven decades.

In his next tutorial session with Granilton, Thalen relayed that

Irinia was exploring whether Oro mining might explain the tainted water.

"The deeper you mine into the volcanic mountains, the more you risk running into seams of metallic ores. Irinia thinks that these might be toxins."

Granilton leaned forward eagerly. "So in their desire for the wealth of their gems and precious metals, the Oros might be poisoning their own water supply?"

"That's what we suspect."

"How interesting! But why would the Oros themselves not have figured this out?"

"Maybe because it's been happening slowly? And don't people overlook what they don't want to see?" Thalen shifted uncomfortably, recalling Gustie's warning about the match between himself and Deganah. "After all, the Oros' economy is built around their mining."

Granilton took off his spectacles and wiped them. "So intriguing. Immediate gain leading to long-term decline. I don't suppose there would be any way of convincing the Oros to halt their mining?"

"How?" said Thalen, raising his hands in a gesture of hopelessness. "At the moment we can't prove a thing."

"Young man, this also links up with a theory of mine I'm contemplating writing up someday. Often a country's strength also becomes its undoing. Take the Free States: we are so proud of our electoral system. But having our sizeable Assembly of Electors means the assembly is often torn by rival interests and everyone must compromise and persuade until the geese grow fat. We dither and dither, and no one can act decisively.

"Or take Weirandale, which relies too much on its queen. Without her, the realm flounders."

Several weeks later, when the Assembly of Electors of the Free States invited Granilton to another emergency session, he asked Thalen to accompany him to Jutterdam. The tutor had aged in the years since Thalen began studying with him—his back had taken on a definite hunch, and his eyes looked filmy, so he genuinely needed a strong arm to lean on and someone to carry his case and books. Granilton had always had few readers, and Thalen was currently the one who had studied with him the longest. Yet from the steady stream of lecturing and quizzing Granilton peppered him with throughout the journey, Thalen suspected that his tutor also wanted his company so he could cram in every last drop of his knowledge. His hectoring carried an urgency that Thalen found distressing.

Under other circumstances Thalen would have relished the journey. His long love affair with Deganah had ended with bruised feelings on both sides, and he found it refreshing to get away from campus. The Long Roads Cart took them through parts of the Free States that Thalen had never seen before. But Granilton's dark mood made enjoyment impossible; he repeatedly made comments on the order of, "Look at that peaceful picture of peasants sowing, young man; imprint it in your memory. Alas, this field will never be so bucolic again." Every vista thus took on an aura of melancholy and fear.

Finding this atmosphere upsetting, Thalen cast around for something that might sidetrack his tutor's bleak mood.

"Sir, see with our forearms close together? See that my skin is darker than yours?"

"What?" said Granilton, startled by the topic. "All right, I suppose, now that you mention it."

"What accounts for the different skin shades amongst people?"

Granilton frowned. "I don't know. *You* brought up the subject."

"I think it might have something to do with being in the sun. Hyllidore often works outside, and his skin is darker. But what actually confounds me is that we all see these differences, but we don't actually notice them—or at least not the way we pay attention to hair color."

He'd managed to capture Granilton's attention. "Hmm. Skin color is a meaningless variation. It doesn't register because . . . our culture doesn't stress it. We can't notice everything, so we pay attention to what society tells us is important. We all know, for instance, that hair color indicates country of origin and traditional social standing, so we notice.

"Ennea Món will be a better place when everyone's hair is brown," Thalen opined.

"Will it?" Granilton mused. "Or will people just settle on other marks of difference, other reasons to hate one another?"

When they approached Jutterdam, the largest city in the Free States, the famous walled city on the sea, they crossed the Jutter River at Kings Bridge. Thalen had only a few glimpses of streets and buildings—he noted that like Sutterdam, the skyline was dotted with churches built to all the Spirits—before Granilton hustled him straight to the assembly.

They met in a small and overheated amphitheater in which rows of participants seated on cushioned benches looked down on a stage area that held an assortment of tables, chairs, maps, and high-ranking functionaries. Each of the Free States—Vígat, Fígat, Jígat, and Wígat—had sent a team of seven electors, and other notables had volunteered to testify. The conversation swung back and forth between disbelief, fear, and bravado in the loud and contentious debates.

"She would sell her country for a handful of deer scat," said Granilton during a woman's long lament about how a war would be bad for business.

"Tutor, I beg you to keep your voice down," Thalen whispered, shrinking smaller in his seat.

The next man who moved to the front argued that the Protectors would turn back when they reached the causeway because it was impossible to cross.

"That man makes a carrot look smart," his venerable teacher said at full volume. "Does he think the Oros have marched all that way just to retreat?"

Thalen pulled at his sleeve. "Tutor, please. They have slated you to speak tomorrow. Perhaps you should sit quietly and not make any enemies. I'm taking notes so you can rebut—"

"Shhh!" someone shushed the pair from the Scoláiríum.

"I tell you, we have the situation in hand," said a different man in a military uniform. "We have placed a detachment at the causeway. More importantly, we have taken the precaution of obtaining—all the way from Agfador, mind you!—the very latest advance in military technology!" The officer crossed over to a table where something bulky lay beneath a canvas cloth. "Behold!!! The fabled repeating crossbow! Where before precious time elapsed while the archer nocked, now he can shoot up to eight quarrels at a time! And they all fly with crossbow strength—sufficient to penetrate Oro armor! With this weapon we can defend against any invading force."

The amphitheater broke into delighted applause. People in the front pounded the officer's back while others passed the sample around.

Granilton alone wore a pronounced scowl. He shook Thalen's calming hand off and stood up, interrupting the speaker.

"Do you have all of these weapons in hand?"

Someone shouted, "You are out of order, Granilton!" But other voices called out, "Let him speak."

"Doldrums delayed the shipment, but we allowed for this. We expect them any day now."

"Will you have time for the men to train with them?" Granilton pressed.

"From this sample we know the mechanism is simple and easy to use."

Granilton's skepticism colored his voice, "How many did you order?"

"One thousand!" said the officer, with a wide flourish of his hands.

The room burst into more applause. A man called out, "Won't

those Oros be surprised!" Another commented, "Free States ingenuity will win out every time! To our glorious victory."

"Putting the crossbows aside," said Granilton, *"have you sent a company to blockade* the Causeway of Stones?"

"We have a squad of archers stationed there, and they may turn the Oros back. However, if the Oros persevere we don't intend the bridge to serve as the site of our decisive battle. We have considered our position with these weapons in mind," he said, gesturing toward the bow. "Because the enemy will be strung out on the causeway, we wouldn't get full advantage from our 'rain of death.' We want the enemy massed before us in a field so we can mow them down all at once. Also, these bows tend to scatter their shot. Which is why we don't want these expensive, custom-made quarrels being wasted in the sea.

"And when you fixate on the causeway, Granilton, you leave out of consideration our cavalry, which must be given an equal chance. As you can see, we have taken many other factors into consideration."

"Other factors?" The old scholar's voice rose through the four short syllables.

"Master, calm yourself." The military officer smiled with condescension. "We are experienced in military matters, while all your notions come from books. We—"

"Sit down and shut up, you imbecilic—you ill-taught, illogical, ILLITERATE!" Spittle gathered in the corners of Granilton's mouth. "You wouldn't listen to me years ago about blocking off the causeway. You wouldn't listen to me about hiring mercenaries or sending emissaries to our allies. Now it is too late for all such measures!

"We have lost our chance to forestall an invasion. Lost it due to your pride, dithering, and misjudgment! All we can do today is mitigate the damage."

The room fell silent as Granilton's fury infected some of the participants with doubts.

A woman shouted out, "I will withdraw Wígat's forces to protect Wígat!"

"And Fígat's should protect our border!" yelled a heavyset man.

Granilton roared, "No, no, NO! You will each want to circle your armies to protect your own homes. That way lies madness. Our only hope is to join together all our forces to meet the Oro army as a combined force. With some luck, we can inflict serious damage upon the invaders."

A Jígat elector jumped to his feet. "But who would command a joint force? Jígat has the most distinguished military force."

"That may be true, but Vígat will be the site of the attack," countered a man in uniform. "Vígat's generals should be in command; to them should go the glory."

"*Glory?* You want *glory?*" Granilton's raised bony fist actually shook with anger. "Finally, I understand; you dither on the causeway because totally forestalling an invasion would not provide enough *glory.* You think that you will decimate the Oro army with your new toy and win *glory.* Instead of thinking about *glory,* you should have been thinking of the welfare of your countrymen. Oh, you fools . . ." Thalen's teacher held his head in his hands.

The room grew quiet. When Granilton spoke again, his voice was soft and despairing: "Appoint a commander—any commander—posthaste and start making all preparations. We may not be ready for war, but war is upon us. Every second you posture and argue costs more Free States lives! I, for one, will not sit here discussing nonsense a moment longer."

He hustled Thalen out of the hall—Thalen heard the shouting immediately recommence as they left—and hired a coach for Latham. Thalen suffered a pang that they didn't even get to spend the night or eat a meal, but his tutor could brook no delay.

At each stop he sent Thalen running to purchase the latest broadsheet and muttered angrily when he discovered it was a week stale. They grabbed cold food when the coachman changed horses.

They arrived in the dark of night, weary from hours of bouncing, but Tutor Granilton had Thalen take him straight to the rector.

Thalen waited outside the door, hearing Granilton's voice yelling at her. Thalen reread the same sentences from *Oromondo Battle Tactics* while time dragged by slowly.

When the rector opened the door after this consultation, her eyes looked puffy and her cheeks moist. But she put on her jolly smile for Thalen and sent him to fetch several other tutors, servants, and even Quinith. When he completed those duties, he escorted Granilton back to his lodgings, holding him up by the elbow.

The aged man collapsed on the edge of his bed while Thalen set his traveling case down and unlatched it.

"Would you like me to pull off your boots for you, sir?"

Granilton waved him away. "That will do. Get some rest, young man. The rector will call a Scoláiríum Meet in the morn on the morrow."

He reached for a heavy volume on a shelf. "For bedtime reading, you might take a glance at this." The book cover he handed Thalen read *Surviving a Siege or Sack*. He saw Thalen's face after he read the title and reconsidered. "No, no, give it back here. What was I thinking of?" he mumbled. "That is not for tonight; it is so late—no reading tonight."


In the morning all the students, tutors, and staff crowded into the Scoláiríum Lecture Hall after fastbreak. Rector Meakey wore a cheery gown of bright yellow and orange, and she had stuck a piece of orange coral in a headpiece at a rakish angle. Just seeing her bobbing and smiling made everyone feel a little less apprehensive.

She mounted the podium and looked out over the throng.

"Oh, my darling scholars! You are so precious! You are more precious than ten walrus skeletons!" She spoke with sincerity and was slightly taken aback by the laughter that rippled through the hall. Then she chuckled and purposely topped herself. "Or even—an intact manatee specimen!"

After the slightly forced laughter died down, she continued with more gravity. "You have all heard that we expect the Oro army to invade sometime in the next moon. Tutor Granilton predicts that the first blow will fall in Vígat, near Sutterdam, because of its proximity to Melladrin.

"So for only the second time in its history—the first time being the grippe epidemic a hundred and seventy-two years ago—I have the singularly unhappy duty of closing the Scoláiríum."

A buzz of conversation overwhelmed the crowd. The rector had to hold up her hands for silence.

"Now, now, no cause for immediate panic.

"Most of you will want to join your families or lend your strength to the Free States army. I learned for the first time yesterday that many of you have long been practicing weaponry without my knowledge or aid. For that, I beg your forgiveness."

Thalen badly wanted a world where the rector could experiment on her fish eggs in undisturbed peace. Her apology made his eyes mist over.

"But before you disperse—readers, tutors, staff—one thing here is more precious even than *you*. The Library of Humility. Hundreds of scholars over hundreds of years have gathered books from all over the world. Our collection holds volumes available nowhere else in Ennea Món.

"Tutor Granilton and I believe that the library faces particular peril. Yes, the barrier of Clear Lake partially protects us and the Oros would find it hard to march here in force. But any enemy soldiers who do venture this far inland would take particular offense from our books, for they record the history of many cultures and religions, and thus their Magi would rule these volumes blasphemous.

"How any person could set a book aflame I do not pretend to understand." She sighed. "But I have been convinced that sacking and burning the library would be the highest priority of any Oros who came here.

"And if the books are burned, we lose the hard-fought knowledge (and ignorance) of generations.

"So. Our duty is clear: we must save the Library of Humility. But how? Tutor Irinia has devised a brilliant plan. She knows of a series of limestone caves in the hills less than two leagues from Latham that are partially hidden and not easily reachable. They might escape Oro notice completely. If we parcel the books out in multiple places, at least they cannot fall from one tinder strike.

"Yet to shift ten thousand books would be a mammoth undertaking. Tutor Kerosh has started to calculate how many cartloads, how many horses, how many ladders, and so on. I must tell you, his calculations make me dizzy!" Here she got them to laugh again.

"Many of you impatiently desire to hurry home to your loved ones. I understand. No one will blame you if you leave this forenoon. Still, I beg of you: stay two weeks and help us hide the books. Then, should we all perish, we will have insured that knowledge remains safe for the next generation, which, we hope, will be blessed to live out *its* days in peace."

Quinith jumped to his feet shouting and raising his fist aloft: "The books! The books! We must save the books!" Tutor Kerosh took up the roar, as did the porter, Hyllidore. All the students and staff in the hall joined in: "The books! The books! We must save the books!" The rafters shook.

Thalen shouted too, because he agreed with the plan. At the same time, a small part of his mind recalled *Motivation of the Populace: Techniques and Recommendations,* which Granilton had assigned him a year ago. He admired how well the rector, through jokes and apologies, had led up to a request, and how she had seeded the audience with enthusiastic advocates.

The community dispersed for a hearty meal in the refectory and then changed into clothing suitable for laboring. They started shifting the books that day. Villagers came to help. Carts, wheelbarrows, buckets, rucksacks, cases, trunks—anything that would hold more than arms—were pressed into service. At first they took care to preserve the books' order, but that soon went by the wayside.

The most physically taxing part of the mammoth task loomed at the cave end. The caves opened some paces above ground level, reachable only by ladder. Initially, the stronger men, such as Thalen, carried the volumes up the ladders by rucksack. When that proved much too slow, Thalen conferred with the tutor of Engineering; together they hooked up a pulley system. Buoyed by a fine spirit of camaraderie, the Scoláiríum and Latham communities worked dusty, arduous days.

When the caves would hold not one more, leaving but a few hundred straggling volumes that had fallen during transport, the rector proclaimed the battle over and dismissed her troops. The volunteers tried hard to erase the signs of their access to the caves. A good rainstorm would complete the job.

In the morn, Thalen packed his own belongings and embraced his friends. Deganah had already left, which saved him both from worrying about her and from an awkward farewell. Many readers said they would follow his footsteps back to Vígat, if not immediately, then after a stop at their family homes. Everyone put on a cheery face and vowed to meet back at the Scoláiríum "when the war is over."

Thalen stopped by the rector's chamber to say goodbye. The door stood open, and he discovered Tutor Granilton already there in the throes of a vehement argument. His tutor insisted that all the women and older girls of the Scoláiríum staff and the town of Latham flee to the hills and forests. The rector protested that she could not abandon her post.

"Meakey, *don't be an arrogant idiot.* I know the depredations of these soldiers. My logic is flawless: One, you are a young and beautiful woman, a woman who would be their prey. Two, you have many more years of scholarship and teaching ahead of you. Three, I, on the other hand, stand here as naught but a shriveled old man. All they can do to me is kill me. I insist that you set an example for the others and leave tomorrow. They will need your leadership and good humor to buoy them in their hideouts."

Thalen had read that war led to rape and the brutalization of civilians, though the concept of such brutality disturbing the peace of the Scoláiríum struck him as an implausible nightmare. Still, Thalen joined Granilton in his entreaties, and together they won the rector over.

Tutor Irinia came running down the stairs from her own office and burst into their discussion. "I thought I heard your voice," she said to Thalen. "Can I borrow him for a minute?" she asked her colleagues.

"As long as you bring him right back," said Granilton. "Now, Rector—"

"We've got to go over to the laboratory," Irinia said to Thalen urgently.

"Tutor, I have to catch the cart to the ferry; I really don't think I have time."

"Then we'll run," said Irinia firmly, and she set across the grass at an awkward lope, bony elbows pumping, holding up her long skirt, her pinned-up hair falling down. Thalen had no choice but to follow her.

Panting, they burst into the laboratory, where his tutor led him to a pan placed on a table.

Thalen started to say, "What's so important," but the words died on his lips because he saw the pan's contents—five small dead fish.

"These are fathead minnows," Irinia explained in a rush. "I was trying different concentrations of solutions on them. During the book shifting I fed them late at night and didn't pay any real attention to them, and this morning I saw they had all died."

Not only had the fish died, but they showed a variety of ill effects. One had a big tumor on its belly; another had lost most of its scales; the eyes of a third had gone cloudy.

Irinia grabbed Thalen's shoulders with both hands. "You've got to run now. But if either of us should perish in the upcoming invasion, at least the other one knows for certain: *the Oros have poisoned their own water through their mining*!" She squeezed him with her long fingers. "Now, go!"

Thalen rushed back to Scholars' House, where Granilton was watching for him impatiently. "Young man, come upstairs with me." They climbed the stairs to his office, the tired elder leaning on his reader.

In his office, Granilton remarked, "Look round." Thalen's sensitized eyes saw the problem: all the tutors' personal chambers still held hundreds of their own books.

"What can we do?" Thalen asked hopelessly.

"There is naught to be done," sighed Granilton. "Let us hope that walking through Scholars' House and setting each separate study alight is too much of a bother for any Oro soldiers. But just in case . . ." The tutor quickly grabbed a book here, one there, one off his shelf, and one off his chair. "Could you find room for these? I judge they are the most precious and the most useful to you. Oh, and this one. Please, take them. Please, *save them*."

Thalen could hardly refuse. He stuffed them in his rucksack, though they doubled its weight.

He held out his hand, trying to think of something comforting to say. "Farewell, Tutor Granilton. You provided the assembly with your wisest advice. You and the others saved the library. You've given the local women prudent counsel. You can be proud of these notable accomplishments."

The elderly scholar shook his hand and then pulled him into an awkward embrace. "I have not done half enough with my life. There were treatises I should have written." He struck his own forehead with his fingertips. "What knowledge will perish when I die? How could I have thought I had more time? How could I have been so lazy and slow?

"Thalen, keep thyself safe. My only son died some years ago, you know." He pointed at Thalen's chest. "*You* have been my most promising pupil. *You* are my legacy."

Thalen left the room quickly before he became emotional. As he ran to catch the last coach to Clear Lake, he realized that this was the sole time Granilton had embraced him, complimented him, or called him by name.

# 45

## Melladrin

Sumroth recognized that another army might have mutinied over its sparse rations. But due to the years of famine, Oro Protectors had become almost inured to hunger, and from childhood they had been trained in unquestioning obedience. The coterie of priests kept them on a tight rein of devotion, and their military discipline kept them dutiful.

Besides, a mutiny wouldn't produce food—it would just leave them in disarray on the steppes. The only hope of filling their stomachs lay in moving forward.

After three moons of hard sloughing, with their belts tightening every day, General Sumroth led his still-formidable army to the western edge of the Causeway of Stones. While his men pitched camp, he and his staff officers—fourth-flamers and above—spurred their aurochs on to examine the course ahead.

The causeway spanned the ocean from Melladrin to the Free States. No one now knew who had built it or how. A series of massive boulders had been laid end to end from one landmass to the other. Sumroth couldn't even imagine how men could have moved these stones into place; each spanned at least six paces in length.

They didn't form a smooth roadway: the boulders jutted jaggedly askew; most boasted slippery pools and lichens; sometimes a gap—large or small—yawned in between rocks. Certainly no one could ever use the causeway for wagons or trade goods.

"We'll have to leave the carts behind," a sixth-flamer growled.

"Well, they're nearly empty anyway," said the officer who Sumroth surmised might be his supply commander. "Tents, hollow casks, medical supplies. Your men have been using them to carry their battle armor, though. They'll have to grab their gear."

"Going to be a mess, getting the right pieces back to the right men," a fifth-flamer sniped. "They should never have stored them on the wagons."

"They are too weak to march with all that metal, and it hasn't been necessary—the Mellies haven't struck many times in the last weeks," retorted the sixth-flamer.

"Men with all their own set of armor, good-fitting armor, will live through the coming battle; those without, won't," said a fifth-flamer sourly. "You weren't strict enough about discipline, and now look at the trouble you've allowed."

Sumroth didn't listen to their dispute. He eyed the route ahead. He would wager that Mellies, so lithe and coordinated, managed to cross when the need arose. He was not confident about Protectors. It should be just possible for a soldier to walk or jump from one rock to the next. Pulling your stinking aurochs behind you would make it trickier. Seaweed markings showed that even in high tide, the rocks stayed above the surface. If you slipped off, of course, you would get smashed into the rocks by the fierce waves. Everyone should expect to get wet from the spray of the surf . . . but if the Protectors were fearless and careful, the general guessed he would get 90 percent across alive.

At least 80 percent.

He'd lost twenty-six hundred soldiers at the Mouth of the Mountains. Harrying, illness, and starvation had reaped another thousand or so. He might lose another three thousand here, especially since none of his men could swim. But if he could invade with close to thirteen thousand . . .

What awaited them on the other side worried him. If the Free Staters had an ounce of strategic sense, they would have blocked the causeway or set up an ambush to pick them off, one by one, as they crossed. His tactics would be useless on this slippery jetty; a child's breath could make his soldiers lose their balance.

"We'll let the men rest this afternoon and tonight," Sumroth declared. "Feed them as best you can. Sixth-flamer, you will bring the second half of the troops tomorrow, so as to cross in daylight."

"Sir, would you allow me the honor of leading the vanguard?" asked an ambitious fifth-flamer.

Sumroth found his eagerness annoying. "Your platoon will need to carry the shields. Are your men strong enough?"

The fifth-flamer turned to other officers. "If we're going first and burdened with shields, you'll have to pull our aurochs." The fellow officers assented with little grace.

The next morning was drizzly, just to add to the overall danger and discomfort, but his supply teams had scavenged seaweed and mollusks to cook up a nourishing if odd-tasting fastbreak. Sumroth couldn't restrain himself from a second portion, though he knew he was running the risk of making himself sick.

Some priests had been out on the foot of the causeway, blessing the rocks, entreating Pozhar to look favorably on their venture. They sacrificed an ailing aurochs and burned it as an offering. The vanguard set off, awkwardly carrying the shield plates.

Brushing the priests aside, Sumroth rode to the first rock, dismounted, and, holding the reins in his left hand, climbed out to the initial slick stone, conscious that thousands of soldiers observed him.

Sumroth slipped on the fourth stone, grazing his knee. On the seventh his aurochs fell heavily and he had to use all his strength grabbing it by the neck to keep it from sliding over into the drink. By the twentieth he had to stop counting because fatigue had already taken its toll. He refused to look backward toward stable ground. Behind him he heard occasional shouts as men or animals slipped into the sea. After a fourth-flamer reported that two men fell in trying to retrieve a comrade, he issued an order forbidding any rescue attempts.

His men followed him. With practice Sumroth got a little better at judging the jumps from one rock to the next and at seeing which areas of the boulders offered the best purchase. His son-of-a-slut aurochs learned nothing from experience—if it hadn't been carrying his armor, his great sword, and his letters from Zea he would have gladly let the sea swallow it.

The hours passed in this dangerous exertion. Daring a glance over his shoulder he saw an extensive contingent of his men keeping up, but in the distance the line became disorderly and broken. Soldiers who hung back would be caught on the rocks in the dark. As treacherous as the causeway might be in the daytime, darkness would mean death for sure.

As daylight waned, he strained to see. The vanguard had nearly reached the far end of the causeway. Sumroth scanned the flat ground ahead and then the trees and hillocks topped with the sun's sinking rays. He saw no fortifications, no lines of cavalry.

But just at that moment a whir of arrows from the nearest tree cover took down the cocky fifth-flamer who led his troops. Protectors shouted and fumbled to raise the shield plates they had lugged. The heavy shields overbalanced some of the men on the slippery rocks; Sumroth saw a dozen fall into the water. But two squads made it off the causeway and onto dry earth.

Stoutly making a wall with their shields, the men, exhausted though they must have been, charged the tree line. Some arrows struck their feet and they tripped; Protectors behind filled in the shield wall. More Oro soldiers made it to firm soil. Now hundreds bunched behind the metal plates, raising their battle cries with passionate voices.

In a short time, no more arrows flew out from the tree cover. The Free States archers had either met their deaths on Oro pikes and swords or turned and fled.

Sumroth smiled with satisfaction and bounded over the last boulders as nimbly as a mountain goat.

# 46

## Latham to Sutterdam

At Latham, Thalen had been isolated from how the rest of the states dealt with the incipient invasion. As he discovered at the landing at Clear Lake, panic bloomed. Women and children had fled Vígat by the hundreds. Because Jígat lay inland and Clear Lake formed a natural barrier, refugees overloaded the ferry from Trout Landing.

Babes wailed while mothers with tense voices scolded small children who strayed too far from their sides. Everyone tried to carry too many heavy cases. Items they decided to toss away littered the ground like strange, multicolored wildflowers.

Thalen pushed his way through the throng. He made it to the ferry just as it shoved off on its reverse trip back to the landing. On the return trip the ferry sailed nearly empty, the only passengers being men bound for the battle. A stringy, older man with an old-fashioned sword. Two twin brothers with dark freckles, turned-up noses, and big ears, of maybe sixteen summers, if that. Thalen wondered how their mother let them go.

The ferrymen would take no fees from any of them.

Thalen caught his breath and tried to calm down for a few minutes by watching the rippling water. Then he examined the five books that Granilton had pressed upon him: *Oromondo Beliefs, Weirandale versus Oromondo over the Centuries, Basic Battlefield Healing, The Magicks of the Magi,* and *A Leader's Duties.*

At first Thalen could not concentrate enough to read. Yet worrying just made him more anxious, so he opened *Basic Battlefield Healing,* which he thought might be the most immediately useful. He predicted he would find the book disturbing, but the information fascinated him. "More soldiers die of blood loss or infection than their wounds," he read. "Always clean and sharpen the saw before starting an amputation." Soon, he lost himself in the pages and the lake slipped by.

The elderly man tapped his book, handing him a hunk of sausage. Thalen looked up to thank him, but he had already moved on to share his bounty with the twins. Thalen hoped the old-timer would talk to them, because the boys quivered like bunnies. But the old man just silently returned to his seat at the front of the ferry.

Sighing, Thalen realized *he* should go tend to the youngsters. So he marked his page and moved to sit beside them. He learned they had not asked their parents for permission; they had slipped out in the night. They deeply regretted leaving their horses behind but had decided they could not abscond with their parents' property. They both claimed to be expert shots with the yew bows they carried. Thalen admired the bows and gently brought up the difference between shooting game and shooting armored Oromondo soldiers. The three of them discussed where they should aim to bring down Protectors. Fortunately, from his reading, Thalen knew the strengths and weaknesses of Oro mail.

When the ferry reached Trout Landing, the anxious crowd of even more hundreds of women and children pressing to board the ferry separated Thalen from the twins. If any carriages waited to take passengers south, Thalen had missed them by the time he pushed through the terrified civilians. So he hoisted his rucksack and started tramping up and down the gently rolling hills.

On his lonely trudge anxious thoughts besieged Thalen. What was happening? Had he already missed the battle? The day waned and he tried to keep his pace. He had walked for a few hours in the gathering darkness when he heard hoofbeats catching up with him. A man in a businessman's wig pulled up beside him. "Headed toward Sutterdam?" he asked.

"Yes," answered Thalen.

"Climb up behind me," said the stranger.

Riding behind a saddle, while uncomfortable, saved Thalen from hiking the whole distance. Each lost in thoughts of his own mortality, the two men did not talk during the trip. When they got close to the midnight city, the horseman hailed passersby, "What word?"

Pointing, a man answered, "They've been spotted by scouts. About five leagues southwest." Thalen had the rider drop him off in the middle of town. As Thalen slid off, the stranger said, "Let's see that sword you've got strapped to your belt." He grimaced at the weapon's poor quality and started to reach for one of his own.

Thalen forestalled him. "Your fine sword would be wasted on me, sir. Give it to someone who will get the best use out of it."

They clasped hands. "Fare you well, young man," said the horseman.

"You too, sir. Thank you for the ride."

The stranger could have ridden off, but he paused to say again, "I really hope you make it."

"Me too. And you too," said Thalen.

The horseman touched his hat and nudged his mount.

Obviously, Thalen could not join a battle carrying his rucksack of books and clothes. Home or Sutterdam Pottery? The factory lay closer at hand. And he might learn something there.

The factory gate swung to his touch, and he heard voices. Thalen pushed the door open, hallooing. Norling's voice called, "Up here!" and Thalen ran up the back stairs to find his aunt and his mother, fully dressed but without shoes or caps.

"What are you doing here!" he shouted, aghast. "You have to leave the city. Both of you. Immediately."

Mater had her hands on her hips before he'd gotten two words out.

"Wait. You listen here, Middle. Your father and your brothers could not get us to evacuate, so save your breath. The way we figure, if anyone's hurt, he'll need us to nurse him. And if the enemy takes the city, they're going to need us to run Sutterdam Pottery. How are they going to get the foodstuffs back to their precious homeland without pots?"

Teta Norling broke in, saying, "Look at you two. Both as stubborn as Clear Lake is long. All your sons are stubborn, Indy, just like you. Give me a hug, Thalen. I am glad to see you, lad, sorry, but glad too. Are you hungry? I've got a little stew warm in the room yonder." She tottered off.

Jerinda hugged him too, fiercely. "Mater," Thalen said in her ear, "the soldiers might leave Norling alone. But you—you're too young and pretty. The Oros—"

She put her hand over his mouth, and Thalen saw tears start to brim. "I could not go, Middle," she whispered. "To think that your brothers or your father might be wounded and calling for me? I know the dangers. It's my choice, and I made it. Why did *you* not stay in Jígat where you would be out of harm's way? At least one of you would be safer. That would've been a comfort to me. We sent you a letter, but maybe it never arrived."

"I could not stay away and let others do the fighting in my stead," Thalen replied.

"Then you know exactly how we feel," answered Jerinda triumphantly.

Teta Norling came back with the stew. As Thalen gobbled it down he asked for news of his brothers and father. Hake had joined the army two moons ago and had been put to good use in the Quartermasters' Corps. Since Harthen now commanded a division of cavalry, he would be right on the front lines. Pater had left to join the troops this very morning. He had no fighting skills, but like many Sutters, he hoped to be useful fetching water or bearing stretchers.

Thalen exaggerated, telling his mother and aunt that he'd picked up a little doctoring; he planned to join the healers' tents. As those tents would be away from the main battle, this stratagem eased their minds a bit.

But first Thalen had to get to the battlefield. He slipped *Basic Battlefield Healing* into a satchel, filled a waterskin, left the rest of his gear in the annex, and hugged his womenfolk one more time. Then he slipped out into the dead of night, trying to shake off the image of the tears dripping down his mater's cheeks.

The streets of Sutterdam had now fallen eerily quiet. Thalen pointed himself in the right direction and kept an eye out for any other latecomers. After he crossed Artisans Bridge, he hit the southern post road. His boots pinched his tired, swollen feet, and he was sorry to find himself solitary once again. He tramped along for an hour, wondering what lay ahead.

Out of the misty darkness, a white horse running loose unexpectedly pounded in his direction. Thalen held his arms out, forcing it to halt or run him down. The poor thing was spooked: its ears pitched way back, and its eyes rolled in terror.

"Shh, shh! You're all right. Everything's all right. I'm a friend." Eventually, the horse allowed him to come closer. A tan saddle blanket identified the mare as belonging to a Vígat regiment. When Thalen squinted in the half moonlight he saw dangling reins, blood all over its belly and one stirrup. He concluded that her rider had been wounded, panicking the horse; she sought to flee back to the safety of her stable.

"I'm sorry, girl. There's no hiding for us tonight." Stroking her seemed to provide comfort and her shaking eased.

Thalen filled his hands with water and offered this to the horse; she sniffed the water but couldn't drink from his small, leaking container.

"See, I mean you no harm. I'll find you water. You must be thirsty. Good girl, you can stop trembling now. You're not alone anymore."

With more soft words and strokes the horse allowed him to mount, and Thalen turned her back in the direction from which she had fled. The skies let down a gentle drizzle for a while, and then the rain stopped. Following the well-maintained post road, after two leagues he found a stream, watered the mare thoroughly, and washed off the bloodstain that distressed her so.

While he was paused at the stream a dispatch rider galloped past him, back in the direction of the city. Thalen would have tried to hail him for he badly wanted to know what was happening, but the man was moving too fast.

As Thalen and dawn approached, the noise of a multitude grew distinguishable. Thalen climbed up a steep rise and was rewarded with a full view of the gently sloping field below. He'd never seen a battlefield before, and he halted, openmouthed in astonishment.

The lack of trees indicated the field had once been farmed, but this year it lay fallow. A brook cut across it diagonally, from southeast to northwest, and a little valley followed the path of the water.

Thousands of Oros, wearing varied pieces of armor, massed at the far end of the clearing on foot or sat on odd, oxen-type creatures. Tall, red-plumed helmets marked the officers. Their command occupied a hillock in the middle left of the field; Thalen could make out a clump of plumed helmets, the Oromondo flag of a mountaintop spewing eight flames, signal bearers, and trumpeters.

The Oros vastly outnumbered the Free Staters. But the Free States had companies of archers positioned midway down the incline and faster horse cavalry assembled at the base.

Thalen nudged the horse up to a squad of twenty archers situated near the road. He discovered that instead of preparing to fire, the archers were in the midst of a pitched argument with one another. Several men showed fresh blood or bruising above their leather jerkins.

"What's going on?" Thalen asked generally.

"These fucking crossbows!" an archer spoke up. "At first light we were set to pepper the blasted Oros with them. But we found they don't have the range from up here, so we crept down into the woods on the right side—over there, see? We got off a few good volleys, but the bolts kept jamming! And then when you fired it, the damn thing bucked back in your face. Men smashed their noses; my pal lost an eye."

"Can I see one?"

A man standing close by handed him his repeating crossbow.

The reloading mechanism turned out to be a wooden box that stacked the quarrels, mounted on top of the shaft. Even in his cursory examination Thalen could tell that the wood had swollen.

"I think they got wet," Thalen said.

"No shit, genius—" interrupted an archer.

"Only a few of us brought along our longbows!" another one said in a tone of desperation. "We're helpless with these. We've tried prying off the top or gouging bigger holes, but—"

"The Oros seem to be waiting," said another archer.

Thalen knew from his books that defensive positions provided more safety; thus one of the primary battle tactics was to bait the other side into an offensive charge. So sure, the Oros would wait. They had little to fear from archers with malfunctioning bows.

One of the men whispered, "Down there . . . Down there lies death."

Thalen looked across the field. The thousands of Oro pikemen had formed up in squares in the deep middle. On the sides, more enemy massed on top of their lumbering creatures, with squads of infantry interspersed between them.

"Listen," Thalen said urgently. "The best plan would be to fall back. Return to Sutterdam. Get your own crossbows or your longbows—get anything that works. Destroy the biggest bridges— like Artisans—and hide in the buildings surrounding the smaller ones. You'd wreak havoc when they approached the city! You could hold them off the bridges for days."

Some of the archers shifted uneasily, and the light of hope came into the eyes of the man who sounded most despondent. But a thick-necked man with an armband who had just rejoined the group approached, asking, "Who are *you*, and wha'd you doing upsetting my squad? We obey our orders. Git you gone, 'fore I report you."

*"Listen to me, I beg you!"*

The squad leader snarled and reached his hand toward his dagger. "Git! You're a troublemaker! A coward!"

Thalen urged the mare to trot a little ways down the hill. He saw that the Free States commanders had divided their horse brigades into three prongs to face the enemy. A standard, predictable move, but one that would never work in this desperate situation. Thalen would have ignored the Oros on the right hand, northern side, counting on their oxen being too slow to rush in as reinforcements and trusting that the brook would slow them down. He would have sent his fastest, bravest cavalry to the left, arcing *behind* the southern arm, flanking them. And he'd have sent the second, larger group as a fist right into the gap between the lines of pikemen and oxen. His two strike forces would meet at that knot of Oro commanders to lop off the snake's head. He could almost see the Free States cavalry overrunning the hillock and the Oros scattering in disarray.

Thalen shook himself a little. He was *not* a general, merely a student who had never even raised a weapon against a foe. He looked around for the healers' stations and the supply tents; he spied their flags almost behind him in the flat and narrow stream valley. He kicked the horse, intending to ride to the tents, but midway down the hill he changed his mind and his direction. This trained cavalry horse might be useful. He trotted instead to the ranks of the horsemen.

Thalen addressed the first mounted Free Stater he saw, resplendent with his striped neck drape showing his regiment and equipped with lance and sword. "Here's an extra horse for you."

"Hey, that's Wareth's mare," the man said. "Where'd *you* get it?"

"She was racing back to Sutterdam."

"Hmm. Look at her sides; she's totally knackered. Give her here anyway; I'll take her to the reserves." Thalen slid off the mare and handed her reins to the outstretched hand.

"Where's the volunteer infantry?" Thalen asked.

"Massing over that way," the man pointed.

Thalen walked over to the crowd of people, mostly men but a few women too. Officers yelled at them to form straight lines and divided them into three sections. Thalen found himself in the right-hand group, several lines deep, but he didn't know if this position was favorable or unfavorable. Anxiously looking around for anyone he knew, he craned his neck in all directions. Hake should be back in the quartermaster tents behind him, but he saw no sign of stretcher-bearers or his father. Occasionally, the wind brought him a noise that sounded like Harthen's laugh, and then he felt a desperate longing to see his brother.

Thalen rose on his toes to survey the length of the field. Many of the hillside archers had thrown away their worthless crossbows; pulled daggers, swords, or axes; and run down the hill to join these ranks of ragged infantrymen. A Free States officer (who looked like an old schoolmate of Thalen's from Sutterdam's Upper Academy) shouted orders at the foot soldiers no one really heeded. They all waited anxiously, silently, as the sun rose hotter. Water boys passed through the lines. No one had any idea of what they were waiting for. Thalen wondered what the Free States generals were doing; he hoped they had some grand strategy in mind, but from his experience at the assembly he thought it was more likely that they were spending these hours arguing with one another.

Harthen's laughter wafted from somewhere closer by.

Thalen stood on his toes, waved his hands, and shouted, "Harthen! Harthen! I'm here!"

Harthen rode up, looking comfortable, even relaxed, on his bay.

"So, Middle! You've come to join us too! I'm glad you won't miss this glorious day. Hey, tie your neck drape around your head so I can spot you better. Don't fret; I'll keep an eye on you."

Thalen opened his mouth to answer, but someone shouted, "Captain! We need you," and Harthen rode off.

Seeing Thalen rearrange his drape gave the men around him ideas. Some wrapped their long scarves around their middles as a pitiful attempt at padding. Laughing, a few stuffed them down the front of their trousers to protect their tenderest spot.

Standing around made Thalen's legs ache, and he wished he had something to eat. He wiped the sweat out of his eyebrows. If he were home in Lantern Lane right now, his teta might be fixing him fastbreak. He could take off these boots and put his feet up . . . He could take a nap and have a wash . . . Thalen's mind drifted away from his uncomfortable surroundings.

A slow drum cadence rolled across the field, and the Oro pikemen marched a few paces forward in formation. *Don't be baited,* Thalen mentally addressed the Free States general. *We could take advantage of the high ground. Back us up the hill and use it.* But he held small hope regarding command's sagacity.

After all the time waiting, Thalen thought he'd be relieved when the Free States horns blew, but when they finally sounded his first thought was, "No, not yet! I'm not ready to die!" The remaining Free States archers let loose volleys of shots. Thalen couldn't tell how much damage they inflicted. When the arrows started to thin, the cavalry began its assault, leveling its lances with a roar of hoofbeats and shouts. A few moments later the officers bellowed to the infantrymen, "Draw and advance!!! Forward!!!"

The foot soldiers started at a brisk walk. The man next to Thalen started a rhythmic chant of, "No. No. No. No. No." Once they forded the little stream, their officers screamed, "Charge!!!"

Like the men around him, Thalen started to run. Ahead he saw a swirl of indecipherable chaos of horses veering, bodies falling, and metal flashing. The noise all around was equal uproar, but somehow Thalen's mind closed out all sound and focused all his attention on his vision.

An Oro Protector appeared in his field of view with his back to Thalen, intent on thrusting his pike at an unhorsed cavalryman prone on the ground. Thalen raised his sword over his own head two-handed and brought it down on the back of the Oro's unprotected neck.

He whirled because he sensed movement: an Oro mounted on an oxen thundered at him, intending to ride him down. Thalen sucked his body away from a sword that reached to stab him, awkwardly slashing upward and perhaps wounding his assailant's underarm. The Oro turned his animal back at Thalen; desperately Thalen dodged the wicked horn and thrust his sword deep into the oxen's haunch. His cheap sword broke off at the hilt, but the animal went berserk from the pain, bellowing and kicking, carrying the enemy rider away.

Thalen grabbed a breath and desperately searched the ground for a weapon. He dived for a blood-slick sword next to a man's body. When he stood up he found himself in the midst of a group of Oros, all of whom, at that particular instant, were engaged in attacking other Free Staters. He tried to help a countryman with a wild slash at an Oro's leg, only to miss his objective completely and stumble from his own momentum.

Thalen could recognize Harthen's laugh in the midst of a windstorm. Against all odds, his brother shouted, "Thalen!!! Hang on! I'm coming!!!" Harthen's well-trained mount cleaved through the chaos, and Harthen reached his free arm down. Desperate, Thalen grabbed it, jumped, and awkwardly landed on his belly on the rump of Harthen's horse.

"Middle, you need practice at that!" Harthen smoothly parried a blow with a deafening clang and then thrust his lance into the man's exposed throat while Thalen pulled himself into a seated position, dropping the sword he'd just picked up but managing to cling fast to his brother's waist. Harthen shone with a kind of light—full of the joy of battle.

Several Free States cavalry wearing similar colors formed up around their dashing captain with practiced precision, and together they turned their horses to face a phalanx of approaching pikemen. "Here we go!" shouted Harthen with glee. Thalen, bumping along as worthless baggage, watched in awe as the cavalrymen managed to rout that group of Oros by breaking their formation, wheeling back, and using their height, lances, and swords to scatter the enemy.

Harthen had dropped his reins; he guided the horse with his knees. His horse veered around a tall man in its path waving metal. Harthen cleaved the stick of a halberd coming at his right side from another foe. This left the middle of his body open, and in that instant a pike struck Harthen smack in the chest. The impact of the blow transferred from Harthen to Thalen as his brother shuddered once violently. Harthen's horse reared, and Thalen slipped backward off the horse's hindquarters. He chased the horse a few steps and reached up to pull down Harthen's slumped form. Bright red blood already saturated his brother's shirt and burbled from his still-smiling lips. Thalen tried to say something, but nothing came out of his throat.

Thalen knelt holding his baby brother, his thoughts aswirl. *The pike broke the ribs, went straight through. Through your body and almost into mine. How could you be so alive one moment and now only this . . . weight? Where are you? I want you back. Is it my fault? So much blood. Youngest, I want you back. You saved my life. Did you suffer? Do you even know I'm here?*

Thalen still knelt holding Harthen's body when a leaping horse accidentally kicked him in the head and sent him sprawling face-down in the mud. Thalen braced his hands into the ground to lever himself up but found his body would not obey.

*I'm not that hurt,* his mind said to him. *I am in shock; I read about that. I'll just lie here a minute and collect my wits.*

Apparently the Oro lines had moved forward, because the battle sounded as if it swirled right on top of him: deafening horses' screams and human grunts and the sound of metal hitting metal. Above the confused sounds Thalen heard a strange, melodic noise. He thought he hallucinated.

Hooves and boots trod on Thalen several times, which vaguely hurt, but still his body refused to move.

His mind drifted. When had he last slept? He was so tired, so very, very tired. The muddy field felt so soft and warm with blood.


Thalen reentered consciousness with a jerk. Laboriously, he pushed up on his knees. The sun had crept over to late afternoon. He had a knot on the back of his head and bruises everywhere else. Otherwise, he seemed to be alive and intact, though parched. The waterskin slung over his shoulder held enough for him to take a long drink, and he used the last handful to make a pass at the mud on his face.

*Harthen.* Thalen looked around in a panic, realizing that he knelt in a tangled sea of broken things, like smashed poles, bits of armor, arrows, and broken bodies. The churned-up mud had splashed everything. Harthen had been right next to him, but either he or his brother had moved some paces when the battle washed over them.

*Must I find his body? I know he's dead.*

He spotted a nearby pike. He used it as support to help him gain his feet and look around. The field, with the battle long over, at present contained only thousands of intermixed dead and wounded. In the distance, two squads of white-haired soldiers combed the pasture, occasionally reaching down.

Thalen dropped back to his belly and started crawling over the bodies, some of which moaned or reached for him. The Scoláiríum student would have stopped to help a wounded stranger, friend or foe. But the man who'd awoken on the battlefield was more single-minded.

*I can't help you. I can't stop. I still have one brother—I have to find Hake.*

When he got a little farther away from watchful Oros, he risked a running crouch. He ran to the supply tent in the rear of the battleground that he had seen earlier. The tent's canvas had been rent and some of its poles broken. Chairs and tables lay overturned and snapped. Corpses, already stinking, buzzing with flies, littered the dirt floor. In the dim light Thalen could not read the uniforms splattered with blood, and he didn't trust himself to recognize Hake by his stature. He began methodically studying each face, turning over men sprawled on their bellies—*Not him*—and forcing himself even to pick up heads detached from their necks—*Not him.*

Thalen found Hake half under a table near the rear of the tent. He lay quite still with his eyes open and unfocused. Crouching on his heels, Thalen stared at him in dismay. Then Hake blinked.

"Hake!" Thalen whispered. "Hake, I'm here. Where are you hurt?" Hake turned his gaze and recognized him.

"Hey," he croaked in a dry voice. "Thalen. Is it really you? Am I dreaming? I have been waiting all day for those bastards to come and cut my throat. Better for you to do it."

"Where are you hurt?"

"I can't move or feel below my waist."

"I've got to get you out of here," Thalen said.

"Leave me. I'm done for. Vígat is done for. Mater and Pater—"

"*Mater* would skin me if I left you. The scavenging crew is far away. I'm going to get you out of here."

Thalen pulled Hake out from under the table and, with difficulty, hoisted him over his shoulder.

As he left the supply tent they passed the entrance to the healers' tent. Thalen peered in at the bodies and gore.

"Anyone alive? Anyone able to walk?" Thalen called softly.

"Wait for me!" came a muffled voice. One of the piles of corpses started to move, and a stab of terror hit Thalen. But a young lad emerged, not a ghost. For a second Thalen thought he might be one of the twins from the ferry and his heart leaped, but a second glance proved him wrong. This scrawny youngster wore ill-fitting, patched clothes, with his hair cropped to his skull. He sported a bandage wrapped around his chest and left shoulder.

"I kin walk," said the lad. "Just hiding to escape notice. Where to, Cap'n?"

"Away from here! Grab one of those swords, some rolls of bandages, and a waterskin."

Creeping round behind the tents, the three made their way into the tree line. Back toward Sutterdam was the only direction that made sense to Thalen. There, he could find help, healers, and food. He could try to hide Hake with Mater; he would heal under her care.

Thalen led them to the right of the road he had trotted down on the white mare, so many eons ago. Now, he had to climb the hill, carrying a heavy burden, and it had grown so very steep. Thalen staggered and panted under the weight. He stopped to pull off his bloody neck drape and make a cushion on his shoulder. Hake made no protest, no matter how much Thalen jostled him.

Once they crested the hill, they paused to catch their breath, and the lad squirted water in Thalen's mouth. "My name's Tristo," he said. "From Yosta. Came down here on a fishing boat with me mates, to help hold off them invaders. They gave me one of those newfangled crossbows and placed me in the woods. But when I goes to fire it—bam! It bites me back. Me mate brought me to the healers' tent, and the man says, 'You're my first patient: you've a broken collarbone, laddie. War's over for you.' Gave me milk of the poppy. I fell asleep, nice as you please. And the next thing I knows damn Oros were crashing through the tent, running through the healers and everyone. I crawled under some poor fellas to hide."

Hake spoke, "Smart thinking, Tristo. I sat in the supply tent, doling out our last weapons, when aurochs came smashing through. One caught its horn on my waistcoat, and then shook me off like a pest. I guess when I landed I broke my spine."

Tristo and Hake shook hands. Thalen said, "Keep your voices soft. Tristo, I'll watch forward; you keep a look out behind."

"Yeah, we don't wanna get captured now," the boy agreed.

Thalen switched Hake to his other shoulder and cautiously led the way. They walked downhill for a while, and then their path flattened. They had covered more than half a league when Thalen's strength completely gave out and he staggered. He led them into sparse cover and tried to set Hake down gently. They all drank a little more from Tristo's waterskin.

"Someone's coming," warned Tristo. Over the rush of blood pounding in his ears, Thalen also detected the rustle in the brush. He grabbed the sword and struggled to his feet.

A man appeared out of the thin undergrowth. His wrinkled, dark brown face showed he was middle-aged, but he looked fit; he wore a splattered Free States uniform of tan and silver, a neck drape of silver and maroon, and boasted impressively thick mutton-chop sideburns. He dragged a stretcher bed on which lay an unconscious Free States soldier whose leg was covered in a repurposed scarf now sopping with blood. The older soldier paid no attention at all to Thalen's sword. He slowly set the litter down and wiped the sweat from his forehead with the back of his sleeve.

"Been hoping to find more survivors. Set off hours ago. Seen many folks caught and trussed up—taken as slaves, I figure. But no one else free. Got to be more of us scattered around. The enemy failed to set up a perimeter."

Hake introduced their threesome. The soldier was Sergeant Codek from Jígat. He did not know the name of the man on the litter.

"Well, now we are five," Thalen said, "and we might pick up a few more. What do you suggest? I know there's a stream not too far ahead; I thought maybe to hole up near it."

"That's as good a plan as any," said the sergeant. He suggested that he and Thalen exchange burdens so as to use different muscles. So Codek hoisted up Hake, while Thalen grabbed the litter handles. Tristo managed to hold up the end of the stretcher for a short distance and they covered ground more quickly, but when Tristo's face twisted with pain Thalen made him let the back end of the stretcher drag.

Just when none of them could manage to lurch another step they reached the stream. Tristo wandered a little ways upstream and Codek a ways down, scouting for a place to hide.

Tristo returned soonest. "I spotted a shed just yonder, like for animals. With straw."

When Codek rejoined them they set out for it. Before they took the comatose soldier into the shed, however, Thalen insisted on taking off his bandage and washing the wounded leg thoroughly in the cold water. In the shed, he rebandaged it tightly in clean bandages. He sent Tristo to clean his collarbone too. Finally, Thalen scrubbed the mud off himself, cleaned his various nicks and the knot on his head, rinsed out his drape, and let the freezing water numb his bruises.

"I will take the first watch," offered Codek. The others sank down in the straw. Thalen expected he might be too distraught to sleep, but exhaustion won out.

When Codek shook Thalen awake, night surrounded the shed. The sergeant whispered, "I hear voices back by the stream. I'm going to check. You watch here."

Thalen grabbed the sword. To reassure himself he placed his palm just above chests to make sure the wounded were still alive. After a few minutes of waiting, Codek returned with three more people: a scout with a broken arm and a cut in his calf who introduced himself as Wareth; an older citizen volunteer, Ikas, who murmured he worked as a wheelwright by trade; and a woman healer named Dwinny.

Thalen took the next watch and let the others collapse in the straw. He watched the sun rise over the pasture mockingly as if it were just another day.

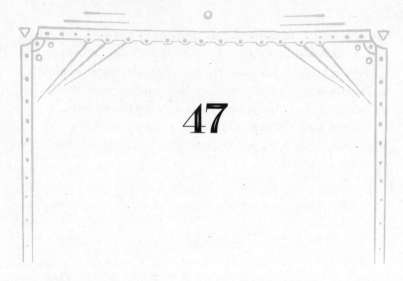

# 47

## Naven's Manor, Androvale

Tenny spent several pleasant days resting at Naven's country manor. Perfectly placed on the side of a gentle hill, the gardens of the well-proportioned estate bloomed with summer's abundance. Tenny's guest room window opened on a tranquil scene of rolling pastures. She particularly admired the vibrant—nearly lifelike—tapestries in the Great Hall depicting historic themes. The duchess mentioned with pride that she had not imported them from Cascada but rather patronized the work of a local weaver.

The duchess's well-trained staff and Tenny's improved temper warded off any scenes like the ones in Gulltown. Tenny hated the guards who watched her like vultures, but she managed to pointedly ignore their existence most of the time.

She brought her attention back to Duchess Naven, who, as they sat in a rose garden sipping summer wine, wanted to unburden herself of her worries about her daughters.

"You don't have children, Lady Tenny. It is so hard, these days, to know what to tell them about Color."

"I'm not sure what you mean, Duchess."

"Well, my lord husband tells me we must not be snobbish, that brown hair is fine, that if one of our girls—you know, we have *five* we must see settled—has a brown-haired suitor, we should not discourage him." Instinctively, her hand traveled up to her own head, where amber locks lay carefully and ostentatiously arranged on top of a darker, brown layer.

"I've traveled a great deal, Duchess," said Tenny. "Let me assure you: Color has nothing to do with character. It is merely a quirk of the past."

"Yes, yes. So you say, so everyone says, and that to think otherwise is narrow and old-fashioned. But we're talking about *marriage* now, and the future of the Naven line. Tell me, honestly, Tenny, don't the Spirits favor Old Color?"

"Do they?" Tenny had to stop and think. "They might . . . in some cases, such as our queen. But then again, given the tragedy of so many Old Color lines—recall how all of Iga's Gold were massacred!—we can't take this as axiomatic."

"My littlest girl once told me that brown color comes from tisane, black teas, and cocoa. Isn't that adorable?" said the duchess.

Tenny didn't usually find anecdotes about children amusing, but this brought a smile to her lips. "So did your daughter turn down her cocoa?"

"For a full week!" They both laughed.

"But seriously, Lady Tenny, next you'll be uttering blasphemies!" said the duchess.

"Well," said Tenny, sipping from her glass, "who's to say the Spirits have always been infallible or incapable of whim? No, really! I'm serious," she forestalled her companion's effort to object. "My own theory about Old Color is that it was more or less a momentary fancy. It's been rich elites who have deliberately bred for Old Colors throughout the centuries as a mark of separation and distinction." Again, she rushed on, this time to take the sting out of indirectly criticizing her hostess. "As for the amber color in Weirandale, I suspect it didn't come from Nargis anyway. Our legends talk about the queen's Blue, but actually say nothing whatsoever about amber. I suspect that it derives from intermarriage between Iga Gold and Rorther Red—in which case you can hardly count it as a sign of Weir nobility!"

"Ah," said Duchess Naven, sitting back in her chair. "I just realized something. You always wear a turban. Is that to cover your hair?"

"Mostly it's because I'm too impatient to sit through the fussing," Tenny admitted with a self-mocking smile. "But yes, I want people to talk to my face, rather than be distracted by my Color."

Tenny reached to lay her hand on top of Duchess Naven's. "You should worry much more about whether the suitors demonstrate compatibility with your girls than about their hair."

Tenny felt the duchess shrink at this last statement, and the involuntary movement confirmed Tenny's private guess about the union between her host and hostess.

Duke Naven, who had needed to attend to some estate concerns, joined them in the rose garden and told his wife all about their experiences searching for the princella.

"Oh my dear, such a scene—comic and tragic at the same time. The peacekeepers and the midwives rounded up any gal who could possibly fit our criteria. We had throngs of girls from fourteen to twenty-four: fat ones, skinny ones, pockmarked, no teeth, dairymaids, and some who smelt strongly of the barnyard. The country lasses acted so confused, fearful they had done something wrong, their parents half-servile and half-offended. I tell you I felt a proper fool.

"Each girl had to have a private audience with Lady Tenny. How did you find them, Tenny?" asked Duke Naven.

"Abashed. And you are being harsh on them in the main, dear Naven. Most were levelheaded and quite lovely, if somewhat untutored. In fact, I had to be quite stern"—here she broke off and glared at the Cascada guards behind her—"with Twitch and Stare that these pretty young women were not to be harassed by glance, word, or touch."

The duchess sighed. "But none of them turned out to be the princella, enchanted and disguised."

"No, no, of course not," said Naven. "They were all Androvale girls. Seen their like all my days. So we have covered all the Northern Wards on this blasted, wasteful quest." He stroked his mustache. "Today and the morrow, my dear, we will rest with you—refortify ourselves, so to speak—and then commence the hunt again in the Middle Wards."

"Will you bring these hordes of girls and their outraged parents here, Lord Husband? They might trample my garden beds or chase the swans. They certainly would disturb my peace." The duchess's voice had taken on an aggrieved and nagging tone.

"Oh no. I plan to host only an initial meeting of the peacekeepers and midwives here. You know the peacekeepers already—respectable chaps all. We are not acquainted with all the goodies, but they do the hamlets great service."

"'Tis so," sighed the duchess. And then, perhaps regretting her first inhospitable response, she said, "I will make arrangements for a nice luncheon for them all. And little gifts, such as bars of my lilac soap. The goodies and the peacekeepers could set a model of cleanliness for the villagers. We needn't raid the wine cellars, though, I do hope."

"Orest will set out cider and ale. Later I will find a centrally located inn so we can conduct additional meetings without disturbing your household's peace." Naven's glance at his wife was almost a glare. "I'll send Orest tomorrow to have a look-see as to which inns would be most accessible and most comfortable for Lady Tenny.

"The Wyndton Arms might work best. Wilim is such a steady chap; put a job in his hands and it's bound to go off well."

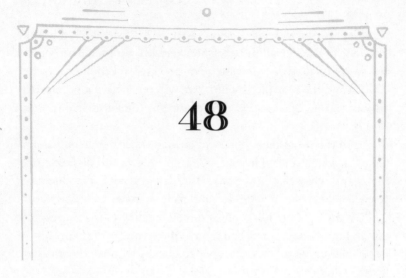

# 48

## Sutterdam

Upon winning the battle outside Sutterdam, General Sumroth pulled his dagger and slit the throat of his aurochs. He recognized this was a wasteful, petty thing to do. But he despised the animal with a passion that exceeded the excruciating blisters it had raised on his backside. He hated its bad temper and the way it continually tried to bite or kick him. He abhorred its stink and its spit.

*Enough! May the wretched beast and its bony spine rot forever.*

He ordered his aide to find him the best horse left alive on the battlefield. Then the general gathered together officers and infantry and rode into the city of Sutterdam, outwardly impassive, but inwardly impressed by the trapping of peace and luxury. The populace hid from the conquerors, but he cared little about them.

Houses with balconies filled with flowers. Watering troughs for horses outside of businesses filled with an unimaginable wealth of goods. Ornate carvings on each bridge. Expensive glass in many windows.

As he and his men rode by, pet dogs barked at the conquerors. Sumroth could hardly recall when he last saw a dog in Oromondo; they had all been eaten long ago. He recalled dog meat being tasty, but he also remembered, faintly, the pleasure of a dog's affection. He had been deprived, all his life, of trivial and grand comforts these people took for granted.

Leading his personal platoon to the center of the city, he decided that the Inn at Golden Bridge would do as officers' quarters and the council house as his army's field office. He sent a squad scavenging for food and drink.

Soon he and his top officers ensconced themselves in the dining room of the tavern and made the quaking staff serve them the best meal they had enjoyed in years: newly baked bread, beef soup, sweet halibut, fresh vegetables, all washed down with goblets of wine and topped with sweets, cheese, and nuts.

Reports started coming in of so many Protectors dead; so many walking wounded; so many enemy killed; so many slaves captured; so many horses rounded up; so many wagonloads of food expropriated; so many quarters for the Protectors requisitioned; etc. etc. etc.

Sumroth nodded at each report and pointed to one of his high officers (choosing them by counting their flame tattoos) as the person responsible for following up on the matter. Personally, he cared only about the number of Oro fatalities, which a fourth-flamer estimated at three thousand, meaning that Sumroth still commanded nearly ten thousand Protectors, more than enough to conquer this nation of artisans and burghers.

The officers' stomachs groaned with the rich food. One fifth-flamer ran from the room sick to his stomach while another started snoring at the table. They ate again and drank more wine. Sumroth felt weary, and after this heavy meal, sleepy. But first he craved a real bath.

He had slaves brought in to fill a bathtub with scalding water. He ordered up a squad of captured women to scrub the blood and grime from his body and wash his hair pure white again. The water soothed some of his aches, but not the most troublesome.

Naked, he walked to his doorway. "You!" he ordered the Protector on duty. "I want you to fetch a healer to me. A Free States healer."

"Yes, General," the soldier saluted.

Sumroth drank a flagon of sweet water and then, still unclothed, walked out onto his balcony. He looked around Sutterdam Square at the merchants' rich dwellings and the Statue of the Martyrs in the middle of the park. How he hated these softlings, these weaklings who had everything without sacrifice, so drugged by their prosperity they didn't even know how to defend it properly.

Sumroth felt drunk now—drunk on wine, exhaustion, and victory. *What did these lardwits ever do to deserve the plenty they take so for granted? I own their country now.*

Deliberately, he pissed off the balcony, showering his spray in a victorious arc.

A knock at the door interrupted his gesture. Sumroth finished emptying his bladder, and gave himself a little shake before shouting, "Enter." His soldiers had brought a haggard healer, his apron splashed with blood, carrying a satchel. A big bruise started to puff out his jaw.

"Ah. Took long enough!" Sumroth grumbled.

"He gave us lip about coming, sir."

"I was trying to save a life," said the man, his eyes still ablaze.

"How could that matter—one Free Stater more or less?" Sumroth said. "Soldiers, you will wait outside."

After they closed the door the general addressed the healer. "I have painful blisters on my bum. You will lance them and dress them."

If the captive considered complaining about being dragged away from a life-and-death situation for this medical emergency, he kept his thoughts to himself. Sumroth stretched himself out on the bed so the healer could get to the inflammations. He knew the little coward didn't have the nerve to use the knife in his hand to injure or kill the man who had just taken his country. And sure enough, the healer just docilely lanced the blisters—which hurt like fire, though Sumroth wouldn't allow himself even to blink. Then the man disinfected the area.

"You may go now, back to your patients—or to blazes." Sumroth waved a dismissal.

Then he gave a prayer of thanks to Pozhar and tumbled into the feather bed, wishing that Zea snuggled here beside him.

# 49

*Outside Sutterdam*

To Thalen's relief, in the morning Dwinny took charge of the injured hiding in the cowshed. Her satchel held needle and thread, unguents, willow bark tincture, and milk of the poppy.

She sewed up the unconscious archer's thigh first. He'd lost so much blood, but they hoped that he would survive.

The scout, Wareth, had a wide smile, a high forehead, and curly hair. He stood a tad shorter than Thalen, but his muscular frame stretched more broadly. He sat still while Dwinny sewed up the pike gash on his calf, and though he pressed his lips together, he told Thalen and Codek to keep going as they fashioned a splint for his broken arm.

"Thanks, fellas. Whoa, that feels more secure."

Thalen tied a neck drape around Wareth's neck as a sling so he could rest his bad arm. "You know, I think I heard your name on the battlefield. Do you own a white mare?"

"Rosie? Yeah. How do you know about Rosie?"

Wareth and Thalen marveled over the coincidence of Thalen finding his white mare.

"She was always a little skittish, that one. My captain sent me south, scouting for the Oros, only I ran into a forward squad. Got my wound there—took a pike to the leg."

"How'd you break your arm?"

"I tried to tie my drape around my calf, and I lost my balance and fell off! Rosie hightailed it out of the woods and deserted me!"

Dwinny smeared her unguents on every wound she could find. Though she gave the archer with the leg wound milk of the poppy, she made the others take willow bark drops. Thalen had not even realized how much his head ached from the horse's kick until the medicine ameliorated the throb. Dwinny said the only remedy to try for Hake was to sit him in the cold stream; if his back was merely bruised, the swelling might subside. They left him there until his legs turned bluish, but no sensation returned.

At midafternoon, Thalen called them all to council.

"We need food. We need to find out what is going on back in Sutterdam. Dwinny wants fresh bandages. I propose that Ikas and I try to sneak into town for supplies and information."

"I could go," Codek offered.

"But your fighting skills are better deployed guarding the wounded. And Ikas and I have lived in Sutterdam for years and know our way around well."

Codek grunted assent.

Oros on stolen horses rode in every direction on the major roads, so Ikas and Thalen crept through cover on a parallel line. When they got close to Sutterdam they hid in a gulch until night fell. In the distance they could see dozens of small fires raging.

"Fucking Oros sure love their fires," muttered Ikas, rubbing his dark beard. "Where are we going? Oros will have gathered all the food from the markets, and they'll probably be watching the major bridges."

"We will break into some homes," said Thalen, who had never stolen anything before in his life.

The modest cottages on the outskirts of town had already been thoroughly ransacked by hungry invaders. Thalen and Ikas snuck toward the center of Sutterdam, where the lodgings bunched closer together. Ikas kicked in the door of one quiet house, but the owners had evacuated, taking all foodstuffs with them. They tried another with the same result, though Thalen scrounged pieces of clean linen that held promise as bandages.

They were about to force the back door of the third, when a tiny old woman holding a fire poker over her head jerked the door open. When she saw they were Free Staters, she let them in. Though they judged it risky to light a lantern, she fixed them tisane in the dark while she packed a basket with all the provisions she had in her larder.

"Do you know what's going on?" Thalen asked avidly. "Where are the Oros? Where are they holding their prisoners?"

The ancient lady knew nothing. Thalen and Ikas were the first people she had seen since the battle.

"Why didn't you evacuate?" Ikas asked her.

"And let those invaders drive me out of the house I've lived in for years? The house we built with our own hands? Couldn't do that."

"Do you have kin here?" she asked. Ikas had sent his wife and daughters to Jígat, but Thalen told her how much he worried about his family at Sutterdam Pottery.

"Well, then. I'll just pop down to Hartling's place and find out what's what. Bought my milk jug there and my oil jar too. You men have another cup of tisane, and I'll be back in a tick."

"It's too dangerous for you to go abroad."

"Pshaw! No one will bother with an old woman. Can't hide under my bed forever. Feel kind of shamed for staying under cover for so long." And she tottered off, carrying a shaded lantern, before they could talk sense into her.

Ikas and Thalen waited in the small, unlit house. How long had she been gone? Surely she should be back by now? Had she been captured?

After an anxious interval, they heard lightweight feet returning round the back door. When the door opened to Ikas standing guard with the poker, Thalen saw that the homeowner had brought Norling with her!

Norling hugged Thalen tightly and wiped her tears with her apron. "Your brothers?" she asked.

"I'm hiding Hake," Thalen said, quickly adding, "he's injured but he'll live. Harthen—" Thalen could not say the words. Norling put her hand on his mouth and nodded.

"I heard that your father lives," she told him in return. "The Oros gathered him up with the other captives and locked them all in the shipping hall. No one has said he's hurt, and I think they would have mentioned that if he were.

"But . . . your mother . . ." Norling took a breath. "Soldiers broke into the factory, and Jerinda—I tried to help her, Thalen, but I wasn't strong enough, they pushed me away. And she screamed and fought so—I think she done it on purpose-like to make them kill her quickly, and this one Oro got so angry he pulled out his dagger . . ."

Thalen buried his face on the table and cried while Norling pulled her apron over her face and wept again too, hugging his shoulders from behind. At first the homeowner made soothing, sympathetic noises. But after a few moments she got angry and slapped them both on the back of their heads.

"There's no time for this grieving now," she hissed at them. "The living's got to live. You've got to be made of tougher clay. You've got hungry folk and wounded soldiers waiting for you. Norling, show what you brought from the pottery."

His aunt had grabbed Thalen's rucksack, a string bag of food, and a handful of coin.

"Thalen, don't come home," she said. "Mother Rellia here says she'll help me. I'll find out about Hartling's condition, and I'll bury your mother. You don't come home while this filth holds our city. I'm counting on you to stay free and safe and look after Hake."

On their way out the back door, both Ikas and Thalen solemnly kissed Rellia's and Norling's foreheads. Laden down with their burdens, they headed back out into the night. Then by starlight and fire shadows they hurried back to their pasture.

The group of survivors stayed one more day in the cowshed. The pasture belonged to a dairy farm northwest of Sutterdam; the rambling stone farmhouse and barn, both deserted, stood a short way from their hiding place. They relocated on the second day after the battle, as soon as night covered their movements. Abandoned barn cats pestered them with frantic meows until Wareth figured out they needed water pumped into the trough.

Although Hake's paralysis had not changed, due to Dwinny's care the rest of the wounded began to recover. The archer with the vicious leg wound rose to semiconsciousness, too weak to talk but able to swallow broth. The chatty lad, Tristo, turned out to have a flair with food, and if others helped with any task that required two working hands, he turned the edibles cadged from Sutterdam, mixed with foraging in the farm's garden and larder, into decent meals.

Hake and Thalen stayed close to one another—finding a modicum of comfort in proximity—in the ground floor common room, but they avoided talking about family or anything else. Images of Harthen dead in his arms, images he did not want to share with Hake, plagued Thalen.

*At least I never have to tell Mater about Hake's injury or Harthen's death. The news would have killed her if the Oros hadn't.*

When not needed, Thalen took refuge in a book or pretended to read the pages before him while his mind frantically ruffled through earlier volumes. Hake stared off into space, absently worrying the tatty quilt they had thrown over his legs, as if hiding the legs from his sight would hide the knowledge of their uselessness. Hoping to catch a breeze, they kept the shutters and doors agape against the summer heat; flies from the manure pile plagued everyone.

On the fourth day after the battle, the survivors (excluding the still-drugged archer) gathered around the sloping farmhouse table on crude stools eating an evening meal. Hake, in his chair, sat at the head. The open shutters let in the early evening air, which smelled of the marigolds planted in the kitchen garden mixed with smoke that had blown from town and funeral pyres.

Tristo spoke up. "I have peas, cheese, and some greens left. We could live for a while, but this is hardly good eats."

"We can't hide here forever anyway. Who's got a plan?" Ikas asked.

"Yes, what's the plan, Thalen?" asked Dwinny.

Thalen wanted to say, "Why are you looking at me?" He wanted to say, "My brother can run a business," or "Sergeant Codek has more experience." But, in truth, he had been reviewing his reading, weighing their options, and working on a proposal.

"You're right; we can't stay here any longer. And not just because we'll run out of food. Hiding from the Oros may keep us free, but it does nothing to liberate Vígat or the rest of the Alliance.

"So. What is the situation? The Oros are much stronger than us militarily. I doubt that any other country is going to come to our aid now that the Oros are entrenched in Sutterdam. We could organize those of us who escaped capture to harry them, but they might squash such resistance activities with reprisals on citizens.

"We are not strong enough to *make* them withdraw. So they have to *want* to withdraw. What would do this?"

Thalen turned to the scout, Wareth, asking, "What do the Oromondo soldiers call themselves?"

Wareth frowned at such a stupid question. "The Protectors."

Thalen turned to Hake, prodding, "What do the Protectors protect?"

Hake answered, "Oromondo. They call it 'the Land,' as if other realms don't count.

"Thalen, where are you going with this?"

Thalen made a "patience" movement with his hand. "Dwinny, if your whole purpose in life was to 'protect the Land,' what would make you withdraw from elsewhere and scurry home?"

"If someone attacked Oromondo," she answered.

"Exactly." Thalen allowed the thought to sink in. "So that is what I intend to do."

Ikas broke in testily. "Are you barkin' mad? How're you going to get there? And with what army? You do not just walk into Oro-mondo!"

"I don't need an army—an army actually would be an encumbrance. I need a lightning-fast troop, a troop able to sting and sting again." Thalen stared off into the distance, seeing his plan, not the kitchen. "I need cavalry. We saw what cavalry can do against Oro foot soldiers. Harthen and his comrades were amazing."

"Go on," said Tristo, leaning forward on his healthy elbow.

"So I figure two dozen men—on good horses—striking their precious mining shipments and burning down their worship citadels, striking and fleeing, hiding and bedeviling. Oromondo has always lived in fear of invaders; in fact it is completely crazy paranoid on the subject. You bring battle to the heart of Oromondo, and I guarantee the Magi will call their army back."

"Thalen," Hake interjected, "in that school of yours didn't they teach you that crops have failed in Oromondo? That is why those animals have come here to begin with."

"I know. So when they return they will bring what they can steal from the Free States. But they *will* go scurrying back. Even if your cupboard were bare, if you thought ruffians were invading your home, threatening your people, burning your church, you would leave off your hunting expedition and return."

"But isn't Oromondo guarded against invasion?" asked Hake.

"Yes," said Thalen. "Eight watchtowers. Each the home of one of their Magi. I'm not sure how we'll sneak past them. But we'll find a way."

"The Oros would squash such a troop like a bug. Look what they did to our whole army," said Wareth, the scout.

"Not if we are clever and fast enough. Not if we find ingenious hideaways. Look, the eight of us, even wounded and without horses, have been able to escape capture. The Oros rely on brute force. They have never faced an enemy with nothing more to lose bent on creating terror and vanishing."

"Could be this attacking their homeland is a good strategy,"

Wareth grudgingly admitted. "But two dozen men! Horses, weapons, food, and supplies in a barren country! How would you raise those? How would you even get there?"

Thalen turned to Hake. "This is where you come in, Quartermaster."

Hake thought out loud. "Obviously, first, you'd need money. The horses and the food would need to be bought—men eager for revenge you could get for no cost. Free States merchants and artisans would be happy to contribute if they believed this would liberate them of these invaders that have ruined their commerce. Sutterdam Pottery has contacts all over the Free States, the Green Isles, and elsewhere. I could write to them. . . ." He played with his fork a moment, looking down, calculating under his breath. "I could raise the funds. Easily, I'd wager, though some folks might have to accept credit to start."

Thalen nodded. "I figure the Oros are still feasting and celebrating their victory. Probably commandeering a few ships and crews to rush foodstuffs back home and thinking about solidifying their hold on the Free States. But I'd bet they haven't bothered about Yosta yet. So that is where I would muster the men. And Yosta boasts a serious port." Thalen's voice turned dreamy, "I think sailing would be the best method of transport. Riding would take too long, and they must be guarding the causeway. . . ."

"Wait, one moment. How are you going to get to Yosta? We know that Oros are patrolling all the main roads now. We were lucky to get here in the confusion," said the sergeant, Codek, who had yet to speak during this conversation, though he'd eyed Thalen intently.

"Tristo traveled here by fishing boat, so I plan to go back the same way." Turning to the wheelwright, Ikas, Thalen asked, "Do you know any fisherfolk who would take me?"

Ikas stroked his beard. "Could be. If they still live. If I can find them. If the docks aren't cordoned off, if—"

"That's a lot of 'ifs.'" Thalen smiled. "But some of them will break in our favor."

The room fell quiet while everyone considered Thalen's proposal and the lack of other options.

"It's a damn-fool, batshit-crazy plan." Codek hit the table with his palm. "But I don't have another, and I'll be damned if I'll just lie down and die for those Oros. I'm in."

Tristo quickly added, "Me too."

Wareth chimed in, "Aye."

Dwinny sighed. "Thalen, many folk have been injured. My skills belong here, with my people. I need to get myself to one of the healing centers, to tend our wounded."

"Of course."

"I have a wife and two young daughters here," Ikas said. "I'll not flee the country and leave them behind." He rubbed his beard. "But, tell you what—I'll find you a fishing boat. I'll see to it that Dwinny gets safely to her healing center, along with that poor sod." He jerked his head in the direction of the room where the drugged archer slept. "And I'll go one better: I'll make Hake here a chair with metal wheels."

Thalen turned to Hake. "Neither you nor the archer are strong enough to travel or fight. But I need you here anyway. I need you to quietly spread the word, find more survivors, and send them to Yosta." Briefly he put his hand on top of his brother's. "Hake, I can't pull this off without the funding. I don't know how . . ."

Hake shook off his hand. "Just leave it to me. I may be crippled, but I'm neither helpless nor dumb."

Looking around at all of them, Thalen said, "Possibly we all know of particular people we would like to find alive and who would be right for this mission. We could give their names to those who remain in Vígat, and Hake, Ikas, and Dwinny could whisper in the right ears."

"I wonder if we could find me mates," Tristo said longingly. "What I wouldn't give to see their ugly pugs again! I don't even know if they lived or died."

Thalen answered, "So here is what we do: first, we write down for those who are staying the names of those we would most like to muster in Yosta. Second, we gather together what we need for the trip."

"When do you plan to leave?" Ikas asked.

Thalen pushed back from the table, taking a load of trenchers to the wash bucket. "When the dishes are dry," he answered.

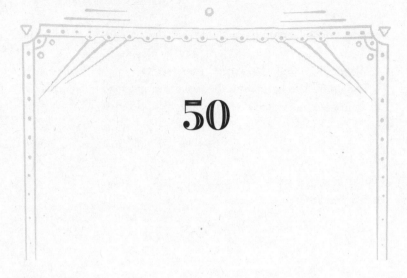

# 50

*Wyndton*

Wren had been harvesting greens from their garden for Stahlia when she saw Wilim and Syrup trot down their lane. She hadn't seen him leave early in the morning, though her teta had said that Duke Naven had called all the peacekeepers to his manor.

Wilim paused Syrup by the vegetable patch. "Take your basket in, Birdie, and then come help me with the horse." The whites of his eyes looked red, and sweat had stained his shirt though the day was only moderately warm. Wonderingly, Wren complied.

After they both entered the barn, Wilim shut the door. On fine summer evenings like this, when pink laced through the sky, they always left the doors open to air the horses.

At first Wilim said nothing about what troubled him; he just uncinched the saddle. When Wren started to unbridle Syrup, as usual the horse bent his head all the way down to make the reach easy for her and nuzzled her neck.

"Birdie." Wilim stopped. Then he started again. "You've never minded my calling you 'Birdie,' have you?"

Wren just looked at him in amazement. He had been calling

her that for twelve summers. Why would he fret about it now? She grabbed the curry brush and started on Syrup's neck.

Wilim picked up each of Syrup's feet and cleaned them in turn. He cleared his throat and started again.

"Today, Duke Naven gathered all the peacekeepers and mid-wives of the Middle Wards of the duchy at the manor. He and this lady—she's gentry all the way from Cascada!—are seeking . . . any woman of around twenty summers. They asked if anyone had shown up in the villages or farms the winter the late queen—may the Waters bless her!—left Cascada."

He added, "The woman they seek is uncommonly fond of animals."

Wren said nothing because she couldn't speak if she wanted to. She moved on down to Syrup's back.

"They said that, being as the late queen was an Enchanter, folk might not know what they know, if you get my meaning. They might have been *enchanted*. The noblewoman asked all the peace-keepers if any of us could think of any girl-child who just appeared twelve years ago." He continued in a rush, "Of course, I couldn't think of anyone who fit that description. They asked all the mid-wives too, if they knew of any girls whose birth they hadn't attended. Of course, Goody Gintie only settled here two years before Tilim, so she couldn't say who was born here and who wasn't."

Wilim took the brush from her to work on his side of Syrup. He avoided looking at his foster daughter, and Wren moved on to Syrup's mane and tail with the comb, gently working out any snarls while her teto finished the brushing.

He left the stall to grab a large armful of hay while Wren poured a small portion of oats into Syrup's bucket. The gelding attacked his feed eagerly, so the two of them slipped out of the stall to let him eat without distraction.

Wren was still gripping the currying implements in her hands.

"Is his water bucket fresh?" Wilim asked.

She nodded.

Rubbing his hands through his hair, Wilim continued, "They

said that if they don't find the woman they seek with these questions, they are going to post a reward, asking all the folk in Androvale for tips." He continued, in a soft voice, "I know some fools that got their backsides cut who might be eager to do a low deed and get paid for it too. In my experience, people caught doing an ill turn never let bygones go."

Hearing the strain in Wilim's voice, Syrup pulled his head up from his feed, hay sticking out of the sides of his mouth; he moved his back hooves uneasily, and his ears went down. Meanwhile, Baki scratched on the barn door and barked, *Let one in.*

Wren swallowed. "It could be that anyone who sheltered or protected the woman they seek would be in peril."

Wilim lifted both his hands, spread-fingered, into the air; Wren read the gesture as half-dismissive and half-defeated.

They had finished with Syrup and had no further excuse to dally in the barn. Wilim ran a hand through his hair again and chewed his thumbnail.

"I'm going in now," he said, and left the barn door swinging open.

Baki rushed inside, leaning hard against her legs, and Wren steadied herself from his weight and her shock by grabbing onto the wood slats that separated Barley's and Syrup's stalls. Instinctively, she craved the darkness of the barn, as if hiding behind the bales of hay would save her.

*What ails thee?* asked Baki, sniffing the familiar barn scents, wondering what had caused her such emotional distress.

*Now it has come, what I've feared all these years.*

Syrup stamped his back hooves. *One does nay understand. No enemies here, Your Majesty.*

*One smells no strangers,* Baki confirmed.

*They aren't here yet. But they are so close—only hours away. They might already be on my trail.*

*One will protect thee,* vowed Baki.

*And this one,* said Syrup.

*I am in danger. This family is in danger. If I am discovered here, will they be questioned, jailed, killed?*

Barley, whom she had earlier turned out into the paddock behind the barn, called, *What happens?*

*Hush,* Wren sent to her animal friends. *I have to think; I have to plan.*

Wren slowly wandered into the yard, lingering, trying to slow her pulse, looking at the pink sunset, feeling the warmth of the day rising from the ground, and the cool of the evening starting to freshen the smells of horse, garden, and soil. Then she washed her hands in the pump and went inside the cottage she had called home for most of her life.

Tilim, now eight summers, watched Stahlia's dinner preparation with the eagerness of a hungry boy.

"What did the duke want, Husband?" asked Stahlia as she tasted from the cook pot.

"Naught to do with Wyndton," said Wilim firmly, sitting down.

Stahlia brought the pot to the table, and the three others took their accustomed places.

"May ye never know thirst," said Tilim quickly; then he tore a corner off the bread before him.

"Is he keeping himself well? And the duchess?" Stahlia asked, ladling the thick potage into each bowl.

"I didn't see the duchess this visit," Wilim replied. "She made us a present of this soap, though." He fished a packet out of his purse and handed it to his wife. "The duke looked hale."

"Birdie and I went swimming in the creek today, Pa," said Tilim. "The water was so cold! Then we made little boats for my soldiers to sail. But they weren't sound enough—they took on water and sank, and then we had to find them in the rocks."

"Sounds like a good day, Son. You know, you need to help more with the horses."

"I fetched them their water like always. You know the horses love Birdie best, Pa."

Wilim changed the subject. "How was the 'torture' loom today?"

"Slow, but steady. Another moon or two. I can hardly wait to take it to Pattengale Manor and see how it looks hanging in their Great Hall. What would you think, Wilim, if for a holiday, I took Wren with me? We womenfolk could go cavorting, and you and Tilim could get into mischief together?"

"Sure. I would take Tilim out with me on my circuits."

Tilim pulled his face out of his food with excitement. "Pa, take me tomorrow!"

"See, Wren," said Stahlia to her foster daughter. "I told you he would agree. No nonsense about two women traveling alone—he knows that in Naven's and Pattengale's duchies, the post roads are safe enough. Besides, we'll take Baki with us, just for extra surety."

"I can't protect my family against all threats," said Wilim, looking down at his bowl.

"What a queer thing to say!" said Stahlia. "Are you feeling all right?" She stared at him for a moment, then turned to Wren. "Soon you can look at Duchess Pattengale's shelves and see if she owns any books I need to borrow for you."

Stahlia cut more slices of bread. "You might need a new hat for this trip," she added, waving the knife thoughtfully. "Next time you're in town see what's in the mercers. Never mind whether you like the way the bonnet's been trimmed—just look at the shape. I can decorate it any way you like. I have plenty of green ribbon left from your summer gown—green might be becoming."

"Mama's trying to find you a beau!" teased Tilim.

"And what would be the matter with that?" Stahlia challenged the table. "It's about time both of my girls settled down. Grandchildren don't grow on tomato plants, you know."

"Yes'm," said Wren.

"You're not eating, Wren," said Wilim. "You need to eat."

"Are *you* feeling poorly?" asked Stahlia, her brow furrowing.

"Just a little. Would you mind—I would fain lie down."

When she got up from the table, Wilim held out his arms. They weren't a family that embraced often. Wren lingered half a second with her head on his shoulder.

She just kept herself from running up the steep stairs to the attic bedroom, Baki—this time—following on her heels.

He sniffed the room thoroughly. *Trouble? One still scents no strangers by.*

*My enemies seek me. I must flee tonight.*

The thought of pursuit petrified Wren. But she felt equal anguish at the thought of leaving this family: she hadn't known how much she cared for them until just this moment.

When Tilim came in to crawl into his small bed under the eaves, he whispered, "Hey, are you awake? Do you feel any better?"

"I feel much better. Go to sleep now, and—Tilim—"

"What?"

"—dream of happy days," she called softly.

Not long after, she heard Wilim and Stahlia climb the stairs. Wilim was talking about money: that what with Stahlia's commission for this tapestry their household prospered. "Someone could even take my purse, and I wouldn't begrudge him the monies," said Wilim, rather loudly. "Not in the slightest. I would just wish I had more to give to that poor soul."

"Tush, Husband. What nonsense you talk," said her teta.

"Do you want to hear more nonsense?" said Wilim. "You and me have the best family in all of Wyndton. Tilim is growing up so strong, no blow would knock him down. And course the same is true of Percia. And Wren, well, we'll love and honor her all our days."

"Wilim, come to bed. You're rambling as if you have been in your cups. And tush. You will wake those treasures, and I want Wren to sleep well tonight. She looked a bit peaked at supper, don't you think?"

Wren waited, all senses on alert, until everyone in the household fell asleep. She heard a rabbit scream: that plaintive cry—so like a baby's—when a predator cuts its life short. Then she dressed in dark leather breeches, a shirt, and a black lace-up over-bodice, and crept down the stairs, a handful of undergarments clutched under her arm. Her boots stood by the door.

On the table she saw Wilim's money purse left out for her.

She had to flee. Every second she stayed she put them in terrible danger. But she could hardly leave without some kind of farewell. What would Stahlia think? Or Percia or Tilim? They needed an answer for the townspeople about where she had gone and why. Otherwise her flight would raise more suspicion, maybe even pursuit.

Lying in her bed, waiting, she had concocted a story. She found the tale totally humiliating, but she hoped that Wilim would read between the lines.

She found the family's small inkpot on the bookshelf, and she tore a piece of paper out of one of Stahlia's books.

> My dear family—
> During our visits to Gulltown to visit Percia I have fallen in love with a sailor. I thought you wouldn't approve, so I never told you. I am with child. You will say, "Like mother, like daughter." I don't want to bring disgrace on you, so I am leaving. Pray forgive me for the sorrow I have brought you. I love you so.
>                              Your ever grateful, Wren

She left the letter on the front room table where they would be sure to see it.

She grabbed Wilim's game bag and stuffed in a few items: the remainder of a loaf of bread, three pears, her dagger, her underclothes, her cloak, and one of Wilim's caps. A metal soldier of Tilim's standing at attention on the mantelpiece glinted in the banked-down fire. She seized it as a keepsake.

At the last moment she remembered her hair tonic; she rushed to the washhouse where they stored it. Then she ran to the barn and threw a bridle and saddle on Barley.

*Speckles, will you escort me to the bounds of the valley? Will you keep watch?*

*It will be one's honor. One has hunted all the bats in this valley, but if thou goest farther, thou shouldst change thy scent—bats hunt by smell.*

Wren looked around the barn frantically for anything odorous. Wilim kept mink oil to moisturize the saddles; Wren stuck a finger in and drew thin lines down her arms and legs and around her hairline. She stuffed the jar in her sack, mounted up, turned in her saddle for one more look at the cottage that had welcomed and sheltered her, and then, under a clear sky brocaded with bright stars, she headed Barley toward Gulltown.

Sensing her urgency, Barley started off so briskly that Baki had to lope to keep up.

In Gulltown she would get a ship. Where to? Lortherrod seemed the only sensible choice. Even though she'd never met her grandfather or uncles, surely they would welcome, counsel, and protect Cressa's daughter.

Every noise made Wren jump, imagining red-eyed bats or a squad of assassins coming to snatch her. Yet she passed no one as she rode by sleeping apple orchards and quiet beech tree sentinels; the horizon remained clear, and Baki raised no alarms.

As they passed out of Wyndton Valley, Speckles hooted.

*Your Majesty, one stays in one's territory.*

*I understand, Speckles. You've been a constant friend to me all these years. I want you to know how grateful I am.*

*One will miss thee. But fledglings must find their own territory.*

Though she stopped to rest and water the animals, Wren made it to Gulltown in less than six hours; dawn had not yet erased the stars that guided her.

Gulltown was not as still and quiet as a country village. Rough-looking men already headed toward their daily labor on the dark streets along with drunks, cutthroats, and prostitutes too. Wren saw more than a few guards wearing the brown sash of Androvale, but she kept riding steadily and no one challenged her. It probably helped that in the dark—in her trousers, short hair, and Wilim's cap—she could pass for a lad.

She had to fight herself to keep from heading in the direction of

Percia's lodgings. Instead she aimed Barley toward the docks. At a horse trough she watered the horse and dog well.

*Barley and Baki. You can stay with me for another hour or two, while I wait for light. Then you must head back home, because I can't take you with me.*

Barley agreed to go back to his familiar stall in Wyndton. Baki, however, opposed her.

*One is thy guard dog. Where thou goest, one goes.*

*I want you to protect the family for me.* Wren reached inside herself. She felt an odd sensation, as if a thin membrane had given way and she had discovered beneath the chamber of her Talent a deeper and wider pool. She knew now that she could Command beasts and they would have to obey her orders.

She found a scrap of grass in a vacant lot for Barley to graze; she dismounted, lay down, and dozed, trying to take full advantage of the safety the animals provided. When the dark began to cede to dawn, she took off Barley's bridle and tied it up on his saddle, so that catching him would be harder for anyone who figured a loose horse made a nice windfall. She bent down to look in Baki's yellow eyes, told him to see to it that no one captured Barley, scratched him behind his ears, and thanked him for his vigilance. After one more pat on Barley's neck, she ordered them to return to the cottage. She stood alone, watching her last tie with home recede until the duo disappeared out of sight down a cobblestone street.

Behind her a market took down its shutters and opened its door. From a sleepy old shopkeep she bought her favorite Gulltown treat: a mug of coffee mixed with milk. She squatted outside a building, cupping the warm mug in her hands, and ate a corner of her loaf of bread and a pear. The gulls screamed overhead; several swooped down to see if she would feed them her crumbs.

Light broke on a mild day with low clouds lying stretched like a ribbon on the horizon. Wren found the booking hall closed and locked. In the slanting light of dawn, a board outside announced that today's second sailing would be Lortherrod's *Porpoise Racer,* heading east on the morning tide. She killed time waiting for the of-

fice to open by reading a tacked-up broadsheet, recounting the news
that an Oromondian army approached the Free States.

When she turned back down the road to the booking office, the
official had just unbolted the doors.

"I would like to book passage on *Porpoise Racer,*" she said across
the counter, reaching for Wilim's purse. "It sails to Liddlecup, right?"

The official looked at her closely. "You're a woman?" he asked.

"So? Aren't women allowed to book passage?"

"Oh surely, surely. Just one moment." The man went to talk to a
figure in the inner cabinet.

Wren grew anxious. She turned and started to walk smartly
toward the front door and had almost made it when she heard boot
steps running behind her: a man grabbed her elbow.

"Miss, you need to come with us," said an Androvale guard with
a brown sash. Wren's hand reached for her knife, but she then saw
another soldier right behind the first.

"What for?"

"We have orders to hold any young woman trying to ship out of
Gulltown. Come this way, please."

So they didn't know *her;* they were questioning everyone. The
guards marched her in between them several blocks to a high-class
inn. There an officer in a tricornered hat took over; he regretted the
inconvenience; she would have to wait until the proper person came
to question her and the other young ladies who waited; refreshments
would be provided.

"But I'll miss my ship!" Wren protested.

"I am sorry, miss. But I just follow my orders."

He showed her into a fine sitting room with one wall occupied by
a mural of a nautical scene. Three women dozed on matching fur-
nishings of white upholstery. One was clearly too old to be Cerúlia,
but she had been caught up in their net too. Another had discolor-
ations all over her broad face. Those two women wore the resigned
expressions of poor folk accustomed to getting pushed around. The
third, and the angriest, turned out to be a fine-featured woman of
the right age and of obvious means, dressed in a lovely burgundy

frock with a pink apron and bodice with a matching hat and feather on the table beside her.

"This treatment is outrageous!" she railed at the officer. "I hope you've considered what will happen to you when my father and my fiancé find out that you've held me against my will!"

"Yes, miss. I'm sorry, but I am bound to follow my orders," replied the officer as if he had heard her complaints before.

The older woman nodded toward Wren in acknowledgment. The rather talkative freckled girl explained that she had been there the longest—"Two days and a half!" Her companions had appeared yesterday, both trying to board a Cascada-bound ship.

"What's this all about?" Wren asked.

"Dunno," said the girl with freckles. "They don't tell us nothin'. All I know is the officer said that the person who can clear us is due this afternoon."

Wren briefly considered breaking out a window, but she couldn't rely on the other women keeping quiet during such a brazen act. Nor did she know what she'd do on the run in Gulltown.

So she settled down on a divan, covered herself up with her cloak, and tried to rest. Servants appeared at midday, bringing the four women a generous meal of fresh cod, roasted potatoes, and summer corn. When they gathered round the table the lady in burgundy dropped her condescension, though she did wrinkle her nose a bit at the lingering odor of mink.

The older woman had visited sick family in Androvale; she had been starting her long journey home to Prairyvale, one of the far Western Duchies.

"I don't know what's going on here in Gulltown," she commented, "but I ain't really surprised. I had heard that Androvale was peaceable, kind of like the before times, but nowhere is really safe nowadays, 'specially for a female. Prairyvale, now, hard times has us in its talons there. You don't dare speak back to a guard," she said, looking at the woman in burgundy. "You liable to get a swat that would bust your jaw. If'n they don't take you to the guardhouse for their sport."

The young lady's eyes went wide.

Wren tried out her story on her table companions: her brother, her only kin because their parents had died two years ago, had preceded her to Liddlecup, the capital of Lortherrod. Now that he had gotten a good position as an assistant in a furrier's business, he had sent for her. The women accepted this tale without question; no one asked probing questions or accused her of lying. As she ate Wren embroidered her tale a little in her mind to prepare for any cross-examination.

A guard escorted each woman to the jakes, to a washing room, and then back to their sitting room. Waiting preyed upon Wren's nerves. She looked at the books on the shelves longingly, but decided that a farm girl wouldn't read to pass the time.

A few hours into the afternoon a bustle of horses and carriage outside and footsteps and shouted orders indicated that an important party had arrived.

The officer unlocked their sitting room. He ushered into the room a noblewoman with a wide-awake appearance whose hair was wrapped in a blue-and-white turban. As the young women rose and curtsied, she glanced at the four of them; then she looked back at Wren, but she pointed to the fine lady.

"We'll start with her."

"All right, miss, please come with us," said the officer, and the group left the room.

After ten minutes or so, he came back for the Prairyvale woman. Then the frightened runaway. Left alone in the sitting room, Wren hurried to the window, thinking that maybe now she could hazard an escape. But through the glass she spotted a group of half a dozen guards, probably the carriage escorts, smoking and chatting in the courtyard.

So Wren returned to her footstool to wait, trying to calm herself. She kept chewing over the older woman's remarks about injustices in Prairyvale. Anger helped to steady her, anger and shame. While she'd been going through the peaceful, daily routines in Wyndton—hiding—others had been suffering. If Matwyck hadn't sought her out, how much longer would she have stayed safe and sheltered? She was grown now and had no excuses for dallying.

Maybe this flight would turn out to be a blessing; maybe (if she could just get out of this trap), she could set out to fulfill her duties.

Finally, the officer returned.

"This way, if you please."

He led her up a flight of stairs to a suite of fine rooms in the front of the inn where a noblewoman sat at a card table, sipping wine from a fancy goblet in front of two floor-to-ceiling glass windows. Behind her stood two guards in their white Cascada sashes, both heavily armed and more alert than the Gulltown guards; they stared at her with glances compounded of leering, contempt, and intimidation. A linen cloth folded several times occupied the table in front of her.

"Please sit across from me, miss," said the noblewoman. "I regret we have disrupted your travel plans."

Wren did as the lady bid her but said nothing.

"I will tell you what I told the others. I am Lady Tenny, from Cascada. Once I served as a member of Queen Cressa's council. I meant well, but in the end I failed my queen. Now I seek her daughter, the princella, on behalf of Lord Regent Matwyck. I wish to do her a good turn.

"Officers detained you because the harbor watch judged you to be of about twenty summers. They have instructions to question all young women and to hold anyone traveling alone. We have begun a systematic search of the Eastern Duchies, and there is some fear that she might try to flee."

Wren forced herself to snort and then let her mouth fall open. "You reckon I might be *the missing princella*? That's a laugh. Would I be mucking cow pens if'n I was royalty?"

"I can see that you've been living a rural life. But we must be thorough; I am bound to follow the same procedure with each detainee. I have here an item that helps me know when someone is telling the truth." She looked straight into Wren's eyes, and Wren could have sworn she winked at her. "You have naught to fear from the Stone, my dear."

Lady Tenny pulled something out of the lower fold of the linen cloth. On the table lay a flat stone, a bit larger than her palm.

"May I have your hand?" When Wren hesitated, Lady Tenny repeated, "It's all right. I swear this procedure will not harm you."

The lady took Wren's hand and placed it on top of the stone, holding it there firmly. In the presence of a highborn woman with soft, smooth hands, Wren abruptly became self-conscious about the state of her own hands—the calluses, the ground-in dirt, the chipped nails, the innumerable small scars earned through years of harvest, cottage, and stable. Even to her roughened skin, however, the stone felt bumpy; it had gravelly bits embedded in it that dug into her palm.

"Now, tell us your name." Lady Tenny gave her hand a slight squeeze.

"My name is Robin," said Wren. Nothing happened with this Stone.

"And where are you from?"

"Eight leagues west of Millburg. A farming hamlet. We call it Donen."

"Ah. I'll probably visit there soon. Who are your mother and father?"

"My mother was Hanna, my father, Wellman. Both died two springs ago."

"Oh, I *am* sorry, my dear. So hard to be alone in the world."

One of the guards broke in. "The Stone proves she's not the one. So let's get on with it." He said to his partner, "This grubby slut in breeches! Hardly. I would have picked the first beauty. *She* had the bearing."

Tenny turned to the guards with asperity in her tone. "Which just goes to show, does it not, that appearances can be deceiving? You *will* be quiet, Twitch, I insist!"

"My dear," she said to Wren. "I am giving you a note with my seal on it. That way whenever you buy your passage you will not be molested again. You plan to sail to . . ."

Wren remembered her cover story. "Lortherrod, milady. My older brother set himself up there in a good trade. He's a furrier, you see, and he's finally sent for me to—"

The guard on the left-hand side purposely interrupted her by hacking up phlegm and spitting into the cold fireplace.

The noblewoman closed her lids a moment and shuddered.

"Here, my dear," she said, passing her the sheet of paper. "You can't know how much I wish you a pleasant voyage."

"I thank you, milady," said Wren, meaning for more than the note.

"Don't mention it. Least I can do. I mean, making you miss your sailing and all."

Wren took the note. *Lady Tenny.* As she made her way to the front door, the officer handed her the game bag.

"I regret detaining you," he said.

Wren nodded at him and headed back to the quay's booking office.

"I missed the Lorther ship," she told the same clerk from the morning. "When is the next one?"

"Hard to say. Gulltown ain't such a big port that the Lorthers stop here often. Could be two weeks, could be a moon."

"Two weeks! But I see so many ships here!"

"You see mostly fishing boats or ferries that only cross the Bay of Cinda. Oceangoing vessels don't stop here so often. They have much bigger hulls and three masts, and they—"

Wren interrupted the lesson in ship construction. "What's the next oceangoing vessel you have leaving?"

"Ah, *Island Flyer.* Sailing on tonight's tide for the Green Isles."

Wren stood paralyzed with indecision.

"You know," the clerk said in a kind tone, possibly feeling guilty about turning Wren over to the harbor watch, "the Green Isles is a major transit hub and kind of in the right direction. If you want to get to Liddlecup, for certain you can catch a ship from there."

*Well, I can't stay here.* Wren paid for her passage (showing the ticket seller her note), walked down the dock (showing the watch stationed there her note), and boarded the swaying gangway. She had bought a bunk in the women's room, a narrow stateroom that held six stacked bunks for women and children tucked into the hull. It smelled of brine and unwashed bodies. She stowed her bag in her locker and then went on deck to watch the ship cast off. A sailor yelled at her to get out of his way, but when she moved elsewhere, another sailor called, "Not there, you lubber!" Finally she found a spot at the rail where she could stand without anyone yelling at her.

As *Island Flyer* slipped out of port headed toward the clouded horizon, Wren watched Gulltown, Androvale, and Weirandale grow smaller and smaller until she could see nothing at all behind her.

She had powerful enemies in her own country who would stop at nothing to maintain their rule. And even stronger adversaries who could wield Magic much more developed than her own undeveloped Talent. These usurpers, these carrion birds, were pecking at the eyes and still-beating heart of her country. How she longed to sweep down on them, like a mighty wind or a scouring river!

But she had no shields and no army; she'd even had to leave her dog behind. She was neither an Enchanter nor a Warrior.

*Humble anonymity has been my cloak. I will wear it a bit longer.*

# EPILOGUE

## Cascada

Every day, usually at dawn, Nana slipped out of the palace and trod down the hill to the Courtyard of the Star. She would disperse the foodstuffs she and Besi had cadged from the noblemen's waste to the many hungry and homeless folk who gathered near the Fountain. She would pull out any leaves or debris that had fallen into the pool, sit on its edge, listen to the Water's music, and pray for Cerúlia's safe return.

The last few weeks she had been plagued by a nameless dread, waking often in the night and unable to fall back asleep. Each morning when she reached the Fountain, its unceasing flow soothed her, though Nana kept worrying that the Water arced less high each year since Cressa's death.

This morning the water sparkled in the sun. Closing her eyes a moment, Nana, fatigued, could almost fancy that she heard voices in the tumbling water. She heard her own voice, pledging to Queen Cressa so long ago, "I will be waiting right here," and a melodic voice murmuring in return. Nana strained to decipher the words. Perchance her overtired mind played tricks on her, but she thought she heard the following:

*Thou hast proven to be rare amongst mortals. I choose thee as my servant and my Agent.*

A gust of wind rained Fountain droplets on her white cap in a quick patter.

A man's voice startled Nana from her joyous reverie.

"Why, 'tis Nana, 'tis it not?"

Nana opened her eyes. In front of her, blocking the morning light, stood a tall, elderly Brother of Sorrow—

Nana smiled in recognition. "Whoa-ho! Brother Whitsury! Well met! Have you rotated back to Cascada again?"

"Indeed, as you see." Brother Whitsury smiled. "They posted me in the far west for many years, and then I took a turn in the middle duchies. Now I'm back here for a spell."

"How do the duchies fare? How does Cascada strike you after so many years away?"

"Ach! I don't know, Nana. Morale has dropped everywhere, and the folk are frightened. The people have no hope. The dukes lay on such high taxes, even when crops come scant. I've seen horrible things; things that shouldn't have happened. Tenants driven off their farms; guards behaving like brutes. A Sister of Sorrow beaten by a lordling!"

"Someone struck a Sister! Whatever for?" asked Nana, scandalized.

"She had interceded for a young woman whose father sold her to a lustful merchant to pay his debts! Such things would never be allowed if Catreena or Cressa still ruled. When that ship went down we lost more than a sovereign. Mercy and decency have fled the realm too.

"Cascada, now," he paused. "Cascada has changed the most."

"Aye. So you feel it too, Whitsury?"

The elderly Brother allowed his face to show his concern. "The tension? As if the whole city is holding its breath? Folk all suspicious of one another and afraid to look a fellow in the eye? Children growing up stunted for lack of good victuals? I tell you, frankly, Nana, unless the princella—" He broke off from whatever he was about to say and looked around. When he spoke again, he took up a different theme.

"But you, Nana, you have hardly aged at all! Before my eyes is the proud woman who cradled that babe during Cerúlia's Naming Ceremony. Grandest day of my life."

Nana laughed with remembrance and affection. "Oh go on, you rogue! Full of flattery as ever. I'm an old woman, now, and I've let out my seams so often there's no slack left. Though this morn I do feel spry and strong. And ready to take on any enemies of the throne."

"One mystery solved, at any rate."

Nana was confused. "What mystery?"

"At the Abbey table last eve, Sorrowers talked with reverence about someone who always visited the Fountain. They called her 'The Faithful One.' 'Tis *you*, Nana."

"Hmmph," Nana replied. "I don't know as there's anything mysterious about me. And I hope I can count on your faithfulness, Whitsury?"

"Nana!" he replied with a hint of outrage. "Do you have to ask? Hey, have you heard the verse going around?"

"What verse?"

Brother Whitsury spoke softly, looking at the Fountain, not at Nana.

> *Though dusty sits the Nargis Throne*
> *While tyrants befoul and bluster;*
> *Though citizens do their yoke bemoan,*
> *And the Fountain's lost its luster:*
> *Someday the drought shall be broken,*
> *And the wondrous Waters course clean,*
> *One dawn the words shall be spoken,*
> *As the long-lost heir becomes queen.*

"Ah, me-oh-my," *tsk*ed Nana, as she daubed her eyes with her apron. "Well, the faithful wait for that day."

A Sister of Sorrow interrupted them. "Brother Whitsury, could you assist us? There's some pilgrims here, quite distraught—"

The Brother squeezed Nana's hands and sped off to his duties.

Nana watched him thoughtfully a moment and then turned her attention back to the Nargis Fountain. In the turbulent water below her something caught her eye. She pushed up her sleeve and reached for it. She grasped a beautiful blue feather.

*It's a gift. A badge of sorts.*

Nana took out one of the pins that affixed her cap on her hair and pinned the blue feather to her collar. She squared her shoulders and set off back to her post in the palace to wait.

# APPENDIX ONE

## CHARACTERS AND PLACES IN ENNEA MÓN

### The Spirits

'Chamen, Spirit of Stone
    Agent "Mason," chosen realm, Rortherrod
Ghibli, Spirit of the Wind
    Agent "Hunter," chooses no country
Lautan, Spirit of the Sea
    Agent "Sailor," chosen realm, Lortherrod
Nargis, Spirit of Fresh Water
    Agent "Water Bearer" (Tiklok), chosen realm, Weirandale
Pozhar, Spirit of Fire
    Agent "Smithy," chosen realm, Oromondo
Restaurà, Spirit of Sleep and Health
    Agent "Healer," chosen realm, Wyeland
Saulė, Spirit of the Sun
    Agent "Peddler," chosen realm, Alpetar
Vertia, Spirit of Growth
    Agent "Gardener," chosen realm, the Green Isles

# Countries and inhabitants

## Weirandale

### THE EIGHT WESTERN DUCHIES (WEST TO EAST)

Northvale

Prairyvale

Woodsdale

Lakevale

Maritima—includes city of Queen's Harbor

Riverine—includes Cascada

Crenovale

Vittorine

### THE THREE EASTERN DUCHIES ACROSS THE BAY OF CINDA (WEST TO EAST)

Androvale—contains Gulltown (port city) and Wyndton (country village)

Patenroux

Bailiwick—contains Barston (major city)

### THE FORMER GENERATION ON THE THRONE

Queen Catreena the Strategist (deceased)

    Consort: King Nithanil of Lortherrod (abdicated)

    Nikil, male baby (deceased)

### THE CURRENT ROYALS

Queen Cressa the Enchanter

    Consort: Ambrice, Lord of the Ships

    Cerúlia, the princella

## People in Cascada, the Capital City

Alix, a Cascadian involved with the Parity Party

Besi, a cook

Borta, a baker

Eyevie, a toymaker

 Sotteson, her lover

Geesilla, primarily a hair maid but also a room maid

Hiccuth, a stableman

Kiltti, a scullery maid

Nana, a nursemaid, later Water Bearer

Platsy, a room maid

Ryton, Cerúlia's tutor

 Rysta, his elderly mother

Sewel, the royal chronicler

 Rowatag, the former royal chronicler (deceased)

Teonora, the chamberlaine

 Martza, Teonora's second, and temporary chamberlaine

Thum, the envoy from Oromondo

Tiklok, a lackey and Water Bearer

Whitsury, a Brother of Sorrow

## Queen Cressa's Councilors

Lord Steward, later Lord Regent, Matwyck

 Lady Tirinella, his wife

 Lordling Marcot, his son

 Heathclaw, his secretary

Belcazar

 Engeliqua, his wife

Duchess Latlie

Prigent, also treasurer of the realm

Lord Retzel, a landowner

Lady Tenny, specializes in diplomacy

Yurgn, also general of the Armed Forces

    Captain Lurgn, eldest son of General Yurgn

    Captain Murgn, nephew of general and head of Matwyck's
       Marauders

## QUEEN CRESSA'S LADIES-IN-WAITING

Duchette Aubrie (plays the lyre)

Lady Dinista (mistress of the wardrobe), marries one of Lord
Retzel's sons

Lady Fanyah (witty)

Duchette Lumetta (relation of Councilor Duchess Latlie)

## MEMBERS OF THE QUEEN'S SHIELD

Captain Clemçon

Sergeant Bristle

Shields:

    Branwise

    Dariush

    Gathleigh

    Kinley

    Pontole

    Seena

    Yanath

## WEIR SEAMASTERS

Bashkim

Gourdo

Wilamara

## IN OR NEAR WYNDTON, A SMALL HAMLET IN THE DUCHY OF ANDROVALE

Duke Naven

    Duchess Naven

    Five daughters

    Orest, the duke's chamberlain

    Walmunt, the captain of the Duke's guard

Duke Burdis, the duke of a neighboring duchy

Duchess Pattengale, the duchess of a neighboring duchy

Wilim, a peacekeeper

    Stahlia, a weaver, Wilim's wife

    Percia, their daughter

        Dewva, friend of Percia

        Nettie, friend of Percia

    Tilim, their son

Alat, a local ruffian

    Halat, Alat's father, a drunk

    Corburret, a local ruffian

    Ferl, a local ruffian

    Nowltin, a local ruffian

Carneigh, a blacksmith

Cupist, an assassin sent to Androvale

    Johin, an assassin sent to Androvale

Goody Gintie, the midwife

Lemle, Wren's friend

    Rooks, a retired/injured sergeant, Lemle's uncle

Nellsapeta, a Sister of Sorrow

Raynr, the peacekeeper in the ward south of Wyndton

Volthain, the apothecary's son

*Alliance of Free States, once a unified country
called "Iga," now four smaller nation-states*
Fígat—contains Latham and the Scoláiríum
Vígat—contains Sutterdam
Jígat—contains Jutterdam
Wígat—contains Yosta

## IN SUTTERDAM (SECOND-LARGEST CITY)

Hartling, a potter and owner of a thriving pottery business
    Jerinda (Indy), his wife and business manager
    Hake, their eldest son
    Thalen, their middle son
    Harthen, their youngest son
    Norling, Hartling's older sister
Codek, a sergeant
Dwinny, a healer
Ikas, a wheelwright
Rellia, an old lady
Tristo, a street orphan from Yosta
Wareth, a cavalry scout

## THE SCOLÁIRÍUM OF THE FREE STATES
## LOCATED IN THE TOWN OF LATHAM, REACHED BY FERRY FROM TROUT LANDING

Rector Meakey
Andreata, a tutor of Ancient Languages
Granilton, a tutor of History
Irinia, a tutor of Earth and Water
Kerosh, a tutor of Engineering
Deganah, a reader of Comparative Magic
Gustie, a reader of Ancient Languages
Quinith, a reader of Music

Hyllidore, a porter for the Scoláiríum

*Lortherrod, capital city Liddlecup, castle Tidewater Keep*

King Nithanil, abdicated
King Rikil, the current king
    wife and two sons
      Prince Mikil, King Rikil's younger brother

## *The Green Isles*

### PILAGOS (LARGEST ISLAND AND CAPITAL)

Magistrar Destra, the head of the government, originally from
   the Free States
Arlettie, a general ladies' maid
Peketta, a hair maid
Simonetta, a tradeswoman
   Jaret, boat navigator, her kinsman
   Laret, boat navigator, her kinsman

## *Oromondo*

### FEMTURAN (CAPITAL CITY)

The Magi, One through Eight
Sumroth, rises from fourth-flamer to seventh-flamer
   Zea, his wife, works for the Library of Reverence
Chumelle, a high-ranking officer
Umrat, a high-ranking officer

## *Rortherrod*

### FELDSPAR (CAPITAL CITY)

King Kentros

# Appendix Two

## Notable Historic Queens of Weirandale in Chronological Order

Cayla the Foremother

Carra the Royal

Chista the Builder

Cayleethia the Artist

Carlina the Gryphling

Charmana the Fighter

Cinda the Conqueror

Chyneza the Wise

Crylinda the Fertile

Cashala the Enchanter

Catorie the Swimmer

Ciella the Patient

Cenika the Protector

Chanta the Musical

Carmena the Perseverant

Callindra the Faithful

Cymena the Proud

Clesindra the Kind

Crilisa the Just

# ACKNOWLEDGMENTS

In the years that I worked on this series I incurred debts, large and small, to those who guided, helped, and encouraged me.

I am grateful to Vassar College, which has always valued creative pursuits on an equal plane with traditional scholarship, for travel funds and the William R. Kenan Jr. Endowed Chair.

Throughout the drafting, Lt. Colonel Sean Sculley, academy professor and chief of the American History Division at West Point, generously shared his military, historical, strategic, and sailing expertise. (I drew specialized information from Angus Konstam's *Renaissance War Galley, 1470–1590* and Sean McGrail's *Ancient Boats in North-West Europe*.)

Professors Kirsten Menking and Jeff Walker of Vassar's Earth Science Department led me away from grievous errors concerning world-building.

Stefan Ekman, professor of English at the University of Gothenburg, took the time to share his unique knowledge regarding fantasy maps.

Professor Leslie Dunn of Vassar's English Department, a Shakespeare scholar, studied my poetry with the seriousness and skill she applies to more exalted works.

Professor Darrell James, who teaches stage combat in Drama, showed me his swords and taught me about their use.

I was fortunate indeed to find Penelope Duus, Vassar '17, who was trained in cartography. She started the map of Ennea Món when she was a senior and has patiently, loyally tweaked it for years. For the final corrections I am grateful to Amy Laughlin of Vassar's Academic Computing office.

A professional editor, Linda Branham, critiqued the first fifty pages. Friends who read drafts—in whole or in part—provided comments and encouragement that kept my roots watered. Thank you for your time, Fred Chromey, Joanne Davies, Madelynn Meigs '18, and Molly Shanley. Feedback from Madeline Kozloff, Daniel Kozloff, Bobbie Lucas '16, and Dawn Freer came at particularly timely moments or was particularly influential.

I tapped Theodore Lechterman for his knowledge of the Levelers (the historical analogue of the Parity Party) and his linguistic skills. Tom Racek '18, captain of the fencing team, helped me choreograph some of the fight scenes.

Rather late in my writing process I was lucky to find a writing partner with whom I exchanged manuscripts. The fantasy author James E. Graham provided irreplaceable assistance by reading nearly all of the series and filling the margins with passionate comments.

Others were kind and patient in giving a novice advice about how to publish in a new field, including Susan Chang (Tor), Alicia Condon (Kensington), Diana Frost (Macmillan), and Eddie Gamarra (The Gotham Group). Without their guidance these manuscripts might never have been published.

My husband, Robert Lechterman, supported me in this endeavor as selflessly as he has throughout our life together. Without him, the appliances would have just stayed broken and I would have subsisted on frozen fish sticks.

Martha Millard—my original agent at Sterling Lord Literistic—knew and delighted in the fact that she was changing my life when she pursued me as a client and sold the series. She has retired and I shall miss her, but Nell Pierce of SLL has now ably filled her shoes.

At Tor my manuscripts fell into the hands of Rafal Gibek (production editor) and Deanna Hoak (copy editor), who saved me from myself.

My editor, Jennifer Gunnels of Tor, took a leap of faith on a nontraditional debut author, a four-volume series, and a rapid publication schedule. She also found the balance between corralling me when I wandered astray and giving me freedom. "You really need to research X," she would advise, and I would obediently get busy. Other times, when I fretted over whether I should change something, she'd remind me, "It's *your* book, Sarah."

It *is* my book, Jen, but in a larger sense it belongs to everyone mentioned here, to a dozen others who offered a hand, not to mention the books, films, and teachers who formed me. Except the mistakes and infelicities, which pool around my feet, mewling like attention-mongering kittens—those poor things are mine own.

# THE QUEEN OF RAIDERS

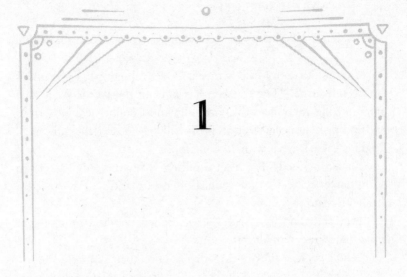

# 1

## Yosta, The Free States

*Thalen's Tally Book: 4 Men*

Codek tipped his glass upside down to reach the clinging drops of wine while Wareth sucked on a chicken leg, getting the last shreds of meat and flavor. Thalen himself scarfed down the bread crust that Tristo had left behind on his plate. Meanwhile, the fire reached some pockets of sap in the burning logs, causing loud pops.

They had supped in silence in this small sitting room normally saved for visitors too genteel for the common room and easiest for the innkeep to heat in these empty hours before dawn. A moth-eaten rug held court to a jar of withered flowers, but the diners found even these details homey; they were starved for food and comfort after their desperate trip hiding in the dark, leaky hold of a small fishing vessel, fleeing from now-occupied Sutterdam to the seacoast city of Yosta on the other side of the Free States.

The fire lifted curdles of briny steam from their damp clothes. Faintly, the men heard the clang of the fog bell guiding ships to harbor.

Thalen broke the quiet. "How long do you think we'll be safe here?"

"Best not to dally," said Sergeant Codek, absently tugging on his bushy sideburns. "The innkeep has put out the word. We'll start interviewing candidates this morning, and I doubt we'll have trouble finding volunteers. Our problem will be choosing the right men. Light cavalry is what we're looking for."

Thalen nodded. "I've been thinking. They not only have to be formidable fighters—they should offer extra skills. We'll need a healer, for sure."

"And someone good with horses," added Wareth. "I'm going to miss that white mare of mine."

"And a cook," said Codek. "Men fight on their stomachs."

They all contemplated the carcass of the cold chicken they'd just devoured.

"You know we can't take him with us," Sergeant Codek said as he nodded toward Tristo. After leading them to the Three Coins Inn, cajoling the owner into heating them up a late-night supper, and shoveling in enough to fill his own empty belly, the youth had curled up on a short bench in front of the fire and fallen asleep. With his dirty, small face relaxed on his cushioning hands, Tristo looked even younger than the fifteen summers he claimed.

Wareth, the Vígat cavalry scout, resettled his broken arm in its sling. "Ach. You can't leave him behind. You'd crush him."

"But we're putting together a troop of skilled fighters," Codek argued. "Tristo can't ride and can't shoot; fuck, he's never held a real sword. He'd just be an encumbrance. And it would be murder."

Both Codek and Wareth looked to Thalen for a ruling.

*This is how it's going to be, from now on. A thousand decisions: from trivial things to matters of life and death. I didn't ask for this role.*

Nevertheless, Thalen found himself the leader of this small group, a group he thought of as "the original survivors." Thalen was the one who had hatched the plan of invading Oromondo with a tiny strike force to terrorize their enemy's native land, in hopes that such an incursion would lift the occupation of the Free States. So he turned his blue eyes on the sleeping street urchin he'd known for about three weeks, since they met amongst the corpses after the battle. Tristo's collarbone had healed quickly, and the lad had not complained once during their voyage.

"We are all taking a suicidal gamble," Thalen said slowly. "Tristo has as much of a right to make his life count as the rest of us. As to what he'd contribute . . . he offers something just as valuable as fighting skills—we've all seen how resourceful he is. If he wants to come, I want him with us."

It might have been a quirk of the fire shadows, but Thalen thought he saw the sleeping boy's mouth twitch up at the corners.

Free Staters had lost many kin in the battle they now self-derisively called "the Rout," and in the days thereafter Oro soldiers had rampaged farther east, burning, looting, enslaving, and raping. The friends Thalen had left behind in Sutterdam had fanned rumors of Thalen's plans. Men who escaped followed these murmurs about Thalen's gamble to Yosta. Free Staters' humiliation, desire for revenge, and willingness to do anything to rid their countries of these conquerors led to a crowd of men jostling outside the Three Coins Inn the next morning.

The first person in line turned out to be the Three Coins' own man-of-all-work.

"I wanna go with ya," he said.

"We need to engage professional soldiers," said Codek. "Have much experience in that line?"

"A bit. Give us a chance, won't ya?"

The four original survivors exchanged glances.

"Just a chance," urged the man. "It's only fair."

"Auditions in the yard out back?" Thalen asked his comrades.

"All right," agreed Codek. He turned to the applicant. "We'll test your fencing and archery."

Thalen watched from a back window. Tristo ran about drawing a rough target on the woodshed wall. In the meantime, Wareth, who couldn't fight with his broken arm, offered the candidate his own sword.

Codek pushed his sleeves out of his way, pulled on the gauntlet tucked through his belt, and slashed the air a few times to warm up. Then he turned to the inn employee.

"Whenever you're ready."

The man grabbed Wareth's sword too tightly. He raised it over his head two-handed—treating it as if it were an axe—and rushed at Codek, yelling, "Aargh!"

Codek stepped forward, his sword blocking the overhead blow at a diagonal. He pushed outward in such a way that his attacker's own momentum carried his sword wildly to the outside, while Codek deftly circled his point to the man's throat. The inn worker scowled with embarrassment.

Tristo broke the uncomfortable moment, coming forward to put his hand on the applicant's sleeve. "It's not fair, you know. Only soldiers like this sergeant get fencing lessons, and they practice for years. You, you've got something more special—you've got guts.

"Maybe you'd do us a service? I need paint for this target here; you're just the person who could help me find some. Where should we look for it?"

Soon the survivors developed a ritual. Thalen and Wareth would conduct an initial interview, and then Tristo would escort the man to the backyard. If he passed Codek's audition, Tristo would then escort the applicant into the kitchen for something to drink. Growing up as a street orphan in Yosta, the boy, with his cropped hair and stunted growth, had developed a disarming facility in getting strangers to confide in him. Within moments they would be telling Tristo their darkest secrets. The "Mead Test," once institutionalized, washed out blackguards and troublemakers. While Thalen wasn't looking for under schoolteachers, he couldn't sign up anyone so difficult he would disrupt their troop.

After a few hours Codek grew bored humiliating farmers and dockworkers. He varied his audition routine by ambushing candidates in the inn's shabby hallways: Wareth would escort them toward the sitting room where Thalen waited at a little table while Codek stood, dagger drawn, hiding in a recess.

On that first afternoon, a muscled bald man wearing a silver ear-bob in his left ear smelled the ambush from six paces' distance. He drew back with lowered brows and a suspicious smile.

"What are you playing at?" he asked.

Codek stepped out of hiding and held out his hand. "Who might you be?"

"I'm Kambey," said the stranger. "I've been the weapons master of Yosta's Upper Academy for twenty years."

"And why do you want to join up with us?" asked Thalen.

"I just told you," Kambey growled in a gravelly voice. "I've taught hundreds of Yosta's youths. How many did I send to the Rout? How many were slaughtered?"

The original survivors exchanged looks. "Glad to have you with us, Kambey," said Thalen. "Your skills will be invaluable. Could you confer with Sergeant Codek about our arms and equipment? We have no time or money to fashion armor—can we buy it second-hand from Yostamen?"

"I doubt if there's a breastplate left in town," said Kambey. "But we could get gambesons or leathers fashioned. We'll set Tailors Row to work."

In the morning of the second day they found their healer, a middle-aged man named Cerf who had lost his sons in the Rout and his grief-addled wife to suicide. And the original survivors were also gratified by the arrival of three trained Vígat cavalrymen—Fedak, Latof, and Jothile—who had escaped the chaos of the Rout as a group.

These three worried that Thalen would think them cowards for fleeing the battlefield.

"Set your minds at rest," said Thalen. "I was *there*. I cursed the generals for not falling back to regroup. Retreating would have been far wiser and more effective."

"Besides." Codek pointed to the grimy neck drape wrapping about Fedak's throat and Latof's bandaged foot and crutch. "Your scars show you engaged before you fled the field."

"Men, understand this," Thalen said, "I won't ask you to charge the whole Oro army—that's not tactics, that's folly. But we will be setting off to gain Oro attention and pull them back from the Free States, possibly at the cost of our lives. Nobody should harbor hopes of coming home. If you want to rethink volunteering, do it now."

The cavalrymen's faces turned somber, but none of them backed out.

Wareth asked to examine how well their horses had weathered the stress of the battle and the long journey. "Healthy, trained cavalry chargers are almost more valuable than men to us," he reminded them all.

In the afternoon, Kambey, the weapons master, who had taken over the tryouts, reported that a bodyguard to a rich Jutterdam merchant had a powerful arm. Moreover, his father had skill as a swordsmith. Though Tristo warned Thalen that this applicant, a stocky man named Kran, had a hot temper, Thalen decided that his skills made him worth the risk.

After a break, Thalen, returning to the sitting room, was surprised to discover a stranger perched on the edge of his table, carefully cleaning caked dirt off the bottoms of his fine leather boots with the tip of his dagger.

"How did you get in here?" Thalen asked. They had their newest recruits monitoring the line outside.

The interloper was slender, with coiled muscles; he wore a neck drape and beret of shimmering black velvet, with his chestnut hair hanging in a long tail down his back. He motioned upward with his knife. "I jumped from the store next door onto the roof and then came down the stairs."

Wareth overheard this as he entered and emitted a low whistle of appreciation. "Huh. Nimble, I take it. And stealthy."

"I'd prefer to say I'm quiet," said the stranger. "I'm the best scout in the Free States."

"Why didn't you wait in line with the others?" asked Thalen.

"Because," said Kambey in his guttural tones, scowling, "folk might have recognized him."

Thalen turned to Kambey. "You know this man?"

"Well, we haven't spoken before, but I can guess who he is. Gentlemen, may I present Adair, the leader of the Wígat Waylayers."

"At your service," said Adair, with a graceful bow.

"No shit?" said Tristo. "The Waylayers are the most fearsome band in Wígat!"

"In the Free States," Adair corrected him mildly. "We're respected because we always get our haul."

"Modest too, I see," said Thalen.

"I don't see the point of modesty or of waiting in lines," said Adair. "I have certain"—he waved his dagger in a graceful circle—"talents. And I'd like to offer them to your team." He turned to face Thalen, intuiting who made the final decisions.

"But how could we trust you?" asked Kambey.

"I doubt there's much to steal where we're going," said Adair with a dazzling smile.

"No, of course not. But we could be double-crossed," said Thalen.

"Double-crossing is too much trouble. I relieve travelers of their goods because I'm lazy. I make it a point not to injure them—much—because riling up the law causes too much trouble. Besides, consider: if I wanted to turn you in to the Oros, I could tell them you're gathering here."

"I'd run you through!" Kambey growled.

"You could try," Adair replied, with that same smile.

"How about we spar a bit in the yard so I can test your skill with that fancy piece of steel you're carting round your waist?" Kambey challenged him.

When they left the room, Thalen turned to Tristo. "Forget about the mead. This one's too poised. But bring him back to me after the fencing."

"You already know he'll pass the audition?" asked Tristo.

"Without a doubt. No one's that cocky without reason," Thalen replied.

To the clang of metal and the roar of Kambey's curses, Thalen gently turned away an archer with a hacking cough whom Cerf, the healer, had vetoed, saying he doubted the man would survive the winter. Thalen then updated his notebook tally of the list of volunteers, considering their strengths and skills. As of now Wareth was their only trained scout.

Tristo escorted Adair to Thalen with an admiring light in his eyes.

Thalen expected Adair to swagger, but the man who sat in front of him grew serious as he met Thalen's gaze. He kept his body still—he didn't fidget or show nervousness—but Thalen sensed that he could spring into action any second.

"Tell me, *why* do you want to enlist?"

"Just because a man's a thief doesn't mean he can't be a patriot."

"Well, let's think about that," said Thalen. "Patriotism implies caring about your fellow countrymen, while stealing from them implies the opposite."

"Maybe a man wants a second chance?"

"A second chance at what? Be specific," said Thalen.

Adair paused a moment. "Freedom," he answered. "I'd rather be dead than an Oro slave."

Thalen held his glance, wondering if he dared trust him.

"And I have more to offer," said the highwayman. "Do you have a cobbler? You're going to need one. Men travel and fight on their feet, and boots can make all the difference. Before I joined my current 'trade,' I apprenticed to a cobbler." He thrust his feet forward, showing off his elegant boots.

"I hadn't thought about that; you have a point. But how do I know you made these? After all, you could afford to buy the best boots available—or you could have stolen those."

"I sign each pair with my mark." Adair turned down the leather on his calf; Thalen saw the carving of an intricate "A" floating on a sword.

Perhaps the whimsy and conceitedness amused Thalen, or perhaps he felt drawn to someone with artisanal skill. He decided.

"Be sure you gather all the shoemaking tools you need."

Adair stood up, his cocky smile back in place. "'Gather' as in 'purchase,' or 'gather' as in 'collect'?"

"Purchase," Thalen said firmly, and he reached in the box on the table for some coin Hake had already sent.

"Save your money," said Adair. "Come to think of it—catch!" He tossed Thalen a coin purse.

"Ill-gotten gains?" Thalen asked, hefting the weighty leather bag.

"Too proud to use it?" Adair asked.

"Maybe once," Thalen admitted, "but I left a lot of pride on a field outside of Sutterdam."

Adair stopped at the doorway. "By the way, one of the men queuing outside goes by the name Slown. You might be tempted not to take him because he has a hitch in his stride. That would be a mistake. Slown's got the best aim I've ever seen. He can hit a sparrow midflight."

"I'll keep that in mind," said Thalen.

Although the people who lived in Yosta were busy trying to prepare for the upcoming Oro invasion, Yostamen who had been turned down for the expedition still wanted to contribute to their venture. Thalen gratefully accepted their help: he asked volunteers to obtain supplies and to find them a ship. For both the town's safety and his own purposes, he also sent men and women out to relay stations, watching the roads for any sign of Oro approach. Each additional day they remained they gathered essential fighters and supplies, but these preparations would all go for naught if Oros arrived en masse and captured them.

A tailor was pinning a quilted, deep brown gambeson around Thalen when Tristo burst into the shabby sitting room grinning from ear to ear. "One of me mates has shown up!" The boy's infectious delight pulled the other three survivors to the long kitchen table, where his ravenous friend now sat catching up on missed meals.

Thalen managed to turn his gasp into a cough: Tristo's "mate" turned out to be a woman of about thirty summers. She wore men's clothes, including a leather weskit, and wore her hair cut above her ears. She was in the midst of scarfing down cubes of venison on the point of a wicked-looking dagger with a thick hand grasp. She nodded but kept chewing.

Codek said to Tristo, "Lad, I am happy you're reunited with a mate from happier times. That'll be important to all of us. We're pleased to meet your friend. But we can't take any women on this expedition. She wouldn't be strong enough. No offense, ma'am."

Tristo chortled. The woman swallowed her mouthful and wiped her lips on the back of her hand. She stood up; Thalen could see her muscled shoulders and thighs. She walked over to Wareth, who was younger and taller than Codek, holding out a rough hand.

Wareth smiled his broad smile, which lit up his whole friendly face, and held out his hand too. "Ma'am, pleased to make—" In a blink she threw Wareth down to the ground on his back, though she took care not to jostle his splinted arm. Her dagger glittered at his throat.

"My pleasure, horse soldier," she rasped. "Name's Ooma." She threw the knife in the air so that it twirled end over end, and then she snatched it out of the air by its handle. She held her hand out to Wareth to pull him up. As he regained his feet, she pivoted to face Codek; before he could react her dagger had snagged a patch of his bushy sideburn.

Tristo, grinning, said, "Ooma's awful clever with her knives."

"What about swords or bows?" asked Wareth.

"Haven't had much use for them in the back alleys of Yosta," she said. "Now, my knives . . ." She advanced toward Thalen.

Thalen held his hands in front of himself. "Peace, Ooma. You have proved your point. I am such a poor fighter that besting me would be no sport."

"What good are *you* to the expedition then?" she asked. "I recognize the military man's experience and straight talk, and this tall fella's got the bowlegs of cavalry. Why should *we* take *you*?"

"Good question, Ooma. I ask myself that five times a day."

"And what do you answer yourself?" she asked in her raspy voice, not rudely, but not backing down.

"I thought up this plan, and I am going to make it succeed."

Codek put in sternly, "Thalen is our commander."

"Huh!" she answered, reserving judgment, and sat back to her meat and bread.

Tristo said to his new comrades, "Ooma led our gang here. She kept us all alive. Taught us all everything we know. Ooma, how many Oros did you gut in the Rout?"

"Didn't gut a one, lad. Had to go for arteries in the leg or neck 'cause of that rat-fuckin' armor. Bloody work."

With more respect in his tone, Codek persisted. "Still, having a woman around could bring all kinds of trouble."

Ooma grinned. "I don't lie with men, old fella. Men around me usually catch on. And if they stay mule-stupid, my dagger teaches a lesson."

So Ooma joined the group. And despite Codek's reservations, she was not going to be the only woman after all. They chose a husband and wife, Moorvale and Maribel, as their cooks after asking them to prepare a midmeal out of restricted supplies for the partially assembled troop.

"The grub is great," said Codek through a mouthful of food. "But ma'am, I wonder if you're strong enough for the rigors of this venture."

"Call me 'Cookie,'" she said. "Let me show you something." Much to their horror this middle-aged woman put her foot on the bench on the side of the kitchen table and started to pull up her skirt. "Hey, handsome," she said to Adair, "squeeze them muscles in my legs."

"Rock solid, Madam Cookie," Adair pronounced.

"I'd like to see *you* lot work on your feet from morning to dusk and cart bags of flour and buckets of water." She grew angrier as she spoke. "*Strong enough!* I'll show you *strong enough*! Wait till you see my muscles!" And she started to unlace her tapestry bodice.

"No, no," said Thalen hastily. "We'll take your word for it."

But Cookie's dander kept rising. "Strong enough! Why're *you pups* doubting me? *He's* the one"—she pointed to her husband—"who complains he needs to sit! He's the one you should be mis-giving!"

"Calm down, will ya," said Moorvale. "True, I have my aches and pains. Sometimes in the middle of the day I sit for a spell and work on my sideline trade—a trade I wager might interest you." He crossed to the side of the kitchen, where he had parked a large, lumpy burlap bag before they started to cook. He brought it to Kambey.

The instant Kambey grabbed the covered-up contents he said, "A crossbow. Quarrels."

"Let's see," said Codek.

Kambey drew out the items and passed them around. Slown whistled over the workmanship as Kran sampled the pull of the bow.

"An atilliator!" said Thalen. "Were we really so idiotic as to think to set off without one! Moorvale, I want to talk to you about the repeating crossbows from the Rout. I've been wondering if we enlarged the feed slot—"

"I won't go without my wife," Moorvale interrupted. "Not only does she bake a mean biscuit, but she's a crack shot."

"And I won't go without my lardwit of a husband," said Cookie. "Gonna take death's dirty breath to part us."

Codek, stubborn, looked at Thalen. Thalen grinned and held up his hands in mock helplessness.

"Well then," said Cookie. "Now that's settled, who's for more biscuits and gravy?"

Many people raised up their plates.

Gathering sufficient healthy horses trained for fighting became Thalen's biggest concern. In this, the group was aided by the Oros' brutality. The stable master of one of Fígat's cavalry stations, a man named Gentain, had had daughters of eleven and twelve summers. When Oros molested his girls and then slashed their throats, Gentain vowed they would not lay their hands on the last thing left to him of value—the horses still in his stable. In the dregs of night he snuck up behind each Oro guard and strangled him with his daughter's shawl. His twelve well-trained coursers became the backbone of their string.

On the fifth morning, the original survivors chose four more cavalrymen (friends from a Jígat regiment), an archer, and a man who—though slow-witted—wielded a six-foot quarterstaff of red oak with fluid strength.

Rumor reached them that the Oros had moved en masse into Jutterdam. The Three Coins innkeep told his female servants to pack up and flee.

On the afternoon of their sixth day Wareth interrupted Thalen's intense study of maps with a little whistle. "Here's a gentleman says he knows you from before."

Quinith, Thalen's close friend from the Scoláiríum, entered the sitting room. Soiled bandages festooned his head, and his cream silk coat hung stiff with mud and sweat.

"Quinith!" Thalen embraced his friend. "What happened to you? Sit, sit. Drink a glass of wine."

"Here's to freedom." Quinith raised the glass, then drank it down without stopping to breathe. "Ah, Thalen! I'm so glad to see you. I was so afraid I'd miss you, I rode like a madman."

"Have another drink. Do you know anything about the Oros' movements?"

"No, I skirted towns and came overland.

"As to what happened . . ." Quinith set down his glass. "Well, from the Scoláiríum, I traveled to my family's manse. I helped my mother and my young sisters hide with a woodsman's family and then returned to guard the estate with my father. A small squad of Oros showed up after two weeks. We would have stood by if they'd just pillaged food or horses, but they bludgeoned our butler and my father intervened, which meant I had to jump in too. In the scuffle the Oros went down, but my father did as well."

"I'm sorry, Quinith," said Thalen. "And that's when you took that blow on your head? Were you knocked cold? We have a healer—let's get Cerf to look at it and change the bandage."

Quinith waved away Thalen's concern for his health. "Everyone has lost kin, and in truth, I did not harbor much love for my sire," he said with somewhat elaborate casualness. "I came as soon as whispers reached me where you were."

Thalen felt torn. "Quinith, you are a feast for my eyes, yet we can't take you with us. We have as many fighters as we can engage. Food and supplies keep me awake at night."

"You mistake me, Thalen. I know I am not fit to join your band. Aye, at the Scoláiríum I taught you basic fencing, but I'm hardly a warrior. After my little engagement I puked and shook for days. Obviously, I am not cut out to be a fighter; I belong at the Scoláiríum singing about real heroes. But I came to offer the talents I do have— you know I'm a terrific manager. Tell me how I can help."

So, over the sounds of Kambey drilling the recruits in the inn's cobbled courtyard, Thalen and Quinith conferred all afternoon about sneaking into Melladrin, setting up a long supply chain, and communicating from the field to suppliers. Quinith advised creating a quartermaster base in the Green Isles out of the reach of the Oros; Thalen begged Quinith to find a way to smuggle Hake to that base to make use of Sutterdam Pottery's contacts (and to get his injured brother out of the occupied city).

As the shadows lengthened, Thalen inquired, "What tidings of Gustie?"

Quinith looked away at the mention of his lover from the Scoláiríum. "Ill rumors, but naught confirmed." He changed the subject by asking, "What do you call your group?"

"I hadn't given it a thought."

"You need to have a name."

Thalen mused aloud, "Well, let's think about that. We're not 'soldiers,' really; but I don't plan to plunder, like highwaymen. 'Trespassers'? 'Invaders'?"

"Hmmm. 'Raiders,'" said Quinith definitively.

"Fine. But why?"

"Two syllables always works better in songs," said Quinith.

Thalen shook his head, bemused that even under these circumstances Quinith fell back on his expertise.

Quinith continued, "Do you have a good sword for this venture?"

"Good steel is wasted on me."

Quinith drew his own weapon out of a leather scabbard embellished with gold and silver: the rapier had gold-and-silver filigree on the pommel and intricate handguard, and the blade glistened. He offered it to Thalen with formal grace, the handle resting across his waist-high hands.

"If you will take my grandfather's sword, then I will feel part of the vengeance."

Thalen tried to refuse, but Quinith wouldn't listen.

He spoke over Thalen's protestations. "And I have another weapon I insist you accept. Follow me." Quinith led Thalen out to the street. There, next to his mud-splashed palfrey, lay an even dirtier wolfhound, with amber eyes and a lolling tongue.

"This hound belonged to my father. When we fought the Oros, he chalked up more kills than either of us. He's invaluable."

"No, Quinith, thank you, but no. I don't want to take a dog." Thalen was peeved. "If he's that vicious, how can I control him?"

Quinith would not accept his refusal. He claimed that if Thalen became the one who fed the dog, the wolfhound would transfer its loyalty to him. When Sergeant Codek joined the argument he—traitorously—agreed with Quinith. "Them wolfhounds are worth gold in a scrap; we'd be muckwits not to take him."

Thalen stared at the wiry gray dog with annoyance and tried to marshal another argument.

Quinith said, "The dog answers to 'Maki'; the sword, my grandfather named—"

But at that moment two Yostamen came galloping down the street, their horses foaming and trembling.

"A company of Oros approaches!" one shouted.

"Where are they?" Thalen shouted back.

"On the Coast Road traveling north from Jutterdam. When we first spotted 'em, they was maybe two days away; but it's taken us relays at least half a day to get here."

Thalen took a breath, raised the glistening rapier in the air to capture everyone's attention, and began issuing orders.

Some hours before dawn, the wolfhound, Maki, trotted alongside Thalen's Raiders as they hastily loaded their ship. Thalen had twenty-six horses and twenty-two men.

We've got two scouts, Adair and Wareth; three dedicated archers, Slown, Cookie, and Yislan; two pros at hand-to-hand, Weddle and Ooma. Swordsmen aplenty. Kambey and Kran may be the strongest, but Britmank and Jothile are the swiftest.

Divide the troop another way—I've got two cooks, a healer, a horse master, a cobbler, an atilliator, a swordsmith, a weapons master, and a sergeant. And a brace of quartermasters.

What I don't have is a wisp of a plan of getting these Raiders into Oromondo to let loose the kind of havoc we need to raise.

The Oros are just about to set upon Yosta to ransack, murder, and rape. It feels wrong to flee . . . unless this wild gamble is the only way of saving my country.

*Tally: 4 Original Survivors + 18 Recruits = 22 Raiders*